The Greatest Challenge Of Them All

A nobleman devoted to defending queen and country and a noblewoman wild enough to match his every step race to disrupt the plans of a malignant intelligence intent on shaking England to its very foundations.

Lord Drake Varisey, Marquess of Winch... nd heir of the Duke of Wolverstone. ... 'ns to shake the foundations o' ... -nay, noblewoman—he needs ... 'ter, known throughout the ton.

For the past nine years, L... ...ed that Drake might well be the ideal husband f... ...ven though he's assiduous in avoiding her. But she's now twenty-seven and enough is enough. She believes propinquity will reveal exactly what it is that lies between them, and what better opportunity to work closely with Drake than this latest mission with which he patently needs her help?

Unable to deny Louisa's abilities or the value of her assistance and powerless to curb her willfulness, Drake is forced to grit his teeth and acquiesce to her sticking by his side if only to ensure her safety. But all too soon, his true feelings for her surface sufficiently for her, perspicacious as she is, to see through his denials, which she then interprets as a challenge.

Even while they gather information, tease out clues, increasingly desperately search for the missing gunpowder, and doggedly pursue the killer responsible for an ever-escalating tally of dead men, thrown together through the hours, he and she learn to trust and appreciate each other. And fed by constant exposure—and blatantly encouraged by her—their desires and hungers swell and grow...

As the barriers between them crumble, the attraction he has for so long restrained burgeons and balloons, until goaded by her near-death, it erupts, and he seizes her—only to be seized in return.

Linked irrevocably and with their wills melded and merged by passion's fire, with time running out and the evil mastermind's deadline looming, together, they focus their considerable talents and make one last push to learn the critical truths—to find the gunpowder and unmask the villain behind this far-reaching plot.

Only to discover that they have significantly less time than they'd thought, that the villain's target is even more crucially fundamental to the realm than they'd imagined, and it's going to take all that Drake is—as well as all that Louisa as Lady Wild can bring to bear—to defuse the threat, capture the villain, and make all safe and right again.

As they race to the ultimate confrontation, the future of all England rests on their shoulders.

Third volume in a trilogy. A historical romance with gothic overtones layered over an intrigue. A full length novel of 129,000 words.

Praise for the works of Stephanie Laurens

Praise for "The Greatest Challenge Of Them All"

Other Titles from Stephanie Laurens

In memory of

Larry

Murphy

STEPHANIE LAURENS

The Greatest Challenge Of Them All

A Cynster Next Generation Novel

Savdek Management Pty. Ltd.

THE GREATEST CHALLENGE OF THEM ALL
Copyright © 2017 by Savdek Management Proprietary Limited
ISBN: 978-1-925559-05-7

Cover design by Savdek Management Pty. Ltd.
Cover and inside front couple photography and photographic composition by Period Images © 2017

Savdek Management Proprietary Limited, Melbourne, Australia.
www.stephanielaurens.com
Email: admin@stephanielaurens.com

The names Stephanie Laurens, the SL Logo and the Cynsters are registered trademarks of Savdek Management Proprietary Ltd.

The Greatest Challenge
Of Them All

Cast Of Characters

Principal Characters

Varisey, Lord Drake, Marquess of Winchelsea – *eldest son of Royce Varisey, Duke of Wolverstone, and Minerva, née Chesterton; heir to the dukedom of Wolverstone*

Cynster, Lady Louisa – *only daughter of Devil Cynster, Duke of St. Ives, and Honoria, née Anstruther-Wetherby; widely known as Lady Wild*

At Wolverstone House, Grosvenor Square

Varisey, Lord Royce, Duke of Wolverstone aka Dalziel – *Drake's father*

Varisey, Lady Minerva, Duchess of Wolverstone – *Drake's mother; née Chesterton*

Varisey, Lord Tobias – *second son of Royce Varisey, Duke of Wolverstone, and Minerva, née Chesterton; Drake's brother*

Hamilton – *the Wolverstones' London butler*

Finnegan – *Drake's gentleman's gentleman*

Henry – *Drake's personal coachman-cum-groom*

At St. Ives House, Grosvenor Square

Cynster, Lord Sebastian, Marquess of Earith – *eldest son of Devil Cynster, Duke of St. Ives, and Honoria, née Anstruther-Wetherby; heir to the dukedom of St. Ives; now engaged to Lady Antonia Rawlings*

Cynster, Lord Michael Magnus – *second son of Devil Cynster, Duke of St. Ives, and Honoria, née Anstruther-Wetherby; now unofficially engaged to Miss Cleome Hendon*

Cynster, Lord Sylvester (Devil), Duke of St. Ives – *Sebastian's, Michael's, and Louisa's father*

Cynster, Lady Honoria, Duchess of St. Ives – *Sebastian's, Michael's, and Louisa's mother; née Anstruther-Wetherby*

Cynster, Lady Helena, Dowager Duchess of St. Ives – *Sebastian's, Michael's, and Louisa's grandmother; arch-grande dame of the ton*

Osbaldestone, Therese, Lady Osbaldestone – *old friend of the family; widow; arch-grande dame of the ton*

Crewe – *the Cynsters' London butler*

Sukie – *Louisa's maid*

Tom – *Michael's gentleman's gentleman-cum-groom-cum-driver*

Tully – *a footman*

Gregory – *another footman*

Ned – *Sebastian's groom*

The footmen army – *footmen and grooms from the Cynster households in*

London

At the Hendon town house, Clarges Street
Hendon, Miss Cleome (Cleo) – *only daughter of Jack, Lord Hendon and Katherine (Kit), née Cranmer; now unofficially engaged to Lord Michael Cynster*
Hendon, Jack, Lord Hendon – *Cleo's father*
Hendon, Katherine (Kit), Lady Hendon – *Cleo's mother; née Cranmer*

At the Chillingworth town house, Green Street
Rawlings, Lady Antonia – *eldest daughter of Gyles Rawlings, Earl of Chillingworth, and Francesca, née Rawlings; now engaged to Lord Sebastian Cynster, Marquess of Earith*
Rawlings, Lord Gyles, Earl of Chillingworth – *Antonia's father*
Rawlings, Lady Francesca, Countess of Chillingworth – *Gyles's wife and Antonia's mother*

In Southwark
Flock, Mr. – *manager of the Phoenix Brewery*
Jones, Michael (Mike) – *master cooper at the brewery*
Blunt, Cecil (Cec) – *stableman at the brewery*
Triggs, Malcolm (Mal) – *driver at the brewery*
Sawyer, Jed – *cooper's apprentice at the brewery*
Cook, Martin – *bargeman working for the brewery*
Mellon, Herbert – *bargeman working for the brewery*
Sawyer, Mrs. Suzie – *Jed Sawyer's wife*

In Kennington
Beam, Mr. – *secretary of the London Working Men's Association*
Johnstone, Mr., Neill, Mr., and one other – *militia leaders; missing*
In Cross Lane
Chilburn, the Honorable Lawton – *fourth son of Lord Chilburn, Viscount Hawesley and Lavinia, Lady Chilburn, Viscountess Hawesley, née Nagle; deceased*
Badger – *Lawton's gentleman's gentleman*

In George Street
Griswade, Mr. Bevis – *fourth son of Lord Griswade and Alice, Lady Griswade, née Nagle*

In Whitehall
Greville, Sir George – *the Home Secretary*
Waltham, Sir Harold – *the Home Secretary's principal private secretary*

At Scotland Yard
Crawford, Inspector – *in charge of investigating the murders*
Cranthorpe, Sir Martin – *surgeon; chief pathologist in charge of the morgue*
Chartwell, Assistant Commissioner

Elsewhere in London
Chilburn, Lord, Viscount Hawesley – *Lawton Chilburn's father*
Chilburn, Lavinia, Viscountess Hawesley – *Lawton Chilburn's mother; née Nagle*
Chilburn, the Honorable Robert – *Lawton Chilburn's eldest brother*
Chilburn, the Honorable Gerrard – *Lawton Chilburn's second oldest brother*
Chilburn, the Honorable Basil – *Lawton Chilburn's older brother*
Harriet, Gloria, and Aileen – *Lawton Chilburn's sisters, older, all married*
Tippet, Miss – *cousin to the Chilburns*
Trevallayan, Monica, Mrs. – *cousin to the Chilburns*
Nagle, Lord, Marquess of Faringdale – *nephew of Lady Chilburn*
Hunstable, Mr. – *owner of Hunstable's Wines and Ales*
Higgins – *Hunstable's clerk*
Proudfoot, Mr. – *the Keeper of the Crown Jewels*
Proudfoot, Mrs. – *wife of Mr. Proudfoot*

In Kent
Boyne, William, Lord Ennis – *of Pressingstoke Hall; deceased*
Boyne, Cecilia, Lady Ennis – *of Pressingstoke Hall; deceased*
Boyne, Connell – *Lord Ennis's brother; also deceased*

At Midgham Manor in Berkshire
An old gentleman – *pulling the strings of the plot*
Reed – *the old gentleman's manservant*

PREVIOUSLY...

In "The Lady by His Side"

When the Duke of Wolverstone, known to many as Dalziel, retired from active involvement in political intrigues, his eldest son, Lord Drake Varisey, Marquess of Winchelsea, was prevailed upon to take up his father's mantle. Specifically, Drake steps in where the authorities fear to go.

It's mid-October 1850, and Drake has been asked by the Home Office to investigate rumors of a Young Irelander plot, the Young Irelanders being a sometimes-militant group calling for Irish self-rule. To do so, Drake needs to travel to Ireland in person, but he has also received a strange letter from Lord Ennis, an Anglo-Irish peer living in England. Ennis claims he possesses information he believes Drake needs to know, but insists he must meet with Drake face-to-face. To that end, Ennis has invited Drake to a house party at Ennis's estate on the east coast of Kent. Not knowing if the two matters are connected and unable to be in two places at once, Drake inveigles Lord Sebastian Cynster to stand in for him at Ennis's house party while Drake himself goes to Ireland.

In the guise of escort to childhood friend Lady Antonia Rawlings, Sebastian arrives at the house party, and Lord Ennis agrees to meet privately with him as Drake's surrogate. But in the minutes before Sebastian reaches Ennis's study, his lordship is stabbed and left dying. Ennis's last words, gasped to Sebastian, are "Gunpowder. Here."

Assisted by the local magistrate and the inspector sent by Scotland Yard to investigate Ennis's murder, Sebastian and Antonia search the house, gardens, grounds, and fields for any trace of gunpowder. And then Lady Ennis is murdered as well. Finally, in a cave off the shore, Sebastian and Antonia discover the imprints left by ten large barrels, only to be shot at by the villain responsible for the murders. They and others identify the villain as Connell Boyne, Ennis's younger brother who manages the family estate in Ireland. They give chase, only to find Boyne dead, apparently killed by whomever he had been working with.

Sebastian and Antonia return to London and report to Drake, who has just returned from Ireland. From all the evidence they have gathered, they conclude that, although Young Irelander foot soldiers like Connell Boyne may have been involved, the movement's leaders know nothing about the plot. However, ten barrels of gunpowder, enough to blow up a significant building, have been smuggled into England and, subsequently, taken into London by cart.

The questions Drake, Sebastian, and Antonia are left with are: Where is the gunpowder? Who is behind the plot? What is their target? And why?

In "An Irresistible Alliance"

Sebastian and Antonia, now engaged and swept up in the resulting social whirl, no longer have sufficient time to devote to the intrigue.

Consequently, Drake recruits Sebastian's brother, Lord Michael Cynster, to search for the gunpowder while Drake heads north to learn if the Chartists, another group agitating for political change and now rumored to be involved, are in fact behind the plot.

Michael's pursuit of information about barrels being carted into London leads him to Miss Cleome Hendon, daughter of Jack and Kit Hendon and de facto manager of the Hendon Shipping Company. Cleo views the intrigue as the answer to her yearning for adventure. With Michael at her heels, she sets out to find the gunpowder-carter who collected the ten barrels from Kent.

Together, Cleo and Michael doggedly follow a trail of missing men and—at last!—locate the gunpowder. But that night, before they have a chance to nullify the threat the gunpowder poses, a gentleman arrives on horseback with two drays driven by two other men and takes the barrels away. Cleo and Michael had been keeping watch. They follow the man, hoping to learn who he is and to where the barrels are being moved. But in the fog, Cleo is captured by the gentleman-villain. She fights free, then Michael arrives, and in the ensuing struggle, the gentleman is shot dead. Worse, they realize they've lost track of the drays carrying the gunpowder.

But Michael had placed a cordon of men around the neighborhood and can state with certainty that the barrels haven't left that area of dockside factories and warehouses.

Leaving the cordon of watchers in place, Michael and Cleo take the body of the dead mystery gentleman to Drake's home. Hours later, Drake returns from the north. Later that morning, Drake summons Sebastian and Antonia to join them, and the five pool all they have learned.

At this point, the sum of their knowledge is:

- Ten barrels of gunpowder—over a thousand pounds of explosive—lie secreted within an area of London that the authorities cannot search without causing a riot.

- Although low-ranking foot soldiers of the Young Irelander movement, and possibly of the Chartist movement, have assisted with the plot, believing it to be an action approved by their leaders, neither the Young Irelander generals nor the Chartist leaders know anything about the gunpowder. It appears both politically radical organizations are being set up as scapegoats for whatever heinous explosion the gunpowder is intended to create.

- From what the late gentleman-villain let fall, there is at least one other higher-level villain directing the gullible men recruited as helpers.

- The higher-level villains are consistently killing said gullible men after their tasks are completed, presumably on the grounds that dead men can tell no tales.

- There has to be a mastermind behind the plot, and he is cautious, careful, Machiavellian, and politically adept, using the Young Irelander and Chartist movements to disguise, deflect, and most importantly, effectively tie Drake's hands over raising any general alert via the constabulary and guard regiments about the capital.

- The identity of the dead gentleman-villain is yet to be determined, but his bootmaker is one possible source—Drake's man, Finnegan, is checking.

At the end of their cogitations, the questions still before our heroes and heroines are:

- Where exactly is the gunpowder? If they can locate it, they can substitute something non-explosive and wait to see who collects the barrels and follow them to the true villains and, ultimately, to the mastermind.
- Who is the mastermind?
- What is the mastermind's target, and why?

In the final scene from "An Irresistible Alliance" that leads in to the opening scene of "The Greatest Challenge of Them All"

Later that same day, our five investigators meet again and agree that they have little hope of identifying the target without knowing who the mastermind is.

They decide that:
- Learning the dead gentleman's identity is their clearest route to identifying the mastermind. At that moment, they are awaiting information; once they learn his name, Drake, Sebastian, and Antonia will pursue that line of investigation.

- They need to learn whether the man who killed Connell Boyne was the dead gentleman or another of the mastermind's lieutenants. Armed with a description of the dead gentleman, Sebastian and Antonia will approach Inspector Crawford at Scotland Yard, who must by now have a description of the man who shot Boyne.

- Michael will keep his watchers in place in case the barrels of gunpowder are moved again, but could the gunpowder be disguised by being put into other containers? Cleo and Michael will check with those likely to know, as well as subtly asking around inside the critical area, hoping to catch a whisper of the gunpowder's specific location.

- Meanwhile, Drake will investigate any further dead bodies in the hope their identities might indicate where the gunpowder has gone. For instance, who drove the two drays on which the gunpowder vanished into the fog? Even if the men are already dead, they might have spoken to someone about the plot.

- Drake will also follow up with the local branch of the Chartists in case any of their men have been lured into assisting with the plot. If any have and are still alive, they might know where the gunpowder is. Also, alerting the Chartists will deny the villains further manpower from that source and possibly slow the deployment of the gunpowder to the intended target.

Finally, the five investigators attempt to place themselves in the mastermind's shoes, and by working through the logistics and accounting for his cautiousness, they reason that they have a few days, possibly as long as a week, before everything would be in place to detonate the gunpowder. They also hypothesize that given the way the mastermind operates, the men he chooses to move the gunpowder to his final target site are unlikely to be attached to any group and might well be innocent of what they are doing—implying that the gunpowder will be disguised as something ordinary. How such a transformation might be achieved remains a mystery.

They have reached this point when Finnegan returns bearing news of the dead gentleman-villain's identity. His bootmaker has identified him as Mr. Lawton Chilburn. The name means nothing to Drake, nor to Sebastian, Michael, Antonia, or Cleo. Frustrated, Drake demands of the world at large, "Who the devil is Lawton Chilburn?"

The answer comes in a voice Drake instantly recognizes.

Lady Louisa Cynster, Sebastian and Michael's sister, sweeps in. She has eavesdropped, overheard all, and knows the critical answer: Lawton Chilburn is the youngest of Viscount Hawesley's four sons.
Louisa makes it abundantly plain that she is dealing herself into the investigation.

Even though Drake is beyond certain that the very last person he needs assisting him is the lady widely known—for excellent reasons—as Lady Wild, he discovers he, who is otherwise unfailingly in control of his world, is helpless to prevent it.

TUESDAY, OCTOBER 29, 1850

CHAPTER 1

*E*nthroned in an armchair in the back parlor of St. Ives House, Lady
Louisa Helena Horatia Cynster watched Lord Drake Varisey, Marquess
of Winchelsea, struggle to accept the inevitable. Could his reluctance be
any more obvious? Well, he would simply have to get used to it. She'd
had enough of playing by his rules.

She knew all about Drake's "missions" and his coterie of gentlemen
known as the "sons of the nobility." What she wanted to know was: What
about the daughters of the nobility? Weren't they allowed to play a part in
defending their country?

What about Boadicea?

Besides, as it appeared that Antonia Rawlings and Miss Hendon had
been included in this intrigue, Louisa saw no reason why she—a duke's
daughter accomplished in wielding the power such standing bestowed—
couldn't play a part. An active part.

Naturally, she understood why Drake, and her brothers, too, wished to
keep her far from their enterprise. But her brothers knew their place.
Drake would simply have to grow accustomed to his.

It was time. And more, truth be told.

She could remember the precise moment when she'd realized that from
her point of view, Drake was the outstanding candidate for the position of

her husband. She could also remember perfectly well when she'd realized he knew that, too.

He, however, had evidently decided to avoid addressing the issue for as long as he possibly could.

They were not in love. How could they be when he'd ensured he spent as little time within ten yards of her as humanly possible?

Which, of course, was a very large part of the reason he didn't want her anywhere near his precious mission.

Too bad. She was dealing herself into his game.

"I understand," she said, allowing her words, clear and even, to fall into the pervasive silence, "what your intentions are at this point." Briskly, she summarized, "Sebastian and Antonia to hold the social fort and, now we know the dead gentleman's name, to learn as much as possible about him from those they meet in the ballrooms. Also, they will inquire of Scotland Yard as to whether Lawton was the man who shot Connell Boyne in Kent. If not, it would seem we have more than one killer involved in this intrigue."

Drake opened his mouth, but she gave him no quarter—no chance to interrupt and seize the reins. "Meanwhile, Michael and Cleo— " She broke off to smile at the fair-haired lady sitting beside Michael. "I do hope I may call you Cleo?"

Cleo's resulting smile held a touch of fascination. "As we are to be sisters-in-law, I hope you will."

Louisa felt her smile spontaneously deepen; she rather thought she and Cleo would get on. She inclined her head and continued, "Michael and Cleo will make inquiries as to whether gunpowder can be transported in containers other than barrels specially made for the purpose." She arched a brow at Michael. "I assume the men you have watching the area in Southwark are the footmen army."

Michael blinked; it seemed he hadn't realized she knew about his and Sebastian's previous exploits that had led to the formation of said army. Slowly, warily, he nodded. "They know what they're doing—we can trust them to keep watch."

"And respond appropriately should they spot the barrels once again in transit." She switched her gaze to Drake.

Apparently accepting that she was not about to withdraw, he'd subsided into the armchair he'd previously occupied and was regarding her through eyes of beaten gold; his expression said little other than that he was very definitely not amused.

She inwardly grinned. "As it's already well past five o'clock"—on cue, the others all glanced at the mantelpiece on which a large ormolu clock resided—"then I assume it's too late to call at the London Working Men's Association." At the slight flaring of Drake's eyes—which for him denoted startled surprise—she smiled a touch patronizingly. "I understand that's the headquarters of the London Chartists. However, like most such offices, they will have closed at five o'clock, so pursuing that line of inquiry will need to wait until morning."

Drake nearly spoke—no doubt to insist she went nowhere near the London Working Men's Association—but at the last second, his gaze steady on her face, presumably reading her preparedness to verbally engage, he bit the words back.

Smoothly, she continued, "Our most pressing need—and also the avenue most amenable to immediate pursuit—is to learn of Lawton Chilburn's connections. His friends, his family, those with whom he associated. Anyone who might know with whom he was involved in recent days—or, indeed, who might themselves be his fellow conspirators."

"You knew who he was." Drake's tone was studiously level. "What do you know of his family?"

"Three older brothers and three sisters—two much older, the other younger, yet still older than Lawton. All his siblings are married." She paused to consult her memory. "His father is Viscount Hawesley of Ludworth, near Durham. His mother was a Nagle—she's aunt to the current Marquess of Faringdale." She met Drake's eyes. "The branches of both family trees are numerous, so Lawton has a large number of cousins."

She switched her gaze to Sebastian and Antonia. "Which events are you planning to attend tonight?"

From his expression, Sebastian had no clue. He glanced at Antonia, who recited, "The Carnabys' dinner, Lady Ormond's soiree, and the Marchmains' gala."

Louisa nodded. "I have to make an appearance at the Marchmains', but as you're covering those events, I'll try my hand at Lady Chisholm's ball and at the Mountjoys' soiree, then end at Lady Cottlesloe's. Most of the Chilburns should be in town, and at least some of them should be out and about in the ton tonight."

Michael glanced at Cleo. "We need to compose and dispatch a letter to Cleo's parents."

"And I must return home before my household raises a hue and cry," Cleo added.

"But later"—Michael looked at Louisa, then switched his gaze to Drake—"I can circulate through the clubs and see if I can turn up any of Chilburn's friends. At the very least, I should get some inkling of what crowd he ran with."

"Then tomorrow," Cleo said, "we'll check with the footmen and learn what types of containers are commonly passing out of that area, then I believe we'll visit the office of the Inspector General of Gunpowder. Someone there should be able to tell us definitively whether any other sort of receptacle can be used to transport gunpowder." Gathering her reticule, she glanced at the clock and rose. "And as it's past six o'clock, I need to be on my way."

The men stood. Michael declared he would see Cleo home.

Louisa rose, clasped Cleo's hand, and smiled warmly. "We haven't had a chance to grow acquainted, yet I'm already certain we'll be friends."

Cleo's smile was delighted and also intrigued. "I feel the same. Until tomorrow and whatever it brings."

Louisa watched Michael and Cleo leave, then turned to see Sebastian arching a black brow at Antonia.

"Yes, I agree." Antonia glanced at Louisa. "The Carnabys' dinner is at eight, so we, too, must get on."

They'd been acquainted all their lives; Louisa touched cheeks with Antonia. For her ears alone, Louisa whispered, "I can barely believe he finally came to his senses. How on earth did you manage it?"

Antonia's smile turned mischievous. "It wasn't that hard. I just needed the right time and the right place. And the right incentive."

Barred by the company from requesting further clarification, Louisa released Antonia to Sebastian, whom she farewelled with a regal nod.

She and Drake watched the pair pass through the parlor door, leaving the two of them standing in the space between the sofas, separated by a perfectly decent two yards.

Although she wasn't looking at him—was rather careful not to—she sensed his hesitation, his equivocation over being alone with her even in such innocuous and understandable circumstances. And it wasn't any consideration of propriety that provoked the itch beneath his skin. She was twenty-seven years old, for heaven's sake, and they were in her parents' house with staff only a good scream distant.

No. It was the attraction that had always simmered between them that was making him glance at the door. To this day, she didn't know if he was as affected by it as she was—if he felt it to the same extent, with the same unrelenting intensity. Like a roughened hand passing over already sensitized nerves in a manner that was simultaneously unsettling and the ultimate in temptation.

She didn't know if that compulsive attraction presaged anything more than lust or if it might be a harbinger of something deeper. Something more profound, like love.

The most irritating aspect of her ignorance was the lowering thought that his reaction to her over the past decade was due to him—so much more experienced in such matters than she—correctly interpreting her fascination with him, not reciprocating it, and because of their families' connection, rather than bluntly repudiating her interest, he'd elected to simply avoid her.

Presumably in the hope that she would turn away and, eventually, marry someone else.

She might have done just that—no lady of her ilk willingly remained a virgin for so long—except that from her earliest years in society, she'd measured every other gentleman against him, and invariably, those others had failed to meet his mark. Until she—and he—confronted whatever fueled their attraction, until they gave it its head and allowed it to rise or die as it would, she wasn't going to be able to get on with her life.

With him or with some other gentleman. She was already twenty-seven years old. Waiting for Drake to make his feelings known—to accept or reject her in some unequivocal fashion—hadn't borne fruit. It was time to learn the truth, one way or the other.

"What are you imagining?"

She glanced at him and found him regarding her through narrowed eyes. His demand—for demand it unquestionably was—was no longer couched in any gentle tone. His voice had turned hard, even harsh, with an undertone that was faintly menacing.

She quelled an urge to grin; if he was trying to send her running, she had the upper hand. "I believe I'll concentrate on tracking down Lawton's sisters and possibly his mother and see what they can tell me about him. I'm sure they'll frequently send notes, even if only summonses to family events. They must know his address."

Learning of Chilburn's address was Drake's top priority. With the man dead, the sooner Drake gained access to his rooms and any papers therein, the better.

Her limpid gaze on his face, Louisa arched her brows. "How are you planning on spending your evening?"

Avoiding you. "I'm going to start at Arthur's, then quarter the likely clubs." He hesitated, then acknowledged, "I—we—need to learn Chilburn's address with all speed." Of course, she'd focused on the critical next step.

Her lips curved playfully. "I wonder which of us will learn it first?" For a second, her eyes quizzed him.

Then before he could insist she promise that, if she did learn of Chilburn's address, she wouldn't venture there herself, Lady Wild's smile deepened, and with a swish of her skirts, she swept past him and on toward the door. Without looking back, she raised her right hand and waggled her fingers. "Good luck."

And then she was gone, leaving him staring after her, inwardly swearing while wrestling with a host of contradictory impulses.

A minute passed, then he set his lips. He felt his jaw clench, tried to ease the telltale sign, and failed.

With a muttered oath, he stalked out of the room and headed for the front hall.

CHAPTER 2

*S*eated at the scarred desk in his rooms above a tailor's shop, Bevis Griswade stared at the old man's missive and wondered what had gone wrong.

From the first, he'd been confident of winning the unstated competition between Lawton and himself for the right to direct the third stage of the old man's plot. After his faultless execution of the first stage, culminating in the delivery of the gunpowder into the warehouse in London, he'd felt all but assured of gaining a full two-thirds of the old man's estate, rather than just one third. When the old man had changed his mind over allowing him, Griswade, any insight into Lawton's second stage and had sent a copy of the instructions Lawton had been given, Griswade had felt even more certain of victory, or at least that the old man was leaning his way.

He'd dutifully surveilled the yard in Southwark during the day on Monday and had returned late that night to watch the arrival of the barrels after Lawton and his helpers had collected them from the warehouse. He'd hung back in the shadows and watched the drays roll up and turn through the gates. Fired by curiosity, he'd used the fog for cover and had silently crept closer—close enough to observe the beginnings of the transfer.

Very clever. He had to admit the old man constantly amazed him. He'd watched the process; it had seemed that Lawton, too, had performed as required. He'd heard enough of the men's mutterings to gather that Lawton had hung back to check for anyone taking too close an interest in the drays' route. As he hadn't wanted Lawton to see him—to ask why he was there—he'd let the shadows swallow him and had quietly left the area before Lawton had arrived.

Griswade reread the old man's most recent communiqué. The only construction he could place upon it was that Lawton had been permanently delayed.

At no point had Griswade foreseen any such happening. On the one hand, it was all well and good; more for him once the old man shuffled off. Yet on the other hand, Lawton's disappearance—or more accurately, his failure to report to the old man in Berkshire—indicated that someone had stumbled on the plot.

Intentionally? Or had the interference been accidental, as it were?

More to the point, if, somehow, Lawton had been taken up by the authorities, would he talk?

After several minutes of weighing the prospect, Griswade decided it wasn't all that likely. However much he denigrated Lawton, it was unquestionably true that Lawton was clever enough to realize that talking wouldn't save his skin. Let alone his neck. Lawton might not be as clever or as cunning—and he definitely wasn't as ruthless—as Griswade, but Lawton was far from stupid.

That left two alternatives. Either Lawton was locked up and not talking, or Lawton was dead. In either case, how safe was the gunpowder? Had the transfer been properly completed? The old man had, as usual, cut to the heart of the matter in demanding that Griswade obtain answers to those questions.

He glanced at the clock. It was too late to do anything about gaining the required answers tonight. He would go to Southwark tomorrow and find out what they—he as well as the old man—needed to know.

However, there was also the question of the four men who had performed the transfer. If Lawton had been taken out of the game before or even immediately after the transfer had been completed, he wouldn't have had time to snip those loose ends.

That needed to be done; Griswade knew the old man wouldn't agree to the third stage rolling ahead until the second was completed to the last detail. Griswade could and would kill two birds with one stone.

The ends of his lips kicked upward in a brief smile. He would verify that the transfer had been successfully completed and then…

For several minutes, he indulged his imagination, then another thought intruded.

He looked again at the letter the old man had sent. Yes—there it was. The old man had received word that Lawton hadn't returned home last night. That word assuredly came via Badger, Lawton's man; no one else would have known of Lawton's disappearance in time to send word to Berkshire sufficiently early for Griswade to have received a communication that night.

That left another outstanding issue. What about Badger?

CHAPTER 3

*D*rake climbed the stairs to Lady Cottlesloe's ballroom. His feet felt like lead. In one part of his brain, impatience reigned, whipping him on; in the larger part, a bone-deep reluctance held sway. What he was about to do wasn't wise, not on any count. Unfortunately, finding Louisa and learning if she'd discovered Chilburn's address was absolutely mandatory if he wished to get any sleep that night.

Lady Louisa Cynster was the bane of his life. For the past nine years, he'd been all too aware that, for him, she radiated an almost hypnotic attraction, one that operated on multiple levels—intellectually, sexually, emotionally. Even socially.

Nine years ago, he'd recognized that if he gave in to that potent attraction, if he indulged it and pursued her in any way, he might well fall in love with her.

To him, as to his father before him, love was a trap to be avoided for as long as possible. Love was a power he inherently distrusted—a power strong enough to influence him, to bend him to its will.

Love was definitely not a power to be trifled with.

Hence his decision to steer clear of Louisa to the best of his considerable ability.

Of course, in order to avoid her, he'd had to know where she was.

What her circles were, her favorite haunts. Whose arm she'd been seen on. Consequently, he knew that, despite a positive army of would-be suitors, she couldn't be said to have encouraged any gentleman. Much to the grandes dames' and the gossipmongers' disappointment, she'd never given the slightest sign of being even vaguely interested in any other man.

He'd suspected, and the undercurrents alive during the meeting that afternoon had proved, that she'd retained her interest in him—something that had bloomed long ago—as well as a sexual awareness of him that had grown with the years.

Even more unsettling, that afternoon, there'd been a certain intensity in her gaze, a purpose that had blazed behind the translucent pale green of her eyes.

Unless he missed his guess, she intended to use the situation thrown up by his current mission to challenge him. Privately, between him and her—on a personal plane.

If he could, he would have clung to safety, turned, and walked away, maintaining his habitual wall of distance and separation from her.

But he needed her help. This time, he—and unfortunately, she—knew he needed her assistance. Now they'd established that the perpetrators came from the ranks of the social elite—and he would take an oath that the mastermind was even more solidly haut ton than Chilburn—then of all those he might tap on the shoulder, Louisa was unquestionably the best qualified to render the type of support he required. She was widely regarded as the natural successor to her grandmother's and Lady Osbaldestone's mantles; she would either know the answers to his questions or know from whom to get them.

He reached the top of the long flight of stairs and stepped into the foyer before the crowded ballroom. The few guests he'd passed had nodded politely—and tried their best to hide their surprise and the speculation that immediately followed. Lady Cottlesloe would have sent him an invitation, but no more than her guests would she expect him to appear given he so rarely waltzed to society's tune.

The ballroom doors stood open; he could see the usual throng of ladies garbed in all the colors of the rainbow, in silks and satins bedecked with ribbons and bows, with diamonds, rubies, emeralds, and sapphires flashing from about their throats, bobbing from their earlobes, circling their wrists, and even gleaming from amid the artfully arranged curls of their upswept hair. In contrast, the gentlemen, including him, formed a regiment in black and white, providing sharp contrast to the ladies' peacock hues.

He knew he was hesitating, all but dithering, reluctance still dragging at his feet. But he'd weighed all the prospects, and his way forward was clear.

This mission was too important for him to walk away from Louisa and the help she could and would give.

He had no choice but to engage with his nemesis and let Fate play out her hand.

It was nearly midnight, and Lady Cottlesloe had long ago abandoned her position by the door. Drake found her seated on a chaise against one wall and made his bow—predictably to unfeigned and delighted surprise, rapidly followed by effusive welcome.

He managed to extricate himself and, being tall enough to see over most heads, swiftly quartered the room. He spotted Louisa, also predictably surrounded by a circle of the fashionable—ladies and gentlemen both, but with the gentlemen heavily outnumbering the ladies.

She was wearing a gown of pale-green satin, the shimmering hue contrasting sharply with the lustrous tumble of her black curls. The cut and fit of her gown and the stylish scalloping of the two-tiered skirt and the top of her bodice were the epitome of haute couture, with not a single flounce or even lace edging to distract the eye from the superb lines.

As ever to him, she shone like a beacon in a shifting sea and drew him like a lodestone.

When he was still several feet away, she swung around, her eyes widening, her gaze instantly colliding with his. Typically, she made no attempt to excuse the awareness that had prompted her to so suddenly look for him. Instead, after a second of studying his eyes, his expression, her finely arched black brows rose interrogatively.

He halted at her elbow, and the circle shifted to include him. Perforce, he had to acknowledge the others. He bowed slightly to the ladies.

Understanding his difficulty, Louisa stepped in. "Lord Winchelsea— allow me to present Lady Anne Colby, Mrs. Hendricks, and Miss Dunstable."

The ladies bobbed curtsies and murmured excited welcomes.

Drake exchanged nods and brief greetings with the other men, all of whom he could place. They eyed him measuringly. Were he a betting man, he would have wagered that, despite the presence of the three other ladies, the true focus of the gentlemen's attentions and intentions was Louisa; the other men were wondering what he was doing there and whether he would queer their pitch.

He turned to Louisa, met her gaze, and saw the suppressed laughter there… Only then did he realize he hadn't greeted her.

And that his unexpected—indeed, unprecedented—appearance by her side, combined with his familiarity in not formally acknowledging her, had already started hares running in far too many minds.

He mentally gritted his teeth. He avoided society, especially of this sort; obviously, he was rusty.

He was also apparently too slow. Before he could draw Louisa away, Viscount Coleman leapt in. "I say, Lady Louisa, Lady Anne—have you seen the latest play at the Theatre Royal? The farce is quite hilarious."

Louisa admitted she had yet to see Drury Lane's most recent offering. The other gentlemen weighed in with their opinions, and a lively discussion ensued.

Too lively. Standing in silence beside Louisa, Drake had no doubt the intent was to keep her engaged and away from him.

His temper was already abraded by his misstep in approaching her so directly; even without turning his head, he was aware of the glances bent on him and her and the whispered comments being exchanged behind raised hands.

He gritted his teeth in earnest and reminded himself he didn't care what society thought—he just needed to talk to her, and this wasn't working.

The instant the first chord in the summons for the next waltz floated over the coiffured heads, he seized her hand.

She glanced at his face, her eyes widening.

He met those eyes, his gaze a warning, and stated, "My dance, I believe."

She opened her eyes even wider. "I don't have a dance card."

"So there's nothing to prevent you granting me this dance." With the briefest of nods to the others, he stepped out of the circle, drawing her with him.

She chuckled, acquiesced, and allowed him to lead her to the floor.

On reaching the area of parquet that was rapidly clearing, he halted, drew her into his arms, and stepped out—and she followed light as thistledown, supple and responsive.

They were both scions of noble houses; they could waltz in their sleep. That should have freed their minds for conversation. Instead, sensation blossomed, bloomed, geysered. Despite all his many shields, his senses heightened and fixed on the feeling of her however acceptably whirling in his arms, on the weight of her palm riding on his shoulder, and the way her fingers curled in his. Slender, but strong. Without thought, their paces matched perfectly; her body mirrored his without hesitation as they whirled through a turn.

The impulse to hold her closer yet was a drumbeat in his brain. The compulsion was strong enough to jolt his wits into place.

He looked into her eyes; for several instants, he felt as if he was drowning, then he drew in a breath, pulled back from the tangle of feelings and emotions swirling through him, and focused on her face. On her expression.

Only to realize that she'd been distracted, too.

"Have you learned anything about Chilburn?" The question was abrupt, his tone hard—an attempt to jerk them both back to the here and now of the mission.

Louisa blinked. Reluctantly, she corralled her senses, her wits, until then whirling along with their feet. What she'd seen in his eyes as he'd gazed into hers... It took effort to turn her mind to his question, then she refocused on his face. "Not a great deal. Apparently, all his family are in town, but at this time of year, the events are so much smaller than during the Season that if you want to hunt someone down, unless you're lucky, it means attending many more events." She paused, then reported, "I met Sebastian and Antonia at the Marchmains'. They hadn't had any luck at all and were going to call it a night. After the Marchmains', I stopped by Lady Ortolan's soiree on the off chance and caught up with one of Lawton's sisters-in-law there."

She paused as they whirled through the turn at the end of the oval dance floor, then as they once more precessed up the room, continued, "Lawton's sister-in-law apparently has no time for Lawton—very definitely no love lost there. I gathered he's regarded as the family wastrel. She didn't know his address, only that he has lodgings somewhere in town. Oh—and he has a man who goes by the name of Badger."

She studied Drake's face—the lean planes of his cheeks, his hooded eyes, the blade of his patrician nose. His thin, mobile lips were presently set in a rather rigid line. "Did you learn anything?" She wondered if he would tell her.

He hesitated, but then admitted, "No. In fact, nothing—a dearth of information so complete that I have to wonder if Chilburn had dropped out of society—our circles, at least—altogether. His name is known, but only vaguely, a distant acquaintance met somewhere, sometime. I couldn't find anyone who called him friend—not even acquaintance—at any of the major clubs or hells. And he's not a member of any of those establishments, either."

"Hmm. That does rather fit with him being a wastrel. Presumably, he doesn't have the wherewithal to play in those circles anymore. His sister-in-law hinted that he lived a hand-to-mouth existence funded by gambling and what she termed 'crazy wagers.'" She thought, then suggested, "You might have more luck in the clubs frequented by ex-cavalry officers."

Drake grunted. After two revolutions, he said, "We'll need to check, but if he's chronically short of funds, those doors will be closed to him, too."

The waltz whirled them on. With nothing further to say or ask, she allowed her senses to rise again, to take hold again and draw her awareness back into the dance—into all it revealed. All it confirmed.

When the last bar sounded and Drake released her, while he bowed and she curtsied, she felt even more vindicated in pursuing the path she'd decided to take. Regardless of his ineffable control, his all-but-impenetrable emotional shields, there'd been an instant there, in the second that followed the last note of the music, when his reluctance to release her, to let her move out of his arms, had shone through.

He was attracted to her—just how deeply she could not as yet tell—but he was determined to fight it. To hold the compulsion at bay and keep her at a distance.

She rose from her curtsy and smiled at him. Propinquity should trump even his control.

His eyes, already fixed on hers, narrowed.

She fought not to let her smile deepen. "I believe I'll call it a night." She swung toward the door. "It's Tuesday, after all. Sebastian, Antonia, and I are more likely to find the Hawesleys, or at least the viscountess, tomorrow evening, when more of the major hostesses will be hosting events."

Drake paced alongside her, listening as she mused, "I particularly want to speak with Lawton's sisters. Of all the family, they're the most likely to have recent and accurate insights into his present life and any friends or associates he might have taken up with. I'll try at the at-homes and afternoon teas tomorrow..."

He glanced at her and saw her pull a face.

"Sadly, those events are much less well attended at this time of year." She caught his eye. "They're not the same source of boundless information they are during the Season."

They came upon their hostess in the crowd and took their leave. Drake ignored the speculative glances and walked out of the ballroom by Louisa's side.

They paused in the front hall while the butler collected her cloak; noticing the direction of the man's gaze, Drake reached out, took the garment, and draped it over Louisa's bare white shoulders. She thanked him with an absentminded smile...or at least a smile that appeared to be so. He knew better than to trust outward appearances with her.

He walked with her out of the house and down the steps to where her carriage—a neat black town carriage that, he noted with some disapproval, did not bear the St. Ives crest on the door—waited. He waved the footman back and opened the door.

Louisa stepped past him, gathered her full skirts, then held out her gloved hand.

He steeled himself and grasped it.

She paused and met his eyes, then arched a brow. "Are you coming?"

He held her gaze. He'd come to the ball to assure himself that she hadn't learned Chilburn's address and gone haring off to investigate by herself. His intention had been to see her safely home...and she wasn't home yet.

Her home lay a mere fifty yards or so from his, and he didn't have anything more planned for tonight.

And there was enough challenge in her eyes to make the thought of retreat unappealing.

He nodded, gripped her fingers, and handed her up, then with a mental shrug, followed. *Why not?*

He shut the door, then sat beside her on the leather seat. He leaned back as the horses took up the slack in the traces, and the carriage rolled smoothly forward.

Within a minute, he'd realized that there were, in fact, several reasons why walking home might have been the better option. Sitting beside Louisa in the dark dimness of the carriage, aware of her satin skirts sliding against his trousered leg. Inhaling the subtle scent that screamed *her* in a shadowed, quiet, private place perfect for...

He drew breath, with effort hauled his mind from that track, and desperately seeking distraction, voiced the first words that came into his head. "Neville—why the devil didn't you marry him?" He crossed his arms and sank into a brooding sprawl. "Or Chifley, come to that."

Louisa blinked. She managed not to turn and stare, but really? He'd kept track of her suitors—including, apparently, the few who'd refused to accept her subtle dismissals and had insisted on bringing matters to a head with a formal proposal. Which, of course, she'd refused.

Before she'd decided how best to respond, Drake grumbled, the sound seeming to come from the depths of his chest, "Or Carris, even, although I suppose I can understand that. And Morffet was no great prize."

She pressed her lips together in an attempt to stifle her laugh, but his disgruntled tone defeated her, and a chuckle broke free.

The sultry sound feathered over Drake's senses, made him hold his breath, made much of him grow predator-still while other parts hardened.

Eventually, through the dimness, he cast his bane a dark glance. "What's so funny?"

"You."

He couldn't make out her expression, but her tone suggested she found him distinctly amusing.

"You're trying to sound like—trying to cast yourself as—a big brother. Like Sebastian."

He realized she wasn't wrong. He'd instinctively reached for a guise, a façade he'd assumed would keep him safe. He hesitated, then asked, "Is it working?"

"No. Not at all."

He sighed, uncrossed his arms, and straightened in the seat. "Just as long as you understand that that's the only relationship that can exist between us—and as we're together alone at night in this carriage, that better be our pseudo-relationship."

He wasn't sure what response he'd imagined that declaration would elicit, but it certainly hadn't been an unsettlingly calm, "Ah. Is that what's behind your pantomime?"

An offhand "Of course" seemed the safest response.

Louisa tried hard not to snort. After a minute of cogitation—of defining her best avenue of attack—she said, "After that dance...you do realize it was only the second dance we've ever shared?"

"Yes."

"Well," she said, flicking out a fold in her skirt, "I started this evening not knowing whether the attraction I've always felt for you was reciprocated." Beside her, he stilled, but if the gloves were going to come off between them, she was only too ready to oblige. "Given you've assiduously avoided me for the past nine years, I really had no clue—I was seventeen when we last waltzed and hardly an expert in what *I* was feeling, let alone able to read you. But after tonight's dance, and even more after what you've just revealed..." Tipping her head, she slanted him a glance. "You do know that pretending a fundamental reality isn't real never actually works?"

Several seconds passed, then, through the shadows, he spoke—from the sound of his diction, she suspected through clenched teeth. "You would do well to accept that although an *attraction* might be there, I am not going to act on it."

She let a heartbeat pass, then in her most provocative tone, purred, "Are you sure?"

"I am not, ever, going to find my way to your bed."

"Well, of course not. What use would that be?"

Drake felt as if she'd swung him around and around, and he'd lost track of the conversation. He debated the wisdom of asking for clarification. Confusion was not a state with which he was comfortable, but caution suggested that any continuing exchange might be fraught with imperfectly perceived dangers...

The carriage drew up and rocked to a halt. He glanced out of the window and confirmed they'd reached St. Ives House in Grosvenor Square. Feeling unexpectedly grateful—knowing escape from her irritating, annoying, unsettling presence was mere seconds away—he reached for the door handle, swung the door open, and stepped down to the pavement. He drew in a deep, somewhat freer breath, then extended his hand to help her down.

She gripped his fingers, and he supported her as she descended the steps to the pavement.

Her hand still in his, he led her to the steps leading up to the porch before the St. Ives House door. And unbidden, unscripted, the words slipped out. "What did you mean by 'what use would that be?' If not that, then what?"

With one hand clutching his and the other raising her voluminous skirt and petticoats, she started up the steps. Her eyes on the stone, she calmly stated, "What I meant is that there would be no sense in you coming to my bed. Far more to the point, I fully intend to join you in yours."

They gained the porch, and he halted. Her reasoning blazed clear in his mind. He looked down and met her as-ever limpid gaze. "No."

He made the negative, the denial, as forceful, as absolute, as he could.

Instead of deflating, she smiled, apparently delightedly, up at him. "Oh, Drake." He was still holding her hand. She gripped his fingers and stretched up—he thought to kiss his cheek, so he didn't draw back.

At the very last second, she shifted to face him, and her lips brushed—tantalizingly, alluringly, in the very lightest of caresses—over his.

His pulse leapt. His senses surged. Every instinct he possessed reared up and shrieked at him to *seize*.

Struggling to hold against the tide, he felt himself sway.

Throughout, in the faint light falling through the fanlight, she held his gaze—saw what he fought to suppress, to contain.

Her lips still curved, she murmured, "It's never wise to fling down a gauntlet you don't want someone to pick up."

Before he could reply—before he could find breath or master his tongue—she slipped her fingers from his hold, reached for the latch, opened the door, and with a last, deliberately provocative glance, one filled with steely promise, she swept inside and softly shut the door.

Leaving him frozen, utterly in thrall, but whether to his desire or hers, he couldn't have said.

Beyond the door, he heard the fading click of her heels on the tiles.

Finally—finally!—the vise clamped about his chest eased, and he managed to fill his lungs.

That broke the spell. He shook his head as if to free his mind of the lingering remnants of her enchantment, then he turned, went quickly down the steps, and strode for the safety of Wolverstone House.

WEDNESDAY, OCTOBER 30, 1850

CHAPTER 4

*A*t nine o'clock the next morning, Drake arrived outside the building in Kennington that housed the London Working Men's Association. On his descent from the hackney he'd caught in Grosvenor Square, the first sight that met his eyes was a suspiciously familiar plain black town carriage drawn up by the curb fifteen yards farther along.

Somewhat dourly, he paid off the jarvey, then stalked toward the other carriage. He didn't waste energy wondering how Louisa had known the Association's location and that he would be there at that hour; he didn't doubt she had her ways.

Before he reached the carriage, the door swung open, and she leaned out. "There you are." Imperiously, she held out her hand.

He told himself there was no point seizing her hand, pushing her back into the carriage, and slamming the door. Her coachman wouldn't take orders from him. Lips compressed, he grasped her gloved fingers and assisted her to the pavement. "I suppose I should have guessed."

"Indeed, you should have."

She was wearing a fashionable walking dress in twill the color of a forest at midnight; the very dark green accentuated the luminous, much paler green of her eyes.

After briskly shaking down her skirts and settling her reticule on her wrist, she looked at the building before them.

Built of red brick, it was substantial, but lacked any ornamentation. The double front doors were set in a plain wooden frame, white-painted, as were the window frames.

"Very utilitarian. Appropriate, I daresay. Shall we?" Without waiting for any response, she swept forward.

She always swept or glided rather than walked like other mortals... Drake started after her, rapidly lengthening his stride.

She reached the door first, tried it, and when it opened, swept boldly in.

He swallowed a curse, caught the door, and followed at her heels.

The large room they walked into was set up as a general meeting area. Men of all sizes and shapes were gathered in groups, some about tables, others in chairs, some standing, all chatting—or rather they had been. The opening door had drawn all eyes, and the vision that had entered had stilled all tongues.

The rumble of conversation died, and silence took hold as every last man turned to stare at Louisa. They noticed Drake, too, but without exception, their gazes deflected back to her.

She halted and smiled brightly. Her gaze swept the gathering, then she noticed a long window in the side wall that formed a partition between this room and the next. Beyond the window lay a counter, and shelves full of ledgers lined the far wall. Wooden cabinets formed an orderly rank against an inner partition.

Drake spoke before she could. "I've a letter from O'Connor." Moving unhurriedly, he reached into his coat pocket and drew out O'Connor's letter, in which the ultimate leader of the Chartists directed the London chapter of the organization to render all assistance to Drake as Lord Winchelsea. "If someone could direct me to whoever's in charge?"

The men exchanged glances. Some shifted their feet.

Drake wondered at the reaction. True, they would have picked him for an aristocrat; he hadn't considered it necessary to approach in disguise. He glanced briefly at Louisa, but she was simply standing beside him, her expression serene, her eyes observant and watchful, but definitely not challenging. The men weren't being made nervous by her.

The sound of a throat being cleared—nervously—reached him. With Louisa, he glanced at the window to the office, which had silently slid open. A tall, thin, not to say gangly man leaned over the counter. "I'm the association secretary. I...er...believe that, at the present moment, I'm the...ah...most senior man here."

Drake moved to the window. To his relief, Louisa drifted by his side.

The secretary reached for the letter. "I'm Mr. Beam."

Drake handed him the missive and waited as Beam unfolded it and read. Beam wasn't any poker player; his expression had appeared troubled even before he'd started to read, and the farther down the letter his eyes tracked, the more transparent his anxiety became.

Behind Drake and Louisa, Drake was aware of the other men congregating and edging nearer, but none came close enough for him to consider them a threat.

Finally, Beam lowered the letter. "This, um, appears to be genuine."

Drake couldn't stop his eyebrows from faintly rising. "It is—I received it from O'Connor himself."

Beam blinked. His gaze rose to Drake's face. "In Liverpool?"

"No." Drake didn't appreciate being tested. "In Leeds. Or rather at Tamworth Grange, O'Connor's house just outside the city."

Beam looked suitably chastened. "Ah—yes, of course." He glanced again at the letter. "It says here that we—meaning the London Working Men's Association—should answer whatever questions you have and render all possible assistance..." He paused, as if weighing the necessity of uttering what came next, then continued, "Because you are investigating a matter that threatens the entire Chartist cause." Beam looked at Drake, then straightened. "O'Connor says you're Winchelsea?"

Curtly, Drake nodded. The silence from behind them was absolute; every man there was listening for all he was worth.

"So...um, what do you want to know?"

"I need the names of your three militia leaders." Drake glanced around. "Are any of them here?"

"Ah...no." Beam's expression grew even more troubled.

"In that case, I'll need their addresses as well."

"I'm...ah... If I might ask, why do you need that information?"

Drake considered Beam. The man had been unsettled even before they'd arrived. "Is something wrong?"

"Well..."

One of the men behind Drake and Louisa spoke up. "It's just that we're unused to having your sort come in and ask for our leaders—not without there being some trouble following close behind. Trouble for us, that is."

Drake shifted so he could keep the men in view. "There's no trouble following us. Quite the opposite—it's likely the trouble is already here. As O'Connor wrote, I'm investigating a situation where some conniving soul is trying his damnedest to use your cause, your association, as his scapegoat. I need to speak with your leaders to warn them, and if they have been drawn in, to help them pull their men back from any further involvement in this plot." He paused, then, continuing to speak more to the gathered men than to Beam, added, "It's the mastermind behind this plot who's a danger to the Chartists, not me."

Silence reigned for several seconds, then the men exchanged glances again. Their resistance to the notion of trusting him with their leaders' whereabouts was palpable.

"Oh, for heaven's sake!" Louisa's voice cut through the tension. All heads swung her way, and she blithely rolled on, her haughty, duchess-like tones effortlessly carrying superiority along with imperious command, "You can't seriously imagine that Lord Winchelsea would be here, waving a letter with Mr. O'Connor's signature"—with a flick of her hand, she gestured at Beam—"a signature your secretary has verified as authentic, if Mr. O'Connor, your ultimate leader, didn't believe that cooperating with Lord Winchelsea is in the Chartist movement's best interests."

Drake had already said as much, albeit not in such a forthright way. Yet as he glanced around, he noted that the men were regarding Louisa as if she was some strange, exotic species, one who stated the obvious truth and, most telling to their minds, as a female, could have no possible connection with Whitehall or the authorities.

She swayed them.

Beam sensed the change in the atmosphere. "Ah—I'll just write down the names and addresses."

None of the men made any move to stop him.

When Beam handed over the single sheet, Drake perused the information, then glanced at Beam. "One thing." He swept his gaze over the gathered men, including them in his inquiry. "Did a gentleman call here, perhaps last week, asking to meet with these three leaders?"

Beam glanced at the others, then looked back at Drake and nodded. "Yes, a man called. A gentleman, but not like you, begging your pardon, my lord."

"Did this gentleman have a scar running from the corner of his lips to his ear?" Louisa demonstrated on her own face. "Like that?"

"Yes, miss. Ma'am." Beam looked uncomfortable having to speak to a lady of such degree. "It was him who called."

Drake took back the reins. "And your leaders met with him?"

Beam grimaced. "I wasn't keen—he said he had a message from O'Connor, but he didn't have a letter." Beam nodded at the letter he'd laid on the counter. "Not like yours."

The man who'd spoken earlier shifted. "The other gentleman said as he had some secret message from O'Connor about some action O'Connor and the others wanted taken. That was all he would say."

"Just that, and all three of your leaders went to meet with him?" Drake tried hard to mute his incredulousness.

The men shuffled.

Beam coughed. "I warned them they were leaping in, but they said things had gone too quiet, and the men were restless, so they would go and hear what he had to say." Beam spread his hands. "So they went."

Drake glanced at the men. He was getting a bad feeling about this. "When was the meeting?"

"Last Thursday," Beam replied.

"And you've seen your three leaders since?" Drake asked.

Nods came from all around.

He fought not to narrow his eyes. "Are they expected today?"

And there it was—shifty, uncertain looks all around. Drake inwardly sighed and bluntly asked, "What is it?"

Beam sent a helpless look at the other men, then said, "We've seen none of our leaders"—he nodded at the list in Drake's hand—"since Saturday. Their wives were around here on Monday, and again yesterday, asking after them, but they—our three leaders—haven't come in since Saturday."

Drake exchanged a look with Louisa; he didn't need to ask to know what she was thinking. The odds were good the three leaders were dead. Drake met Beam's gaze and nodded. "If I learn anything about their whereabouts, I'll let you know."

"Thank you, my lord." Beam hesitated, then asked, "Is there anything else?"

"This is all I require at the moment. If I need more information, I'll be back."

Beam held up the letter. "I'll keep this on file."

Drake nodded and, gathering Louisa with a gesture, turned toward the door. The gathered men fell back, breaking into various groups. Their talk was now hushed; worry etched their faces.

Louisa led the way outside. When she paused just beyond the door, Drake urged her on with a hand at her back. "It seems," he murmured, "that the London Chartists were ripe for the plucking. I wonder how Chilburn—or even the mastermind—knew?"

"Did he know? Or was it just an educated guess?"

"Even an educated guess requires prior knowledge."

"True." She halted on the pavement and glanced at the list of names and addresses he still held.

He folded the sheet and tucked it into his coat pocket. Should he assume and head straight for Scotland Yard or...?

Louisa headed for her carriage. "As we're already on this side of the river, I suggest we check at those addresses first. Who knows? We might learn more from their wives. Not all men are as tight-lipped as you."

She halted beside the carriage door and swung to face him; he hadn't moved.

He studied her; she'd barely glanced at the list. "Where are you going?"

Her smile grew edged. "First to Swanston Street, then to Gilray Close, and finally to Milton Avenue."

He swore beneath his breath and went after her.

She turned to the carriage, and her footman opened the door. She called up to her coachman, giving the first address, which wasn't all that far away.

His jaw clenched, Drake waved the footman back, gripped her hand, and helped her into the carriage, then followed and sat beside her.

The footman closed the door, then clambered up behind as the carriage started rolling.

Drake waited until he was sure he had his temper under control before, with what he felt was commendable evenness, stating, "This is not a game."

Her response came in decidedly clipped accents. "Obviously. It sounds as if we have three more men dead." She shot him a glance from very green eyes. "Regardless of whether the wives have had the deaths confirmed or not, you will do very much better with me than without."

He hadn't thought of that. Dealing with grieving women...definitely wasn't his forte.

He slumped back against the seat. He was in no way resigned to her dogging his every step. Unfortunately, he was helpless to prevent her—Lady Wild—doing precisely as she pleased.

For a nobleman of his ilk, that grated.

CHAPTER 5

*H*e hated killing in daylight—the risks associated with hiding the bodies were, to his mind, unacceptable. Unnecessary. So much easier to strike at night and slip his victims into the waiting river.

The river confused things, too. No telling where a victim had been killed, and consequently, less chance of a body being identified rapidly. All of that worked to his advantage.

Not today. Luckily, the area near the yard included pockets of near-slum. He left his second body of the morning under a pile of rubble sheltered by the remains of a ramshackle stable in the minuscule yard of a dwelling that appeared deserted. Good enough. With luck, the body would remain undiscovered for at least a few days.

He didn't want anyone realizing where his latest victims worked, not until the gunpowder was well away.

But if the old man's third stage was going to succeed—if he, Bevis Griswade, was going to make himself the old man's sole heir—then he needed to make sure of all four men Lawton had recruited to make the critical transfer. Thank God he'd been curious enough to check on Lawton's Monday night activities. If he hadn't been there and seen the men's faces, he wouldn't know who among the large body of workers he needed to remove.

As usual, the old man's foresight in sharing Lawton's instructions with him smacked of near-omniscience. That, or a canny understanding that transcended the norm.

Walking steadily, he made his way back to the larger lanes. As he drew within sight of the yard gates, presently set wide, the city's bells started pealing. Ten o'clock. The other two men would be in the yard and hard at work by now. He would have to deal with them later. Even if he had to scour the neighborhood, he would find them. He knew where they worked; they wouldn't escape him.

Now, however, the fading echoes of the bells reminded him that he needed to be on his way. The old man would be waiting for his report, and he had no intention of disappointing.

Before he'd silenced his latest victims, he'd confirmed that the gunpowder was safely stored as planned, and the transfer had gone without a hitch.

He would ride into Berkshire, make his report, and then learn what the old man's plans were for the last and final stage in his thus-far remarkably ingenious plot.

CHAPTER 6

$\mathcal{B}$y the time they reached the third address on Beam's list, the one in Milton Avenue, Drake was exceedingly thankful that Louisa had insisted on accompanying him.

The wives of the men who had lived at the first and second addresses had been notified that morning by Scotland Yard that bodies believed to be those of their husbands had been found in alleys not far from their homes. Apparently, they'd been killed on Saturday evening, but separately, at quite different locations.

Both women had only recently returned from identifying the bodies and were in no fit state to be questioned.

Despite that, Louisa had won the trust of the females manning both doors and had learned that there was nothing known by either wives or friends of any matter that might conceivably explain the deaths.

"Other than," Drake had grimly observed as he'd handed Louisa back into the carriage, "each dead man having led one of the local Chartist militias."

With no great hope, he trailed Louisa up the short path to the door of the third militia leader's house.

But when the door opened, it was instantly obvious that it was the wife—a Mrs. Neill—who faced them. She wore her anxiety openly; she scanned their faces in hope, but that swiftly faded. Tremulously, she asked, "Yes?"

Louisa lowered and softened her voice. "We've been speaking with the London Working Men's Association. We'd hoped to talk with your husband, but I can see he's not yet back." She hesitated a heartbeat, then ventured, "I take it he's still missing?"

Mrs. Neill nodded. She gripped the door as if it could absorb some of the strain. "Just like the other two—the other leaders, I mean." She scanned their faces. "Have you heard about them?"

Her expression grave, Louisa nodded. "We've already called at their homes."

Mrs. Neill drew breath, then blurted out, "I'm hoping Bill wasn't caught up in it. Whatever it was. He was here on Saturday night, just as usual. I heard the other two never made it home that night, but Bill did."

"When did you last see him?" Louisa asked.

"Sunday morning, about eleven. After church. He set off to walk to the Association."

Drake kept his voice low, his tone undemanding. "Did he often go in on a Sunday?"

"Aye. Quite a few of the men gather there to play cards or darts of a Sunday afternoon."

"I wonder," Louisa said. "We've been asked by the Association's head to look into a certain matter. Did your husband mention anything about some secret effort for the cause?"

Mrs. Neill looked troubled. "I know he went with the other two leaders to meet with some man last Thursday night. He came back in a good mood—happier than he's been for some time. He said as how things were finally under way. I asked what he meant, but he said he didn't actually know—it wasn't anything he needed to do himself, just a matter of sitting back and watching what happened."

"He didn't have any idea what was supposed to happen?" Drake asked gently.

Mrs. Neill shook her head. "No—he said it was a secret." She looked at Louisa. "Like you mentioned."

Louisa nodded and thanked her for her time and tendered their sincere hopes that her husband might turn up hale and whole soon.

Mrs. Neill smiled wanly, bobbed, then shut the door.

Louisa turned and, inwardly grimacing, walked beside Drake to the carriage.

Drake murmured as he opened the door, "Neill's body will most likely turn up in some ginnel near the Association's office."

She glanced at him. "So it's off to Scotland Yard?"

From across the river, the bells started their long peal for midday.

Drake's gaze grew distant, then he focused on her face. After a moment of studying it—of reading her resolution, or so she hoped—he said, "Let's head back over the river and get something to eat. After that…don't you have calls to make? People to interrogate over the teacups as to Chilburn's friends and acquaintances, not to mention his address."

She tipped her head and considered the prospect, then shook her head. "I'll almost certainly do better on that front this evening. There are two major balls, and the Hawesleys are sure to be at one or the other. Hawesley at least will know his son's address." She met Drake's eyes. "But we can't call at Scotland Yard in the evening, so I suggest we head there once you've satisfied your appetite."

Drake swallowed a comment regarding appetites—no need to encourage her. He handed her into the carriage. "Aren't you going to eat, too?"

Her lips curved. "Not on your scale. I'll nibble."

He directed her coachman to take them across the river to Whitehall, to a lane on which lay a small public house with an excellent menu, then followed her into the carriage and sat.

He wasn't going to waste energy attempting to put his foot down over a duke's daughter venturing into the halls of Scotland Yard. Scotland Yard would just have to cope.

CHAPTER 7

"*L*et me get this straight." Inspector Crawford leaned forward, clasped his hands on his blotter, and fixed Sebastian and Antonia, seated before his desk, with a level look. "You believe the killing of Boyne in Kent is linked to the deaths of two carters who, shortly after, were found garroted and floating in the Thames. On top of that, you say that some blighter, possibly a gentleman, tried to kill your brother and, perhaps unsurprisingly, wound up dead, and you want to know if he—the dead gentleman—was Boyne's killer."

Antonia nodded decisively. "That's correct."

The inspector looked faintly harassed.

"Do you have a description of the man in Kent?" Sebastian asked.

Crawford frowned and started searching through a pile of stacked papers. "We didn't get much, I'm afraid. An ostler and a stableman saw the man we think must have been Boyne's killer. He was riding a good-looking hack and stopped to water it—truth be told, we've a better description of the horse than of him."

"If it's any help," Antonia put in, "the dead gentleman had a scar on his face, from the corner of his lips to the point of his jaw—possibly a sword cut. If the ostler and stableman were at all close or spoke to the man, they would have noticed."

Crawford glanced up. "Is that so?" He drew out a page covered with tiny writing, placed it before him, and read, then he grunted. "It seems the ostler spoke with our man—received a penny for fetching a bucket of water for the horse—and as a rule, ostlers are sharp-eyed. His description of the man would fit thousands—nothing remarkable about his face at all." Crawford humphed. "Seems to me the ostler would have remembered a scar like that, so it appears your dead gentleman wasn't Boyne's killer."

Sebastian exchanged a grim glance with Antonia. "So we have at least two killers."

Crawford looked up. "As to that, I should mention that while finding bodies floating in the river is no great surprise, the ones we find are rarely garroted. That's not a common method of killing. Our surgeon tells us that the men were stunned first, then strangled."

"That," Sebastian admitted, "is a point we haven't dwelled on. But if Boyne's killer is also the one wielding the garrote…" He focused on Crawford. "Would you say your description of Boyne's killer is that of an Englishman?"

Crawford glanced at the page before him. "He couldn't rightly be anything else—the locals down that way are quick to note foreigners of any stripe, and the point about the description was that it would fit millions of Englishmen and, consequently, was no real use."

"But if we hypothesize that Boyne's killer is the garrote-wielder and he's English, then where did he learn to use the garrote? As you say, it's not a common form of killing in this country."

"Hmm. They do sometimes see it on the Continent," Crawford said. "But if you gave me that clue—a garrote-wielding Englishman—then I'd be looking for a gentleman who'd spent time in the east. Or…" He picked up the page and scanned it. "Yes—I thought they'd said that. Both the ostler and the stableman mentioned that although the man wasn't in uniform, he had guardsman stamped all over him."

"So," Antonia said, "possibly a guardsman who served in India."

Crawford nodded. "They use the garrote a great deal over there, or so I understand."

"That's interesting," Sebastian said. "Our dead gentleman carried a cavalry saber and knew how to use it, so there may be a connection between the two men via the army."

Crawford harrumphed. "I suppose there's no reason I shouldn't tell you that the River Police hauled another body from the river yesterday morning—garroted like the first two. After that tip-off from Lord Michael, we had the clerk from that warehouse in Morgan's Lane around, and he said it's their missing foreman right enough." Crawford met Sebastian's gaze. "Can I leave it to you to pass the word to your brother?"

Sebastian nodded. "We're all working together on this, albeit on different aspects."

"I thought as much. I have to tell you these garroting murders are all the talk of the higher-ups around here. That's not something they want the public getting wind of—too likely to cause a panic."

Sebastian glanced at Antonia. "We should go. Thank you for your help." He picked up his cane and rose. He gave Antonia his hand, and she came to her feet.

Crawford hurriedly got to his. "I don't suppose you know who your dead gentleman is?"

Sebastian hesitated. "We do have some notion, but as the matter is rather sensitive at the moment, and as you know, this is all a part of a mission Winchelsea's running, I'd prefer to leave it to him to make any disclosures."

Crawford frowned, but nodded. "Quite. Quite. I'll walk you out."

He followed Sebastian and Antonia out of his small office, and they started down the corridor.

They reached the main stairs leading to the ground floor just as another group descended from the upper floor—Louisa, Drake, and a uniformed individual with braid on his shoulders.

Louisa smiled, transparently delighted. Her gaze passed over Sebastian and Antonia and fixed on Crawford. Her smile brightened. "Inspector Crawford, I presume?"

Her husky contralto sounded entirely out of place in the gruff, rather bleak halls of the Yard.

Smoothly, Drake stepped in and made the introductions. "Lord Sebastian Cynster, Lady Antonia Rawlings—allow me to present Assistant Commissioner Chartwell."

Sebastian shook hands, then introduced Crawford to Louisa and Drake. Sebastian then gave Drake—and perforce Louisa, given she was standing beside Drake and avidly listening—a concise report of what he and Antonia had learned from the inspector and what they'd deduced.

"So the foreman has been found dead, garroted like the two carters," Drake summarized. "And Boyne's killer wasn't our dead gentleman, but we don't yet know if Boyne's killer is the man wielding the garrote."

Sebastian stirred. "Boyne was facing his killer. If it was as we suspect and Boyne was working with the man, and was agitated and pleading to be spirited away, then there might not have been time for the killer to have calmed Boyne sufficiently to let him get close enough behind Boyne to use the garrote."

"No, indeed." Drake nodded. "When killing Boyne, from the murderer's point of view, time was definitely of the essence. Much faster to simply shoot Boyne. So he did."

Chartwell shifted uneasily. "That suggests that there's no reason to *discount* the possibility that Boyne's murderer and the man garroting people and slipping their bodies into the Thames are one and the same."

A second's pause ensued, then Drake looked at Sebastian. "Two of the three leaders of the local Chartist militias have been found murdered in alleys in the area around the London Working Men's Association. A third body, most likely that of the third leader, is awaiting identification." A constable had already been dispatched to summon Mrs. Neill by the time Drake and Louisa had arrived at the Yard. "All separate killings—two on Saturday night and the other on Sunday." He glanced briefly at Louisa, then returned his gaze to Sebastian. "I'm on my way to the morgue to speak with Sir Martin Cranthorpe, the surgeon who examined the bodies. Care to join me?"

"Ah—perhaps," Assistant Commissioner Chartwell said, "the ladies would prefer to wait in my office."

To Drake's ears, Chartwell sounded faintly desperate.

Predictably, Louisa and Antonia exchanged a swift glance, then both turned sweet smiles on Chartwell. Louisa patted the man's forearm. "Thank you for the kind offer, Assistant Commissioner, but actually, Lady Antonia and I would much prefer to hear what Sir Martin has to say directly."

Chartwell sent a helpless look at Drake, which Drake ignored in favor of exchanging a resigned glance with Sebastian.

Crawford read the exchange correctly. He waved down the stairs. "The morgue's in the basement."

"Actually, Crawford," Chartwell said, "I was intending to speak with you about this case. As it seems all these murders are connected in some way, and as you were the investigator for the first of the deaths, it might be best were you to continue as investigator-in-charge of our activities in unraveling this...." Chartwell gestured vaguely.

"Plot," Drake dryly supplied.

"Indeed." Chartwell bowed to Drake and Louisa, and to Sebastian and Antonia. "I will leave you in the inspector's capable hands." His gaze flicked to Crawford. "Needless to say, you may be assured of having the full resources of the Yard at your disposal in this matter."

Drake murmured their thanks, and after another bow, Chartwell withdrew, turning and ascending the stairs.

Crawford grunted and shot a look at Drake and Sebastian. "I'm not sure if being in charge of this one will be a good thing or not. But"—he gestured onward—"we may as well see what Sir Martin will deign to tell us."

Crawford led the way. Sebastian and Antonia followed, with Drake and Louisa bringing up the rear.

"Somehow," Louisa murmured, "I feel as if I'm walking into a lion's den. Knowing more about Sir Martin might be helpful."

After a moment, Drake replied sotto voce, "He's an experienced surgeon and the Yard's chief pathologist. He considers the morgue his domain and all those who enter little more than students. He's often irascible and difficult, but he misses very little."

"Ah—I see." Louisa's lips curved. "One of those."

Drake refrained from asking for clarification; he doubted any answer she gave would be intelligible to a male.

They continued down the stairs to the basement. Crawford led them along the tiled corridor to the heavy swinging doors of the morgue; even from outside, the smell of the various fluids used by Sir Martin and his acolytes was strong.

Crawford held open the door and waved them in. Louisa wrinkled her nose, but without hesitation, followed Antonia into Sir Martin's domain.

Sir Martin was seated at his desk to one side of the large chamber. He glanced up as they entered, his usual contemptuous snort of greeting halfway to utterance, but the sight that met his eyes momentarily froze him.

Drake hid a smile as Louisa, a distractingly gracious smile on her lips, swept forward.

"Sir Martin?" She halted as Sir Martin, a large man, hastily clambered to his feet, then she held out a gloved hand. "I'm Lady Louisa Cynster." She looked on approvingly as Sir Martin bowed over her hand. As he straightened, she waved toward the rest of them. "I understand you're acquainted with Lord Winchelsea and, of course, Inspector Crawford. The other gentleman is my brother, Lord Earith, and the lady is his fiancée, Lady Antonia Rawlings."

Sir Martin bowed to Sebastian and Antonia.

Her expression turning expectant, Louisa swung her gaze over the room. "I believe you have some dead bodies to show us. I confess I'm intrigued by what deductions you can make from the manner of their killing."

It took effort to keep his grin from his lips; Drake almost felt sorry for Sir Martin as that redoubtable martinet blinked and battled to come to grips with a situation he could not possibly have foreseen.

Unsurprisingly, Sir Martin's gaze eventually shifted to Drake in something close to appeal. "Ah—yes." As if the sight of Drake had given him some recognizable rock to cling to, Sir Martin more briskly said, "We have several that I believe will be of interest. One brought in dripping yesterday morning—that one's from your garrote-wielder. His signature hasn't varied." Having found his stride, Sir Martin enthusiastically demonstrated on an imaginary victim, his actions mirroring his words. "He stuns his victims first with a blow to the head, struck from behind, right-handed blow, then he uses a wire garrote to finish them off, and it's into the river, all neat and tidy. We've now got three to his score. However," Sir Martin had steadied and continued in his lecturing voice, "yesterday we had two others brought in, with another found this morning, and they were quite different to the garrote killings."

Sir Martin rounded on Drake. "Are you interested in the latest three as well?"

"It seems so," Drake replied. "The first two—the ones from yesterday—have already been identified as the bodies of two men we were seeking to question."

"In relation to the same plot?" Sir Martin's brows beetled as he looked searchingly at Drake.

"Yes. What can you tell us about the actual killings?"

Sir Martin humphed. "Of those first two—they were killed separately, but within a few hours and in the same area, a few blocks apart. Very definitely killed by the same man—his signature is almost as definite as the garrote-wielder."

"How so?" It was Louisa who asked.

"It's the angle of the thrust." Again, Sir Martin demonstrated, with his right hand thrusting an imaginary knife sharply upward, angling the phantom blade a little to the right. "He uses a dagger of some sort—longish, smooth-edged, double-sided blade, wider than a stiletto—and he stands in front of his victim. The tricky part is that he has to be close to send the blade up under the lower edge of the ribs, straight into the heart. He has to be well practiced—such strikes have to be very quick and absolutely precise. The other difference is that our dagger-wielder leaves his victims more or less where he kills them. Oh, he might stuff them in the nearest dark nook, but he doesn't bother with the river or, indeed, trying to conceal the bodies as such. I suspect he only sticks them somewhere so they remain out of sight long enough for him to make himself scarce. Just his luck that in this case, it's taken a few days for someone to stumble over them."

"And the third body?" Drake asked. "The one found today?"

Sir Martin stroked his chin. "I'd say that one was killed on Sunday, possibly around noon."

Louisa glanced at Drake. "Mrs. Neill said her husband left home at about eleven to walk to the Association office."

Sir Martin humphed. "That fits. His body was found a few blocks from the Association building. Saturday's two—and I think they were killed early evening—were in the same general area."

"Most likely as they left the Association offices." Drake looked at Sir Martin. "Would there have been any blood on the killer's clothes? Either of our killers?"

"Little to none," Sir Martin replied. "With the garrote, none, of course, and as for the dagger-wielder, that's one of the advantages of the way he strikes. There's little bleeding outside the body and no reason the killer would have been wearing any blood."

After a moment, Sir Martin grunted. "One thing I can add is that this dagger-wielder is extremely coolheaded. There might not have been many people about on the streets in that area on Saturday early evening or on Sunday before noon, but there would have been some. Yet he killed in the open street—we've found the actual spots in all three cases—and his aim didn't waver an inch. More, he had to have known his victims—he was close when he struck, and none of them even suspected. There was no sign they fought or resisted in any way. Whoever he is, they thought he was a friend."

Drake exchanged a glance with Sebastian. From the corner of his eye, he saw Louisa and Antonia glance at each other, too.

He looked at Sir Martin. "Thank you. We'll need to know if"—he broke off, then faintly grimaced—"when other bodies killed in the same way turn up."

Sir Martin frowned. "Are you telling me there'll be more?"

"Sadly, yes. There are at least two other men we know of who've been lured into this plot and have, therefore, however unwittingly, signed their own death warrants. We haven't yet identified who the pair are, but they drive carts, possibly for a living, so you might find the usual calluses on their hands."

Sir Martin and Crawford exchanged a look, then Sir Martin asked, "Same killer?"

Drake paused, then said, "I think we've removed one of them. If I had to guess, I would say the one we've eliminated was the dagger-wielder. That said, we can't be sure he hadn't killed others before we stopped him, but he definitely didn't have time to kill the two cart drivers. They were still alive when he...wasn't."

Sir Martin humphed.

Crawford grunted. "I'll get the word out to keep all eyes peeled for more bodies killed by either means."

Drake had already started steering Louisa toward the door. She paused to bend a regal look on Sir Martin and the inspector and say, "Do be sure to let us know immediately if—or when—you find any."

With that and an inclination of her head, she passed through the door Drake held open.

After bestowing a similarly regal nod, Antonia followed.

Leaving all four men to exchange speaking glances, then Drake and Sebastian followed the two ladies. Still resigned. Still holding their tongues.

CHAPTER 8

*M*ichael followed Cleo into the office of the Inspector General of Gunpowder. As Michael understood it, the purpose of the office was to examine and approve the quality of the gunpowder sourced to supply Her Majesty's forces from the many gunpowder mills scattered around the country. Now that almost all the mills were in private hands, the Admiralty and the army considered such checks critical in assuring the performance of gunpowder dispatched to the various outposts of empire.

As was fast becoming their investigative modus operandi, Michael used his title to gain immediate attention, then stepped back and let Cleo use her knowledge to extract the information they required.

In this case, they quickly found themselves seated before the desk of a Mr. Crimmins, who, they were assured, was the most experienced of the office's testers.

Her hands clasped on her reticule, set in her lap, Cleo explained, "We are assisting the authorities in a rather complicated matter, and the question has arisen of whether it's possible to transport gunpowder in some container—be it barrel or bag—other than a barrel expressly manufactured for that purpose." She fixed bright eyes on Mr. Crimmins, a small, neat man of indeterminate years. "We hoped you—or at least this office—would be able to give us valuable insight into the possibilities."

Mr. Crimmins all but preened. "Well, as to that, Miss Hendon, I can say with certainty that in all my years of assessing gunpowder, I have never come across a satisfactory means of transporting it—especially over any distance and even more if water is to be crossed—other than by sealing it within barrels specifically made for the purpose. You see"—Crimmins leaned forward, using his hands to demonstrate—"the staves from which gunpowder barrels are constructed must be not just overlapping but perfectly fitted and, indeed, airtight. Virtually all other barrel types fall into two categories—they are either for storing and transporting liquids or for storing and transporting powders and solids that do not need to be kept airtight. The latter type of barrel is obviously useless for your purpose—exposure to air, and the moisture air inevitably carries, very quickly degrades gunpowder. I've known breached barrels to become useless in just a few days if there's a body of water anywhere near."

"What about barrels made for storing liquids?" Michael asked. "I would have thought they would be airtight."

Folding his hands before him, Mr. Crimmins nodded earnestly. "Indeed, so one would think. However, such barrels—for instance, those used for storing and transporting beer, wine, or spirits—are not *constructed* as airtight. That sort of barrel relies on the liquid itself to soak into and swell the staves. That's what creates the seal and makes those barrels airtight. And that's why gunpowder barrels are made by specially trained coopers—the staves have to be made to a much higher standard of fit to create a seal that's entirely airtight without the benefit of any later swelling."

"What if," Cleo asked, "one were to use old wine casks emptied of wine and dried out? Could those be used to transport gunpowder without ruining it?"

Mr. Crimmins's smile was patronizing. "Oh, dear me, no. That has been tried. For instance, it's certain that the famous Guy Fawkes plot, even had the perpetrators not been betrayed, would have come to naught—or as we in the trade say, would have merely fizzled—because they had thought to disguise their gunpowder in beer kegs in order to smuggle it into the cellars beneath Parliament and, thus, had ruined the gunpowder. No matter how well dried the barrel, once it has been used to store liquid—any liquid—there will always be too much residual dampness in the wood. Or alternatively, if the barrels truly are fully dried out, the gaps between the staves will open, and the barrels will no longer be airtight. Either way, that's not a useful way to proceed—not if one wants the gunpowder to perform to any acceptable standard."

Cleo exchanged a glance with Michael. She and he had spent the morning checking with the numerous Cynster footmen in the cordon encircling the neighborhood in which the ten barrels of gunpowder had gone to ground. They'd made a list of the different types of containers that their watchers had seen being moved out of the area on drays, carts, barges—any possible alternative to gunpowder barrels that might conceivably be used to disguise the gunpowder and move it onward, presumably to the intended target site.

Mr. Crimmins's experience seemed to negate that possibility.

She looked again at the clerk and stated, just to be sure, "So there's no other way of transporting gunpowder other than in specially made gunpowder barrels."

Mr. Crimmins nodded. "I would say that's so—unless, of course, one was merely transporting small amounts. Then old-fashioned skins might be employed—the type musketeers used to carry their powder in days gone by."

Cleo wrinkled her nose. "We're looking into the transport of multiple barrels' worth, so it can't be that." She stifled a sigh and rose. "Thank you, Mr. Crimmins. You've been most helpful."

Beaming, the clerk rose. They shook hands all around, then Cleo led the way out.

CHAPTER 9

*G*riswade stood at ease in the upstairs parlor of the old manor house—a house he was starting to view through the eyes of pending ownership. Facing the old man sunk in his Bath chair, he stated, "All is in readiness exactly as you'd planned. The gunpowder has been efficiently transferred and is now safely stored, correctly labeled, and awaiting delivery. I confirmed that with two of the men involved in the transfer before I silenced them."

The old man's head, which now appeared overlarge for his shrunken frame, bobbed on his wrinkled, scrawny neck. "So Lawton succeeded in executing his part of the plan...well, all except removing the men he'd used. Still, it's a pity he was caught."

"Has he been caught?" Griswade hadn't heard anything of that.

"Oh, I think so." The old man looked up and met Griswade's eyes. "He would be here instead of you if he hadn't been."

Griswade acknowledged that was true and that Lawton vanishing of his own accord made no sense. Yet...

Through shrewd, calculating eyes, the old man had been watching Griswade's face. Now, a slight smile curved his lips. "Assuming Lawton is still alive—and we have no reason to think he isn't—then I seriously doubt he will reveal anything at all about our plan. There would be no point, and Lawton is cunning enough to realize that. As long as he remains silent, what can they possibly charge him with? Breaking and entering? But he had the keys. And what did he steal? As far as anyone knows, nothing is missing from that warehouse. In short, there is no charge on which they might hold him, at least not beyond a few days."

Although he'd thought of the possibility of Lawton being captured, Griswade had largely discounted it; being taken up for burglary or stealing in that area of Southwark didn't seem all that likely to him. More likely to his mind was that Lawton had fallen foul of someone and been killed, but either way, he, Griswade, was in the box seat regarding the third stage of the old man's plan. "So," he asked, "what's next?"

That, more than anything else, was what he'd ridden into Berkshire to learn.

Speaking slowly and clearly, the old man laid out the details—exactly what was to happen, how each step would play out, and most importantly, why. Griswade had to admit that every little step that moved the gunpowder nearer to the target was masterly in concept and in proposed execution. There was very little that could go wrong.

Despite the old man's fervor, Griswade felt no personal attachment to the end result, yet if that was what the old man wanted to happen in exchange for his estate and fortune, Griswade was more than happy to transform the old man's dream into reality.

After dwelling for some minutes in silent appreciation of the final act—the explosion and the chaos it would cause—the old man refocused on Griswade and rather querulously snapped, "Any questions?"

Griswade didn't let the old man's tone disturb him; now he was about to embark on the final stage, no doubt the old man was feeling a touch anxious. Griswade took his time going over the entire third stage in his mind, looking for potential problems, for gaps in the progression—anything he wasn't clear about, or the old man's orders failed to cover...

Eventually, he shook his head. "No—not about your plan. But I assume that with Lawton unable to act, I should silence the other two men who helped with the transfer?"

"Indeed, you should," the old man replied. "Even at this stage—*especially* at this stage—we cannot risk leaving any source of possible clues."

Griswade hesitated, then felt he should ask, "Clues for whom? Is it likely I'll encounter any opposition?"

The old man grunted. "I have long found it helpful to think ahead and, metaphorically speaking, spike every pistol that might be pointed my way." His gaze shifted to the chessboard on a nearby table. "Between your earlier efforts implicating the Young Irelanders and Lawton's seeding of rumors about the Chartists, I believe that those who might otherwise interfere will have too much on their plates to find any true thread and follow it sufficiently rapidly to catch up with your movements—at least not in time."

Griswade was relieved. He preferred—indeed, had expected—a relatively trouble-free path to his inheritance. Murder was one thing. Battling the authorities was something else again. "One other point." Griswade met the old man's still-sharp eyes. "What about Badger? I assume it was he who sent you word that Lawton hadn't returned home."

"Yes." The old man studied Griswade. "You haven't been to Lawton's lodgings yet?"

Griswade suspected the question was a test. He opted for honesty. "I thought it wiser to check with you first."

The old man's fleeting smile was approving. "You are a careful and cautious man—those are the right sort of attributes for an intrigue such as this." He paused, clearly considering, then nodded. "Yes, Badger has outlived his usefulness. Remove him as well. And search Lawton's rooms while you're about it. As I did with you, I insisted that Lawton committed nothing to paper, but it won't hurt to make sure."

Careful and cautious to the last. Griswade nodded. "I'll take care of that as soon as possible."

He shifted, preparing to depart. The old man fixed him with a wintry eye, and he stilled.

After a momentary hesitation, the old man said, "There should be no further need to report here until all is finished and done. I will, of course, expect to hear from you then. My final advice to you is this: On no account, no matter what happens, deviate from the plan. There may be slips—matters you can't control. Don't panic. Simply proceed, step by small step, and follow my directions to the end…" The old man's gaze grew distant, then he smiled beatifically, as if viewing his scripted climax, and murmured, "And all will be well."

Griswade waited for several seconds, but when the old man said nothing more—when his gaze did not return to Griswade but remained focused on some imagined vision—Griswade bowed, then turned and left the room.

He walked out of the manor into the failing light. He paused to tug on his riding gloves—and to shake off the conviction, underscored by the quality of the old man's final smile, that he was acting as the agent of a madman.

He didn't care. The price was right. He considered his next step. First things first—he would search Lawton's rooms and deal with Badger, who now knew too much.

Griswade caught his horse's trailing reins, swung up to the broad back, and turned the horse's head toward London.

CHAPTER 10

*L*ouisa arrived in Lady Harrington's front hall at eleven o'clock that evening.

She allowed the butler to remove her cloak, paused to shake her absinthe-green silk skirt straight, then turned toward the stairs leading up to the ballroom on the floor above. She'd stepped onto the first stair when a stir amongst the bevy of ladies who had arrived after her had her glancing back—to see Drake striding swiftly up the front steps.

He barely checked on the threshold; he spotted her and, with a curt nod to the butler, who bowed low and murmured, "My lord," made a beeline for her.

Completely ignoring the gaggle of other ladies filling the hall between them—a frothing tide of bright silks and lace that parted like the Red Sea.

On reaching her, he didn't pause but, taking her elbow, started them climbing.

Bemused—and amused—she acquiesced. Three steps on, she cast a swift glance back at the milling ladies. Avid eyes were fixed on them; hands were raised as whispers abounded.

The instant they were out of earshot of the hall, Drake stated, "I've spent the evening trawling through the clubs and hells one step below those I and my peers would normally frequent and have signally failed to turn up anyone who has seen or had contact with Chilburn recently. And by recently, I mean in the past year. The most I succeeded in wringing from what was mostly stone was that Chilburn had been known to be short of the ready for some considerable time."

They reached the head of the stairs, turned left, and strolled through an archway onto the tiles of the ballroom's foyer. Ahead, the doors to the large room stood wide, and it appeared their host and hostess were still receiving. A short queue of arriving guests led into the ballroom.

Drake eased his grip. As his fingers slid from her satin-sheathed elbow, Louisa suppressed a too-revealing, rather too-appreciative shiver. Together, they joined the receiving line.

"Is this the first event you've attended tonight?" Drake murmured.

"No. I went to Lady Osterich's for dinner. Sebastian and Antonia were there, and my parents as well. After that, I went on to the Framlinghams' rout." Louisa lowered her voice as the line moved forward and the ladies from the front hall bustled up behind them; tipping her head closer to Drake, she murmured, "I found another of Lawton's sisters-in-law there. While she didn't know Lawton's address or anything about the company he's been keeping, she confirmed that he is not in good odor with the rest of the family, primarily as a result of his insistent and persistent cadging from them, year after year, to gamble and generally laze about. Disapproval appears to be universal."

Fleetingly, Drake grimaced. "That fits with what I've learned. It appears he'd dropped out of the expected social circles."

The couple ahead of them moved forward to greet Lady Harrington and her spouse, then it was their turn.

Louisa smiled serenely and congratulated her ladyship on an excellent turnout. She might as well have been speaking to the wall; Lady Harrington's gaze had fixed on Drake, and her mouth fractionally agape, her ladyship was staring as if she couldn't believe her eyes.

Drake inwardly sighed and smoothly bowed. "Lady Harrington."

Her ladyship finally found her tongue. "Lord Winchelsea—it's a pleasure to welcome you, my lord."

"The pleasure is all mine, I assure you." With an elegant inclination of his head, Drake moved on, with a hand at the back of Louisa's waist, steering her before him. They exchanged nods and greetings with his lordship, a genial, rotund gentleman entirely devoid of his wife's transparent curiosity.

As Drake, with Louisa, passed into the crowd, he could feel Lady Harrington's gaze boring into his skull. Arriving with Louisa had undoubtedly put the cat among the pigeons, but...he wasn't sure he cared.

He glanced at Louisa; as far as he could tell from her demeanor, she didn't care—wasn't the least bit fussed by a reaction that he would take an oath she hadn't missed—either. She seemed far more intent on scanning the throng around them.

"Given the Hawesleys weren't at Lady Framlingham's, and as I know they're longtime acquaintances of the Harringtons, then with any luck at all, they should be here." She glanced at him. "From your lofty height, can you see his lordship?"

"Hawesley?" He looked around, then grimaced. "Truth be told, I'm not sure I would recognize him."

Louisa heaved a put-upon sigh. "In that case, I'll have to work my way around the ballroom." Without further ado, she started on her quest. She'd said nothing about Drake accompanying her, but he seemed intent on hovering.

She was forced to stop every few feet to exchange greetings and occasionally indulge in the usual conversations. Drake, too, was frequently waylaid, mostly by gentlemen, but occasionally by ladies. Not unmarried ones—matrons of the ton. Louisa needed no clues to guess why such ladies wished to corner him, to hang on his arm and whisper in his ear.

Much good did their machinations do them; whenever she moved on, he materialized by her side in less than a minute.

She wasn't immune to feeling smug but endeavored to keep all signs of gloating from her face.

Indeed, she wasn't entirely sure what Drake thought he was doing. His appearance at the ball, apparently as her escort, had sparked a veritable wildfire of conjecture that, at that very moment, was burning out of control through the assembled ladies; she was perfectly aware of that, but was far too experienced to react. Ignoring all speculation was the best way to deal with overcurious, overly imaginative ladies.

Meanwhile, she was intent on finding Viscount Hawesley and learning Lawton's address. If she missed his lordship that evening, she wasn't confident she would get another chance to question him within the next few days. As she didn't know how long they would have to solve the riddle of Drake's mission, making every effort to learn Lawton's address as soon as possible seemed wise.

And if Lawton had deserted the usual ton circles, his family—those nearest and dearest—were the only certain source of the required information.

As she tacked through the crowd, surreptitiously searching for the viscount's robust figure, she considered alternative paths. If she failed to locate his lordship tonight, she might fabricate a reason and call on the viscountess tomorrow.

She hadn't succeeded in thinking of a believable reason when, through a gap in the crowd, she spotted Lord Hawesley. Drake had been distracted by an inquiry from a friend of his parents; as he returned to her side, she glanced at him.

If she approached Hawesley with Drake at her shoulder...

She faced him and heaved a huge sigh. "You, my lord, are cramping my style."

His only response was a slowly raised, highly skeptical eyebrow.

Ignoring that, she pointed over his shoulder. "The cardroom appears to be crowded. I haven't checked in there. Even if you can't recognize Hawesley, there's sure to be someone there from whom you might inquire. At the very least you might run across one of Lawton's brothers, and they are among the few who are sure to know where he lived."

He studied her, making no effort to hide the calculation in his golden eyes; he was evaluating and weighing the possible reasons for her request.

She returned his gaze with untrammeled calm.

Eventually, he snorted softly. He glanced in the direction in which she'd pointed, then looked back at her. "Don't leave this room without informing me."

She widened her eyes, but before she could inform him what she thought of that outright order, he turned on his heel and walked off toward the cardroom.

As that was precisely what she'd wanted, she contented herself with a glare. How did he imagine she might abide by his dictate? If he was in the cardroom, but she couldn't leave the ballroom...? "Idiot man." She turned, fixed her sights on Viscount Hawesley, plotted her path to his side, then set off to corner her quarry.

She didn't approach directly; Hawesley was no fool. Instead, she chatted with a neighboring group, eventually parting from them with a gay laugh and a wave—which brought her turning, all but stumbling, into the gentleman standing beside Hawesley.

The exchange of apologies on both sides brought her neatly into the small group formed by Hawesley and two gentlemen she recognized as the viscount's close friends. Apparently only then noticing the viscount, she smiled delightedly and held out her hand. "My lord—we haven't met in an age."

"Lady Louisa." Hawesley beamed; he was no less flattered than the next man when a fashionable beauty deigned to recognize him. He took her hand, bowed over it, then introduced her to his friends.

After the usual exchange of greetings, she adroitly steered the conversation to horse racing, a topic gentlemen almost always appreciated and one on which, courtesy of her father's cousin, Demon Cynster, the reigning king of Thoroughbred breeders, she possessed a more than adequate insight.

Unexpectedly, she was visited by several qualms over questioning Hawesley about a son he didn't yet know was dead. But the safety of who knew whom was at stake, so she stiffened her resolve and held her course.

Using the skills she'd learned at her mother's and grandmother's knees, she encouraged the conversation to run freely. Only when it started to flag naturally did she evince any sign of being about to move on—then as if struck by a thought, she stilled. With utter ingenuousness, she smiled and met Hawesley's eyes. "That's it—I knew there was something tickling the back of my mind when I first set eyes on you, my lord."

"Oh?" Hawesley arched his brows. "I'm not entirely sure I want to know what that is, my dear."

She laughed. "Oh, it's entirely innocent. One of my cousins recently met your son Lawton at a race meeting, and my cousin was left holding some winnings that were paid out after Lawton left. He—my cousin—has been trying to discover Lawton's address to deliver the sum to him, but to no avail." She smiled beguilingly at Hawesley. "If you would be so good as to give me Lawton's address, my lord, I'll pass it on. My cousin's quite put out about it—I know he'll be grateful for the information."

Hawesley hesitated. His reluctance was palpable. She'd given him no excuse to refuse, yet he clearly didn't want to give her Lawton's address...

She allowed a little of her surprise and the resulting curiosity to seep into her expression.

Hawesley stirred, coughed—then his expression cleared. He hunted in his pocket and pulled out a card case. "I'll write the address down for you, my dear, and then you can pass it on to your cousin." He pulled out a pencil and swiftly scribbled on the back of a card. "Which of your cousins was it?"

She didn't miss a beat. "Toby." At that time of year, Tobias, third child and second son of Demon Cynster and his wife, Felicity, would be immersed in all things racing and almost certainly not in London for Hawesley to trip over. Moreover, at twenty-four, Toby was horse-mad and was likely to frequent all race meetings, as well as being the trustworthy sort that other gentlemen might delegate to collect their winnings.

"There, then." Hawesley handed her the card and tucked away his card case.

She let her smile brighten. She made no move to read the address but immediately slipped the card into her reticule and snapped it shut. "Thank you, my lord. And now I must leave you. *Such* a crowd—Lady Harrington must be feeling quite chuffed."

After curtsying gracefully in response to the gentlemen's bows, with a last brilliant smile, she moved into the crowd.

Without being obvious about it, she set a direct course for the ballroom doors.

When Drake abruptly appeared at her side, she struggled to hide her grin.

"Did you get Chilburn's address?"

She'd thought he'd been watching her—while tacking through the guests and speaking with Hawesley, a subtle tingle of awareness had frequently brushed her nape before slithering down her spine. "You were supposed to be in the cardroom."

He made a dismissive sound. As, side by side, they maneuvered toward the door, he repeated, "Did you get it?"

"Yes. I wouldn't have if you'd been with me."

He didn't respond, at least not with words. To her surprise—to her senses' shock—he caught her hand and smoothly twined her arm with his. When she glanced at his face, he nodded ahead. "Our hostess."

They tacked around the last knot of guests, and she saw Lady Harrington still at her post even though the arrivals had slowed to a trickle.

Her ladyship saw them approaching. Her face fell. "Leaving so soon, my dear? I had hoped to have a chance to catch up with you."

"Sadly, we must be getting on." Louisa glibly thanked her ladyship for the pleasure of the company and congratulated her on the success of her evening. Louisa and her ladyship exchanged curtsies, and Drake made his bow. Then with all due nonchalance, they quit the ballroom and, within seconds, were descending the stairs.

In the front hall, Drake collected her cloak from the butler and draped it over her shoulders.

She clutched the velvet folds close as they emerged onto the porch.

Her carriage, already summoned by a footman, rolled up and halted at the curb.

Drake led her down the steps, opened the carriage door, and handed her inside, then demanded, "Where?"

Dropping all pretense, she hunted in her reticule and hauled out Hawesley's card. "His lordship wouldn't tell me—he wrote it down." She angled the card to catch the light from the carriage lamp. "Number sixteen, Cross Lane." She looked at Drake. "Do you know where that is?"

"Off Long Acre." He stared at her, then his jaw firmed. "You can't go into that area, especially not at night."

She opened her eyes wide and raised her brows high. "And how, my lord, do you propose to stop me?" Before he could respond—because she suspected he would—she amended, "Or let me put it another way—won't I be safer if I go with you rather than venture there alone?"

That, of course, won her the round.

Narrow-eyed, Drake looked at her for several long seconds, then glanced at her coachman and relayed the address.

Then, with his jaw clenched against the urge to utter words he knew all too well were unwise, he climbed into the carriage and, very precisely, with the utmost gentleness, shut the door.

THURSDAY, OCTOBER 31, 1850

CHAPTER 11

*T*he city's bells tolled midnight as the carriage turned out of the streets of Mayfair and headed east along Piccadilly. From there, their route lay through Piccadilly Circus, then straight on via Coventry Street, along the north side of Leicester Square, on across St. Martin's Lane, and into Long Acre.

Despite the directness of their path, at that time of night, they ran into a certain amount of traffic—patrons from the various theaters, from the Opera, from the hells and clubs and elsewhere returning home. The hour was well advanced by the time the carriage drew to a halt in Long Acre. Peering out of the window, Louisa saw the corner of Cross Lane just ahead.

Drake descended, swiftly checked the surroundings, then handed her down. She drew her dark-green-velvet cloak close, both against the rising chill and for the relative concealment. Beside her, Drake conferred with her coachman, agreeing with the coachman's assessment that it was preferable to halt the carriage in the wider street rather than attempt to negotiate the narrower confines of the lane.

She glanced about. In Long Acre, streetlights were reasonably plentiful and shed enough light to illuminate the denizens still on the street—men and women both, some clearly the worse for drink, others more intent on commerce of various sorts. But in the lanes to either side, the streetlights were spaced much farther apart, leaving swaths of darkness between cones of yellow light. Although they were some way from the river, wisps of fog were thickening the air as the temperature dropped and the cold intensified.

"Come on." Drake took her arm and steered her to the mouth of Cross Lane. As soon as they entered the lane, shadows engulfed them.

She was grateful that Drake didn't stride rapidly but kept his pace to one she could match, steady, sure, and even. In the gloom, she had to manage her full skirts and cloak as well as being careful of her footing; evening slippers weren't ideal for negotiating damp cobbles in the dark. Not that she entertained any thought of complaining; she was intent on seeing what they might find in Lawton Chilburn's rooms.

Drake scanned the façades ahead. There were others walking in the lane, some couples, mostly men striding along. All exuded the air of people knowing where they were going; by walking relatively purposefully, he endeavored to make Louisa and himself likewise appear to have a known destination in mind.

He finally saw it. "Ahead on the right," he murmured and from the corner of his eye saw Louisa raise her head and look.

After a moment, she softly said, "The door between the bakery and the stationer's shop?"

"That would be my guess. Let's see."

They angled across the lane. On closer inspection, the number sixteen was carved into the stone lintel above the black-painted wooden door.

Drake tried the door and found it unlocked. "Interesting." He let the door swing inward and stepped over the threshold. A yard ahead, a set of stairs led upward into relative darkness; very faint light shone down from a skylight in the ceiling above the upper landing. He reached back, grasped Louisa's hand, and quietly ordered, "Stay close and shut the door."

He moved forward and waited while she stepped into the hall and closed the door behind her. Gloom engulfed them. He let several seconds tick past to allow their eyes to adjust, then he started up the stairs.

She had to manage her full skirts; her foot slipped once, but he held her steady.

They finally gained the small landing. A single door was set in the wall to the left. Chilburn's lodgings occupied the rooms above the stationer's shop.

Drake released Louisa's hand. Expecting to need his lock picks, he reached into his pocket as he closed his other hand about the doorknob, only to feel the knob turn freely. "Ah." He paused, then murmured, "I suspect someone else has been before us."

He twisted the knob and sent the door swinging wide. With one hand, he held it back while he scanned the room beyond.

All remained silent and still. There was no light burning; there was no one there.

Easing out the breath he'd instinctively held, he walked into the room. The curtains were open, and sufficient light seeped in to allow them to see the furniture. He looked to his left and saw a sconce on the wall; he walked across, turned up the gas, and lit the flame. As it steadied, he replaced the glass, turned, glanced swiftly around, and grimaced. "Someone has searched the place."

Louisa halted beside him, scanning the room, noting the papers left scattered on the central table and a writing desk, the disarranged cushions on the simple sofa. "Who? And what were they looking for?"

"Given his family doesn't yet know Chilburn's dead, I think we can assume that the search was ordered or done by whoever he was working for or with. Possibly the man who killed Connell Boyne, but there might be others acting for the mastermind as well."

"Hmm. Are we also to assume that they took away anything incriminating and that there's no point us searching as there'll be nothing left to find?"

Drake stepped back and closed the door, then walked to an old-fashioned escritoire set against the wall a few feet from the door. The front of the escritoire was down, forming a desk that was covered in a welter of papers. "No. We still search. You would be amazed at what people trying to hide their tracks leave behind." Another sconce was set on the wall above the escritoire; he lit that as well, casting light throughout the room.

Louisa moved past him, deeper into the room. She went to first one, then the other of the two open doorways that led to adjoining rooms. "As there's no one here…where's Lawton's man? What was his name? Badger?"

Drake drew out the chair before the escritoire. "I have no idea." He sat and started sorting the piles of disarranged papers. "See if you can find any clues."

Louisa humphed. She debated, then approached the rickety circular table that stood a yard or so in front of the battered sideboard that ran along the main room's rear wall. The sideboard's drawers were half out, and the doors of its cupboards were open; like the desk, it appeared to have been thoroughly searched. She gathered the papers scattered haphazardly over the table's surface, then swiftly flicked through them. "Nothing but playbills and notices of events—no letters or personal communications."

Drake grunted. After a second, he added, "These appear to be primarily vowels or bills, with the odd letter or note thrown in."

He continued to work his way through the bundles he'd assembled on the desk.

She studied him, then left the table and its uninteresting offerings and walked into the larger of the two other rooms. The bed, chest of drawers, and a rod across one corner from which hung several coats confirmed that this was Lawton's bedchamber. It, too, had been ransacked. Regardless, she dutifully searched, including checking all the coat pockets, feeling under the papers used to line the drawers, and lifting the horsehair mattress enough to peer beneath.

She emerged into the main room, shaking her head. "Nothing in there." She walked into the other, smaller room. It was little more than an airless closet containing a narrow truckle bed; pushed into one corner and running along one wall, the bed took up most of the space. Unlike the main room and Lawton's bedroom, this room appeared untouched. That might have been because there was nowhere to hide anything—no chest, not even a small side table. A shelf crossed the wall above the head of the bed; a single glance over the items ranged upon it was enough to establish that there were no papers of any sort hidden there.

She ran her hands over the thin blanket neatly stretched over the bed, picked up the pillow and shook it, but heard no crackling, then lifted the mattress, yet as she'd expected, there was nothing to be found.

"Huh." She returned to the main room.

Drake had divided the papers he'd found into three piles. He looked up as she neared. "Nothing?"

When she shook her head, he handed her one of the piles. "These are his unpaid bills—see if there's anything that stands out. I've gone through his letters—all are from his siblings and contain nothing relevant to the plot. These"—he waved at the pile he was still working through—"are demands and vowels. He seems to have owed a lot of people money, and he made a lot of promises."

Louisa took the stack of bills. She drew a straight-backed chair to the circular table, sat, and started working through the pile.

By "search," she had thought they would be opening drawers, poking into cupboards, and looking for concealed hiding places. Pausing in her task, she raised her head and scanned the room once more. Other than the sideboard and the desk, there wasn't any of the usual furniture that had drawers, and there were no other cupboards. Just tables and chairs, and all the cushions had been disarranged.

You would be amazed at what people trying to hide their tracks leave behind.

She turned in the chair and looked at the small room—the closet in which Lawton's man had slept. "That's Badger's room, that's his bed, and his brush and comb are still there. There's a perfectly wearable suit hanging on the back of the door." She turned back and met Drake's eyes. "So where is Badger?"

Drake held her gaze for an instant, then looked down at the papers through which he was rifling. "Once he realized Lawton wasn't coming back, then given the creditors who, judging by these demands, were guaranteed to come knocking, if there'd been anything worth taking, if he had any sense at all, Badger would have taken it in lieu of his wages and gone."

"Without his brush, his comb, and his extra suit?"

When Drake only grimaced and continued working through his pile, she looked around the room again. "Perhaps it was Badger who searched?" She glanced at Drake.

Without looking up, he shook his head. "Badger would have known where everything of value was kept—he wouldn't have had to turn the place upside down."

"So someone else came here and searched. Was that before or after Badger left?"

Finally, Drake met her gaze, and this time, his expression was grim. "That, indeed, is the question, and your observations make it unlikely that Badger left of his own accord. However, there's no sign of a struggle, so I suspect Badger went out, expecting to return, but either changed his mind and fled or he was waylaid somewhere and never made it back here. Then later, someone searched."

"You think they—the others in the plot—have killed Badger." She didn't make it a question.

Nevertheless, Drake nodded. "They've killed everyone else who might conceivably know anything. Now Lawton's gone, they have no need of Badger. It's possible he realized that and fled before they found him, but I think it's certain his name is on our garrotter's list."

"Hmm." She returned to the bills she was supposed to be checking—to what purpose, she wasn't sure. But when she reached the bottom of the pile, she frowned. Quickly, she flicked through the stack again, then set it down and looked at Drake. "There's no bill from any landlord here. Have you seen any accounting or an invoice?"

Drake glanced at her. "No. Nothing about rent."

She tapped a nail on the table. "I can't see Lawton owning this place, so I wonder if that means the landlord lives near—for instance, downstairs."

His expression arrested, Drake met her gaze. "That's...very likely." He set down the pile of papers he'd been leafing through. "Beyond that, there's nothing in these papers that hints at anything other than that Chilburn's pockets were perennially to let."

"Perhaps the landlord might have noticed something."

Drake got to his feet. "Someone living close with an interest in what goes on here, in who comes and goes, might well have noticed something. However, it's already long past midnight—we aren't going to get cooperation from any landlord by waking him at this hour. I'll send Finnegan to ask around tomorrow...well, later today."

She rose and handed back the stack of bills.

Drake took them and set them on the desk, then reached up, turned off the lamp, and waved her to the door.

She passed through it and waited as he turned off the second lamp, then joined her on the ill-lit landing, drawing the door closed behind him.

Realizing the dimness made it impossible to see his eyes, she led the way down the stairs and out of the door into the lane. There, she paused. Once he'd joined her and shut the black-painted door, she bluntly asked, "What are you planning on doing today?"

Drake met her eyes and lied. "Thinking things through and making plans."

She narrowed her eyes at him, her expression eloquently conveying dismissive disbelief.

Ignoring that, he took her elbow. "Come on. There's nothing more we can learn here—we need to be gone."

CHAPTER 12

*L*ouisa sat in the darkened carriage as it bowled toward Mayfair,
rolling freely now the traffic had eased, and pondered the state of her
personal campaign.

Her goal was straightforward: To discover what the seething attraction
between them sprang from, what it truly presaged.

The propinquity of the past thirty hours spent together focused on a
common cause was, she judged, producing the anticipated results and
escalating awareness, at least on her part.

Her nerves and all her senses seemed significantly more attuned to the
reality of Drake, sitting beside her only inches away on the carriage's
well-padded seat. The warmth radiating from his muscled body, the aura
of reined power, and the physical intensity she'd always associated with
him all impinged on her mind, while the subtle scent of his cologne
wafted like a miasma tempting enough to addle her brain.

After that all-but-phantom kiss the previous night, that ever-present
awareness had deepened and broadened; that part of her mind engrossed
with him seemed to have expanded and grown.

And if she was truthful, beneath her calm serenity, her outward control,
a sense of hunger had bloomed.

Yet she had no idea if he had been similarly affected by their interactions over the past two days. She had no way of telling.

A situation that, she decided, left her in a state of ignorance she couldn't afford to allow to continue.

When the horses turned into Grosvenor Square and slowed, Drake stirred. The instant the carriage halted outside St. Ives House, he reached for the handle, opened the door, and stepped out.

Swift glances left and right confirmed that no one was presently on that stretch of pavement. He turned and held out his hand to assist Louisa down.

She shuffled forward and paused in the doorway. With her skirts gathered in both hands, she looked down—at the edge of the step. At where the tips of her slippers should have been visible. "Damn!" she muttered.

Then she tipped and pitched forward.

Instinctively, he reached for her, to catch her before she fell.

Only to have her straighten and land breast to chest against him, fully within his arms.

Before he'd done more than register that—before his mind shook free of the physical shock of her slender, supple, subtly curvaceous, and far-too-alluring form plastered against him from shoulders to thighs   she'd reached up with both hands, framed his face, and pressed her lips, not in the least bit tentatively, to his.

His traitorous arms locked about her.

His traitorous lips responded to her challenge.

His traitorous tongue—

The instant she parted her lips, whether by his design or hers he hadn't the slightest clue or the slightest desire to know, he plunged into the heated haven of her surrendered mouth and claimed.

Took, sought, and with a hunger he couldn't rein in, couldn't tame— couldn't, it seemed, any longer restrain—he devoured and savored.

And she did the same.

She met him and matched him breath for breath, heartbeat for heartbeat, in a giddily escalating exchange.

Louisa clung and gloried—and did her level best to spin the engagement out. She reveled in the flagrant passion that laced each and every touch, each and every hungry caress—heated, blatant, powerfully inciting.

Evocative. Her whole being responded to the burgeoning flame, to the desire that sprang to life and the elemental hunger that prowled behind.

His lips and hers had all but melded. She no longer needed to frame his face. She slid her hands to his shoulders and gripped hard, fingertips sinking through layers of cloth to thrill at the tension investing the thick muscles there.

He responded with a kiss so scalding it all but curled her toes.

Emboldened and not to be outdone, she reached one hand to his nape, cupped it as she slid the fingers of her other hand into his thick dark hair and clutched, and held him to the kiss.

Held herself to the searing heat of their shared passions and wallowed.

Drake was mentally reeling. She wanted; he wanted. At this point, they should be looking for a bed.

His whirling senses drew back enough to assess...

Sheer shock gave him the strength to break from the kiss—to raise his head and drag his lips free of hers.

He glanced around—as if he'd never seen Grosvenor Square before. Then he looked down at her—took in the glow, the incipiently radiant expression that, as she surfaced, was slowly infusing her features. "Good God!" The imprecation was all but breathless.

She—the kiss—had dragged him under. So far under, he'd come up like a drowning man breaking the surface. He filled his lungs with much the same desperation and fought to steady his giddy head. "Damn it," he muttered. "We're in public."

He had to exert significant effort to force his arms to ease from about her, to release her—then he had to grip her waist to steady her.

From beneath her long lashes, her eyes gleamed. Her gaze traveled his face, then her lids rose fully, and her lips curved in a smug, cat-who-had-found-the-cream-bowl smile. "I'll bear that in mind next time."

The sultry words made his libido leap, made his cock, already iron hard, throb. He wanted to glare, but his features were not yet responding.

She grinned, then swiftly stretched up and touched her lips to his again.

With a muttered oath, he set her away from him and released her. Compressing his lips to a thin line, curtly, he waved her to the steps to her parents' front door.

Her lips still curved, her eyes dancing with entirely unsuppressed amusement, she consented to swing around, walk across the pavement, and mount the steps.

He trailed her as far as the bottom of the steps, ignoring the carriage—one of her family's town carriages driven by her coachman and with her groom up behind—as it rattled off to the mews.

On reaching the door, she turned her head and, over her shoulder, regarded him.

In triumph.

He narrowed his eyes at her. Through gritted teeth, he muttered, "You should be whipped."

She laughed, sultry and low, then she opened the door. As she walked inside, she had the temerity to call, "Goodnight."

He spun on his heel and stalked along the pavement. Reaching the steps to Wolverstone House, he all but snarled, "*Good* night? Huh!"

He leapt up the steps, opened the front door, and managed—just—not to slam it behind him.

CHAPTER 13

Step by quick, silent step, Griswade slid through the thick early-morning fog that blanketed the south bank of the Thames. His quarry lay ahead, walking purposefully through the maze of lanes that filled the blocks adjacent to the riverbank.

Griswade had disposed of one man already that morning—the third of Lawton's helpers. Luck had been on his side; the spot in which he'd chosen to lurk, entirely concealed by the helpful pea-souper, had turned out to be close to the man's house. Silent as a ghost, he'd trailed the man as he'd headed for his workplace.

Griswade had bided his time, then had come up behind the man. He'd stunned the fellow, looped the wire about the man's neck, and pulled it tight as he'd dragged the man down a narrow ginnel that led to the water. Slipping the body into the waiting river had taken no time at all.

Then he'd started after the last man.

From what Griswade had seen of the four men as they'd worked to transfer the gunpowder, this man was the youngest—the most junior. He should be the easiest to bring down.

Because of his earlier appointment, Griswade had accepted he would need to intercept this man closer to the yard. He'd noted the route the man invariably took to work and had plotted just where to attack.

But either the man had been early, or Griswade had fractionally mistimed his appearance. The man had already passed Griswade's chosen spot when Griswade had reached it, but luckily, the fellow had just been visible walking away into the fog.

Griswade had followed.

The slap of the man's shoes on the cobbles was Griswade's beacon. The fog grew even thicker; silently, he closed the distance between him and his prey.

In the fog, keeping track of where they were and attacking at just the right spot, where an alley or gap between buildings would give him cover against someone accidentally coming upon them, was easier planned than done.

Suddenly, the man's footsteps stuttered. Not stopping, but...dancing?

Griswade halted. Blind in the fog, he strained his ears. What was going on?

Then the man's footsteps resumed, louder but more rapid and fading as the man took to his heels and ran.

Instinctively, Griswade gave chase, but after three strides, abruptly pulled up. Chasing his prey through an area the prey knew better than he did—heading toward the man's workplace and workmates, no less—was the act of an amateur.

Griswade blew out a breath. He would have sworn he'd done nothing to alert his quarry, yet for whatever reason, the man had panicked.

Jaw setting, hands fisting, Griswade stared into the fog.

After several seconds, he stuffed his garrote into his pocket. One more day wouldn't matter. He knew what his quarry looked like. He knew where he worked.

He would find him later. Whether later today or tomorrow, it would make no difference to the old man's plan.

And when it came down to it, steering that plan to its conclusion was all that mattered.

Griswade swung about and strode out of the warren of lanes toward Tooley Street, his mind shifting to finding a hackney, rattling across the river, and buying himself a good breakfast.

CHAPTER 14

*W*hen, with the city's bells pealing nine o'clock, Drake descended from a hackney outside the London Working Men's Association, he wasn't the least surprised to discover Louisa's carriage drawn up to the curb as it had been the day before.

At the sight of him, her footman, who had been lounging against the carriage, rushed to open the carriage door and hand his mistress down.

Drake halted on the pavement where the short path led to the Association's front door and watched Louisa glide toward him. Today, she'd opted for a walking dress in a shade of rich burgundy. With barely a flounce, only a narrow band of ribbon marking the waist, and no lace whatsoever, the gown shouldn't have appeared fashionable, but it was cut superbly to showcase a figure guaranteed to draw eyes—not simply flattering but powerfully distracting.

Just the sort of quality he could use in a partner in the interviews to come.

Not that he had any intention of owning to that.

She halted before him, her expression serene and untroubled.

Swiftly, he searched her eyes and confirmed she truly did not feel any awkwardness over their interlude eight hours before—not in the slightest.

Her eyes held mild challenge, but to his relief, that challenge wasn't sexual.

God only knew how he might have responded had she chosen to play such a card.

Which, he realized, left him with nothing he wanted to say. No feeling he wanted to risk airing, not—as he'd so sapiently if belatedly noted in the small hours—while they were in public.

Having kept his own expression inscrutable throughout, he stepped aside and waved her to the door. "Shall we?"

A quick, quirky smile curved her lips, and with a dip of her head, she led the way.

Once again, they found a small crowd of men lounging in the main room. And, as before, she and he immediately became the cynosure of all attention; conversations died, and the men turned to regard them. The scrutiny, however, wasn't hostile but watchful.

Louisa swept the gathering with a reassuring social smile, then headed for the office window.

Alerted by the fading voices, Mr. Beam came to look out. The instant he saw them, he looked anxious. As, with Drake beside her, she halted before his counter, Beam blurted, "We've heard. All three of them dead." He swallowed and lifted his gaze to Drake's face. "Was it because of this false plot you were telling us about?"

Drake nodded. "That seems certain. I can't think of any other reason they would have been killed—all murdered within hours in exactly the same way, by the same man."

The man who'd spoken up the day before did so again. "Was it that other gent who came? The one they went to meet with?"

Again, Drake nodded. "However, that man is now dead as well." He glanced at Beam, then at the gathering men. "What I need to know now is what your three leaders agreed to do for that man."

The men exchanged glances, shifted and stirred, but no one volunteered a word.

Drake continued, his tone even, yet compelling, "I have to warn you that regardless of that man's demise, the plot with which your leaders unwittingly assisted him is still afoot. As matters stand, if the plot continues to fruition—to its intended end—then the Chartists may well be held accountable. The only way in which the organization might avoid that is by you telling me all you know and helping me to stop this plot."

Mutters arose, but no one stepped forward. The men turned inward, murmuring among themselves.

It was, it seemed, a difficult thing for them to break with years of habit and trust such a figure of authority as Drake inescapably cut.

Louisa glanced at Mr. Beam. The secretary was plainly torn, but he was, perhaps wisely, waiting on his members to give him some direction…or perhaps, given the way he was watching the milling group, Beam didn't know enough to be helpful but knew some of the others did.

She'd inserted herself into Drake's mission not just in order to spend time by his side but also because the mission intrigued her, and she'd wanted to see what contribution she could make—and ultimately, she'd wanted Drake to see that having her working with him, alongside him, in this sphere was to his advantage.

That said, she was loath to take the reins—to usurp his authority for however short a time—with this group. Yesterday, she'd lost patience and had spoken up, but once she'd said her piece and made her point and the men had fallen in with her directive, she'd stepped back and let Drake steer the resulting exchange.

He was infinitely more intimidating than she was.

However, when it came to persuasion…

And this mission had become far too serious for her not to do every last thing—pull every last string—she possibly could.

When the men showed no signs of coming to any quick, much less sensible decision, she drew breath and stated, "I would have thought you would have been all for avenging your leaders." Her cool, clear words drew and trapped every man's attention. Assured of her audience, she arched her brows lightly and boldly, one by one, met their eyes. "I hesitate to mention it, but from where I stand, you—by your underlying impatience for action in support of the Chartist cause and through passing the gentleman's message to your leaders without urging caution, without, indeed, heeding Mr. Beam's advice—contributed to your three leaders' deaths. You gave them to that gentleman. You set the stage and encouraged them to take to it. They were killed by the man into whose company you steered them—the gentleman with the scar across his face."

She paused to gauge their reaction; several of the men looked belligerent, but most appeared chastened, worried, and abashed. She moderated her tone. "Given all that, shouldn't you, every last one of you, now work with Lord Winchelsea"—she waved a hand at Drake, looming, expressionless, beside her; she knew his teeth were gritted, yet he'd made no move to silence her—"to foil this plot and find justice for your leaders who have been so callously sacrificed? Shouldn't you now take up the call and do all you can to bring down the others behind this plot and ensure that the Chartist cause—the cause your leaders believed so strongly in along with all of you—is saved from being besmirched and dragged down?"

The men blinked. It was an emotional appeal, rather than a rational one.

She kept her gaze steady, unflinching, and waited.

Beside her, Drake remained unmoving.

Mr. Beam, as well, studied the milling men without any sign of equivocation.

Eventually, the men glanced at each other, and muttered questions started to circulate. "Did you...?"

"Did anyone see?"

"Perhaps...?"

Finally, a man at the rear of the group volunteered, "Our three were to meet the man—the one with the scar who said he came from O'Connor—in the tavern in Weaver's Lane."

Others nodded. One said, "That were last Thursday evening."

"All right." Drake surveyed the men. "Does anyone know anything more?"

A man to one side frowned, then, speaking slowly, said, "I was in the Weaver's Lane tavern that night. I saw our three meet a man. I hadn't heard they were to meet with anyone—I hadn't been in here for a couple of days. And I can't tell you if it was your man with the scar because I never saw the man's face. He kept his hat pulled low the whole time, even when he got up and left."

"He left before the others? Your three?" Drake asked.

The man, now the center of attention, nodded. "Aye. He did. Left our three with a fresh round before them and strolled out of the door. By the way he moved, I got the impression he—the man who left—was pleased."

"Did you hear anything of what was said?" Beam asked.

The man shook his head. "Nah—I was at the bar, and they was in the corner. But later, Johnstone came to the bar, and we had a natter."

Johnstone was one of the dead leaders.

Without further prompting, the man continued, "O' course, I asked him—Johnstone— what the strange meeting was about. He said the man had brought word of some plot that O'Connor and the others up north had hatched, one set to make the cause front and center again. He said the man—the one they'd met—was running it and a right careful cove he was. He hadn't even told them any of the details—he'd said that information was only for those who needed to know." Frowning, the man paused, then went on, "That seemed strange, so I said that if he didn't give them the details of the plot, what was the point of him meeting with them? Just to tell them—and us—that there was a plot on?"

When, apparently caught in recollection, the man fell silent, Drake prompted, "And?"

The man stirred and glanced at his mates, who were hanging on his words as much as Drake, Louisa, and Beam were. "And Johnstone said as the man had just wanted manpower. That the stranger had asked for four men to be sent to meet him at some other watering hole. I said he could have hired four men from anywhere, but Johnstone grinned and shook his head. He said the four had to be of certain trades and with a certain business, but between them, him and the other two leaders knew just the right men to tap on the shoulder."

The man looked at his friends. "Well, of course I asked what sort of men—what trades—were needed, but Johnstone just tapped his nose and said he shouldn't say. That he'd already said too much." The man's face creased as, clearly, he wracked his memory. "Johnstone blathered a bit more about how great it was going to be to see the cause written up in the news sheets again." The man raised his gaze to Drake's face and met his eyes. "But he never said anything more about the four men the stranger had wanted."

Drake inclined his head in thanks. "So…the stranger wanted four particular men of your group, who worked at a particular business, and your leaders agreed to send the necessary four men his way." With his gaze, Drake raked the assembled company. "Does anyone have any inkling at all as to which four men your leaders sent to meet with the scar-faced gentleman?"

This time, the talk was a great deal more animated. Sadly, it soon became apparent that no one in the group had any idea what sort of tradesmen had been recruited, much less which individuals had been sent.

Finally, Beam cleared his throat loudly, then rapped on the counter until the talk quieted, and the men looked his way. Beam looked back at them almost defiantly. "Now we've lost all three of our militia leaders, and with Mr. Lovett and Mr. Hethcrington away in the country, it's me who has to run this show—and I say it's in our best interests, the best interests of the cause, to help the gentleman"—he nodded at Drake—"Lord Winchelsea here, and the lady, too, to find out what's going on." Beam's Adam's apple bobbled as he swallowed. "I say we should get the word out and see if we can learn which four men the leaders sent to meet with the scar-faced man."

The consensus was instant and unanimous. The group had, it seemed, been fired with the need to avenge their fallen leaders and protect their cause.

Drake inclined his head to the men. While Louisa beamed her thanks, he turned and offered his hand to Beam. "Thank you."

Somewhat tentatively, Beam gripped the proffered hand, and they briefly shook.

Drake released Beam's hand, drew out his card case, extracted a card, and handed it to Beam. "A message for me delivered by anyone to that address—to the front door or the back as best suits—will always reach me."

Beam studied the card. "Thank you, my lord." The secretary looked up and met Drake's gaze. "I don't rightly understand why you're doing this—helping the cause—but you were right about the danger the scar-faced man brought to our leaders. If you're right about the rest..."

His expression grim, Drake replied, "Sadly, Beam, I fear I'm all too correct about the danger these plotters pose to the cause."

Apparently registering Drake's use of "the cause" rather than "your cause," Beam tipped his head quizzically, but when Drake only met his gaze levelly, Beam nodded. "We'll send word the instant we learn anything, my lord. Anything at all about those four men."

Drake reached for Louisa's arm. "In turn, if we learn any relevant information from elsewhere, we'll be back."

With a last, heartening smile for Mr. Beam and a gracious nod to the other men, Louisa allowed Drake to escort her from the building.

Once on the pavement, he released her, and she turned to study him. As usual, his expression gave nothing away. She fixed her gaze on his face and waited.

He met her gaze—waited as well...

Eventually, he sighed and volunteered, "I'm going to start trawling through the military clubs."

She arched her brows consideringly, then suggested, "If you first check with the army, you should be able to learn what branch of the service Lawton was in. We've assumed he was in the cavalry, but that was based purely on his use of a cavalry saber—a saber he might have picked up anywhere. For all we know, he might have merely been an enthusiast over fighting with such a blade."

Drake conceded the point with a grunt. "I'll go first to Horse Guards and confirm his regiment and the dates he served, then I'll call at the most appropriate clubs." He waved her to her carriage.

Turning, she walked in that direction, with him keeping pace by her side.

"How are you planning to spend your day?"

"First, I'm going to call on several ladies," she said. "Hostesses I know well enough to call on so early. I want to glean all I can about the Chilburn family before I approach any more of its members." She glanced at Drake as they halted beside the carriage. "I keep remembering that comment Lawton made to Cleo about his cousin. If we can discover which cousin he meant, we might find someone with greater insight into Lawton's recent life and acquaintances. Also," she went on, "Grandmama and Lady Osbaldestone arrived last night, and I want to pick their brains."

Drake snorted. "Better you than me." Her grandmother and Lady Osbaldestone terrified his generation even more than they had his parents'. He thought, then added, "I'm going to call a meeting of our group at Wolverstone House at four o'clock." He met Louisa's gaze. "We need to learn if any of us has picked up any clue as to where the gunpowder is or who is behind the plot."

He opened the carriage door and handed her up.

After releasing her hand, he stepped back.

Surprised, she peered out at him. "Aren't you coming? I can easily drop you at the barracks as I go past."

He looked at her. The question revolving in his mind was, quite simply: *Is it safe?*

She must have read something of his uncharacteristic hesitancy, of the thoughts giving rise to it, in his eyes.

Slowly, haughtily, but with a faintly amused and challenging air, one black brow rose...

He wasn't such a coward. Lips thin, he nodded. "Thank you."

He glanced up at her coachman. "Whitehall. Horse Guards." Then he stepped up into the carriage.

She scooted across the seat.

He shut the door and settled beside her. Inwardly stiff and very much on guard.

Of course, this time, almost certainly because she delighted in confounding him, she behaved in an exemplary fashion and refrained from inciting him to madness in any way whatever.

After half an hour of easy, almost companionable silence, the carriage drew up across the street from the entrance to Horse Guards. He opened the carriage door, swung down to the pavement, saluted her, then shut the door and waved the coachman on.

He stood on the pavement and watched the carriage roll away. And felt faintly disgusted that, instead of feeling relieved over his escape from further temptation, he felt...disappointed.

She'd warped his mind.

He shook himself as if to shake off her disturbing influence, then crossed the street, nodded to the guards in their boxes flanking the gates, and stalked into army headquarters.

CHAPTER 15

*J*ust before four o'clock, Louisa started down the grand staircase of St. Ives House. As she'd intimated to Drake, she'd spent a busy morning calling on three ladies, all hostesses of significant standing, and being entertained with hot chocolate and tiny cakes while subtly seeking information on the Chilburn family.

All her endeavors had revealed was the apparently universally held view that the family was unremarkable if not boring, with no scandals or whispers of misdemeanors, much less odd political leanings, to lend the slightest spice. The current viscount and viscountess were held in mild respect. As for Lawton, their youngest son, no one knew much about him at all, other than to agree that he'd largely dropped from social sight over the past five or more years.

Defeated to some degree, she had returned home in time to enjoy a late luncheon in her grandmother's apartments with her grandmother, Helena, Dowager Duchess of St. Ives, and her grandmother's bosom-bow, Therese, Lady Osbaldestone. Although now very old, not to say ancient, and rarely appearing in public, both ladies still managed to keep their fingertips firmly on the pulse of the ton. Indeed, to most of the ton, the pair figured as society's éminences grises. Courtesy of their steel-trap memories, the two old ladies knew more about the elite families that made up the ton than any other living source.

True to form, in keeping with Louisa's fond expectations, the old ladies had had a little more to offer regarding the Chilburns and Lawton, some of which might possibly cast some light on the current investigation.

Eager to learn what the others had discovered—and hoping it was more than she had—she reached the front hall and walked swiftly toward the door. On hearing footsteps hurrying after her, she turned, smiled at Crewe, and waved him back. "I'm just heading to Wolverstone House. I daresay I'll be back with the others in an hour or so. I'll certainly be in for dinner."

"Very good, my lady." Despite her attempt at dismissal, Crewe insisted on hurrying past her, opening the front door, and bowing her through.

After bestowing an appreciatively gracious smile, she walked onto the porch and started down the steps.

"Heading for the meeting?"

The question had her looking up—at Antonia, who was walking along the pavement on Sebastian's arm.

Louisa smiled upon them both. "Yes." She fell in beside Antonia, and they continued along the street. "Have you been at Green Street?" Antonia's parents lived in a town house in Green Street.

"We have." Sebastian exchanged a glance with Antonia. "The Chillingworths are almost as curious about Drake's mission as Mama and Papa, but like them, appear to accept that dealing with such matters now falls to us rather than to them."

"Even Mama has been entirely supportive," Antonia declared. "I had thought she would be more difficult, what with our engagement ball so close and our wedding pending."

Louisa waggled her head. "On the other hand, having you both distracted with Drake's intrigue leaves the reins of both ball and wedding more firmly in their hands—meaning your mama's and our mama's. You have to admit that's an outcome they are unlikely to rail against."

Sebastian snorted.

Antonia grinned. "True. But regardless, everything seems to be working out for all of us."

"Let's hope," Sebastian said as they approached the Wolverstone House steps, "that grace extends to Drake's mission as well."

A clatter of hooves had them turning. They paused as a hackney drew up beside them. The carriage door opened, and Michael stepped out. "What-ho! It appears we're all here." He reached into the hackney and helped Cleo to the pavement.

Cleo grinned at them, then shook out her skirts and resettled her reticule while Michael paid off the driver.

In a group, they climbed the Wolverstone House steps. Hamilton responded immediately to their knock; he'd clearly been waiting to conduct them into the library. There, they found Drake standing before the fireplace and Finnegan hovering unobtrusively before one long window.

Drake waved them to the chairs and sofa. Cleo, Antonia, and Sebastian claimed the long sofa, with Michael taking the armchair beside the end at which Cleo sat. For her part, Louisa elected to sit in the armchair directly opposite the one Drake plainly favored, leaving her seated to Sebastian's right, with Drake to Michael's left.

Finnegan, Louisa noted, remained where he was. She was wondering why when Drake stated, "I suggest we report one by one on our activities and findings since last we met."

His gaze came to rest on Louisa.

She arched a questioning brow at him and received a faint nod in response. "Very well—I'll start. I spent some time searching for the Hawesleys with a view to discovering Lawton's address in town. Finally, I cornered his lordship and discovered that Lawton's rooms were in Cross Street, off Long Acre. Drake and I went there immediately—this was last night, or rather early this morning."

She paused and looked at Drake.

As usual, she'd leapt ahead. "I suggest we describe what we found in Chilburn's rooms later. First, Michael and Cleo need to hear what the rest of us learned when we called at Scotland Yard yesterday." Drake smoothly added, "And what sent all four of us there, which takes us to our interviews at the London Working Men's Association, both yesterday and again today."

Louisa adjusted her mental direction. "We—Drake and I—called at the association first thing yesterday morning and, again, first thing today." Swiftly, she outlined what they'd heard and subsequently suspected when they'd called at the three Chartist militia leaders' homes, suspicions that had been confirmed when they'd gone to Scotland Yard.

Drake stepped in to describe the salient point of the method of dispatch.

"In addition to that," Sebastian said, "Antonia and I had a word with Inspector Crawford. He confirmed that the description of the man who is believed to have killed Connell Boyne was sufficient to establish that Boyne's killer wasn't Chilburn. Whether Boyne's killer is the one who also wields a garrote is something we can't yet say, but as Boyne's killer was presumably the one who arranged for the carters to transport the barrels to London, and they were subsequently killed by garrote, then that seems a strong possibility."

"So all three leaders are dead, but killed by some killer quite different to the garrotter." Cleo grimaced. "So we have two killers. At least."

"Had," Drake said. "I strongly suspect Chilburn was the dagger-wielder, and it was he who killed the three Chartist leaders—the ones he'd spoken with, the ones who knew his face."

Antonia frowned. "But Chilburn was the gentleman-rider, the scar-faced man who worked with the two men who drove the gunpowder off into the fog." She glanced at the others. "Will he have killed those men, too?"

"He couldn't have," Sebastian pointed out. "Michael and Cleo removed him while the drays were driven on."

Drake shifted. "That said, as we know we have a second killer associated with this plot, then I doubt those men, if they are still alive, are safe. However, I haven't heard from Scotland Yard of any more dead bodies, and we"—his gaze switched to Louisa—"have at least made a start on identifying those men. Incidentally, there were four of them, not just the two who drove the drays."

Dutifully, Louisa related the bare bones of what had occurred when they'd called at the Chartist headquarters that morning. "We finally convinced them that finding out which four men the leaders sent to meet with Chilburn was in their and the association's and the cause's best interests. The association secretary, a Mr. Beam, is driving that search at this very moment."

Drake noted her use of the royal "we" when it would have been more accurate for her to say "I," but let the point slide. To his mind, there was no need to confess to her already-nervous brothers that her presence and active assistance had been invaluable. Bad enough that he knew, that he'd been forced to accept and face that fact.

His gaze on her arresting, animated face, he murmured, "You intended to spend the rest of your morning chasing information about the Chilburns. Did you get any further forward?"

She pulled an expressive face. "Not all that much." She sketched what she termed the general view of the Chilburn family and the viscount and viscountess. "But I did learn a little more from Grandmama and Lady Osbaldestone. Apparently there are a lot of branches and therefore twigs on the Chilburn family tree, so Lawton has lots of cousins of varying degrees. That said, Grandmama and Lady Osbaldestone were not aware of any tension or situation that might inspire one of his cousins to spy on Lawton and his doings. However, they did go on to say that as Lawton had several male cousins of similar age, his 'spy' comment might have been occasioned by some competition or attempt to gain advantage—to find out what Lawton was doing so as to interfere and possibly gain something for themselves. In that respect, there are eight cousins who might be the one Lawton referred to." Louisa closed her eyes and, after an instant's pause, reeled off the eight names.

She opened her eyes and looked at Drake, then at Michael and Sebastian. "Do those names ring any bells?"

Together with Michael and Sebastian, Drake volunteered his thoughts on several of those named. Between them, they could claim nodding acquaintance with four of the eight. "All thoroughly and entirely law-abiding souls," Drake summarized for the three ladies. "In fact, that entire family is not one you would expect to be drawn into a situation—an intrigue—such as this. They are dull, rather boring, and staunchly conservative."

Louisa nodded. "That was Grandmama's and Lady Osbaldestone's opinion, too. They were puzzled by the suggestion of wider family involvement."

Sebastian snorted. "If those two are puzzled, it's no wonder the six of us aren't making much headway with the Chilburns." He glanced at Antonia. "We've been quietly asking around, too, much the same as Louisa, but with different sources."

"We called in at Lady Oliphant's breakfast, then went on to a luncheon in Green Street with my Rawlings connections," Antonia said. "There was no notion anywhere of anything at all strange about the Chilburn family or their connections."

Drake humphed and shifted his gaze to Michael and Cleo.

Michael straightened. "We, on the other hand, called on the footmen on duty in Southwark this morning." He glanced at Cleo. "Aside from confirming that ten barrels of gunpowder have not been taken from the area, with the men's help, Cleo put together a list of all the different sorts of containers exported, as it were, from those particular lanes."

"If the gunpowder was to be transferred to some other receptacle, it seems reasonable to assume that the plotters would choose a type frequently seen moving out of the area," Cleo said. "That reduces the possibilities to just two. Either barrels of pickled herrings or barrels of beer or ale." She glanced at a list she'd pulled from her reticule. "I discounted the barrels used for spirits because they're so much smaller. The gunpowder would fill so very many, the number would be problematic and draw attention to the hoard."

She looked at Drake, then at the others. "We then went to the office of the Inspector General of Gunpowder and talked to the most experienced clerk. According to him, there is no known way of safely transporting a large quantity of gunpowder, especially near or over water, other than by using properly made gunpowder barrels. And those, as we know, will be stamped."

"He—the clerk—poured cold water over any notion of using brewery barrels, much less herring barrels," Michael said.

All of those seated frowned. Eventually, Drake voiced the conundrum all were wrestling with. "If they're not planning on disguising the gunpowder as something else, then… I'm finding it difficult to imagine how they propose to move the gunpowder into place at their chosen target."

Sebastian raised a shoulder. "Regardless, if they leave the gunpowder in gunpowder barrels, even if they change the stamp, the instant they try to move them out of Southwark, we'll see and swoop on the barrels."

"Hmm, no." Her frown lightening, Louisa looked around the circle. "You're forgetting—Chilburn hired *four* men of *certain trades and with a certain business.* Two were the drivers of the carts—that's one trade. So who—and what—were the other two? If he wasn't intending to disguise the gunpowder by putting it into some other sort of receptacle, then…"

Drake was nodding. "Then it's hard to see what those other two men would have been needed for."

"If they were transferring the gunpowder into other containers," Michael pointed out, "then Chilburn might well have needed all four men to get the transfer done before the morning."

"Perhaps," Drake said. "However, given this plot has been so exceptionally well planned from the start, I can't imagine them leaving such an obvious weakness—that of the gunpowder remaining in readily identifiable gunpowder barrels when moved to the target site— unaddressed." He glanced at the others. "We've discussed this before. Their best and surest way to get the gunpowder safely to the target site is to disguise it as something else—something normally found at the target site." He looked at Cleo. "Is there any chance we're missing something with regard to transporting gunpowder?"

Cleo bit her lower lip, then said, "There might be—indeed, I've a feeling there has to be." She glanced at Michael. "There's an old gunnery officer who used to work for Hendon Shipping. He's retired now, but if anyone would know of other means of safely transporting gunpowder, it would be him. We should go and see him tomorrow."

"Do that." Drake tapped his steepled fingers before his face. "They have to have some ploy in mind to get that gunpowder out of Southwark. Even though they don't know we're watching, the instant those barrels left the firework supply warehouse, they became very difficult to hide, much less excuse. Ten barrels of a hundredweight each. It's hard to imagine normal people overlooking such a cache."

Michael met Cleo's eyes. "We'll go and find your old gunnery officer tomorrow."

Drake mentally reviewed all they'd discussed, then said, "That brings us to Chilburn's rooms in Cross Lane." He caught Louisa's eyes and smoothly went on, "It was after midnight when Louisa and I reached there. The doors at street level and on the landing were unlocked, and the rooms had already been searched. Badger, Lawton's man, wasn't there, but as his clothes and brush and comb were, we're not sure what conclusion to draw from that. He might have fled in panic. We searched all Chilburn's papers that were still there—mostly bills and demands for payment. He had a lot of creditors, and many were growing insistent. However, Louisa noted that there were no accounts relating to rental payments. We decided that might mean that Chilburn's landlord lived close by."

Drake turned his head and looked at Finnegan. "I sent Finnegan to Cross Lane this morning to hunt down the landlord and ask for any insights that individual might have regarding Chilburn and any frequent visitors to his rooms, and to see if the elusive Badger had returned."

With a lift of his brow, Drake invited Finnegan to relate his findings.

As irrepressible as ever, Finnegan stepped forward, clasped his hands behind his back, and grinned. "The landlord was easy to find—he's the baker who owns and works in the bakery next door. In return for a few shillings, he was willing to chat about Chilburn. Apparently, the rent's up to date. According to the baker, who lives above his shop—so next door to Chilburn's rooms—Chilburn rarely had company of any sort. He usually came home in the early hours and left about lunchtime—he often came into the bakery for a pie. The baker saw him as a charmer, easygoing but with his pockets forever to let. I suspect the baker sized Chilburn up from the start and was careful to always demand the rent on time and in person—big, heavy chap, the baker. He also thought Chilburn had been in the cavalry because of the sword he sometimes sported and the scar, but other than that and the suspicion Chilburn came from a good family, the baker knew nothing else about his background."

"He—this baker—hadn't seen any friends visit? Any close acquaintances calling?" Michael asked.

"No, my lord. He—the baker—seemed fairly confident he'd have noticed any frequent visitors 'cause he's almost always in his shop, and the window gives a decent view of the street and the approach to Chilburn's door." Finnegan paused to draw a portentous breath, then revealed, "What he *had* noticed was that a message arrived for Chilburn last week. It was brought by a shifty-looking sort. The baker thinks it was on Wednesday. He noted the incident particularly because this shifty-looking cove wouldn't leave the message with Badger—the baker heard the argument on the stoop next door. The shifty cove insisted on hanging around in the lane until Chilburn came home. Of course, when Chilburn did arrive, the baker was all curiosity and watched from his shop. The cove stopped Chilburn in the street and gave him a sealed note. The baker swears Chilburn knew the man and was pleased to see him, pleased to get the note. Chilburn read the note then and there, then he asked a question, and the shifty cove handed him something—the baker didn't see what, but Chilburn put it in his jacket pocket, and it was bulky enough to see a bulge. Then Chilburn dismissed the shifty cove, and the cove hied off."

Drake frowned. He'd heard Finnegan's report before, but it had only just struck him… "Chilburn didn't tip or pay the messenger?"

"No, my lord. The baker was quite clear. He was watching closely by that point, and he noticed that particularly—it was something he'd expected to see happen, but it didn't."

There was a pause as they all considered that, then Sebastian uncrossed his long legs. "The only messenger you wouldn't normally tip is a man employed by someone you know." Sebastian looked at Finnegan. "For instance, I wouldn't tip Finnegan if he brought me a message."

Drake nodded. "And I wouldn't tip one of the St. Ives grooms. So the messenger came from someone Chilburn knew. He was pleased to see the man, so he'd been expecting the message, and he was pleased by the contents of the message, too. And the messenger delivered something as well."

"The messenger," Cleo stated, "handed over the keys to Shepherd's warehouse in Morgan's Lane."

"That must be it," Michael said. "The timing fits. We know the warehouse foreman and the drivers who delivered the gunpowder to Morgan's Lane were killed using a garrote. So it was the garrotter who took the keys off the warehouse foreman, O'Toole. But it was Chilburn who was in charge of the subsequent arrangements. He was the one who supervised moving the barrels out of Shepherd's warehouse, so he had to have the keys."

Drake tapped his steepled fingers together. "Yes, and the passing of those keys testifies to the link between our two killers, Chilburn and the garrotter." He paused, then more dryly went on, "That side of things—the immediate past—now fits together neatly. Sadly, that doesn't get us all that far with respect to the immediate future."

After a moment of cogitation, he continued, "I still haven't found hide nor hair of any gentleman willing to own to recent acquaintance with Chilburn. I checked with army headquarters. Chilburn had, indeed, served with the cavalry, but only a short stint. He sold out nearly eight years ago. Money, or the lack thereof, was a problem for him even then. I tracked down two officers who had known him. They hadn't much to add—a good man in a fight, drank and gambled with the best of them, but always short of the ready. He'd borrowed from several sources and hadn't paid them back, so wasn't welcome at any of the main military clubs. I tried a few of the lower-ranking clubs, but the porters all denied he was a member or even a frequent guest, and I doubt any were lying."

Drake paused, then said, "The picture we're assembling is of a younger son with no income and fewer prospects, who his family have largely abandoned due to his rampant profligacy, but who otherwise has no real strikes against his name, not before this enterprise."

Sebastian stirred. "It sounds as if he's been steadily sinking through the social strata. That wouldn't have been to his liking."

Drake inclined his head. "No, indeed. His situation would, very likely, have made him easy to recruit if someone dangled the right carrot before his face. A carrot of sufficient funds to come about and live at the level to which he'd been born."

No one disagreed.

After a moment, Louisa crisply stated, "So that's Lawton Chilburn, but I can't see that it gets us any further in identifying *who* he was working for—who it was who dangled the right carrot before him."

"Or," Drake added, "who sent him the warehouse keys—almost certainly the man we believe to be the garrotter."

"And"—Michael grimaced—"we still haven't a clue where the gunpowder is."

"Or where it might be heading," Sebastian grimly said.

Antonia looked at the others. "So what are we going to do next?"

Drake glanced around the circle and saw unwavering commitment in everyone's face. Gripping his chair's arms, he sat up. "As before, Cleo and Michael are pursuing the gunpowder. The rest of us are pursuing the villains. We have the mastermind and the garrotter in our sights. We need to identify them."

Cleo blinked. "Brewers' drays." She looked at Michael. "The barrels were spirited away on brewers' drays. We keep forgetting that."

Drake nodded. "It's too late now, but unless your old gunnery officer gives you any other clear direction, you should check the breweries inside our cordon." He hesitated, then said, "You might ask if any of their men have gone missing."

"You think Lawton's four helpers have been killed?" The sharp question came from Louisa.

"I think it's all too likely," Drake grimly replied. "We may have removed Chilburn, but the garrotter is still out there. The way this plot has been run, I suspect he'll be directed to eliminate all outstanding evidence before he or the mastermind feels all is satisfactorily in place to take the next step and make their next move."

Antonia asked Cleo and Michael, "How many breweries are there in that area?"

"Three," Cleo replied. "Four if you count the minnow."

"Check all four." Drake glanced at Louisa. "Meanwhile, in the morning, Louisa and I will return to the London Working Men's

Association in case Beam, the secretary there, has managed to turn up a clue."

"Even if," Louisa bleakly added, "it's only that they've found more of their members missing."

"Indeed." After a moment, Drake said, "Missing men might well be our best signposts to where the gunpowder is and how the plotters have thought to disguise it."

He paused.

The others looked at each other, their expressions clearly questioning whether there was anything else.

Drake grimaced and said, "Given we've been unable to turn up anything regarding Chilburn's friends or even close family connections— anyone who might know who he's been consorting with—I believe my next move should be to notify his family and release his body. That, and the funeral, might flush out someone or at least some information."

Louisa frowned. "How, exactly, do you propose to do that—the notification and release?"

"I stopped at Scotland Yard earlier and had a word with Inspector Crawford." To Michael and Cleo, he added in an aside, "Crawford has been put in charge of the entire case, which is fortuitous." To the group at large, he continued, "Crawford agreed that it would be best for someone known to the family to break the news, meaning to tell them that Chilburn is believed to be dead based on an identification by his bootmaker, and that the body is in the morgue awaiting formal identification by one of the family."

Louisa arched her brows. "By 'someone known to the family,' I assume Crawford means you?"

"Actually, I thought"—he looked at the others—"that it would be useful if we were all present. It will be to our advantage to gather as many of the family as possible and break the news to them all at once. As Louisa has verified, there are a lot of Chilburns, and we need as many observers as possible present to catch any telltale reaction, no matter how fleeting." The others all looked keen. He glanced at Louisa. "I understand there's a major ball tonight."

She was frowning at the carpet, but nodded. "At the Herricks'."

He drew breath and asked, "Will Lady Herrick mind us hijacking her function in such a fashion?"

Louisa raised her head and looked at him as if he'd lost his mind. "Good Lord, no! Such a happening is guaranteed to make all those who declined her invitation eat their feathers. If you like, I can speak to her now"—she glanced at the clock—"before dinner, and arrange everything without telling her what it's actually about."

He tried not to look overly impressed. He nodded. "Very well—do that. Then we'll all attend the event, and at suppertime when everyone else is distracted, we'll gather the attending Chilburns in some room and tell them of Lawton's demise." He glanced at Michael and Cleo. "I intend telling them that the body was found in an out-of-the-way spot in Mayfair, although it appeared he'd been killed elsewhere and the body dumped there. That should confuse things sufficiently." He looked at Finnegan, then returned his gaze to Michael. "Finnegan removed Chilburn's gun from your greatcoat the other morning. It's obviously been discharged, and we'll say that was found by the body."

Antonia and Louisa had been conferring in hushed tones. Now Antonia asked, "You think that in the shock of the moment, someone will react or let something fall."

"That's what I'm hoping." Drake let his gaze travel the circle of faces. "We'll need to spread ourselves and cover as many of the family members as we can. Be sympathetic and supportive, a shoulder to weep on—you all know how to do that—then let them tell you whatever they know of dearest Lawton."

Louisa's chin firmed. "I'll sit with his youngest sister."

"I'll hold his other sisters' hands," Antonia said. "We're distantly acquainted."

Cleo looked from Louisa to Antonia. "Who should I focus on?"

"Not his sisters-in-law," Louisa warned. "They have no time for Lawton and will probably be pleased that he, and any chance of family scandal, have turned into ghosts." She considered Cleo, then said, "I think you might make his mother, the viscountess, your target. Aside from his sisters, Lady Hawesley would be the other one I would most suspect of knowing more than she will readily divulge."

Cleo nodded and turned to the three men. Having been shown the way, they put their heads together and in short order had identified the males of the family who, in their estimation, were most likely to let fall information hitherto held close.

"Mind you"—Drake rose as the ladies gathered their reticules and prepared to depart—"that's assuming they'll all be there."

"Most if not all will be." Louisa rose and led the way to the door. "The Chilburns are connections of the Herricks."

Drake exchanged a look with Sebastian and Michael; all three were mentally shaking their heads at the sort of mind required to absorb and keep straight the myriad crossings of the many branches that existed in most ton families' trees.

The other two ladies strolled after Louisa. Drake waved Sebastian and Michael on and followed.

In the front hall, Louisa had paused, a frown marring the beauty of her face. "Damn. I'm going to have to go home for my cloak and bonnet before I call on Lady Herrick." She smiled at Hamilton. "I'd better get on."

As Hamilton moved majestically to open the front door, Drake said, "If Lady Herrick has any qualms, send for me."

Louisa laughed and stepped out of the door. Without turning, she replied, "She won't, but if she does, I'll threaten to do so." Her voice carried a definite hint of amusement. With a wave, she hurried down the steps.

Drake inwardly shook his head. He turned to the other four. "It appears we'll meet later at Lady Herrick's ball."

The others nodded. With "At Lady Herrick's" and "Until then," they followed Louisa down the steps.

CHAPTER 16

*G*riswade knew he wasn't as accomplished in the art of charming men as Lawton. He had to rely on appearances and on simple deceit.

He sat nursing a pint of ale in the small tavern in Parish Street, a cobbled way not much larger than a lane that ran south off the end of Tooley Street. He would have preferred to meet his soon-to-be-latest recruits on the other side of the river, farther from the sites of his recent mopping-up operations, but these two would have grown suspicious if he hadn't come "looking for them" and met them outside their place of work.

A place he was now very familiar with, but they weren't to know that.

As usual, the old man's intelligence was nothing short of uncanny; of all the many men who worked in that place, these two were definitely the right ones for the old man's purpose. Griswade had approached cautiously, feeling his way, but the instant he'd asked if the pair would like to make a little money on the side, no risk to them, he'd seen the avarice gleaming in their eyes and known he would have their cooperation.

Now, idly sipping, he waited for them to join him. Given the story he'd concocted for their edification, the attributes that still marked him as ex-military, indeed, as an ex-guardsman, would, for once, work to his advantage.

They arrived, as he'd been sure they would, more or less on time. The bells had rung for five o'clock about ten minutes ago. It would have taken them ten minutes to walk there from the brewery, which meant they'd come there directly, eager to hear his proposition.

As they made their way to the table at which he sat, Griswade beckoned the serving girl. She arrived along with the men, took their orders, and was back with their pints by the time Griswade had exchanged names and handshakes with his latest assistants.

Both were middle aged, of average height, large and heavyset, with barrel chests and strong, muscular arms and legs.

"So"—the one named Herbert settled on the bench opposite—"what's this job you've got going, then?"

Griswade allowed his lips to ease in a gesture that would pass for a smile. "I'll tell it to you straight—it's a practical joke of sorts."

The other, slightly older man, Martin, didn't look impressed.

Ignoring him, Griswade continued, "I'm here on behalf of my regiment—we want to play a joke on a company of our brothers-in-arms."

"How so?" Martin took a long swallow, his eyes on Griswade's face.

"It's simple. When you come to make your next delivery to Hunstable's across the river—"

"That'd be tomorrow." Herbert exchanged a glance with Martin, then looked at Griswade. "You mean our usual Friday run?"

"Yes." Griswade hated being interrupted, but reined in his temper and continued, "When you load up for Hunstable's, one group of barrels, fifteen of them, will feel different. That's because some of my friends arranged with the brewer to have his best ale replaced with sand. I won't go into the details, but there's a reason for that—a point to be made, a score to settle, if you like, with this other regiment. The barrels are destined for their mess, you see."

"And the boss agreed?" Martin looked surprised.

Griswade nodded. "That he did—well, he was well paid to do so. But the thing is, he wants to be able to say he and the brewery had nothing to do with it—that the barrels that left the brewery were full of ale as ordered." Griswade looked Martin, then Herbert in the eye. "It was your boss who told me about you two—he said you'd be the crew to make the delivery to Hunstable's. Anyone in the business would know that experienced men like you would know if barrels didn't contain ale the instant you lifted them—"

"Oh, aye." Herbert nodded. "We'd know."

"Precisely." Griswade bit off the word, then drew a swift breath and continued, "That's why your boss thought it should be you two—because if later the other side comes asking about what happened, no one would think the pair of you could load barrels of sand without knowing. And your boss felt you both would be agreeable to doing my regiment the favor of overlooking the oddness of the barrels for the other regiment—for a suitable consideration, of course."

Martin and Herbert exchanged a long look, then Herbert turned back to Griswade. "That's all very well, but what about Hunstable? If we deliver doctored barrels to him and he passes them on—"

"He already knows." Griswade grinned at their surprised expressions. "Well, think of it—he would have to know, wouldn't he? Just like you, his deliverymen will realize something's off the instant they lift the first barrel. But he and his men are already in—we've paid them well to turn a blind eye and deliver the doctored barrels to our brother-regiment's mess. Of course, like your boss, Hunstable wants to be able to say he knows nothing of it, so you'll want to keep mum when you're doing the delivery." Griswade looked at Martin, then at Herbert. "We've paid them, just as we're willing to pay you." He waited a heartbeat, then asked, "So what about it?"

Martin looked at Herbert.

Herbert looked back and shrugged. "No skin off our noses if the bosses are in on it."

Martin stared into his ale mug, then raised his gaze and fixed it on Griswade's face. "I'm thinking that five guineas would cover it."

Herbert blinked, but quickly nodded. "Aye—that seems fair."

Griswade straightened and pushed back from the table. "Two," he said. After a second, he added, "Each."

Herbert and Martin exchanged another glance, then nodded.

"Done." Martin slapped the table.

Griswade reached into his pocket and drew out two shiny gold guineas. He laid them on the table, one in front of each man, then pushed them across the pitted surface. "Half now, half later. I'll meet you here tomorrow night, say about ten o'clock, and pay you the rest."

Two weathered hands reached out, and the guineas disappeared. Herbert and Martin engaged in another wordless exchange, then Martin said, "If'n you come from t'other side of the river, and it sounds as if you might, we'd take it kindly if we could meet somewhere over there." Martin grinned conspiratorially. "Our deliveries finish that side, see, and with your money in our pockets, well, we've no need to hurry back this side, where the entertainment's not so great. No sense us going back and forth for no reason."

Griswade hid a wolfish grin; these two were making his job ridiculously easy. His lips curving in easy acquiescence, he shrugged. "That suits me. What say we meet at the Crown and Anchor in Castle

Street. Do you know it?"

"Oh, aye—we know it," Herbert assured him.

"That would suit us fine," Martin said.

"Good." Griswade pushed back his stool. "In that case, I'll see you in the Crown and Anchor at about ten tomorrow night." He stood, nodded genially to the pair, and headed for the door.

Easy and done.

As Griswade stepped into the darkening street, he reviewed the events he had scheduled for the next day—and now, into the next night. With any luck, by an hour or so after ten o'clock tomorrow night, the fog would be up, and Castle Street helpfully angled as it descended toward the river, so much so that the riverbank was out of sight of the Crown and Anchor's door.

All in all, matters could not have fallen out more fortuitously.

Grinning to himself, Griswade thrust his hands in his pockets and walked off into the night.

CHAPTER 17

*D*rake arrived in Lady Herrick's ballroom as late as he possibly could.

After greeting his hostess and coping with the blatant evidence that, along with her cronies, Lady Herrick had been indulging in rampant speculation as to what lay behind his recent uncharacteristic appearances at their events, he was forced to accept that all the gossipmongers had already firmly linked his name with Louisa's.

He didn't know what Louisa had told her ladyship regarding his need to speak in strict privacy with the Hawesleys and their family; while Lady Herrick lowered her voice and assured him of her absolute discretion, he was left with the impression that Louisa's appeal on his behalf had only heightened her ladyship's belief in the nature of the connection between him and Louisa.

As he cut through the crowd, searching for her dark head, he fought to tamp down his irritation over such over-avid interest in his personal life. Avoiding such intense speculation was one reason he eschewed the ballrooms. That and the fact that the usual social round bored him witless. As he smiled easily, nodded, and adroitly sidestepped all attempts to detain him, he comforted himself that the gossipmongers' assumption would at least provide cover for his true purpose in being there.

While dreaming of matrimonial mayhem, the ton's ladies were unlikely to imagine treachery and murder.

He finally spotted his quarry whirling down the floor in the arms of one of his peers. She appeared radiant, glimmering and shimmering in a full-skirted gown of peridot green, the same hue as her eyes. Her attention was focused on her partner to the exclusion of the rest of the world.

He truly was rusty socially speaking; he misjudged the spot where she would fetch up at the end of the dance, and by the time he tacked through the throng—a horrendous crush even by ton standards—she was deep in conversation with a circle of admirers, sprinkled with two other young ladies for leavening.

By dint of approaching the group at the right angle, the gentleman beside Louisa startled and stepped back in surprise—allowing Drake to claim the vacated spot by her side.

She glanced at him; her expression declared that she was delighted to see him, while her eyes—those vivacious, perspicacious, beguiling eyes—signaled wholly feminine amusement.

Recognizing that fact did his temper no good, but he was up to the challenge of exchanging greetings with her as well as the other members of the group, then pretending to a wholly spurious interest in the conversations being bandied back and forth.

He soon discerned that Lord Gareth Rampling, the Earl of Gisborne's heir, and Lord Philip Devenish, the Duke of Ashford's younger son, both gentlemen Drake would have labeled benign acquaintances, were regarding his arrival with less felicity than Drake would have expected... He nearly blinked.

Surely not. He glanced at Louisa and caught her smiling with her usual mesmerizing abandon at Philip.

Drake had always known she was dangerous, but it had never occurred to him to dwell on just how vulnerable to her effortless dazzle so many of his peers were likely to be.

Under her subtle but definite encouragement, the poor sods—not just Gareth and Philip but the three others in the group as well—clambered through innumerable hoops in an ever-escalating competition for her smiles. They had to have heard the rumors, yet...

It took him several minutes to accept that his benign acquaintances were doing their damnedest to cut him out.

Inwardly tight-lipped, he watched and observed; be damned if he would allow himself to get drawn into that game. He set his jaw and bided his time. The instant he detected the first squeak of bow on string, he reached out, closed his hand around one of Louisa's—at that moment transcribing an arc in midair—and in a tone that allowed for no disagreement from her or anyone else, stated, "My dance, I believe."

Louisa swallowed a laugh. His grip on her hand was just a little too definite to hide his aggravation; she had to wonder if he had any real idea of how that emotion, projected in such steely fashion, was being interpreted by the interested spectators surrounding them. Opening her eyes wide, she turned them on him. "Is it, my lord?" She paused for a heartbeat, then inquired, "Are you sure?"

"Quite." His eyes, golden and gleaming, snapped along with his tone. Reasonably gently, passably smoothly, he drew on her hand, and when she permitted it, wound her arm in his. Only then did he lift his gaze to the faintly shocked and curious ring of onlookers. "If you'll excuse us?"

With a distant dip of his head, he drew her away, into the crowd, and thence onto the dance floor.

With elegant ease, they stepped into a waltz, matching and mirroring each other literally without thought.

For several revolutions, she let her senses hold sway, let them greedily absorb the effect he had on them, on all of her. The leap of her pulse when his hand settled at her waist, the sheer thrill that the harnessed power with which he moved sent racing through her, the way her nerves tightened in anticipation of what might come. A scintillating awareness and a sharpened alertness, physical and mental, gripped her — an expectation of engagement and challenge on multiple planes. This, unquestionably, was what she wanted and needed in a husband—a mutual attraction that operated on significantly more levels than one.

He didn't meet her eyes as he whirled her down the ballroom; his expression remained socially bland, but there was a touch of deepening grimness about his lips. "You do know that Philip Devenish will never be able to support you in the manner to which you're accustomed?"

She opened her eyes wide. "Really?" It was a battle to keep her mask in place, to maintain the air of faintly distant hauteur that she knew would most provoke him rather than laugh delightedly. "I had no idea he was seriously considering supporting me."

His lips thinned; surely he had to know that, from his point of view, such comments were never wise—not on any level. "And Gareth—you would have him under your thumb within a week, and after that, he'd bore you to the point where you'd contemplate murder as an acceptable option."

She considered her best response. Eventually, after they'd negotiated the turn at the end of the floor, she stated, "As I've never considered dear Gareth—under that blustery exterior, a sweet man, I admit—as a gentleman with whom I might share a connection closer than that of dance partner, he'll remain safe, at least from me." Boldly, openly, she studied Drake's face. "Tell me," she murmured, deliberately letting huskiness flow through her tones, "were your comments intended to protect me from them or them from me?"

His jaw tightened; his features hardened. He continued to avoid her eyes.

"Hmm," she continued in the same provocative tone. "Regardless, I believe you can rest easy."

At that, he lowered his gaze and finally met her eyes.

Quick as a flash, she smiled intently and said, "That's something you would know if you attended an occasional social event. None of those gentlemen is the man I dream about."

What with the exigencies of the mission and all that had happened over the past days, Drake had managed to push her earlier declaration—that of her intention of joining him in his bed—to the back of his mind. More, he'd dismissed it, telling himself—however self-delusionally—that she hadn't really meant it, that she'd only said it to shake him, to see if she could.

That those subsequent kisses had merely been an escalation of the curious battle of wits and wills that had, it seemed, always raged between them.

Now…with his gaze locked with hers, with her having lowered her innermost shields thus allowing him to see into her soul, or so it felt, to see and appreciate and know the strength, the very feminine strength, that blazed within her, he realized just how misguided he'd been. Realized, fully and consciously, that she'd meant every word.

And she was Lady Wild—she who took stubbornness to unprecedented heights.

Their feet moved of their own accord. They whirled gracefully, effortlessly elegantly down the room as their minds engaged, will against will, while wordlessly she insisted that this—all he could see and sense here, now—was the truth, and he continued to try to deny…

It was he who had to quell a sudden shudder of reaction and look away, shaken by an unexpected wave of yearning that rose through him, broke over him, and all but swept him from his mental moorings.

He stared blindly across the glittering ballroom. He couldn't deal with this—with her—now. He had a mission to run, a fraught and potentially critical interview to conduct in just a few minutes; he had to regain control.

He dragged in a deep breath, relieved when he felt his head steady. After a second, he fleetingly glanced at her face.

She met his gaze with a faintly teasing, quizzical look.

He raised his gaze and focused on those standing about the dance floor. "From what Lady Herrick whispered when I arrived, I take it all is in train for me to break the news to the Chilburns."

After a second, Louisa obliged and fell in with his direction. "Her ladyship has put her drawing room at our disposal. Supper will be served promptly at eleven o'clock—just prior to that, the butler and footmen will collect the Chilburns and conduct them to the drawing room. And we're in luck—all Lawton's immediate family is here. The viscount and viscountess, his three older brothers with their wives, plus his three sisters and their husbands."

"Pray that one of them, at least, has some inkling of whom Lawton was consorting with."

With a musical flourish, the measure drew to a close. They slowed, then halted and stepped apart; he bowed, and she curtsied. Drake had glimpsed Sebastian and Antonia by the side of the ballroom; determined to avoid any return to more personal interaction, he drew Louisa's hand through his arm and nodded toward her brother. "We should alert the others. They're over there."

She went with him willingly. By the time they reached Sebastian and Antonia, Michael and Cleo had joined them.

Louisa immediately informed the four of the arrangements for the upcoming meeting with the Chilburns. The three couples formed their own circle; Drake noticed that the intensity of their exchanges, their alert but serious expressions, effectively kept the interested observers, many of whom were circling, at bay.

When Louisa finished listing the family members present, Drake and Sebastian drew out their watches.

"It's nearly time." Sebastian shut his watch and slid it back into his pocket. He met Drake's eyes. "Shall we?"

Tucking his own watch away, Drake looked over the heads and saw the Herricks' butler moving in stately fashion through the crowd. "The staff have started rounding up the Chilburns and directing them downstairs." He glanced at the other five. "We'd better get down to the drawing room ourselves, but not all together. Let's try for a little discretion."

By agreement, Drake, with Louisa on his arm, went down first. Sebastian and Antonia tracked the viscount and viscountess and followed them down the stairs. Michael and Cleo held back until the butler, consulted, assured them all the Chilburns present had been collected and dispatched, then followed the last couple down the stairs and into the drawing room.

Drake and Louisa had been in the drawing room when Viscount Hawesley and his wife, both transparently mystified, had walked in.

On seeing Drake, Hawesley had halted and stared. "Winchelsea?" Then Hawesley had seen Louisa, and concern had filled his face. Rather stiffly, he'd bowed. "Lady Louisa." Then Hawesley had switched his gaze to Drake and demanded, not without a certain trepidation, "What's this about?"

Drake had greeted the viscountess and waved her to one of the sofas set perpendicular to the fireplace. He'd met Hawesley's eyes and, in a tone that negated opposition, replied, "In a moment, my lord." Sebastian and Antonia had walked in at that point. Smoothly, Drake had continued, "Given the nature of what I have to convey, it will be preferable to have all your family gathered to hear it."

Louisa had noted Drake hadn't specified for whom the arrangement would be preferable, but other than uttering a harrumph and frowning darkly, Hawesley had sat beside his openly anxious wife and had remained grimly silent as his sons and their wives and his daughters and their husbands filed into the room.

All queries as to what was happening had elicited much the same answer as Hawesley had received. Consequently, when the door finally clicked shut behind Michael and Cleo, the atmosphere in the room was already tense.

Cleo slipped into the vacant spot in the corner of the sofa beside Lady Hawesley. On the longer sofa opposite, Hawesley's three daughters were perched somewhat anxiously, while Hawesley's three daughters-in-law stood behind the sofa, their attitudes distinctly more distant. Unobtrusively, Antonia and Louisa moved to flank the former, who in strained silence made room for them; in a susurration of silks, Louisa and Antonia sat alongside their agreed marks. With the exception of Hawesley, the gentlemen of the family, with Sebastian and Michael hovering close, had congregated in a knot at the other end of the Aubusson rug, facing the fireplace and Drake, who had taken up a stance before the hearth.

Frowning—as were all the family's men—Hawesley eyed Michael and Sebastian, glanced at Cleo and Antonia, then looked at Drake. "I can understand that you might wish to speak with us in private, Winchelsea, but these others…?"

"Earith, Lady Antonia, Lady Louisa, Lord Michael, and Miss Hendon are all actively assisting me in this matter." Smoothly, Drake added, "One which impinges on the safety of the realm." Having successfully quashed all protest and snared the attention of all those present, in steady, measured tones, he went on, "I regret to inform you that a body now believed to be that of Lawton Chilburn was discovered on Monday night. He'd been shot." Drake explained that there had been no identification on the body, and consequently, it had taken a few days to confirm identity via the boots the dead man had worn.

The viscountess had uttered a strangled cry at the mention of her youngest son's name. Cleo had edged nearer; instinctively, Lady Hawesley had reached for and gripped Cleo's hand. But now, clutching a lace-edged handkerchief in her other hand, Lady Hawesley looked up at Drake. "Oh, but it can't be Lawton. He must have given away his old boots, and it was some ruffian who was wearing them—it was the ruffian's body you found."

Drake regarded her with sympathy and gently said, "The bootmaker was quite certain, and the dead man bore a scar—possibly a sword cut—from the left corner of his lips to the point of his jaw."

The viscountess stared unseeing at him, then her eyes filled with tears. On a sob, she bowed her head.

Cleo patted her ladyship's hand and murmured soothingly.

Awkwardly, Hawesley shifted nearer and put his arm around his wife's shoulders. "There, there." His face ashen, he looked at Drake. "I don't understand—how did it happen?"

"And," Robert, Lawton's eldest brother, somewhat belligerently asked, "why has it taken so long for us to hear? Even if he'd been robbed of his purse and all papers, they might have checked with his tailor. I hear that's done all the time."

Drake inclined his head. "Indeed. But sadly, Lawton—or rather, his body—was dressed in clothes that…we believe were not his own."

A collective wordless "Oh" was written on all Lawton's siblings' and in-laws' faces. From their expressions, they were calculating the possibilities raised by Drake's words—and plainly those possibilities were numerous.

"But why was he killed?" Lawton's second-oldest brother, the Honorable Gerrard Chilburn, voiced the question, then shut his lips tightly, as if wishing he hadn't.

"Given the way he was shot," Drake replied, "we believe he might have been involved in a duel. Certainly in some sort of altercation involving pistols." Drake lowered his voice and directed his words to the gentlemen of the family. "Lawton was shot twice in the chest. He would have died quickly."

Drake paused, then glanced around at all the family members. As the silence stretched, most looked up and returned his regard. Finally, he said, "In order to assist the authorities in determining what led to Lawton's death, we would be grateful to hear of any insights or suspicions you might have about Lawton's recent endeavors or those with whom he'd recently been consorting. Any theories at all about what might have led to him being killed."

Louisa—and, she felt sure, Michael and Cleo—appreciated Drake's glib phrasing. It was obvious from the absorbed expressions on the faces of Lawton's nearest and dearest, from the questioning looks this one and that exchanged, that insights, suspicions, and theories abounded.

Although understandably the most affected, it was the viscountess who, through gulping sobs, started the ball rolling. "I always knew he would come to a bad end." Clinging to Cleo's hand, she forced out the words, "The others all knuckled down—they were always responsible. But Lawton…he wanted and expected things to come easily, without the slightest exertion on his part."

That drew forth numerous mutters and dark rumblings from other family members.

Leaving his wife to Cleo's ministrations, Hawesley, who appeared to have aged several years and was disturbed and angry, but not, at the base of it, all that surprised, rose and moved to join his sons and sons-in-law.

Drake walked down the center of the room and joined the group; Hawesley and his two oldest sons acknowledged him with brief nods. All three hesitated, then, haltingly, offered their views of Lawton—a profligate, a bad seed, a man who all three felt had let down the Chilburn name. Drake listened, but heard nothing he hadn't already surmised.

Meanwhile, Sebastian attached himself to Basil Chilburn, Hawesley's third son and the nearest in age to Lawton.

Basil shook his head. "Like Mama said, he was always going to come to a bad end, but shot in the street! The mind boggles." Basil glanced rather shrewdly at Sebastian. "I say, that won't have to come out, will it? How he died?"

Sebastian glanced at Drake. "I shouldn't think so." He looked back at Basil. "Especially if we can get some idea of what was behind it."

"Well"—Basil gestured—"living as he was, a hand-to-mouth existence, borrowing off everyone and never paying it back. Playing fast and loose with money and anything else he could lay his hands on." Basil snorted. "Could be anyone he'd borrowed from."

A few paces away, Michael was listening to Lawton's three brothers-in-law. The consensus there was that Lawton was simply a bad egg—it happened in the best of families. All three agreed that the fact he was—had been—charming had only allowed his borrowing and spending to continue more or less unabated.

"Irresponsible and without shame," one stated. "That should be engraved on his tombstone."

"Hawesley did his best," another opined. "You can't say he didn't. He bought Lawton his commission, yet what did Lawton do? Served for barely a year, then sold out and squandered the cash."

"It was after that," the third of the trio stated, "that Hawesley cried enough. That was…what?" He glanced at the other two for assistance. "Seven years ago?"

They all agreed it was something like that.

"Since then," the first man intoned, "we've seen increasingly little of him. He occasionally honored us with his presence at a family gathering, but he was always there for only one purpose."

"To try to touch us, or Hawesley, or his sisters or mother for more money," the second man supplied.

"Or to try to get us to wager on something," the third reminded them, "even though he couldn't possibly have paid up if he'd lost!"

On the longer sofa, Lawton's three sisters were transparently shocked and saddened. But the eldest, Harriet, next to whom Antonia was sitting, was already recovering. Glancing across at her still-weeping mother, Harriet's face hardened. "As Mama said, Lawton brought about his own end, ignominious as it was. He never would shape up—he always just laughed..." Her words trailed away.

The next sister in age, Gloria, seated in the middle, shook herself. "We all know he went his own way quite purposefully, and he sneered at any suggestion he should lift a finger in honest effort, and he certainly went through more of Papa's money than should have been allowed." She glanced at Harriet. "We might have a duty to mourn and feel sorry for him, but does he deserve it?"

A moot point, it seemed.

Gathered behind the sofa, Hawesley's daughters-in-law, far from mourning Lawton, had made several cynical and dismissive comments which might be accurately described as them giving voice to their relief that the black sheep of the family and the threat of scandal he had personified were no more. Louisa, listening to everything she could while seated in the corner of the sofa beside Lawton's youngest sister, Aileen, heard the three daughters-in-law move on to discussing the latest exploits of their offspring.

Deeming the daughters-in-law to be of no further interest, Louisa waited patiently for Aileen to pull herself together. Several years older than Louisa or even Antonia, Aileen was patently sincerely upset. As Louisa watched, Aileen calmed enough to draw in a deeper breath, then turned to her sisters. "I know he was a bad egg. But he was always kind. You have to admit that."

Harriet pulled a face, but didn't disagree.

Gloria gruffly conceded, "True—he was kind, or at least he used to be. But even you have to agree he'd grown harder of late. Gradually, bit by bit, ever since he sold out."

Aileen nodded glumly and went back to staring at her hands, at her fingers twisting her now-sodden handkerchief.

Across the three sisters, Antonia caught Louisa's gaze and arched a brow.

Louisa looked again at Aileen. "Had you"—she flicked a glance at the other two to include them—"seen him recently?" When none of the three answered, she went on, "Had he said anything—mentioned anything at all—about the people he was spending time with? Or about any scheme to make money?"

Harriet and Gloria frowned in a puzzled way.

"We have to wonder," Louisa explained, "given he was so hard-pressed for funds, if he'd gone looking for ways to make money, and perhaps he fell in with the wrong sort of people, and that was, in effect, the reason he was killed."

After a moment of consulting their memories, Harriet and Gloria shook their heads. Harriet added, "I haven't seen him, much less met him, for weeks—indeed, months."

Gloria nodded in agreement.

"I ran into him not long ago." Her gaze still on the twist of her handkerchief, Aileen cleared her throat and continued, "I was walking in Bond Street about a week—no, two weeks—back. He was sauntering about, looking in the windows. I ribbed him that he couldn't possibly afford the prices there, and…he winked and tapped the side of his nose, and said…" She frowned. "Something about needing to keep up with what was on offer as he had high hopes of securing an inheritance quite soon."

"An inheritance?" Harriet straightened. "From whom, pray tell?"

"I asked him, of course," Aileen went on, "but he just grinned—you know how he did when he refused to share a secret—and said it wasn't anyone I knew." She sighed. "And then he just smiled even more devilishly, tipped me a salute, and walked off." She caught her breath on a sob. "I can still see him…"

Her tears flowed again, and this time, her sisters gathered her in. Louisa rose, and Harriet moved to take her place, sandwiching Aileen between herself and Gloria, and the trio hugged and comforted each other.

Antonia came to join Louisa. They exchanged glances, then turned to Drake.

He'd been waiting, watching from across the room; he met their gazes, nodded, and moved to the bellpull. The Chilburns had disclosed all they were likely to; it was time for them to be allowed to go home.

FRIDAY, NOVEMBER 1, 1850

CHAPTER 18

*L*ady Herrick and her butler rose to the occasion and, with sympathy and sensitivity, arranged for the family's various carriages to be summoned to a side door, thus enabling the bereaved to leave without having to weather the full glare of the ton's curiosity.

As soon as her ladyship ushered the last couple out of the drawing room and down the corridor to the side door, Drake shut the drawing room door and turned to the others. "I didn't learn anything beyond what we might already have inferred."

He glanced at Sebastian and Michael, who grimaced and confirmed that they had fared no better, then Drake turned to Cleo.

Still seated in the corner of the sofa, she said, "I don't think Lady Hawesley knows anything that might help us. I got the impression she'd grown to distrust and censure Lawton to much the same degree as his father. She seemed to see Lawton's character quite clearly and had been disappointed in him for some time."

Drake nodded and turned his gaze on Louisa and Antonia, who were plainly all but bursting with news. "Clearly, you two had better luck. What did you hear?"

Swiftly, Louisa related Lawton's youngest sister's revelations. She added, "I think it's significant that she found him looking in the windows—he was already behaving as if, as he said, he was anticipating an inheritance before he knew she was there. It wasn't something he made up out of the blue to tease her."

Drake inclined his head. "Good point." He paused, frowning, then said, "But none of the sisters knew anything about who might be leaving him this inheritance, and he said it wasn't anyone they knew."

"I'll ask Grandmama and Lady Osbaldestone. One of them is sure to know—" Louisa broke off, then grimaced. "Assuming, of course, that it's a family connection or something similar."

"An inheritance," Sebastian said, moving to sit beside Antonia, who had subsided onto the long sofa again, "can be directed from anyone to anyone. It doesn't have to be via family."

"Worse," Drake said, "Lawton might have been working for some merchant or even for some criminal, and 'an inheritance' is the phrase he opted to use to describe the payment he believed he would shortly receive."

Michael had sat beside Cleo; he leaned forward, his forearms on his thighs, his hands clasped between his knees. "A disguise of sorts to account for a sudden windfall."

Frowning, Louisa resumed her position on the long sofa. "But in terms of concealment, his family, surely, would know that none of their connections had been Lawton's benefactor. Wouldn't that still raise questions, at least with them?"

"It might." Drake moved to sit on the chaise beside Michael, opposite Louisa. "But as we've just seen, Lawton was largely estranged from his family, and labeling such a payment as an inheritance..." Drake leaned back and crossed his legs. "To his family, he could claim it was an inheritance from an old friend whose life he'd once saved. To his acquaintances, he says the money's from a family connection."

"Possibly." Still frowning, Louisa said, "Regardless, just in case he meant it literally, I'll ask Grandmama."

Drake inclined his head. "By all means, check. At this stage, we can't afford to ignore any possible clues." He glanced at the others, then at the clock on the mantelpiece. "Yesterday's gone. Today...we have Cleo and Michael asking at the Southwark breweries to see if any are missing men."

"First"—Cleo glanced at Michael—"we'll check with Ollie March." To the others, she said, "He's the old Hendon Shipping Company gunnery officer I mentioned. I don't know where he lives, but it's likely to be somewhere not too far away, and the address will be in the office. If we go to the office first thing in the morning, we can visit Ollie, just in case he can suggest some way of disguising gunpowder, and then we can check at the breweries."

Michael nodded.

Drake did, too. "So that's you two." He shifted his gaze to Sebastian and Antonia.

Antonia promptly stated, "We have a full day of events." She glanced at Sebastian, who winced.

"Regardless," Drake said, "while you're rubbing shoulders with the most gregarious of the ton, monitor the gossip—which will doubtless be circulating by then—about Lawton's death. Someone who isn't family might know something or have seen Lawton with someone suspicious... We're casting in the dark here and need to seize every opportunity."

Sebastian and Antonia nodded, and Drake finally turned his gaze to Louisa.

Mildly, he suggested, "We were intending to check at Chartist headquarters again, in case their search through their membership has turned up any other missing men, but I can do that myself, and in light of your findings this evening, perhaps following up with your Grandmama and her visitor might be a wiser use of your time."

He could hope.

He didn't hope for long.

Louisa's distracting eyes widened as if she remained in complete and utter ignorance of his tactics. "I can't see how that will work. You might not have noticed, but Grandmama and Lady Osbaldestone were here tonight. And if they've been out in the evening, they do not—absolutely will not, no matter who asks—receive before luncheon, and that's generally rather late. I'll get more help from them in the afternoon." She smiled, as eager and innocent as a happy puppy. "So I'll be free to accompany you to the Working Men's Association." Her brows faintly rose in challenge. "And you must admit, the men have been more forthcoming with me there."

Drake wished, very much, that he could deny that, but... His features tightening, he forced himself to nod. "Very well. I'll call for you at eight-thirty."

As one, all six of them looked at the clock on the mantelpiece. The hands declared the time was nearly one o'clock.

Michael blew out a breath and looked at Cleo. "I believe we'll call it a night."

Cleo nodded and picked up her reticule. Sebastian and Antonia voiced their intention of heading home as well, and all six rose and strolled to the door.

In the front hall, at the base of the stairs, Sebastian, Antonia, Michael, and Cleo collected Antonia's and Cleo's cloaks and bade farewell to Louisa and Drake.

When the other four had vanished into the night and the footmen had closed the doors, and Louisa still stood, apparently lost in thought, Drake inwardly sighed and asked, "What are your plans?"

She glanced at him—almost as if she'd forgotten he was there; in her eyes, he saw calculation, but not of the dangerous kind. "I was thinking... The news of Lawton's death will have started to circulate upstairs by now. People will have been curious as to why the Hawesleys and all their family were summoned like that, then left without returning to the ballroom. No matter how discreet Lady Herrick and her staff have been, someone will have seen something, someone will have overheard something." Raising her head, she stated, "If we truly are pursuing every avenue, then I really should spend another hour or two in the ballroom— you never know what I might hear, or what someone will think to tell me."

One of his least favorite places was a crowded, inevitably noisy ballroom. He imagined the peaceful ambiance of his apartment in Wolverstone House with genuine longing.

Apparently reading his face—something few others were able to do— Louisa widened her eyes at him. "You don't have to stay. I don't need an escort, and I have my carriage."

She was right; she didn't require an escort. She warranted a keeper.

He heard himself somewhat gratingly state, "If you learn anything, I'll need to know. And I'll need to question whoever you learn it from, so..." He turned and waved her up the stairs.

The damned woman smiled understandingly—she understood far too much—then gathered her full skirts and started up the long flight.

He kept pace beside her, up the stairs and back into the milling throng still filling the ballroom.

It was soon borne in on them both, even more than before, that appearing as a couple was escalating speculation to a near frenzy. She was the only daughter of the ducal house of St. Ives, while he was the heir to a wealthy dukedom who, socially speaking, had played least in sight for nearly a decade.

Even worse than the gossipmongers, the grandes dames themselves were leveling narrow-eyed, measuring glances at them.

Louisa wasn't all that perturbed; she was a social adept and had no difficulty deflecting any impertinent inquiry. As for suggestive comments, she allowed those to fly past, responding as if the words had been intended literally, a tactic that confounded and frustrated the overly inquisitive.

What she wasn't quite so happy about was the impact of Drake's looming presence at her shoulder on the loquacity of those she could normally count on to whisper the latest on-dit or scandalous tidbit in her ear. With him there, broodingly menacing, her customarily reliable sources wouldn't even risk leaning close!

When Sir Timothy Gavel, an exceedingly well-connected and garrulous gentleman she could usually rely on to have an inside line on the most recent gossip, became so transfixed by Drake's presence that he turned all but incoherent—literally gabbled!—then made the most ridiculous excuse and fled, she had had enough.

Maintaining a relaxed expression, she sank her fingertips into Drake's sleeve, ignored the fluttery sensation in her stomach at the feel of steely muscles shifting beneath the fabric, and all but towed him into an alcove partially screened by two huge potted palms. Then she released him and swung to face him. "You"—she jabbed a finger at his chest—"are unnerving people. You're frightening them off!"

He looked at her with haughty arrogance. "I've neither said nor done anything to interfere with your rather peculiar methods of interrogation."

"With my usually *successful* methods—and you interfere just by being there!"

"Nonsense! If they had anything of substance to say—"

"The last person they would air it in front of is you! No one here knows how to take you. You've avoided society for so long, no one feels they have your measure. Most know you by name and title, but almost all will have heard whispers enough to make them uneasy. The ladies would like to engage, but aren't sure if it's safe, while the gentlemen are wary because they've heard one too many rumors." She glared at his expression of unperturbed superiority and delivered the most damning indictment of which she could conceive. "When it comes to collecting information among the ton, you are a liability, my lord."

That struck home. His lips tightened; a muscle in the side of his jaw ticked. After several seconds during which she held to her glare, he spoke—so evenly she knew she'd flicked his temper. "So what would you have me do?"

With full dramatic fervor, she raised her hands and gripped her hips. "Literally everyone in sight of us is watching. They'll imagine, correctly, that we're having an argument. That gives you the perfect opportunity to retreat to the cardroom." She took half a step back and waved her hands at him—literally shooing him away. "So go!"

Drake wanted to do something quite different. For several seconds, he stared back at her, his gaze locked unrelentingly with hers as the demands of his mission clashed with a set of far more fundamental needs. Far more visceral wants.

But the mission had to come first. Drawing in a long, slow breath, he carefully enunciated, "Very well. Come and find me when you're finished."

Hardening his resolve—battling his own deep-seated resistance—he hauled his gaze from hers, turned, ducked out from behind the palms, and stalked toward the archway that gave onto the cardroom.

Even he noticed that, after one glance at his face, people quickly got out of his way.

From her position behind the palms, Louisa watched him go; until his verbal capitulation, she hadn't known if he would. He'd been considering—quite definitely weighing up—doing something else. Exactly what, she couldn't guess, but his inner debate had been etched clearly enough in the beaten gold of his eyes.

Viewing his broad back as he retreated through the crowd, she slowly arched her brows. Then she glanced around. He'd given her the clear field she'd demanded; now it was up to her to make good on her boast and learn something worth the angst.

She emerged from the alcove and set about systematically quartering the room.

Drake stalked into the cardroom. He halted just inside the doorway. He scanned the tables only briefly, then looked farther. His features eased a fraction when he spied a footman coming through a service door. When the door swung shut, it was well-nigh invisible, becoming just another part of the paneling.

He skirted the room, acknowledging those who nodded to him. On reaching the area before the service door, he paused as if studying the activity at a nearby table. He waited until all eyes and all attention throughout the room were refixed on the play, then he silently turned, opened the service door, and slipped through.

Inside the narrow corridor, barely wide enough to accommodate his shoulders, he stepped away from the door, put his back to the wall, and waited for his eyes to adjust to the poor light. Luckily, he had an excellent sense of direction. Instead of heading toward the kitchen and the cellars from where the footmen were ferrying bottles to the cardroom's denizens, he turned and walked the other way.

By dint of descending a set of narrow stairs and carefully trying several doors, he found his way to a minor parlor on the ground floor. The room had been left in darkness, but the curtains hadn't been drawn, allowing moonlight to stream in through a set of French doors.

The doors were his goal. He unsnibbed the lock, opened one, and stepped out into the night. After quietly closing the door behind him, he made his way around the corner of the house to the rear garden and the terrace that ran the length of the ballroom.

At both ends and also in the middle, sets of stone steps led up to the flagstone terrace. Although the ballroom had multiple fully glassed French doors giving access to the terrace, November had arrived, and the night was chilly; none of the doors had been opened. Even better, when

Drake climbed the steps at the nearest end and surreptitiously approached the first set of doors, he discovered that Lady Herrick had ordered the filmy curtains to be left drawn across the glass.

The gauzy screen didn't materially affect his view of the well-lit ballroom, but it would make it that much harder for anyone inside the ballroom to see him. In addition, the ivy covering the wall was old and thick and had been cut back from around the doors early in the year; through summer, it had grown back with a vengeance, and vines now encroached over the edges of the frames.

Choosing a particularly dense fall of ivy for extra cover, he lounged against the wall beside the first door, peered past the edge of the frame, and searched the room.

Louisa wasn't difficult to locate; she was skillfully flitting from group to group. In her pale-green silk gown, with her dark hair gleaming, she appeared the epitome of a social butterfly. But the longer Drake watched, the more obvious it became that the circles in which she alighted were not randomly chosen. After ten minutes of observing her gyrations, he'd confirmed that she was targeting gentlemen of a similar age to Lawton Chilburn. Presumably, she was searching for men who might react to the rumors of Chilburn's demise by dropping some useful comment.

Although he couldn't hear a word, now he'd guessed her intentions, he found it easy enough to follow the conversations as she encouraged her various marks to tell her their memories and all else they knew of Chilburn.

One part of Drake's mind—the coolly detached intelligencer—viewed her tactics with considerable appreciation. That part of him could admit that she'd been right to get rid of him; he had been cramping her style.

Whether it was that surfacing of his alter ego, drawn to the front of his mind to observe her expertise in action, that made him glance aside and fix on the movement of a tallish gentleman passing between several chatting groups, he didn't know. But once he'd focused on the man, hyperactive, hypersensitive instincts brought all his hunter's faculties to the fore.

Within a minute, he'd satisfied himself that the man was, indeed, stalking Louisa. Despite chatting with others here and there, he was tracking her through the crowd; every now and then, a calculating expression flitted over his face.

The man's approach, his intent, would have been difficult for anyone in the ballroom to detect. Viewing proceedings from the side, from the distance of the terrace, Drake had a much clearer, much more damning perspective.

Finally, the gentleman made his move. He circled through the crowd and joined the group of guests Louisa would most likely approach next.

Drake straightened away from the wall. He watched as Louisa, having chatted animatedly for several minutes with those with whom she'd been engaged, blithely farewelled them and moved on to the next group, where the tallish gentleman was waiting.

Louisa smiled her engaging smile and spoke with the circle of gentlemen and ladies without apparent favor. Drake saw the gentleman start to speak, then he stopped. Louisa's gaze rested on him measuringly, then she switched to a smiling exchange with two others.

But once that was done, she moved to more specifically engage with her stalker.

Drake had to hand it to the man; he played his part to perfection, giving a flawless performance as a reluctant source. He even had the nous, when Louisa clearly pressed him to explain further, to shake his head and glance around as if seeking escape.

Louisa spoke again, more earnestly, then surreptitiously indicated the middle set of French doors.

The man hesitated, then gave a slight nod.

Predictably, Louisa pantomimed feeling overheated, and the gentleman, still appearing reluctant, played along and, with a great show of solicitousness, gave her his arm and escorted her to the French doors.

Silently, Drake moved along the wall where the shadows fell darkly.

The central pair of French doors opened, and the gentleman ushered Louisa outside.

She stepped into the shadows and signaled to the gentleman to shut the doors, which he did.

Meanwhile, she looked right and left, scanning the terrace, checking to see if anyone else was there. She didn't look behind her, so missed the denser shadow that was Drake, looming against the ivy-covered wall.

Having established, as she thought, that she and the gentleman were alone, she swung to face him. "All right—what is it you know that you can't speak of—"

"Not here." The gentleman roughly seized her arm. "Down there."

He went to sweep her down the stone steps and into the garden, but before he could move, he started to choke.

He let go of Louisa's arm and clutched at his collar as he came up on his toes, gasping and struggling for breath.

Having by then seen Drake, Louisa waited for a few more seconds— allowing Drake to dangle the impertinent man from his own collar, which apparently continued to tighten—before she humphed and said, "Oh, do let him go. I would have kneed him in another second."

Drake looked at her, then opened his hand and released Sir Phineas Painter's collar.

Sir Phineas fell to his feet. He staggered, wheezed, and clutched his throat. He glanced around wildly.

Drake regarded him dispassionately, much as he would a fly, then in his darkest, most menacing voice, said, "It seems you've had a lucky escape. On several fronts. I would flee if I was you."

She promptly added, "While you can."

Whether it was her tone or Drake's that punctured the last of Sir Phineas's bravado, she couldn't tell, but he forced himself upright, stared at them as if they were dangerous beasts, tried to utter words, but they came out in a meaningless gurgle, then, still clutching his throat and his abused cravat, he darted around Drake, opened the French door, dashed over the threshold, and quickly shut the door behind him.

Her gaze on the door, Louisa sighed. "That was Sir Phineas Painter. He spun an excellent tale about having known Lawton and meeting with him just last week."

"No doubt." Drake fought to keep his temper from his voice. "However, I believe his foray suggests that your window of opportunity for learning more tonight has closed." Hauling his gaze from Painter, who was as unobtrusively as possible making his escape via the ballroom, Drake finally allowed himself—the self that was very much uppermost at that moment—to focus on her. "Time to leave."

He gave her no chance to argue, simply took her elbow in an unbreakable grip and drew her along the terrace to the steps at the end.

To all her inquiries, such as "Where are we going?" and "Aren't we going back to the ballroom?" he paid not the slightest heed.

But when, with rising temper ringing in her voice, she acerbically reminded him that she needed her cloak "for God's sake," he clenched his jaw even harder and consented to detour and leave via the front hall.

Lady Herrick's butler took one look at their faces and almost fell over his toes rushing to retrieve her cloak.

Drake seized the garment from the fumbling retainer, shook the folds out, then with exquisitely controlled care, draped the cloak over Louisa's bare shoulders.

She turned her head and shot him a furious glare, then smiled sweetly at the uncertain butler. "Thank you," she said—to the butler.

Immediately, Louisa felt her elbow gripped again; even through the combined thickness of her cloak and evening gloves, Drake's long, hard fingers burned like a brand. Her temper, already beyond simmering, boiled.

He more or less marched her out of the house. Her carriage, summoned by a footman, was waiting by the curb. His expression less informative than a stone carving, Drake steered her—propelled her—down the steps and across the pavement to where her footman stood holding the carriage door open.

Inwardly seething, she allowed herself to be all but thrust inside the carriage. She swept her skirts close, sat, and bided her time. Drake, apparently, had forgotten just who he was dealing with; as Lady Wild, she was only too ready—nay, burning—to remind him.

She waited until he'd entered the carriage, until he'd sat in the dark beside her.

Waited some more while the footman scrambled up and her coachman gave the horses the office.

The Herricks' house was on a side street off Gloucester Place. She peered out of the window at the shadowed façades slipping past and timed her move carefully.

She waited until the now-trotting horses had started to swing into the larger road, then abruptly stood.

Drake was jerked from his battle to keep his tongue leashed. For a split second, he stared as Louisa, facing forward, swayed as the carriage tipped—then her leg hit his knee, and she tumbled.

Instinct overrode caution; he reached for her and gripped her waist, but she was falling toward him, and it was easier to cushion her.

She landed on his lap in a froth of silk skirts, lace petticoats, and soft, silken limbs.

His wits scattered.

Before he could regather them, she wriggled around to face him— annihilating his concentration—clamped her palms to either side of his face, stretched up, leaned in, and drew his head down and kissed him.

It was not a tentative kiss.

More an incitement to madness.

One he, the man he was behind the mask, instantly responded to. Before he knew what he was doing, he was enthusiastically participating in an exchange of bold challenge and flagrant desire, of heat and hunger and erupting need.

Her lips were teasing, tempting, alluring and enticing; her mouth, surrendered, was a honeyed haven of delight, a gifting he hadn't been able to resist.

Pleasure welled, more potent and intense with her than any other.

That realization—that warning—weakened the spell, enough for him to haul in a deeper breath, break the seal of their lips, and demand, "What the devil do you think you're doing?"

He might have all but lost his wits, but he hadn't forgotten who she was.

"You had your way over us leaving the ball. Now it's my turn to dictate."

Then her lips were on his again, and his seemed to have a will of their own—they'd rather taste hers than obey his commands. As for his hands...he couldn't seem to stop them from responding to her blatant enticements; he couldn't seem to rein in his own flaring need.

She leaned into him, the ripe swells of her breasts firm against his chest; everything male in him salivated. She was a bundle of warm, feminine curves, sleek and supple, infinitely tempting; her warm weight across his thighs, the feel of her firm flesh shifting against his harder muscled limbs was pure provocation.

Her hands slid beneath his coat. Splayed, they moved over his chest; the evocative pressure as her fingertips sank into the broad muscles sent heat streaking through him, sent desire spiraling.

There was no power on earth that could have stopped him from reacting. From drawing his hands from their exploration of the silk-clad planes of her back and sending them instead to stroke, caress, then flagrantly possess the firm mounds of her breasts.

He'd expected a gasp from her—at least a hesitation. Instead, she purred low in her throat, and her hands flexed, and her lips blazed, and their kiss turned molten.

Her response, and his to hers, was so shockingly intense, so primal and powerful, he could entertain no doubt about where this would end.

Where, at that moment in time, both he and she wanted this to go.

His head spun as he fought to grapple with that reality, but she only pressed on and, with her kisses, lured him into following...

Abruptly, he found himself teetering on an edge of raging need that was far too close to desperation.

When had it ever been this difficult to exercise control in this sphere?

The answer—*never*—streaked through what remained of his mind. Shaken, he forced his head up and back, breaking the kiss. Through the shadows, he searched her face. "Do you have any notion of what you're doing?"

His voice was nearly gone, the words gravelly and rough.

Through the heated darkness, Louisa stared at him. Their eyes were almost level, but in the gloom, she couldn't read anything in his. Slowly, she swept her tongue over her burning lips. "Yes." She arched one brow. "At least I think so." Deliberately, she wriggled her hips. "Is it working?"

He cursed. Against her hip, his erection felt like forged iron.

She laughed—sultry, low, as provocatively as she could. "It certainly seems—"

He shut her up as she'd hoped he would—by kissing her ferociously and wrenching control of the engagement from her. Or at least attempting to.

She wasn't of a mind to cede everything to him. She was willing to share, but she would not be dominated. Would not be dictated to.

Naturally, her stance led to a tussle of sorts, one that in short order escalated the engagement into realms that should have sent any well-bred lady running screaming...

She was definitely well bred, but she wasn't the sort to run screaming, especially not from this. From an engagement she'd dreamt of for years. From an exchange she'd always felt should be.

She was with him every step of the way, through every hard, heated, and increasingly passionate caress, eager, encouraging, enthusiastically participating.

Equally hungry. Equally wanting.

They broke apart only when the carriage rocked to a halt outside St. Ives House.

Through the heated darkness, they stared at each other. They were both breathing rapidly, his chest rising and falling, her breasts all but heaving.

Drake couldn't be certain of her expression, but he didn't need the evidence of his eyes to sense her burgeoning satisfaction.

Rather breathlessly, she purred, "Very nice." He caught the curving of her lips as she added, "I always thought it would be."

Then with calm efficiency, she gathered herself and rose from his lap.

He fought down a nearly overpowering urge to reach up and haul her back—and damn any and all consequences. Increasingly grim, unforgivingly tense, he managed to rise and reach for the door. He opened it and nearly fell onto the pavement. As smoothly as he could, he recovered and turned to hand her down.

She gripped his hand and leaned on his arm as she alighted.

By the time she'd released his hand, shaken down her skirts, and raised her head, he'd recollected enough of how things were supposed to be. He narrowed his eyes on hers. "This will go no further."

Anything else was too...dangerous.

His words hung between them, an edict backed by his considerable authority.

She tipped her head and studied him for an instant, then her glorious smile bloomed. Lightly, she tapped his arm, then swung toward the house, crossed to the steps, raised her skirts, and started climbing.

He stared after her.

Without looking back, she called, "I'll see you at eight-thirty."

She reached the porch, and Crewe, alerted by the footman, swung open the door. Drake watched her glide inside, then Crewe nodded to him and gently shut the door.

Behind Drake, her carriage rattled off on its way to the mews.

He stared at the closed door, then he set his lips, compressed them, turned, and stalked home.

Sadly, his home was too close to allow him to walk off his mood—aggravated, irritated, and unsettlingly uncertain.

As far as he could recall, he'd never before felt so trepidatious about what the next day might bring.

CHAPTER 19

Griswade watched the last of the workers hurry through the gates into the yard.

He waited and watched until the city's bells pealed seven o'clock before, finally, giving up. Stepping out of the alley in which he'd lounged, he walked up the street.

The fourth man who had helped Lawton transfer the gunpowder on Monday night should have been among those reporting for work. Even though the fog was hanging low, Griswade had had a sufficiently clear view and had watched closely enough to be beyond certain that the man hadn't turned up.

Griswade didn't know the man's address, but if the fellow had gone to ground, he might not even be there.

Still...

After weighing the situation, he decided that if the man had done a bunk, perhaps that would be good enough, at least for the moment. At least until the old man's plans had reached their apogee. Later, once all was successfully achieved...there was really nothing the man could do. He posed no threat to Griswade or the old man because he didn't know they existed.

Griswade preferred to be thorough, but in this case, perhaps accepting the situation and letting the man hide away where he was no threat to anyone was the wiser course.

Regardless, he was approaching Tooley Street, and the fog was thinning. It was time he was away from there.

CHAPTER 20

*W*hen at nine o'clock, with Louisa by his side, Drake walked into the London Working Men's Association building, it was to find a sea of gloomy faces awaiting them.

After nodding to the small crowd, Drake turned to the office and Beam, who had come to the window. "I take it you have no new information."

Beam grimaced. "We're still checking through the membership lists. We've hundreds of names to check—maybe as many as a thousand men to find to make sure they haven't vanished like our leaders."

"I daresay it's a grim business." Louisa's clear voice floated over the gathered men. "Not knowing when you might stumble on another of your colleagues who've fallen victim to this plot."

"That's it exactly," Beam said. "I've persuaded the sergeants of the three militias that we have to make sure no other man's in trouble. They're each combing through the list of their members, but we haven't yet heard of anyone else disappearing." Beam looked at Drake. "The sergeants should send in an update in the next hour."

Drake debated waiting to see if anything turned up. The crowd in the meeting room seemed to ebb and flow; men came in, chatted with their mates for a while, then left, and others arrived. Presumably, many different workplaces would be represented by at least one man each day;

Drake could see how, without all that much effort, the Chartists could spread information through their membership quickly and efficiently.

But searching for missing men—men who were no longer present to hear and respond to any appeal—was another matter entirely.

Louisa had been chatting with Beam. Several other men, drawn like moths to a flame, had sidled closer, and she was now questioning the group about other possible ways to check if any of their members were missing.

She was standing several feet away, yet her perfume niggled at Drake, teasing his senses.

When, at eight-thirty, he'd walked into the St. Ives House front hall to find her coming down the stairs garbed in a severe dark-green walking dress, he'd felt something inside him still. Tense and watchful, he'd waited, but she'd behaved in her usual willful and single-minded fashion, and it had been blatantly clear that her focus was firmly fixed on forging ahead with the mission.

He'd found himself both grateful and perversely irritated that she gave every sign of having completely forgotten that senses-searing kiss they'd shared mere hours before.

Of course, he could blot the incident from his mind, too, but only with the exercise of significant effort. He knew she wouldn't have forgotten it—the heat, the hunger, the overwhelming sensations—any more than he had, but that she could, apparently so effortlessly, set it aside...

He inwardly shook himself back to the here and now. He glanced at her again. It truly was madness to continue to allow her to investigate alongside him. Sadly, he knew what incited such madness—her, Louisa, Lady Wild; if he didn't include her and take her with him, she would plunge in on her own.

The sound of running footsteps on the pavement outside had him and everyone else turning toward the front doors.

Abruptly, both doors were flung wide, and Finnegan rushed in. His gaze locked on Drake. "My lord—" Finnegan halted and, having taken in the crowd, fell silent; he was clearly uncertain whether he should speak in such company.

"If it's about this mission, you can speak freely," Drake said.

"Yes, my lord." Finnegan drew breath and reported, "Inspector Crawford sent an urgent message. A runner from the River Police arrived at the Yard to say they've pulled out another body farther downriver. They're sending the remains up to the Yard. And the inspector says there are two more with Sir Martin that he thinks you need to take a look at. He hopes you can help with identification."

Drake turned to survey the men. To the last man, they'd blanched. Quietly, Drake asked, "Is there anyone willing to see if these three recent bodies belong to members of this association?"

The men glanced at each other. They shuffled, murmured unintelligibly, but no one volunteered.

From the corner of his eye, Drake saw Beam stiffen, then the secretary straightened and cleared his throat.

When Drake looked his way, Beam said, "I'll come. While I might not know every man by name, I believe I would recognize most faces…" He looked down at the papers on the counter before him and frowned. "That is, if the matter can wait for a few minutes while I get things in order?"

Drake nodded crisply. "We can wait. If the body from downriver is still on its way…" He glanced at Finnegan, who nodded. Drake continued, "There's no hurry. Take your time. We'll wait, and you can come with us in the carriage."

CHAPTER 21

*C*leo and Michael stood on the stoop of a tiny but well-kept cottage on the edge of Clapham Common. Michael grasped the knocker and plied it.

After several moments, they heard shuffling footsteps approaching, then the door swung open, and an old sailor—he was instantly recognizable as such—looked out at them through bird-bright blue eyes.

The old man surveyed Michael, then his gaze moved to Cleo, and all reserve evaporated. He beamed. "Miss Hendon! Well, I never. It's a delight to see you again, miss."

Cleo smiled back. "Hello, Ollie." She waved at Michael. "This is Lord Michael Cynster. He's a friend of the family's."

Michael cast her a faintly amused look. "And Miss Hendon's fiancé."

Cleo colored. "Yes. And that." She still hadn't grown accustomed to the fact.

Measuringly, Ollie looked Michael over, but apparently liked what he saw. His beaming smile returned. "Delighted to meet you, sir—my lord." His gaze switched from Michael to Cleo and back again. "But what brings you to my door?"

"If we may, Ollie," Cleo said, "we'd like to pick your brains. We're helping the authorities with a puzzle that involves gunpowder."

"Ah, well, if that's the case, you've come to the right place." Ollie stepped back and waved them in. "Come you on in, and I'll get us a pot of tea, and then we'll see how much I still remember, heh?"

He settled them in chairs in the tiny parlor, then bustled away, to return in five minutes with a tray on which resided a brown teapot and three mugs, a small pitcher of milk, and a plate of shortbread biscuits.

Once he'd seen them supplied to his satisfaction, Ollie sat in what was patently his favorite armchair by the fire and fixed them with an interrogatory look. "Now, what's this you need to know?"

Cleo cradled her mug between her hands. "The situation is this. We believe someone—who, we don't know—has brought gunpowder illicitly into London. We've traced ten barrels to a particular area of Southwark. We've kept a watch on the area since, so either the barrels are still there, which they might be, or—and this is what we're worried about—the gunpowder might have been transferred to some other container as a disguise. In that case, it might still be in the area, or it might have been or might soon be moved." Cleo had fixed her gaze on Ollie's face. "We asked the senior clerk at the office of the Inspector General of Gunpowder, and he said there really was no effective way to store gunpowder, especially near water, except in properly made gunpowder barrels."

Ollie was slowly nodding. "Aye, he's right about that. Goes off so fast you wouldn't credit it, especially if, as it seems, they're holding the stuff near the river. They'd want to keep it properly airtight, or it'd be no use at all."

Cleo grimaced. She glanced at Michael.

Leaning forward, his forearms on his thighs, he was studying Ollie's face. "So there's no other way at all—none whatsoever—to successfully transport gunpowder."

"Well," Ollie temporized, "other than skins, but if you're talking ten barrels' worth, that won't do."

The mention of skins juxtaposed with Ollie... Cleo frowned. "You say skins because once they're treated, they're airtight."

Puzzled, Ollie nodded. "Aye, that's right."

"But," Cleo went on, clearly feeling her way, "does that mean that anything that's airtight might be used?" She met Ollie's bright gaze. "I'm thinking of oilskin bags—like the ones used for flotation. Could they be used?"

Ollie blinked. He thought for several moments, then, slowly, he nodded. "Can't see why properly treated oilskin wouldn't work—not that I've ever tried it."

Michael was searching Cleo's face. "What are you imagining?"

Excitement mounting, Cleo said, "What if our villains used oilskin bags and set the bags inside barrels—the sort of barrels you would never think could be used for gunpowder, like brewery barrels or herring barrels?" She looked at Ollie. "Would that—could that—work?"

Again, Ollie thought. Again, eventually, he nodded. "Aye, it might, but only if these villains of yours know to seal the bags good and tight." He paused, clearly envisaging the construction. "Those flotation bags ships use—well, they're in water all the time or right beside it, and they last for years. If your villains use that sort of oilskin, and as long as they know to get the seal right... Aye, I'd stake my name on it—that would do."

"Thank you!" Cleo set down her mug and all but bounced to her feet. Her eyes shining, she looked at Michael. "Now we know what to search for." She turned to Ollie, who had lumbered up from his chair. She gripped his hands and squeezed. "You've helped us enormously."

"My pleasure, miss." Ollie's smile stated he spoke only the truth.

Michael offered his hand. "And you have the thanks of all of us who are working on this."

Ollie shook Michael's hand. "Aye, you're chasing something important. I can see that." He followed Michael and Cleo as they made for the door. He halted in the doorway, and when they turned to farewell him, he bobbed his head to them both. "Good luck to the pair of you. I hope you find that stuff right quick."

"With your help, Ollie, we will." Cleo waved, then rushed for the carriage.

Michael saluted Ollie, which made the old man grin, then hurried to catch up with Cleo. He helped her into the carriage, then called up to Tom, "Back to Southwark with all speed."

Michael joined Cleo in the carriage. It rocked as Tom turned the horses. The instant Tom had the carriage on the road again and had whipped up the horses, Michael met Cleo's eyes. "Where first? The breweries?"

Cleo thought, then said, "Of all the different things going out of that area day after day, the two that stand out are the barrels of pickled herrings and the barrels of beer and ale. And of those two, the barrels from the breweries…there are just so many of them, and they go out in all directions, far more so than the herring barrels. So yes, I believe the breweries ought to be our next ports of call."

CHAPTER 22

*F*rom the shadows cloaking the top of the water stairs beneath the

northern end of Blackfriars Bridge, Griswade watched a barge carrying a massive number of barrels destined for Hunstable's warehouse inch away from Gun Wharf on the other side of the river.

The heavily weighted flat-bottomed barge, guided by his latest helpful henchmen, rode the currents and, yard by yard, moved steadily across the choppy gray waters.

Once the barge was close enough, Griswade put a spyglass to his eye. He focused, then scanned the barrels, searching for the right markings. Yes—there. Clearly visible on the sides of several barrels was the brand identifying the ultimate destination for those very special barrels.

Lowering the glass, Griswade allowed himself a small smile. So far, so good. All was going perfectly to plan. And after tonight, there would be no one left who might mention to anyone the odd qualities of those particular barrels delivered to Hunstable's that day.

He shut the spyglass, returned it to his pocket, then turned and trudged up to the road and thence onto the bridge. Effectively concealed among the many other pedestrians crossing the bridge, he watched the barge slide alongside the wharf onto which the lower level of Hunstable's huge warehouse opened. The bargemen tied up, then hefted the barrels, the special delivery along with others more mundane, onto the wharf, then the pair rolled the barrels along, through the open double doors and into the dimness of the warehouse.

Griswade counted the special barrels as they went into the warehouse. He waited until the entire delivery was complete, and the bargemen pushed their almost empty barge back onto the river.

All had gone smoothly, without a hitch. Without the slightest suspicion raised.

All was in train for the old man's plot to end with a resounding bang.

CHAPTER 23

*M*r. Beam, poor man, was understandably nervous. As Drake led the way through the doors of the morgue, Louisa smiled reassuringly at the gangly secretary and waved him to precede her inside.

Holding open the door, Drake glanced back.

Beam faced the doorway, drew in a deep breath, clutched his cap even more tightly, and followed Drake into the ivory-tiled room.

Louisa walked in behind Beam, while Finnegan, who seemed to possess an unhealthy curiosity regarding dead bodies and had begged to accompany them, brought up the rear.

It was already after midday; they'd been held up by an accident between two carriages that had blocked Vauxhall Bridge while they were on it. Her coachman hadn't been able to turn the carriage; they'd had to wait until the debris was cleared, and they'd been able to pass.

Sir Martin was sitting at a desk by the wall. He'd been working on reports, but had turned at the sound of their footsteps.

He noted their small procession; as he came to his feet, from under his bushy eyebrows, he directed a particularly ferocious scowl at Louisa, but he knew better than to attempt to exclude a duke's daughter from wherever she wished to go.

Regardless, with the strong smell of preservatives in her nostrils,

Louisa halted just a few yards inside the large room. She didn't feel obliged to view any more dead bodies. She did, however, intend to hear every word said.

Drake led Beam to Sir Martin, who greeted the secretary reasonably politely. After making the introductions, Drake said, "Beam believes he'll be able to identify any local member of his organization should their bodies have found their way here."

Sir Martin eyed the transparently edgy secretary and forbore to bark as was his wont; presumably realizing Beam needed no encouragement to bolt, he nodded approvingly. "Good man." Sir Martin started toward the row of marble-topped benches. "If you'll come this way?"

Three of the five benches in the main part of the room were occupied. Well-washed yet yellowing sheets covered the man-shaped mounds.

Sir Martin led Beam to one end of the row and, almost reverently, one after the other, drew back the sheets from the bodies' heads. "Take your time, sir," he instructed Beam. "It's important that you be sure."

Tentatively, Beam approached the first body.

"Sadly," Sir Martin continued, his tone one of clinical detachment, "they're somewhat the worse for wear, but we've done the best we can to make them presentable. Ignore the fresh scratches and bites."

As if mesmerized, Beam stood staring at the first body's face.

"The first two"—Sir Martin glanced at Drake—"were found in Southwark, in the area your friends have under surveillance, while the third was retrieved from the marshes downstream."

Abruptly, Beam wrenched his gaze from the face of the first body and looked at the face of the second. After several seconds of horrified gazing, he shuffled on and looked down on the face of the third corpse.

After a moment, Beam frowned. He looked back at the first and second bodies. Then he raised his gaze to Drake's face. "The—" Beam had to stop and clear his throat, then he gamely went on, "The first two are ours." He glanced at the bodies in question. "They are—were—brewery workers, I think. I'll need to check the register to see which brewery, but their names are Mike Jones and Cec—Cecil—Blunt."

Sir Martin grabbed paper and pencil and jotted down the names. "Addresses?" He looked at Beam.

The secretary shook his head. "I can't say, but they'll be on the register. That's back at the association." Clutching his cap, twisting it between his hands, Beam edged away from the bodies.

Sir Martin caught Drake's gaze, arched a brow, and with his eyes, signaled to the third body.

Drake focused on Beam. "The third man?"

Beam didn't look again, but shook his head decisively. "He's not one of ours. I've never seen him before."

Finnegan had been circling the three occupied benches. He approached the third corpse and studied the dead man's face. Then he stepped to the side, raised the sheet, and lifted one of the man's hands.

Intrigued, Louisa watched as Finnegan appeared to study the man's nails.

Then Finnegan set down the arm and looked at Drake, who was informing Beam that they would be returning to the association with him in order to determine where the two dead men had lived and worked. "My lord?"

Drake glanced at Finnegan and arched an eyebrow.

"The gentleman—Mr. Chilburn. He had a gentleman's gentleman who has disappeared."

Drake turned and approached the third bench. "You think that's him?"

"He looks the part," Finnegan said. "You might not need to search any further."

Drake halted and studied the face of the dead man, then nodded. "You could be right." He paused, then said, "Go and ask Chilburn's landlord, the baker, to come and identify the body." Drake looked at Louisa. "I doubt any of Chilburn's family will be much help, at least not at the moment, and we need to know."

Drake glanced back at Finnegan. "Return here with the landlord and see what he says, then come and report."

"Yes, my lord." Finnegan hesitated, then asked, "Should I take a constable, my lord? The landlord might not believe me."

Sir Martin snorted. "And even if he does, he might not be inclined to oblige." He nodded at the door. "Ask Jennings on the front desk. Tell him I said to send a man with you."

"Thank you, sir." Finnegan bowed to Drake. "My lord." Finnegan made for the door. As he drew level with Louisa, he bowed smoothly. "My lady."

Drake watched Finnegan go, then turned to Sir Martin. "The same killer, obviously, but he didn't put the first two into the river."

"No," Sir Martin conceded, "but that might have been because he killed them during the day."

"Which day?"

"If I had to guess, I'd say Wednesday. Earlyish. They're not that far gone in decomposition, but rigor has passed, and vermin have had time to get at them."

Louisa had noticed Mr. Beam edging closer and closer to the door. Sir Martin's last comment had eradicated what little color had remained in the secretary's face.

All but plastered against the wall beside the door, Beam managed to croak, "If you don't need me anymore, my lord…"

When Drake glanced his way, Beam pointed toward the door.

Drake straightened. "My apologies, Beam. If you'll wait in the corridor, we'll head back to the association in just a few minutes."

Louisa approached and laid a hand on Beam's arm. When he startled, then stared at her, she smiled reassuringly. "I'll come and wait with you, sir. Let's leave these gentlemen to their morbid discussions."

Beam went readily.

Drake caught the look Louisa threw him as she bundled Beam into the corridor. He had to admit that with Finnegan gone, it was as well to keep the nervous Beam under their collective eye. He turned back to Sir Martin. "Anything more of a morbid nature you care to impart?"

Sir Martin snorted. "Sadly, not a lot. It's definitely the same killer—our garrotter. He stuns them with a blow to the back of the head first, quite neat and precise, almost certainly delivered with a short cosh, then uses his garrote. It's a nasty way to kill—I'd say he enjoys it—but at least it's quick."

"And silent," Drake murmured. "Or as near as makes no odds."

"Indeed. This man is confident enough and coolheaded enough to kill in well-trafficked areas as long as he can find a place out of sight." Sir Martin caught Drake's eye. "Combined with his method of killing, that suggests he's someone with whom all the men he's killed have felt comfortable enough not to be on their guard. They've all turned their backs on him when he's been quite close—they definitely didn't view him as any imminent threat."

When Drake said nothing, Sir Martin added, "You need to catch this bastard, Winchelsea. He's already accounted for six souls, and that's just those we know of. We don't need to find any more."

Drake grunted. "We're doing our best, but…" He drew breath and continued, "Sadly, I suspect there will be more bodies before we catch up with him."

Sir Martin made a sound of disgust. "What a delightful thing to look forward to." He waved Drake away. "Off! Off and catch this beggar."

Drake inclined his head and headed for the door.

CHAPTER 24

*D*rake was out of the carriage the instant it halted. He barely paused to hand Louisa down before striding for the big wooden gates, currently set wide, that gave access to the yard of the Phoenix Brewery.

He'd almost reached the gates when Louisa called, "Drake! Wait!"

He halted and looked back, and saw Michael, with Cleo in tow, descending from an identical black carriage to the one Drake had just quit.

Cleo and Michael joined Louisa, then all three walked quickly to where Drake waited.

As soon as he was within earshot, Michael said, "We've been asking at the breweries in the area—we'll explain later, but we think that's where the gunpowder went, to a brewery. We've checked the other three, and none have any men missing." Michael tipped his head at the ironwork arch spanning the gateway, with a phoenix rising from red-painted flames in an oval at the apex. "This is the last."

"And it's by far the largest." Cleo was peering into the yard.

"And," Drake added, his tones clipped, "two men who belong to the Working Men's Association and work here have turned up dead." He met Michael's eyes. "Killed by our garrotter."

No more needed to be said. With Drake leading the way, they marched into the yard.

They halted in the middle of the cobbled space. A surprised worker approached; while Drake gave his title and asked for the manager, Louisa looked about.

The yard was much larger than was apparent from the street; it extended behind various buildings, stretching north toward the river, while to the south and east, huge buildings squatted, wide and deep. From the one to the east, a strong smell of hops emanated, while through the open doors of the barracks-like building to the south, she glimpsed racks of barrels stretching away into cellar-like dimness.

Behind the buildings facing the street and closer to the river stood other buildings she thought might be workshops, while carts and drays were drawn up before the long low stable that formed the north side of the elongated rectangular yard.

As she was looking, workmen rolled four large empty barrels out of the open door of one workshop and across the flagstones to what she assumed was the brewing house.

Rapid footsteps had her swinging around. A short, rather rotund man, a merchant by his attire, came hurrying from a building wedged between the brewery and the cellar-store.

The man's eyes, wide and slightly protuberant, were fixed on Drake.

After halting several yards away, the man bowed low. "My lord, allow me to present myself." Straightening, he informed them, "I am Mr. Flock, and I'm the manager of this enterprise." Clasping his hands, Mr. Flock inquired, "How may I be of service?"

"Mr. Flock. I'm saddened to be the bearer of ill tidings, but I've just come from Scotland Yard. Two men were recently found murdered, their bodies discovered in streets nearby. They have been identified as Mike Jones and Cecil Blunt, both of whom worked here."

Flock paled, and his jaw fell slack. After a moment of goggle-eyed staring, he made a valiant attempt to pull himself together. "Good Lord! But...*dead?*" He goggled again.

Drake eyed Flock's face, considered his reaction. "I take it you knew they were missing."

"Yes—yes." Flock ran a shaking hand over his balding pate. "Mike Jones was one of our master coopers, and Blunt was in charge of the drays. They've been missing—well, they haven't turned up for work—since Tuesday. Them and two others."

"Others? Whom?" Drake demanded.

"Mal Triggs—one of our drivers. And Jed Sawyer, Mike Jones's apprentice. Those two were here on Wednesday, but we haven't seen them since."

"We'll need Triggs's and Sawyer's addresses." Drake paused to swiftly rescript the truth, then said, "The situation, Mr. Flock, is this. A cargo of contraband material, stored in barrels, was taken from a warehouse in Morgan's Lane on Monday night. The barrels were carted away on two drays." Drake glanced at Cleo and added, "Two brewers' drays." He paused, then stated, relatively mildly, "It might help if we could examine your drays."

"Yes, of course, my lord." Flock waved at what was clearly the brewery's stable, lining the north end of the yard, then led the way. "Of course, not all our drays are presently here. Indeed, most are out doing deliveries."

"If we could just see the design." When Flock, surprised, glanced back at her, Cleo smiled encouragingly. "Are all your drays—the bigger ones capable of carrying six or more large barrels—all the same sort?"

Flock blinked. "I expect so, but I really can't say. We'll have to ask the stableman—although, of course, he's a more junior man. He's had to step up to fill Blunt's shoes."

They reached the stable. Drake paused by the doors, allowing Cleo and Michael to pass him, following Flock. Louisa had slipped away from their group. Scanning the yard, Drake spotted her strolling into one of the workshops. He hesitated, then turned and followed Cleo and Michael. One thing at a time, and in this setting, Louisa, he felt sure, could take care of herself.

He found Flock standing back, with another man beside him, while Cleo and Michael studied a cart—a brewer's dray.

As Drake joined the group, Cleo nodded decisively. "Drays the same as this one—same shape of headboard, same body and paintwork—were the ones used to cart away the barrels from the warehouse." Moving to the dray's side, she raised a hand and traced the company's logo—a phoenix rising over flames—which was picked out in gold against the black paint. "I remember this—the gold paint made it stand out in the weak light—but I wasn't close enough to see what it was. What it depicted."

That was more than good enough for Drake.

The stableman was frowning. "This was Monday night, you say?" When Michael nodded, the man said, "If you'll wait just a minute…" Turning his head, he bellowed down the long stable, "Thomas!"

A tow-headed urchin looked out of a distant stall. The stableman waved at him to join them. Brushing straw from his jerkin, the lad came hurrying up.

When he skidded to a halt beside the stableman, the man nodded at Drake and Michael, and Cleo, who had drifted back to join them. "You tell these folks what you found Tuesday morning." When the boy just stared, the stableman nudged him. "The horses, remember?"

"Oh. Aye." The boy blinked, then volunteered, "When I come in on Tuesday morning, one of the big haulers, he had all four hooves wrapped up with cloth. Took me an age to unwind the strips."

Drake looked at Cleo.

She nodded. "The horses that drew the drays out of Morgan's Lane had their hooves muffled with cloth."

Flock and the stableman exchanged wary glances. Flock had started to recover from the shock of having to deal with a marquess and three others of the aristocracy on top of being informed that several men in his employ had been murdered. He cleared his throat, then drew himself up and rather stridently stated, "My lord, I would like to take this opportunity to assure you that the Phoenix Brewery had absolutely nothing to do with any underhand or unsavory dealings, and if some of those who worked here appropriated our equipment to commit some crime, then while we find that deeply regrettable, I must protest that the brewery itself can in no way be held to blame."

Drake inclined his head. "Naturally not."

Flock didn't take that in. Waxing eloquent in defense of his establishment, the manager spread his arms. "Why, even if our drays and horses were used to move the…er, contraband-containing barrels, there's no saying where the barrels were taken. They might have been transported to anywhere in London!"

"I regret to inform you, Mr. Flock, that the barrels were, indeed, brought here."

Louisa's haughty tones acted like cold water flung over Flock's histrionics. Along with everyone else, Drake turned to see her standing in the open stable door.

She met his gaze and tipped her head toward the workshops. "I believe the barrels—or rather what's left of them—are still here." She shifted her gaze to Cleo. "If you would come and look, Cleo?"

"Of course." Cleo was already bustling toward the door.

Michael quickly caught up with her. Drake followed.

Flock, looking stunned again, trotted behind, trying to keep up, both with Drake's strides and, Drake suspected, the unfolding events and how they might impact his business.

Louisa led them between two workshops to what appeared to be a discard pile for broken barrels. Bending, she picked up one shattered stave and showed it to Cleo. "I found this shoved in toward the base of the pile." She glanced at Michael. "There are many more pieces in there if you look. The wood is a different color to that commonly used here, so it's easy to pick out."

The scent of freshly cut wood was pervasive. Several workmen in carpenters' aprons were standing to one side, watching. One volunteered,

"I'd take my oath the piece the lady's holding is Irish oak. Coopers in London don't use such wood—wherever those barrels came from, they weren't local."

Cleo turned to show the broken stave to Drake. She pointed to a mark on the wood. "That's part of the stamp of the Irish mill—all our contraband barrels had that mark."

Crouching, Michael had been tugging more smashed staves from the pile. He rose and showed Drake two more fragments, both with near-complete Irish gunpowder mill stamps.

Drake nodded. "So the barrels were brought here, then...what? If they broke up the barrels, what did they do with the material in them?"

Michael was looking down, almost hopping on one foot as he tried to shake free a piece of material that had wrapped about his ankle.

"Wait! Stop!" Cleo crouched and caught the material. She unwound it, drew it free, then rose and held it out for Michael, Drake, and Louisa to see. They obediently looked, but it was Michael who realized the significance. "Oilskin!"

Cleo turned to Flock and his men. She displayed the fragment of fabric. "Do you use this type of material anywhere in your business?"

All the men looked; all shook their heads, transparently mystified. "I'm sure I've never ordered such stuff," Flock said.

Drake frowned at Michael and Cleo. "Obviously, you've discovered something we don't know."

"Ah...yes." With a glance at the increasing crowd of onlookers, Cleo lowered her voice. "We learned that it's very likely possible to transport our sensitive contraband material in any barrels at all provided that those barrels are lined with oilskin, which is airtight, and the seals made good."

Over Cleo's head, Drake surveyed the adjacent workshop with its benches crammed with barrels in various stages of construction. "That's why they needed the cooper and his apprentice. Not just as hands to help with the transfer but to ensure the seals were tight."

Louisa had turned to peer into the pile. "There are lots more pieces of that material here. It looks as if they trimmed the pieces—presumably so the lining wouldn't show."

Cleo strung out the piece she held. The inner edge formed a large ring. "I think they put the bags inside, filled them, then sealed the lid with the edges of the bags showing and trimmed off the edges."

Drake turned to Flock. "Mr. Flock, this matter of the contraband material we're seeking is serious, and I am acting with the direct authority of the Home Secretary. We in no way imagine the Phoenix Brewery itself is involved. Even the men who were drawn into this plot and were subsequently murdered were hoodwinked. Our immediate concern now is to locate the contraband material. To accomplish this with the greatest speed, I am appealing for your help."

Flock waved his hands. "Good gracious, but of course! We are all entirely at your service, my lord."

"In that case"—Drake glanced at Cleo, then at Louisa—"I believe the first question we have is…"

Louisa looked at Flock. "What size barrels does the brewery use?"

That wasn't a question Drake had expected, but Cleo nodded. "They would almost certainly have opted for barrels not previously used."

"It will be easiest to show you." Flock gestured and led the way into the adjacent workshop and through it to a large adjoining storeroom. "This is our barrel store."

Most of the store was filled with empty barrels of various capacities, stacked according to size. Two men were rolling newly made barrels from the cooper's workshop into the store, while other men were rolling barrels out of another door into the yard; presumably those barrels were on their way to be filled with the brewery's products.

Flock directed their attention to the side wall, where a line of barrels ranging in size from small brandy casks to massive ale barrels were neatly arranged with labels affixed to the wall above stating what beer, ale, or spirits each size of barrel was used for. Some sizes were used for several different beverages, others for just one. "These are all the different barrels we use."

The sharp smell of wood was intense inside the store. They surveyed the barrels, then Louisa took the fabric ring from Cleo, walked to the second-largest barrel, and laid the circular band around the barrel's lip. It was a good fit.

Cleo had followed Louisa; she nodded crisply. "Yes, that's the size they used."

Drake looked at the sign above the barrel. "Bright Flame Ale."

Flock's nervousness was increasing again. "That's our most popular ale."

Cleo was eyeing the barrel measuringly. "If we assume they intend all the barrels to go to one place, then it's most likely they used only one sort of barrel, so the lot could go all together as one order, in which case, they would, I believe, need fifteen of these to account for the ten barrels of…contraband material."

Michael glanced at Flock. "Are you missing any of these Bright Flame barrels? Can you tell?"

Flock looked blank for an instant, then beckoned one of the carpenters who had hung back at the entrance to the barrel store. "Hinchins is our head cooper. I believe he should know."

Hinchins was a heavyset, grizzled man. When appealed to, he reluctantly nodded. "Aye—I was going to mention it if we hadn't found them by the end of the day. We're missing twelve or maybe fifteen Bright Flames."

"Since Monday night?" Drake asked.

The head cooper considered, then admitted, "Could be, but I only noticed yesterday morning, when I came in here to check, seeing as we're down two men—one of my coopers and his apprentice—and they worked mostly on the Bright Flame barrels."

At the mention of the missing coopers, Flock looked distressed, but he thanked Hinchins and, in response to the man's clearly questioning look, said he'd explain later.

Drake led the way back into the yard. The others followed, and Flock, transparently anxious, brought up the rear.

Flock scurried to catch up with Drake. "My lord—"

Drake held up his hand. "One moment, Mr. Flock." Drake halted in the middle of the yard; as the others gathered around, he turned to Michael. "Is Tom with you?" When Michael nodded, Drake said, "Send Tom to call in your men—all the footmen army. We need them here. Either the barrels are here, or they've been moved out of the area. Whichever it is, we need to find out."

Michael nodded and strode for the gates.

Drake turned to Flock. "Mr. Flock, we'll need to search all the Bright Flame barrels in your store"—Drake tipped his head toward the cellar-like building—"and any other already-filled Bright Flame barrels stacked anywhere in the brewery." Flock paled, and Drake hurried to add, "However, all that requires is to test the weight of the barrels—for our men to lift them. If the barrels contain liquid—ale, beer, or anything else—the men will know. The barrels we're looking for won't feel the same."

Flock's puzzled frown evaporated. "Ah. I see. The contraband material isn't liquid."

"No. It isn't." Drake volunteered nothing more.

Flock looked uncertain, but said, "I'll tell my men to…er, assist as required."

"Thank you. We'll endeavor to be as efficient as possible." Drake glanced toward the gates. The first of the Cynster footmen were walking into the yard.

"Meanwhile…" Louisa waited until Drake looked her way, one dark eyebrow rising. "While you and Michael lead the search"—she was sure they would want to ensure no barrels were overlooked—"I suggest Cleo and I see what information we can glean from the brewery office." She smiled encouragingly at Flock. "We need the addresses of those two missing men—Mal Triggs and Jed Sawyer. And regarding the barrels in question, although a search of these premises must be made, there's a good chance those barrels are no longer here. Given we're short of time plus the likelihood that the barrels have already been moved, then as the transfer to the Bright Flame barrels occurred on Monday night, I believe we need to review all deliveries made from Tuesday morning until today."

Cleo was nodding. She glanced at Drake. "If the barrels aren't here, then they might have been moved on by being sent to fulfill an order of fifteen or more barrels of Bright Flame Ale."

Flock looked horrified. "Bright Flame Ale is the brewery's most popular product."

"That might be why they chose those barrels rather than the larger ones." Louisa arched her brows at Drake.

Curtly, he nodded, then glanced toward the gates. More of the footmen army were pouring into the yard. To Louisa and Cleo, he said, "See what you can find while we get this search done." He looked at Flock. "If you would introduce me to your cellarman, Flock, then perhaps you could accompany the ladies."

"Indeed, my lord." Flock bobbed to Louisa and Cleo. "If you will wait here, ladies, I will return in just a moment."

Louisa inclined her head. She and Cleo watched as Drake, with Flock scurrying beside him, walked into the dimness of the cellar-store, where Flock called several workers to attend them.

Michael strode to the front of the milling crowd of over twenty Cynster footmen and grooms. He called them to order, then led them in Drake's wake.

Then Mr. Flock was hurrying back to Louisa and Cleo. Louisa turned toward the office and, with a wave, invited Flock to precede them.

Once in the office, Flock made Louisa and Cleo known to the two middle-aged and clearly experienced clerks who sat at two desks behind a high counter. "Please supply these ladies with whatever information they wish. Anything at all." Flock was starting to look distinctly harried. "I really should stay with the marquess. There's no saying…"

With that, he briefly bowed and departed in some haste.

Louisa exchanged a glance with Cleo, then as one, they turned to the counter and the suitably attentive clerks.

Their request for the addresses of Triggs and Sawyer was easily dealt with; it appeared both lived nearby.

"Within walking distance, my lady, just a few blocks south." The older clerk indicated the direction with a tip of his head. "Most of our men live close."

Louisa thanked him and tucked the sheet of paper bearing the addresses into her reticule, then calmly stated, "And now we must trouble you for your records of all deliveries made since Tuesday morning that included fifteen barrels of Bright Flame Ale."

Both clerks blinked slowly. They exchanged a look, but then the older clerk's face set, and he nodded. "Yes, my lady."

On the public side of the high counter, Louisa and Cleo sat side by side on two straight-backed chairs the clerks fetched for them and did their best to radiate patience.

When the older clerk handed them a stack of papers, they smiled and eagerly accepted them.

"Mind," the clerk added, retreating toward his domain, "that's just the deliveries done on Tuesday."

As together with Cleo, Louisa sorted through the orders, confirming that each one involved at least fifteen barrels of Bright Flame Ale, her hopes of finding just one or perhaps a handful of such orders were comprehensively dashed. "Clearly," she said, "the Phoenix Brewery is large for a reason."

Approaching with another handful of delivery notices, the second clerk smiled. "Oh yes, miss—my lady. Our ale is the finest, and Londoners like their ale."

"Obviously." Louisa accepted the latest pile and started working through the deliveries made on Wednesday. The number was similar to Tuesday, and as with Tuesday's destinations, not one stood out as in any way noteworthy in terms of gunpowder.

Eventually, between them, she and Cleo held a small pile of delivery notices. There had been a minimum of sixteen potentially relevant deliveries made each day, and sometimes as many as twenty-eight.

While Cleo counted the notices, Louisa looked up at the curious clerks. "The deliveries for Friday—today. Have they all gone out?"

"Yes, ma'am—my lady. All deliveries go out by noon, seeing as it's Friday." The older clerk nodded at the pile of notices. "We've included all that have gone out up to now. Won't be any more due to go out until tomorrow."

Cleo came to the end of her pile and looked up. "There have been ninety-three deliveries that might have included the contraband-containing barrels." She looked at the clerks, then with a certain sympathy, said, "I fear, sirs, that we will need you to make a list, in duplicate, of all these deliveries." She rose, carried the stack to the counter, and set it down, artfully adding, "That will be much faster, and also more useful, than having you copy all these notices." The clerks blanched, and their burgeoning resistance deflated. Louisa hid a grin. Smoothly, Cleo continued, "Here is how we need the list organized."

While Cleo dictated form and substance to the clerks, Louisa sat and thought. She considered the sequence of events as they knew them leading up to the gunpowder being put into the fifteen Bright Flame barrels. Why had the plotters, specifically Drake's mastermind, chosen the Phoenix Brewery? There were hundreds of breweries in London, dozens within easy reach of this area, easy to get to from Morgan's Lane; why choose this one? The only reason she could imagine was because the brewery provided a route to getting the gunpowder to the mastermind's intended target. That meant that target, or at least a step closer to it, was buried somewhere on the list the creation of which Cleo was overseeing.

Both clerks were now seated at their desks, heads down as they worked on assembling the list Cleo had defined—including date of delivery, name of customer, the customer's address, and the number of barrels of Bright Flame Ale delivered. In duplicate.

When the younger clerk handed up the two copies of their first sheet to Cleo, who had remained leaning on the high counter, Louisa rose and joined her soon-to-be sister-in-law.

Cleo handed her one of the copies. "The deliveries made on Tuesday."

Louisa scanned down the list. Previously, she'd been looking at the customers' addresses, but now, with each line detailing one delivery, another point stood out.

Fifteen minutes later, when the clerks had delivered the lists for Wednesday and Thursday and she'd checked those, too, she was even more puzzled.

When the older clerk finished his list for Friday and handed it to his junior to copy and sat back, Louisa leaned over the counter, held up Thursday's list, and pointed to a specific entry. "These orders that are particularly large." She pointed to more on the Wednesday and Tuesday lists. "I noticed that these customers take large deliveries several times a week. Yet surely no inn or public house could possibly go through so much ale in just a day."

The older clerk smiled faintly. "No, my lady. Those customers"—he rose and came to the counter, looked at one of the lists, then tapped one entry—"like this one, Merryjigs—are wine and beer merchants. If we had to supply every tavern and inn directly, we'd need hundreds of drays and drivers. Instead, we send barges of barrels to the merchants, and they sell them on to the public houses, inns, and taverns."

Louisa frowned. "So these very large repeat deliveries are to middlemen, so to speak." She pointed again. "What about ones like these—large, but only once?"

"Those are the larger inns." The clerk scanned to the customer name for the delivery she'd picked out. "For instance, that one is to the Bull Inn in Aldersgate. Being a major coaching inn, they go through enough in a week to have a delivery all to themselves. That said, compared to the merchants, it's a smaller order, one we can do by dray."

"I see. Thank you." Louisa stood puzzling over how the plotters had schemed...

Finally, Cleo handed her the last list of deliveries.

Louisa accepted it, then turned back to the counter and the clerks. "One last thing. If you had a specific group of fifteen barrels of Bright Flame Ale, and you wanted all fifteen barrels to be delivered to one place—one tavern, for example—could that be done?"

"Oh, we do that all the time, my lady," the younger clerk assured her. "Lots of innkeepers prefer to get any given delivery all from the same batch, so as the barrels are filled, we count off and stamp barrels enough for each order."

"Even for those inns supplied via the merchants?"

"For those with standing orders," the older clerk replied, "yes, my lady, we do."

Louisa looked at Cleo, then turned back to the clerks and rather sorrowfully said, "In that case, I fear we'll need to trouble you for a list, in duplicate, of all the individual orders placed through merchants, and so not already on our lists, that included fifteen or more barrels of Bright Flame Ale that have been sent out since Tuesday."

Both clerks stared at her.

Eventually, the head clerk grimaced. "This is important, isn't it?"

"Dreadfully important." Louisa allowed her conviction on that point to invest her voice. "Quite literally, I cannot tell you how important."

The older clerk held her gaze for a second, then nodded. He glanced at his junior. "Come on, Ben. Let's get cracking."

It took both clerks another hour to compile the second set of lists. In duplicate.

Finally, the older clerk brought the extra lists to the counter. "We've numbered them and added the merchant's name like you suggested, so you can see which merchant the individual customer's order goes through. Mostly, these are standing orders, so they go through the same merchant every week."

Louisa accepted the lists. She flicked to the last page, read the number inscribed before the last entry, and her heart sank.

She handed the second copy to Cleo, then looked at the clerks and smiled sincerely. "Thank you so much for your hard work."

Cleo glanced at her copy, then added her equally genuine thanks, and they quit the office.

They'd just emerged into the yard when Drake, with Michael beside him, led the footmen army from the brewing house; presumably, they'd moved on to searching there after finishing in the cellar-store. One look at Drake's set and expressionless face, let alone Michael's, told Louisa all she needed to know about the outcome of their search.

Drake halted beside her and Cleo, and Michael halted beside him. With nods and touched caps, but unsmiling, not to say gloomy faces, the various Cynster footmen and grooms streamed on toward the gates.

"You found nothing," Louisa murmured. There was no question.

"We didn't," Drake confirmed, his diction as sharp as chipped flint.

"We searched everywhere." His hands on his hips, Michael watched his men disappear through the gate. "The workers had heard about the deaths, and they helped by pointing out everywhere an already-filled barrel might be, but no luck."

Drake glanced at Louisa's face, then looked at the lists in her hands. "Any luck with the deliveries?"

"I had high hopes, but sadly, there are an awful lot of deliveries." Louisa handed him the lists.

Drake took them and scanned the entries. His brows slowly rose.

"Ninety-three deliveries in which our barrels might have been included," Cleo stated.

"And"—Louisa directed Drake's attention to the second set of lists—"that translates to two hundred and eighty-seven specifically stamped, individual customer orders for fifteen or more barrels of Bright Flame Ale."

Michael, who had been looking through Cleo's copies, murmured, "Good Lord. No wonder our watchers were adamant that ale barrels were the best bet for moving anything out of this area."

Drake made a disgusted sound, thrust the lists back at Louisa, and stalked out of the yard.

For several seconds, Louisa watched him go, then at a less-agitated pace, followed, with Michael and Cleo walking beside her.

They caught up with Drake—an obviously seriously exercised Drake, which was not a sight often seen—by the side of Louisa's carriage. His hands thrust into his trouser pockets, he was leaning against the carriage, the back of his broad shoulders against the panel, with his gaze directed at the ground in front of the toes of his boots.

"So the powder was here," he said as they reached him.

Neither Louisa, Michael, nor Cleo felt any need to confirm that statement.

Without looking up, Drake continued, his tones clipped, "It was put into fifteen barrels lined with oilskin that were supposed to contain Bright Flame Ale. The four men who made the transfer had been carefully instructed—they knew what they were doing and knew the seals had to be made airtight. They completed the transfer even though Chilburn wasn't there to oversee the work—no doubt the men believed they were acting for the Chartist cause. Given that those fifteen barrels are no longer in the brewery, they've been moved again—"

"Presumably as part of a delivery," Louisa said.

Still staring at the ground, Drake frowned. "Possibly. I don't think we can discount the plotters arranging for the barrels to be fetched away at night. The men Chilburn used for the transfer must have had keys to the yard and the buildings. If the plotters, whoever they are, follow their usual pattern, then those four men are already dead. We know two are, and presumably, the other two are as well. There's no saying that the plotters didn't take the keys from those men."

"Hmm." Louisa glanced at the lists she still held. "Possibly."

Before she could say more, Michael nodded. "We know the barrels have been moved—the question is: How?"

Her gaze still on the lists, Louisa said, "After going to all the trouble of disguising the gunpowder as barrels of Bright Flame Ale...if the purpose for the disguise was to get the barrels into place at the target site, and so presumably these ale barrels would not be out of place at that site...why wouldn't the mastermind simply let them be delivered? If Chilburn had instructed the men he'd suborned to mark the barrels with a given customer's stamp"—she waved the lists—"the barrels would be moved into position without any further intervention."

"Yes, but..." Cleo frowned. "If the barrels were delivered to any inn or tavern, then the instant any innkeeper tried to tap them, he'd know the barrels didn't contain ale."

Michael shrugged. "So the barrels go missing on the way—diverted to somewhere else, perhaps to the target."

"Or," Drake said, "they get delivered, then subsequently diverted to the target nearby." He pushed away from the carriage and straightened. "We can, it seems, dream up any number of possible scenarios for how the barrels left the brewery, but as things stand, we have no way of telling which one, if any, is correct."

Across the street, a high-pitched steam whistle sounded a long note. Seconds later, men started pouring out of the brewery gates. Louisa and the other three had all looked that way, but they were standing on the opposite side of the road, more or less screened by the bodies of their two carriages.

Cleo had already tucked her copies of the lists into her capacious reticule. Michael reached over and filched Louisa's set from her fingers. She humphed, but didn't retaliate. She watched as Michael quickly scanned the entries. Drake shifted and looked over his shoulder.

"Damn," Michael muttered. "The end customers are scattered all over London. Mostly north of the river, but still..."

"From Chelsea to Limehouse." Drake's tone was grim. "If the barrels left the brewery as part of a delivery, they could be anywhere between."

Michael sighed. "And just so you know, it's lucky we learned the barrels are no longer here and unlikely to be in this area anymore, because as of tonight, we'll lose the footmen army." He met Drake's gaze. "Sebastian and Antonia's engagement ball is tomorrow evening, so it's all hands on deck in the Cynster households."

Drake grimaced. He glanced again at the lists.

Louisa reached over, twitched them from Michael's grasp, and started studying them again.

"Whether we have your army to call on or not won't make much difference," Drake said. "There's no way we can search the cellars of two hundred and eighty-seven different inns without creating a wave of rumors—and we definitely can't do it in time."

Michael caught Drake's eye. "You think that wherever the barrels are now, they must be near the target?"

Drake weighed the notion before replying, "Near, at least. It depends on the date chosen for the strike, but this latest move should at the very least take the barrels close to their ultimate position—" He broke off, then continued, "Actually, that's a very good point. It's week's end. If, as we suspect, the mastermind has some government or institutional target in mind, then there's no sense detonating his barrels during the next two days. However, if he intends using the gunpowder on a day next week— and I can't imagine he'll want to wait longer—then yes, the barrels cannot be more than one last step away from their ultimate destination. They must be close, but possibly not quite there."

"Did you notice"—Louisa looked up from her perusal of the list of individual customers—"that there are seventeen army or navy establishments who had fifteen or more barrels of Bright Flame Ale dispatched from the brewery since Tuesday morning?"

Drake grimaced. "Paradoxically, armed service messes will be the hardest to search. Those who watch over their cellars are inherently suspicious of anyone who comes asking questions about anything, let alone wanting to examine their stocks of ale. Major bureaucratic incidents have been caused by less."

Louisa raised her brows. "That sounds like the sort of situation our hypothetical ex-bureaucrat might know and seek to exploit."

Drake straightened. "All this is speculation. What we know is that the gunpowder has been disguised as fifteen barrels of Phoenix Brewery's Bright Flame Ale, and those barrels are no longer in the brewery. If they left via the brewery's delivery system, they could have been delivered or be en route to any of two hundred and eighty-seven cellars across London. If the barrels were removed at night using the dead men's keys to the yard, those barrels could be anywhere at all."

"They might," Cleo said, "even be on a barge." She glanced at Michael. "The sort used to ferry ale barrels."

Michael pulled a face. "Our men weren't watching for ale barrels—

they paid no attention to drays or barges carrying the things."

Looking down, Drake grunted. "Once again, we've been stymied by exceptional planning. Until Cleo asked her old gunnery officer, everyone we know, including the experts, swore that gunpowder couldn't be transported other than in gunpowder barrels."

Louisa shifted. "If we discard all notion of hunting through two hundred and eighty-seven inns, taverns, and service messes, what are our ways forward?" Before anyone else could answer, she raised a hand, clearly intending to tick off her points on her fingers. "One, we have the addresses of the two still-missing brewery workers—the second driver and the cooper's apprentice. We assume both are dead, but we should check." She glanced at the sky, which was steadily darkening. "That's something Drake and I can deal with tomorrow." She didn't look at Drake but continued with her second point. "Then there's the question of whether more relevant bodies have turned up at the morgue, and if so, whose bodies they are, and what their identities might tell us." She glanced briefly at Drake. "You and I can follow up there after checking the two addresses.

"Then," she rolled on, "there's the search for the mastermind's remaining henchman—the one who favors the garrote. We suspect he might be military, or at least ex-military, and has served in India."

Drake cut a glance at Michael. "We should ask in the lowest ranks of military clubs and see if we can turn up anyone who was known to be friendly with Chilburn, or who was recently seen with him."

Tight lipped, Michael nodded. "I'll make a start on that tonight." He looked at Cleo. "In the hells and clubs. You can't come."

Cleo shrugged resignedly. "I ought to check with Fitch and catch up with office business, anyway."

"We also "—Louisa tapped her fourth finger and spoke more firmly— "have the question of Lawton Chilburn and his associates and connections. We know he spoke of receiving some inheritance, but don't know if he meant that literally or used the words as a turn of phrase to disguise a windfall from some less reputable source. When I get back to Grosvenor Square, I'll ask Grandmama and Lady Osbaldestone if there's any known family member or connection who might be Lawton's benefactor, but as Lawton's sisters knew of no one, that doesn't sound likely. More likely, as was suggested, it was a turn of phrase, but I'll check." She drew breath. "Regardless, he was anticipating getting money from some source, and surely someone in the ton must have some inkling of what he's been about."

She frowned and, in distinctly severe accents, stated, "Someone knows more than they're letting on. Sebastian and Antonia will have been monitoring the social reactions to Lawton's death during the events they had to attend today, but there's a range of balls and soirees on tonight, and now the ton has had twenty-four hours to digest the news of Lawton's demise, we need to circulate and see what we can learn."

Drake eyed her without expression. "Why do I get the idea that by 'we,' you mean you and me?"

Louisa smiled tightly. "Because that is what I mean. You, me, Sebastian, and Antonia—we're on duty in the ton tonight."

CHAPTER 25

*B*y ton standards, it was still relatively early in the evening when Drake caught up with Sebastian and Antonia by the side of Lady Ferris's ballroom. The pair had crossed Michael's path as he'd returned to St. Ives House, and he'd filled them in on the day's events and what was expected of them that evening—something Louisa had later verified.

At that moment, a waltz was under way, reducing the ranks of those standing by the walls, thus allowing those not dancing to converse in relative privacy. Antonia had taken to the floor, leaving Drake and Sebastian to their ruminations.

"So," Sebastian said, his eyes tracking his wife-to-be amid the revolving couples, "it comes down to the questions of who moved the gunpowder, now disguised as ale, and to where."

His gaze fixed on the dance floor as well, without glancing at Sebastian, Drake replied, "I was considering dropping a word in Fitzwilliam's and Simmonds's ears." The pair were another two gentlemen he occasionally recruited; like Sebastian and Michael, they were members of the loosely termed "sons of the nobility." "I thought to suggest they spin some yarn and check the cellars of the seventeen service messes on the brewery's delivery list... But if we fall back on the argument of how I would run this plot, then even if we check those locations, I would predict we would find nothing at this point."

"Because if a mess—or the building in which the mess or its cellar is housed—is the intended target, the barrels won't yet be there?"

Drake nodded. "This plot positively reeks of politics. To my way of thinking, that means that, at the earliest, the boom won't come until sometime on Monday..." He let the sentence trail off, momentarily distracted as, sparked by his own words, a notion that—surely—was far too fanciful flitted through his brain.

As his mind flirted with the prospect, the waltz drew to a close. The dancers swirled to a halt, then Antonia was returning, smiling as her brother Julius led her back to Sebastian's side.

And behind Antonia and Julius came Louisa, laughing and angling her intriguingly enchanting smile up at a clearly smitten Lord Peter Wallace, who gave every appearance of being utterly in thrall. Literally entranced. Or ensorcelled.

Inwardly, Drake shook his head. It was an effort to keep his lips from setting in a disapproving line. Tonight, Louisa wore a ball gown of shimmering bronzy-colored silk, a hue that somehow heightened the impact of her striking features—of her lustrous black hair, of her pale skin, rose-tinted lips, and her startlingly clear, peridot eyes. In keeping with the latest styles, her shoulders were bare, but as usual, she'd eschewed all frills and furbelows; her gowns, and she in them, were all the more noticeable because of the lack of ostentatious decoration. That evening, the only addition she'd made to her own bounteous charms was a long—very long—rope of perfect ivory pearls that looped around her neck twice, one loop closely encircling her throat while the other hung over her breasts almost to her waist. The clasp of the pearls, formed from a large, flawless, oval peridot set in a frame of very fine diamonds, nestled just above her collarbones.

As she glided nearer and her gaze rose to meet his, he reminded himself that he had known for decades that she was dangerous. Supremely dangerous.

She was the sort of woman men fought wars for.

And given the effect she had on him, given his reaction to her laughing, teasing—wide-eyed and too-knowing—glance, she was more dangerous to him than to anyone else.

This was, in fact, the second time that evening that their paths had crossed. Earlier, while he'd circled Lady Humphrey's ballroom, speaking to friends and acquaintances and hoping the crush would screen him from the gossipmongers, he'd spied his nemesis in gay converse with a circle of admirers. He'd pretended not to notice and hoped he'd remained out of her sight. Ruthlessly, he'd focused his mind on dredging for clues, hints, innuendos—anything that might cast light on Lawton Chilburn and his recent activities.

Although he'd quartered the large room, he'd heard nothing of any real interest, but judging by her scintillating animation, he'd suspected Louisa had fared better. Concealed—he'd hoped—within the crowd, he'd drawn close enough to overhear her declare that she was heading to Lady Ferris's event. Only then had he recalled she'd intended to speak with her redoubtable grandmama and the even more formidable Lady Osbaldestone about Chilburn.

Now, meeting her vibrant eyes—for just one second, swept by a longing to lose himself in the pale green—he held firm against the temptation, yet he needed to speak with her.

He waited while she greeted Julius and glibly exchanged comments with Antonia about this and that—the usual chatter to be found in a ballroom.

Accepting that no other opportunity was likely to eventuate, resigned, he waited until the musicians commenced tuning up for the next measure. At least Louisa was of an age that he didn't have to wrestle with the restrictions of a dance card.

Ignoring the incipiently dark looks thrown his way by Lord Peter, who clearly viewed him as a competitor of sorts—a thought Drake shoved to the back of his mind—he arched a brow at Louisa, and with the easy charm he could summon when it suited him, half bowed and smoothly inquired, "Dare I hope for the honor of this dance, my lady?"

She smiled her brightest smile; her eyes danced with an appreciation, an understanding, he inspired in no one else. "If you wish it, my lord."

He hoped only he caught the teasing note in her voice, hoped even more that only he could read the blatant challenge in her eyes.

That only he understood its genesis.

He grasped the gloved hand she offered him, feeling her fingers fine-boned and delicate under his while she dismissed Lord Peter with boundless charm and one of her glorious smiles, then excused them to Sebastian, Antonia, and Julius.

When, finally, she turned to him, he drew her arm through his, anchored her hand on his sleeve, and led her to the dance floor. On gaining it, he released her only to draw her into his arms, then he stepped out, and they were whirling, revolving and circling, and for those moments, cocooned in a world of their own.

One in which they could share secrets and talk of matters that needed to remain private.

He looked at her face, surveyed her serenely confident expression, then met her eyes—and lost at least a minute while trapped within their web of enchantment. While the reality of how well they moved together, how effortlessly she matched his stride, how supple and svelte she was in his arms, impinged and distracted him.

As was becoming his norm, even once he'd realized he'd been ensorcelled, it took effort to pull free; he wished, fervently, that his inner self would cease being seduced by her, but that seemed to be nowhere in his stars.

Ruthlessly, he bludgeoned his wits into concentrating on the plot. Gunpowder. Over a thousand pounds of it. Somewhere in London under the control of a warped mastermind. "What have you learned about Chilburn? Did your grandmama and her visitor have any useful insights?"

Unlike him, she seemed to have no difficulty focusing on the plot while whirling down the room. "Insights, they had, although as to how useful, I'm not sure. Apparently, they both view Lawton Chilburn as a weak-willed, feckless younger son, a wastrel in every sense of the word. Worthless, unreliable, and untrustworthy were a few of the epithets they suggested for his gravestone. As for any inheritance, they said there's an ageing bachelor uncle on his mother's side, two spinster aunts on his father's side, and several ancient connections, but Grandmama and Lady Osbaldestone both felt that in all cases, any inheritance was unlikely to come to Lawton. Much more likely that it would fall to his eldest brother or, in the case of his aunts, to one or all of his sisters. Especially as the lack of esteem in which Lawton was held by his nearest and dearest seems to be reasonably well known."

Louisa detected the frown forming behind Drake's golden eyes. Of a curious shade of hammered gold, his eyes were more often than not unreadable, as, in general, was his face. But she'd noticed he was increasingly less on guard with her than he was with others. Nevertheless, as she studied his features, she still couldn't guess what in her report had occasioned that frown.

Boldly, she asked, "So what did you learn?"

Briefly, his gaze dropped to her eyes, then he raised it as they continued to whirl. "In short, not a lot, but I'm struck that, in large part, Lawton's acquaintances echo his family's views. I found a few who had known him from schooldays, but while the general consensus described him as the sort always ready to indulge in some prank, none seemed to retain the slightest affection for him. I was left with the impression that Lawton had either cheated them and they knew or suspected it, or that he'd done something similar to sour them to the extent of severing all contact. Not one of them came even close to being willing to recommend him as a secretary."

She opened her eyes wide. "Is that how you disguised your interest? By putting it about that you were thinking of hiring him as your secretary?" The possibilities rolled through her mind. "What a very good idea."

He made a dismissive sound. "You usually get an accurate idea of how others view a gentleman by asking if his friends are willing to stake their honor on his character."

She was honestly impressed and stored the notion away for future reference.

The waltz proved to be a relatively short one. Drake gave mental thanks as they whirled to a halt, then he realized they were at the other end of the ballroom from where they'd left Sebastian and Antonia. Before he could inquire if Louisa wished to be escorted thence, she claimed his arm—which, he supposed, answered his unvoiced question.

Girding his loins against the inevitable effect of keeping her so close—or at least wishing he could—he steered her up the long room.

The crowd was at its height, and their progression was slow, not least because they were constantly waylaid, their attention claimed by one group after another.

He found the sensation evoked by gimlet eyes, curious and unrelentingly fixed on him, irritating. He responded by affecting a distant, rather chilly mien and leaving the verbal replies to Louisa, which, of course, she handled with aplomb.

As they made their slow way up the room, he became aware that while he viewed such social interactions as dull and boring, having her on his arm lent the exchanges a subtly dangerous, almost threatening edge—one that kept his mind and senses engaged. That kept him on his mental toes.

Several minutes pondering that odd occurrence led him to admit that, in this sphere, he didn't entirely trust Louisa.

In all other public spheres, in all the exchanges and interactions they'd shared while investigating the plot, not trusting her had never occurred to him, not even in some distant recess of his mind.

Socially, however, while they were in a ballroom surrounded by the ton and not actively pursuing some clue, his instincts nagged at him to remain vigilant—over her.

She was Lady Wild; he should never forget that.

She was capable of almost anything.

Couples were gathering for the next dance, and those not intending to indulge stepped toward the sides of the room. Drake was cravenly grateful that Louisa gave no sign of wishing to join those crowding onto the dance floor; the sensations evoked by whirling down a ballroom with her in his arms tugged at impulses and instincts he was finding he needed to expend increasing effort to restrain.

When it comes to waltzing with Louisa, once per evening is enough.

He blinked, then almost laughed at the thought…except it was nothing more than the truth. Keeping his inner door firmly shut on all that she evoked—provoked—keeping his mind away from every last memory of their recent kisses, were battles he had to win. Neither he nor she could afford to be distracted at the moment.

With the waltz under way, their rate of progress increased. Then he noticed she was unobtrusively surveying the guests.

When she caught him glancing at her, she leaned more heavily on his arm, tipped her head closer to his, and murmured, "As one might expect, Lawton's sisters aren't here, but rather surprisingly, his sisters-in-law are, although they are in black and not dancing." She glanced ahead. "It's difficult to see that other than as a statement..."

Her feet halted, and she stilled. Just for an instant, then she was strolling again, as if nothing whatever had occurred.

Drake lowered his head and demanded, "What?"

She glanced up and met his eyes. "Don't look now," she murmured, "but Lawton's oldest two brothers and one of his cousins just slipped out through a side door."

"A side door to where?" Drake obeyed the pressure of her hand on his arm and changed tack for the side wall a little way ahead.

He hadn't actually expected a reply, but she confidently stated, "It leads to an antechamber adjacent to the library."

They drew close to the wall. She looked up at him and smiled gloriously. "Look besotted."

That wouldn't be hard, but he did have some pride. He kept his expression mild, but allowed his gaze to grow intent. "Why?"

"Because we're going to slip through the same door." Then she tipped back her head and gave a husky laugh—that particular laugh that feathered over his senses in the worst possible way—then she opened a door concealed in the paneling and slipped through. Her hand slid down his sleeve, her fingers tangled with his, and she drew him after her.

He didn't resist.

One swift glance confirmed that there was no one in the small antechamber.

He glanced fleetingly back into the ballroom. The view was partially screened by a group of potted palms and a column wreathed in greenery. With most attention focused on the dance floor, it was possible no one had seen them leave.

Silently, he eased the panel closed.

He turned to find Louisa on the other side of the room with her ear pressed to the panel of what he deduced must be a door to the library.

Three strides, and he joined her.

The men couldn't have been that far from the door; he could hear them clearly.

"If he was killed by one of his creditors—well, that could be any one of a dozen or more."

That, Drake thought, came from Lawton's second-oldest brother, Gerrard.

"Never heard of a creditor killing a debtor."

Presumably, that was Lawton's cousin, as Drake hadn't heard the voice before.

The cousin went on, "Why, if creditors made a habit of shooting people who owed them, half the ton would be dead. And it rather defeats the purpose—dunning by way of a gun."

"Creditors"—the pompous tones of Lawton's eldest brother, Robert, Hawesley's heir, were instantly recognizable—"would at least be understandable. Even acceptable. But God alone knows who the damned fool might have become involved with."

A lengthy exchange followed, in which the three men gave voice to their fears that Lawton might have, at last, overstepped himself and cheated someone powerful enough to kill him in retribution. It quickly became clear that all three were concerned that said retribution might not stop with Lawton but extend to his family, root and branch.

Although colorful, the three men's assertions were entirely speculative and transparently lacked any basis in fact.

Or at least facts they knew of.

Finally, the three came to what, apparently, was the crux of their current debate, namely that the investigation into Lawton's murder might turn up something—some collection of facts about Lawton—that the family would prefer remained unknown.

Drake considered that highly likely.

"Having the family name dragged through the courts." Robert sounded dismayed and just a tad frightened. "It would do for m'father—he would have an apoplexy, and that would only make things worse."

"Damned gossips would have a field day," Gerrard opined. "M'sisters and m'mother wouldn't be able to show their faces. Possibly not for years."

"I say," the cousin said, "you don't think that having a word with one of the chappies at Scotland Yard might be in order? Just to hint them away, don't you know? Make it clear that the family isn't pressing for the murderer to be found, although of course you'd phrase it as the family fully understanding the difficulties in tracing such a murderer and so on."

"Hmm." After a moment, Robert agreed, "That might bear thinking about."

"At least," Gerrard said, "that's something we can do."

Silence descended on the other side of the panel.

Drake was about to straighten when the cousin said, "Come on—we'd better get back before the wives start to pout."

The words reached Drake and Louisa clearly—because Lawton's

cousin was now very close to the other side of the door.

For a split second, Louisa and Drake stared at each other.

There was nowhere to hide in the small antechamber—all it contained were two wing chairs angled before a small fireplace.

Louisa glanced at the door to the ballroom. Too far away, but if they could reach it…

She took one step—

Drake seized her, whirled, and dropped into the nearest chair, dragging her down onto his lap. Then he framed her face.

As the door to the library opened, he breathed, "Make this look good." Then he kissed her.

Desperately, rapaciously—to within an inch of her sanity.

Hunger exploded across her senses.

Her hands had fallen to his shoulders; she gripped briefly, then impelled by need, slid her hands upward to thrust her fingers into his hair and clutch. And hold on—cling as a maelstrom of feelings rose and swept her from the world.

Her lips had been parted on a gasp; the hard thrust of his tongue against hers, and the heavy provocative stroking that followed, sent thrills cascading down her spine.

Heat rose in response, geysering from somewhere deep inside her.

And she kissed him back, molding her lips to his, tilting her head to improve the angle so they could feed on each other's lips and race on into a landscape of intense, glorious sensation.

Of passion and desire unleashed. Of need so raw, so powerfully primitive it scored their minds.

From a very great distance came a shocked "Oh my!"

Followed by a rumbling chuckle and a murmur, then the door to the library closed again.

Neither of them looked, much less cared.

Drake couldn't catch his breath. And couldn't assemble enough wit to worry. In that moment, the only goal he possessed was blazoned across his brain. To seize her. Have her. And chain her irrevocably to him.

Through the insistent thud of his heart in his veins, through the tumult of need that drove him, he realized he'd let some part of him loose, a part he never should have acknowledged, let alone freed.

To feel. To yearn. To hunger with a wanting so desperately needful it overthrew his rational mind and controlled him.

Dangerous. So dangerous.

Even more dangerous than her.

Not that she was helping. If anything, the flagrant encouragement of her lips beneath his, the ardor with which she matched his soaring desire, fed that darker, more primitive side of him, gave it strength, and crystalized its purpose.

Focused it, and him, even more unrelentingly on her.

She wriggled in his arms, shifting on his lap to more fully face him. To meet his escalating demands with her own—with her own passion, her own needs.

Both were as clear to him, as intense and definite, as his own; they acted like a clarion call to his deepest instincts.

He ravaged her mouth, unable to rein in such a powerful passion too long restrained.

In answer, she leaned her forearms on his chest, rose up to meet him, and tried to wrest control of the exchange from him. Not to end it—that was blatantly obvious—but to drive it into deeper waters...

His last frayed rein snapped.

And he surrendered.

Completely, unequivocally, he jettisoned all pretense, all resistance, all thought of denying what he felt for her.

What he wanted of her.

What he needed and intended to have.

He'd clung to resistance for so long, it had, he'd thought, become second nature, but there was no way and no hope of denying *this*.

Louisa's mind had blanked; she'd forgotten where they were. Her world had shrunk to the confines of the chair, to the circle of Drake's arms.

He'd released her face long ago. Now, like bands of tempered steel, his arms held her, his strong palms pressed to her back, hard fingers splayed, holding her captive.

She had no intention of escaping.

Her entire being was focused on reveling. On drinking in every last gasp of delight, every shiver of sensation.

She had no idea where the kiss had taken them—onto some other plane, certainly, but not one she knew. Not one she'd previously visited. This heat, this wanting, were new—so novel the awareness alone left her giddy.

Was it her or him—or both of them together? She had no idea, but felt sure she would find out. Eventually. For now, she was content to wallow and learn. And experience each new thrill.

One of her hands had slipped from his hair to rest on his chest. Somehow, that hand had slid beneath his coat, and her palm rested on fine linen. Beneath the soft fabric, she could feel the thud of his heart.

Hard. Driving.

A rhythm her own heart seemed to recognize, to know at some level too deep to comprehend.

The click of a doorlatch—the sudden sound of voices near—jerked them both back to full awareness.

As if doused in cold water, they broke from the kiss on a smothered gasp. Even as they looked toward the door to the ballroom, the realization of the picture they would present to anyone entering—

She wasn't given to panicking, and thank God, he wasn't, either. The very last thing either of them needed was a full-blown scandal resulting in a declaration of marriage.

A declaration of marriage, yes, but in the right time and in the right way.

Not like this.

The door from the ballroom was open, but only just a crack; whoever had opened it had paused on the other side to talk to someone.

They had a fraction of a second to save themselves.

She was scrambling from his lap even as he pushed up from the chair.

Face set, he seized her hand and whisked her to the other door. They had to take the risk that there was no one in the library.

He opened the door and whirled her through, then followed.

Drake glanced back as, silently, he drew the door between the antechamber and the library after him. The last thing he saw before he shut the panel was the other door swinging open.

He turned to look at Louisa. His partner in adventures of multiple kinds.

Her lips were rosy red, swollen and slick. Her hair was still passably anchored; he was too experienced to wantonly disarrange it...regardless, she looked wanton. Her eyes were stars, sparkling pools of peridot green in which desire sparked and passion swirled.

He suspected he wasn't much better. That need she and only she evoked was still riding him with the force of a storm.

In that instant, as they stood in the thankfully deserted library and in the light from dimmed sconces, stared at each other, he felt something in him change.

Some hint must have shown in his face, in his eyes. She studied them for a second, then more tentative than she usually was, she gestured to the door to the corridor. "I suppose we should go."

There was just enough uncertainty in her tone to permit that newly risen reality to take hold.

He caught her wrist, shackled his fingers around the fine bones. "Not so fast." His voice was a gravelly rumble. "There's something I believe we should discuss."

Before she could ask what, he towed her across the library and opened a door he'd spied directly opposite the one from the antechamber. Beyond lay a deserted, unlit parlor.

He didn't waste time smiling; he swung her through the door, followed and shut it, then whirled her, backed her against the panel, and covered her lips with his.

The hunger hadn't died, hadn't faded. Now, released, it roared.

Through him—to find its echo, its mate, in her.

Just as she always did, she rose to meet him, responding to the demanding challenge of the kiss.

And as always, she matched him step for step, heartbeat for thudding heartbeat as he deliberately tested the waters, deliberately let passion have its way.

With them both.

He was every bit as mindless as she self-evidently was.

Every bit as wild, as quintessentially untamed as she.

He'd always assumed that with her, any engagement would be clash after clash—that they were too alike to draw close in this sphere.

It had never occurred to him that, as with their wills in the investigation, their passions, too, if focused on one goal, might collide and merge—and become a greater force.

Each augmented by the other. The passion of one expanded and ignited by the passion of the other.

What was between them—what he'd always known was there— erupted in a fiery conflagration of pure, unadulterated need.

One several orders of magnitude more than he'd bargained for.

Louisa clutched, seized—wanted with an urgency she'd never felt before. Now—she needed something *now*, with a desperation that hovered on the edge of pain.

Her breasts felt heavy, swollen and aching behind the constriction of her tightly fitting bodice and corset. Her nipples, puckered tight, burned with a sharp ache.

Somehow, he guessed. She felt his fingers deftly slipping free the buttons down her spine, then the sleeveless bodice loosened. She tried to pull back from the kiss, but he moved into her; with the hard length of his body, he held her against the door while, between them, his experienced fingers pushed her bodice down and undid the front lacings of her corset.

She couldn't catch her breath; her senses and her wits were reeling— with anticipation, with the startling realization that this was truly happening.

Then her corset loosened, and her breasts sprang free, and he palmed one aching mound and, with his thumb, gently stroked her skin.

She shuddered, wracked to her very bones by the leap of her senses and the torrent of need that flowed in response.

No quarter. She asked for none, and he granted none as his fingers artfully stroked, as his hands weighed, then he bent his head, and his lips came into play.

For uncounted moments, she was awash on a sea of exquisite sensation, but that only seemed to heighten her need rather than slake it. For some reason, he avoided touching the peaks of her breasts, those tight buds that begged for a touch, a caress, for ease.

She needed to touch him, to feel his skin as he was feeling hers—perhaps that would spur him to give her what she ached for.

His coat was unbuttoned; she raised her hands, slid them beneath the sides, and spread her suddenly greedy palms and fingers over the heated expanse of his chest—

He raised his head, caught her hands, trapped both her wrists in one hand, raised them above her head, and pressed them to the cool wood.

She gave vent to an incoherent protest. She tugged, the movement arching her against him, pressing her breasts to his hard chest, rubbing the sensitized skin against the fabric of shirt and coat.

"Later," was all he deigned to growl. Then he bent his head and captured her mouth again, and scrambled her wits with a searing kiss as he closed his free hand about her breast.

She hadn't thought it possible, but the kiss was somehow hotter. More fiery, laced with some promise she didn't fully comprehend. She wanted to know more, wanted to follow the trail and see where it led, yet still he gave her no surcease from the sharp, excruciatingly scintillating pleasure-pain of her tightly furled nipples.

His fingers stroked, caressed—languidly, almost idly. She felt perfectly certain he knew what he was doing, knew what she was feeling; she tried to break from the kiss to berate him, but that was something else he wouldn't allow.

Frustration and need was a potent combination. The building wave was so compelling, she felt as if she might soon explode.

Then his fingers shifted, drifted from her skin.

Through the gasping, needy tumult that was swamping her mind, she managed to focus enough to follow as he found her pearls, draped them over his fingers, then he stroked the smooth curves over and about her areolas, circling her burning nipples, inciting a fresh wave of sensation, sending heat and longing surging through her.

The pearls were too smooth to relieve the ache that gripped her.

Drake knew it. He let the long strand slide through his fingers. Keeping his lips on hers, taking pleasure in the honeyed haven of her mouth, keeping her anchored in and momentarily distracted by the exchange, he blindly searched and found the peridot-and-diamond clasp, and with a few expert flicks of his fingers, shifted the rope of pearls until the clasp dangled, hanging low.

He caught the clasp, turned it between his fingertips, then artfully, with a skill he'd learned long ago, used the rough surface of the cut stones and their gold settings to abrade her nipples.

Her shocked gasp, followed by something very close to a keening whimper of pure pleasure, although trapped and smothered by the kiss, nevertheless purled across his senses.

He pandered to her need, to her immediate desire—stoked and fed the fire that burned so achingly bright, so fierce and unrestrained, within her. For long minutes, he held her on that specific plane of physical sensation, sating her senses just enough to keep her ensnared, floating.

His to steer, to guide.

Ultimately to take, to plunder.

But not tonight.

His iron-hard erection was a pulsing pain, but strategy and tactics were his middle name, a part of his psyche that had long stood him in excellent stead in this sphere.

Campaigns such as this, the one he'd embarked on in a split-second decision he did not yet regret, were best conducted step by step.

If he wished to adhere to that maxim, he needed to draw a line now and bring tonight's engagement to an end.

He'd anticipated some degree of reluctance on his part, the part that would much prefer to seize her now. He hadn't counted on her—on the combination of her inexperience and her usual willful propensity to plunge headlong into the unknown.

When he tried to ease back from the kiss, to retreat by degrees, she took it as an invitation to seize the reins and drive them on.

When he tried to straighten and physically break the kiss, she flung off his restraining hands, wrapped her arms about his neck, flung herself against him, and clung. She nearly overbalanced him with her enthusiasm.

Nearly brought him to his knees as she pressed her body full length to his.

Flickering panic drove him to wrench his lips from hers and hiss, "Louisa!" in, as he thought, his sternest, harshest voice—the word came out sounding like a gravelly plea.

Her lids rose, revealing eyes darkened to spring green and burning with an almost-incandescent passion. "What?" she murmured in a husky, breathless whisper.

The rumble of male voices in the library next door reached them. He seized on the excuse like a drowning man—and given the inevitable effect of having her naked to the waist in his arms, crushed against him, that was precisely what he was, seconds away from sinking under passion's raging sea.

He managed to grasp some vestige of control, metaphorically tightened his grip, then licked his lips and forced out the words, "We have to stop.

Now. It's…late."

Slowly, she blinked; in her fabulous eyes, he could almost see the wheels of her wits turning. Could almost make out her thoughts as she wondered why he was insisting, then recalled that in this sphere, she was a novice while he was not, and finally decided that he must know what he was doing.

Thank God! Relief flowed through him, but did little to cool the fire in his blood.

Her arms slackened from about his neck. "Oh." She blinked again, then looked down at the mounds of her bare breasts, pressed against his chest. "I suppose…"

He didn't wait to hear more. He forced his arms to ease their compulsive hold on her and let her slide down until her feet were once more fully on the floor. She swayed, and he steadied her, then without waiting for any discussion, he swiftly redid her corset laces before stepping around her and rapidly refastening her gown.

She grumbled and wriggled, resetting her breasts within the corset and tight bodice, now even tighter. "I barely fit anymore."

He tried not to think about the bounty of her full breasts; they'd proved a surprisingly lush handful, the fine skin like peach satin… He wrenched his mind back to the buttons and fastened the last.

"Where's my reticule?" She glanced around and spotted the small purse lying on the floor near the door.

While she walked over to collect it, he resettled his coat, smoothed the lapels and the shoulders where she'd clutched, then he saw a mirror and, with quick fingers, rearranged the rumpled folds of his cravat into passable neatness.

He turned to see her standing in the middle of the parlor and frowning at nothing—as if endeavoring to get her wits working again so she could think through what had just occurred.

He crossed to her, grasped her arm, and steered her to the door. He didn't want her thinking too much.

In what was, for her, a strange and unaccustomed daze, one she was having trouble shaking off, Louisa found herself all but propelled into the corridor, to the stairs and down, directly to the front hall. When she tried to suggest they divert into the ballroom and take their leave of Lady Ferris, lips set, Drake shook his head, mumbled something about it being too late for that, and steered her inexorably on.

The butler hurried to fetch her cloak. Drake commandeered it and draped it over her shoulders.

She held the cloak's velvet folds close, grateful for the warmth as they stepped onto the porch, and the November night sent chilly fingers brushing over her still flushed and sensitized skin.

Then her carriage was there, and Drake escorted her down the steps, opened the carriage door, and helped her into the dimness within.

She settled on the leather seat and heard him confirm that the destination was to be St. Ives House.

He was standing on the pavement, framed in the carriage doorway. She looked at him, but he made no move to climb up and in. Instead, he stared at her for a second, then he nodded curtly and stepped back. "I'll walk."

With that, he shut the door, tapped the panel, and the carriage started to roll.

What?

The unexpected outcome jerked her to fully functioning awareness. The hazy veil induced by their sensual encounter evaporated. She blinked into the darkness. "What just happened?"

The answer came in a dozen mental vignettes, all loaded with feeling and underlying insight.

Somehow, between the moment when he'd followed her into the antechamber and the moment he'd towed her through the library and into the little parlor, their roles vis-à-vis each other had reversed. Previously, she'd been the hunter, and she'd been hunting him. But now…

She quelled an evocative shiver and leaned back against the squabs.

Tonight, he'd become the hunter and she his prey.

Wide-eyed, she stared unseeing across the carriage as the implications rose and rolled through her brain.

Her lips set. "Damn him," she muttered. "We can't go that way."

She'd pushed him—she acknowledged that—but she hadn't expected him to react by changing the rules. By, it seemed, reverting to his true nature, dropping all civilized screens, and simply seizing!

If he took that line, used that as his means of dealing with her—and she wasn't fool enough to think he hadn't done so with deliberate intent— then given who he was and who she was, the result would inevitably be marriage.

Admittedly, that was her goal, but if it came about like that—as an outcome driven by the twin imperatives of lust and social acceptability— how would she ever know, ever learn, if he loved her?

For her, love was an absolute requirement for marriage.

For him…she had a strong suspicion that avoiding all mention of that emotion ranked high on his list of life's desires. She knew far too many men like him—she was related to too many—to doubt that.

She'd taken a certain route to test what lay between them, and he'd turned the tables on her and diverted them down his preferred path.

"Well," she stated to the empty carriage. Her eyes narrowed; her chin firmed. "We'll see about that."

CHAPTER 26

*L*eft standing on the pavement before Ferris House, Drake watched Louisa's carriage roll away.

He could have gone with her, except that he no longer trusted either him or her in such a setting, in the cloaking dark, alone, even though Grosvenor Square was only blocks away.

Besides, walking and letting the chill of the night douse the heat still coursing through his veins would do him good.

He crossed the pavement and started pacing in the same direction in which the carriage had gone.

Normally, he would have used the minutes of relative peace to review his position, both personal and with respect to any mission. Tonight, however, he really didn't have all that much to dwell on.

The mission was proceeding as fast as they could drive it; they all knew what they needed to do tomorrow, and there was no point wracking his brains until they had more information. All they'd learned from Chilburn's brothers and cousin was that the family understandably feared a scandal arising through the search for Chilburn's killer.

Mission-wise, all he could do was hope that their endeavors tomorrow would get them further.

On the personal side...to his mind, all questions regarding Louisa were now settled.

He'd expected to be able to drag things out, to avoid her and the potential situation for several more years, but she and the exigencies of the mission had conspired to force him to deal with her now.

So he had. In the instant he'd realized they were teetering on the brink of social exposure—being seen engaging in a heated kiss by three gentlemen was nowhere near the transgression being discovered even more engrossed by half a ballroom would have been—his true self, already in charge courtesy of the kiss, had taken over completely.

In exactly the same way as Louisa, when faced with a challenge, his instinctive reaction was to take decisive action to meet that challenge and win, rather than allow circumstance any chance to interfere with or influence him.

And where she was concerned, his protective instincts, perhaps unsurprisingly, knew no bounds; between one heartbeat and the next, he'd acted to get them out of there, out of danger. No real thought had been required.

Of course, in the aftermath, those same instincts, by then very much in control, had insisted he claim her.

So he had, at least as far as circumstance had allowed.

He knew what he'd done. Had known in the instant in which he'd made the decision to accept the inevitable and stop fighting it.

He knew what his consequent actions had set in train.

Somewhat to his surprise, as of yet, not the slightest regret had surfaced.

As he turned into Grosvenor Square, he considered that—considered, too, that contrary to his expectations, allowing Louisa to contribute to the mission had resulted not in any detrimental battle of will against will, but rather with them both focused on the same goal and their wills conjoined, in a greater degree of energy, a greater drive.

Offering a commensurately greater chance of success.

What if a similar effect occurred when they came together on a personal level?

That thought occupied him all the way to the Wolverstone House steps. As he climbed them, he let himself think of Louisa, of meeting her again—and realized that what he felt at the prospect was expectation and not a little impatience.

He couldn't decide if he should be wary of that or not.

SATURDAY, NOVEMBER 2, 1850

CHAPTER 27

*L*ouisa was determined not to allow Drake to sideline her from the mission; after their previous night's interlude, she wouldn't have been the least surprised had he attempted to do so. Consequently, she was somewhat mollified and appeased—and also suspicious—when he called for her as arranged at eight-thirty and, with nothing more than a mild "Good morning," took her gloved hand and escorted her outside and into the carriage.

She felt no awkwardness over their evening's activities, and she seriously doubted he did. Indeed, if anything, she was looking forward to the next time they had a chance to indulge in that fashion. With luck, next time, they would be in a more amenable setting...

Hauling her mind back to the day, to the moment in hand, she reluctantly set aside all salacious thoughts and turned her mind to the mission.

Their conversation during the drive to Kennington ranged over the lack of anything noteworthy in the discussion they'd overheard between Lawton's relatives, and their prospects for the day, first at the Working Men's Association and, later, at Scotland Yard.

Perhaps unsurprisingly, she discovered that her awareness of Drake had shifted to a new and quite novel plane. It appeared that the minor intimacy of the previous night, rather than leaving her nerves leaping even more sharply, had assured and, to some degree, calmed them—as if the engagement had reassured her inner self that with respect to what lay between them, her desired resolution, if not immediately imminent, was nevertheless certain.

She assumed that any adjustments between them—any getting used to things—would affect him as much as her and deemed that fair enough. Just one of those things couples had to work through—how to interact in public after interacting in private.

When the carriage drew up outside the Association building and Drake descended and handed her down, she was ready and willing, even eager, to forge ahead with the investigation.

Drake opened the building's door for her, and she led the way in. He followed in her wake, unconcerned as long as she remained near, within arm's reach. Indeed, he was feeling more relaxed over her, about her, than he'd anticipated after a night spent tossing and turning.

Possibly his inner calm was due to the certainty that his time would come and, what's more, relatively soon.

Just as soon as they put paid to this infernal plot.

As Louisa approached the office, Mr. Beam appeared at the window.

Predictably, she smiled at Beam, although the effect was commiserating, and her expression remained serious. "Good morning, Mr. Beam. We've come to let you know about our investigations at the Phoenix Brewery."

The previous day, when they'd returned from the morgue with Beam, his ledgers had revealed Mike Jones and Cecil Blunt's workplace and had sent Drake and Louisa tearing off to the brewery.

"Sadly, Beam"—Drake halted beside Louisa—"we have to inform you that two more of your members—a Mal Triggs, a driver, and Jed Sawyer, a cooper's apprentice, both of whom work at the Phoenix Brewery—are also missing."

Beam's expression turned mournful. "The sergeant of their group said he hadn't been able to find them at the brewery, but we'd hoped…" He blinked, hesitated, then asked, "Are they…that is, should we presume they're dead?"

"We fear so," Drake said, "but anything's possible. They might be alive, but in hiding. They, like Jones and Blunt, haven't reported for work, in their cases, not since Wednesday." He gave Beam a moment to digest that, then said, "We've also come to inquire whether you or your members have learned of any other men missing."

Beam's morose expression lightened a fraction. "At least we've had good news on that score." He met Drake's gaze with more confidence. "Our militia sergeants were waiting for me when I opened this morning.

They've finished checking with all the men on their lists and have found no one else missing."

"They've spoken with every man?" Drake asked.

Beam nodded. "Them or one of the other members who helped. Face-to-face took more time, but we decided it was the only way to be sure."

Drake inclined his head. "Please thank your sergeants and their helpers for their thoroughness. It seems we can all rest easy that no more of your members have been—or, we hope, will be—dragged into this."

"We managed to get Mr. Triggs's and Mr. Sawyer's addresses from the brewery." Louisa was hunting in her reticule. She drew out a folded sheet, consulted it, then glanced at Drake. "We might believe both are likely to have been murdered, but we need to check. We can't afford to overlook any possible clue, and if one of the men managed to avoid the garrotter—"

"That man might well know enough about the plot to help us." Drake tipped his head to her, then looked at Beam. "We'll let you know if we learn anything more about Triggs and Sawyer."

Beam allowed that he and the members would appreciate that.

Drake escorted Louisa out of the building. They halted on the pavement beside her carriage. "Where to?" he asked.

"Bermondsey." Looking up, she read out the two addresses to her coachman.

He nodded. "Aye, I know those streets."

Louisa held out her hand to Drake. He helped her into the carriage, then followed.

They were silent as the horses clattered up Kennington Lane. As they rocked and rattled along Lambeth Road, Louisa murmured, "There's not much hope for Triggs and Sawyer, is there?"

Drake considered, then replied, "No. But you're right in insisting we check. In situations like these, one never does know."

As it transpired, there seemed to be little hope entertained at the first address they called at—that of the driver, Triggs.

His son, a young man of about twenty, answered the door. His face pale, he responded to Louisa's gently put question with a shake of his head. "He hasn't been home since Thursday morning. He left for work at his usual time—'bout six-thirty. But his mates at the brewery told us he didn't turn up there."

The youth paused, then added, "We heard 'bout the others—the two who were found strangled-like. Me dad went out on some special job with the pair o' them on Monday night. He was right as rain, happy as a lark the next day, so all seemed fine. But now…" He sniffled and passed the back of his hand beneath his nose. "Me mam's expecting to have the constable around telling her to come to the morgue any time."

Louisa murmured appropriately soothing words without, Drake noticed, giving any most likely false hope. A man with a steady job and a family—a wife and son at least; it was hard to imagine such a man just vanishing with no word.

They returned to the carriage. Louisa paused beside it to allow him to open the door. As he reached past her, she caught his eye. "If Triggs had escaped an attempt on his life, or if he'd grown sufficiently suspicious after Jones and Blunt unexpectedly disappeared, he would have warned his family before going into hiding. That lad wasn't pretending. He and his mother truly are expecting the worst." She sighed and gripped his offered hand. "So Triggs is most likely dead."

Drake handed her up. When the coachman asked if they still wanted to try the other address, Drake nodded, then joined Louisa in the carriage. He sat and used the relative quiet to think, but much as he might wish it was otherwise, Louisa's reasoning was sound.

Sawyer lived in a small, neat house only two long blocks from the brewery. On answering the door, Mrs. Sawyer, a small, tidy, and quite young woman, stared at them, round-eyed. Her hand gripped the edge of the door tightly—very tightly—but when Louisa introduced them, Mrs. Sawyer appeared to relax. She let go of the door and bobbed a curtsy. "Ma'am—my lady. My lord." She nodded gravely to Drake, then returned her gaze to Louisa's face. "What can I do fer you?"

"We're here because we're assisting the Working Men's Association over the disappearance of some of their members." Louisa found it curious that Mrs. Sawyer—several years younger than Louisa herself—should be so relatively composed. "We wondered if you'd had any word from your husband?"

The change in the young woman was marked. Her expression, which had eased, tightened and closed. She clasped her hands, again very tightly, before her. "No, ma'am—m'lady. I ain't heard nothing at all, and I don't know where he is."

Her tone was wooden, and the phrases sounded rehearsed.

Louisa endeavored to keep her frown from her face. "When did you last see him?"

Mrs. Sawyer had to think before she replied, "Thursday morning, it were. He left for work as usual—heading for seven, that would be."

Gently, Louisa nodded. She kept her tone even and unthreatening. "We know he didn't arrive for work on Thursday morning. We, and Mr. Flock and your husband's friends at the brewery, and also Mr. Beam and those at the association, wondered if, by chance, he'd come home...before going off again."

Her jaw tight, Mrs. Sawyer shook her head from side to side. "No, ma'am—m'lady." She now watched Louisa as if she was some dangerous animal liable to pounce. "He ain't been back since he left for work that morning."

Louisa didn't want to pressure the woman—a young wife with a missing husband—yet she felt compelled to say, "Have you heard about the other three men who worked in the brewery and have also gone missing?"

Mrs. Sawyer nodded, another overtly careful gesture. When Louisa waited and said nothing more, Mrs. Sawyer reluctantly conceded, "I did hear there were three others gone missing." After a second's hesitation, she added, "And that two of them have turned up dead. Murdered." Her voice shook on the last word. She clamped her lips shut and gripped her fingers more tightly.

Louisa couldn't decide if Mrs. Sawyer was being open with them or not. Perhaps her stiffness was simply her way of coping with a horribly frightening situation.

"Did your husband go out with those three now-missing men on Monday night?"

Drake's quiet question drew Mrs. Sawyer's gaze to him. For several seconds, she stared, biting her lips and patently debating what to say. Eventually, she offered, "He was out that night—helping someone, he said—but I don't know anything more about that. I don't know if it was them—those three who've gone missing—or some others."

When Drake glanced at Louisa as if to ask if she had any more questions, she fractionally shook her head. She turned back to Mrs. Sawyer and thanked her for her time.

With a nod and another bobbed curtsy, Mrs. Sawyer retreated behind her door, but she didn't close it—not until Louisa and Drake were walking down the street toward the carriage.

When Louisa finally heard a distant click, she glanced back, then, facing forward again, declared, "I'm really not sure what to think of that performance—because that's just it. It felt as if she was parroting a part."

Drake nodded. Halting beside the carriage, he reached for the doorlatch. "Sadly, that doesn't mean that Sawyer is still alive—only, if I read between Mrs. Sawyer's lines correctly, that he escaped a first attempt and, subsequently, went into hiding somewhere."

Louisa sighed and met his eyes. "And we can't even be certain of that. Mrs. Sawyer might just be more given to clinging to hope than the average woman."

Drake opened the door and tipped his head into the carriage. "Let's go to Scotland Yard and see if Triggs and Sawyer and anyone else has turned up there."

CHAPTER 28

*O*n taking Cleo home the previous afternoon, Michael had discovered that her parents had arrived from Norfolk. After greeting them and being warmly embraced by Cleo's mama, he had perforce had to weather an interesting if slightly fraught interview with her father, Jack, Lord Hendon.

In truth, the Hendons had been delighted with his and Cleo's news, and contrary to Cleo's anxious expectations that the older couple would want to derail him and her into discussions of engagement balls and weddings, Lord Hendon and Lady Hendon both had been more eager to hear of Drake's mission and the undertaking that had thrown Michael and Cleo together.

Between them, he and Cleo had given her parents a potted history of the mission to date.

Lord and Lady Hendon had listened closely, thrown in the odd question, then had exchanged a long look before Lady Hendon, backed by Lord Hendon, had made it unequivocally clear that Michael and Cleo, and Drake and the others, too, had their unqualified support in dealing with the threat of the putative plot first.

"Let's get the villains caught and cleared away," Lord Hendon had said, "before we turn our minds to the trappings of matrimony."

Wise words, Michael had thought.

He'd been even more impressed when Lady Hendon had suggested, and Lord Hendon had supported, the hosting of an impromptu dinner— not to spread the news of their engagement, at least not primarily, but to pick the assembled brains of several of the Hendons' friends and Lord Hendon's ex-colleagues.

"While they're all retired from the army and the positions they once held," Lady Hendon had explained, "they all worked at one time or another with Drake's father, and they will assuredly have valuable insights to offer regarding Lawton Chilburn and this other, nasty ex-military man."

Consequently, Michael had returned to Clarges Street an hour later and sat down to dinner with the Marquess of Dearne and Sir Rafe Carstairs, along with their wives. All the company were interested in hearing of the plot, and once Michael and Cleo had outlined the problems and the questions currently before them, everyone, the ladies included, had debated and discussed the possibilities far into the night.

The upshot was that Dearne, Carstairs, and Hendon had all strongly recommended that a connection between Chilburn and an unknown military man should be assumed. "Ask your questions as if that was a known fact," Carstairs had advised, "and see what you uncover."

The three, along with their wives, had also clarified just where he should ask and given him some names that would hopefully prove useful in trawling through the military establishments for some clue as to Chilburn's associates, and especially any hint of any man who might fit the bill of their diabolical garrotter.

Consequently, at nine o'clock on Saturday morning, Michael had presented himself at the adjutant's office in Kensington Barracks, located at Kensington Gate, which was the home of the Household Cavalry. Drake had earlier learned that Chilburn had served with one of the cavalry regiments. On learning that Michael had been sent his way by no less a personage than Dearne, the adjutant had been happy to confirm that Chilburn had been bought a commission by his father, but hadn't stuck the course and had sold out after little more than a year. The adjutant had studied Michael, then rather primly offered, "Not really up to snuff."

Michael had nodded and asked if any there had served with Chilburn. A few stalwarts had, but even with Dearne's recommendation, the experienced guardsmen could offer little help. "He sold out years ago," one explained, "and we haven't seen him since."

Michael had returned to the adjutant and asked about any cavalryman who had served concurrently with Chilburn and had subsequently served with any regiment in India. The adjutant had checked his records, but hadn't turned up any such man.

From Kensington Gate, Michael had headed to Knightsbridge, to the barracks there, the home of the Horse Guards. As he'd been instructed, using Dearne's and Hendon's names, he asked the sergeant in charge of the records if there was anything known of a Chilburn or any member of the connected families—he'd had Louisa make him a list of the relevant surnames—who had served in any of the Horse Guard regiments that had toured overseas, especially to the subcontinent. The sergeant had taken his list and carefully checked, but had turned up precisely nothing.

Now, with the clocks about town standing at well after ten o'clock, Michael approached his final port of call for this exercise—Wellington Barracks off Birdcage Walk. Home to the Foot Guards—the Coldstream, Grenadier, Scots, Irish, and Welsh Guards—the regiments stationed at Wellington Barracks supplied all the guardsmen who protected the two royal residences in London as well as the Tower, still regarded as a royal compound.

Michael knew several officers personally. He found two in their digs. After engaging in the usual banter, Michael asked his questions. Both his friends were fly enough not to inquire why he wanted to know if they could tell him anything about any Chilburn, or any member of the connected families whose names Michael read out for them, or even any acquaintance of the above who had served in the guard regiments in any capacity, especially if that man had at any time served in India.

After duly wracking their brains, his friends shook their heads. However, as both were quick to point out, them not being aware of such a man didn't mean he didn't exist.

Asking them had been a long shot, but Michael would have kicked himself if he hadn't and later discovered the pair had known the identity of the wretched garrotter.

After exchanging news of their shared acquaintance, Michael left them and made his way to the main office.

There, using Carstairs's name to good effect, he obtained a list of all the officers commanding details of guards on duty around the capital over the next week. On scanning the list, he discovered that all of his friends' names were on it, as well as those of some of Sebastian's friends, and it was likely Drake knew others as well.

It had occurred to Michael that if they failed to find the gunpowder over the next few days, then it was likely the officers on his list would be the ones in the front line—the men they might need to alert, even if on the quiet, to the existence of the plot and the terrible threat it posed.

He folded the list, stashed it in an inner pocket, then grimly strode out into Birdcage Walk.

CHAPTER 29

Griswade sat behind the desk in the tiny parlor of his lodgings on the first floor of a respectable building in George Street. In the dim daylight seeping into the room through the uncurtained side window—daylight rendered soft and gray courtesy of the fog hanging low over the nearby river—he was debating which were his most urgent bills when a knock fell on his door.

He hadn't heard anyone climb the stairs, but then, he hadn't been listening, and the stairs led to three other sets of rooms as well as those he occupied.

Frowning, he hesitated. Few called at his rooms.

When the knock came again, rather more forcefully this time, he collected the bills, thrust them under a ledger, then stood and, quickly and silently, crossed to the window that looked over the street.

A lace curtain gave him some cover; he peered past its edge and saw his sister Monica's coachman seated on the box of what Griswade assumed was Monica's carriage.

"Huh." He let the curtain fall and walked to the door, treading heavily so she would know he was coming.

He opened the door and nodded. "Monica."

She stepped forward, came up on her toes, and planted a sisterly peck on his cheek. "Bevis."

She walked into the room and sat in the armchair before the small hearth.

Griswade closed the door and went to stand before the fireplace. When, after settling her skirts, Monica looked up at him, he asked, "What brings you here?"

She considered him for a moment, then said, "I wondered if you'd heard."

"Heard what?"

She sighed. "I thought not. Simply stated, Lawton has been murdered."

He stilled. Then he asked, "Really?" Lawton murdered didn't fit the script he and the old man had written.

Monica frowned. "Yes, of course—really! What do you take me for? That's hardly something I would joke about."

He waved her down. "Yes, of course. My apologies. I was just...surprised."

"As were we all. Even though one half expected to hear Lawton had met a bad end, an actual sordid murder came as something of a shock. As you might imagine, the family is...exercised."

"Do you have any idea how he was killed?"

"We ladies are not supposed to know, but it seems he was shot."

Shot? He managed to keep his lips shut. He reached to the side, drew up a straight-backed chair, and slowly subsided onto the seat. "Do you know when he was killed?"

Monica studied him, clearly wondering why he was interested. "I understand Hawesley was advised of the death on Thursday evening, but the authorities had taken several days to realize the body was Lawton's, so I assume he was killed sometime earlier in the week." Monica's eyes narrowed. "Why? Were you and he involved in something?"

"No." He shook his head. "No—I just wondered. I haven't seen Lawton for...months, it must be."

Not since before the old man had seen fit to pit them against each other.

Logically, some part of him had known that Lawton was dead—there really was other possible explanation for his sudden vanishing act. Any other occurrence, and they—or at least Hawesley—would have heard within a day or two.

But shot?

Thieves, footpads, and London's lowlifes didn't carry guns.

Lawton shot dead was like a trumpet blast announcing that someone—someone backed by the authorities, but playing in the shadows—was after them. That was not good news.

Monica heaved a long-suffering sigh. "Anyway, I just came to make sure you knew Lawton had died and that the funeral will be on Monday. At noon, at St. George's."

Griswade rose as his sister came to her feet. "Sadly, I have a prior engagement." *And a few more funerals to arrange.*

Monica shook her head in resignation. "I'll tell Mama." She met Griswade's eyes. "You might drop in and see her sometime."

He kept his face expressionless. "Perhaps in a few weeks."

Monica sighed again and walked to the door.

Griswade escorted her outside and handed her into her carriage. He stood on the pavement and watched the coach rattle away.

If some opponent had dealt himself into the old man's game, then the very last event at which he needed to be seen was Lawton's funeral.

And regardless of his sister's imaginings, he very much doubted anyone would miss him.

He turned and went inside.

CHAPTER 30

*A*s noon approached, Sebastian stood beside Antonia and did his best to project an appropriately interested and engaged demeanor.

He was the only male in attendance at the gathering in his great-aunt Horatia's drawing room overlooking Berkeley Square.

As virtually all the more than twenty ladies present were either related to him or about to become related to him, he couldn't claim to be cowed into nervousness. He'd tried to make himself invisible, but he was the tallest by far, and even though he'd attempted to hang back, metaphorically hiding behind Antonia's skirts, that hadn't worked, either.

He'd accepted that he'd had to attend if he didn't want to find himself wearing a white suit to the church, or something equally ridiculous, but there seemed to be so many questions and decisions to make, his head literally spun.

How did ladies deal with such things?

He sipped from his teacup and had to own to a newfound and still-evolving respect for his mother, his aunt—who had traveled down from Scotland for the upcoming event—and all the other ladies.

Luckily, Antonia had thus far fielded most of the questions.

He contented himself with listening and nodding when appealed to.

Then one of the few who was not a relation—thank God!—leaned over and, using the end of her confounded cane, stabbed him in the calf. When he set his cup on its saucer and dutifully turned to Lady Osbaldestone, it was to find her regarding him through gimlet black eyes. Obsidian eyes like a basilisk's, as his father and the Cynster males of that generation had always maintained.

"You," Lady Osbaldestone informed him, "whether by luck or remarkable planning, have timed your engagement ball well. There are precious few weeks in this season when all the major families are in town, but with Parliament sitting again, everyone who is anyone is back in residence. I predict you'll have an excellent turnout. Given few others of your station are likely to announce anything similar over this time, you'll have no competition. If you must get engaged at this time of year, it is, in fact, quite a good time to make a splash."

Sebastian murmured some suitable rejoinder, but something in the ancient arch-grande dame's words had sent a ripple of presentiment across his nape and down his spine.

Something she'd said had pricked his instincts.

It took him more than ten minutes of pretending to pay attention to all Antonia was telling him before he worked out what.

CHAPTER 31

*R*ather than rushing straight to Scotland Yard and arriving while Sir Martin was enjoying his lunch in one of the neighborhood taverns, Drake had suggested that he and Louisa—and her long-suffering coachman and groom stop at the Crown and Keys public house on the Strand. The fashionable watering hole was more or less on their way.

On entering the low-ceilinged dining room, Drake had steered Louisa to one of the booths along the wall. Once they were served and the girl had withdrawn, he picked up his cutlery and cut a slice of the house's famous beef pie.

"Perhaps we should"—Louisa set down the glass of wine she'd sipped—"re-examine where we are."

Drawn in by the delicious aroma wafting from the pie, Drake signaled with one hand for her to proceed.

"Well." She poked at the venison stew she'd ordered. "We know the gunpowder is now in fifteen barrels marked as containing Bright Flame Ale. We know those barrels are no longer in the Phoenix Brewery, and we can surmise that they've been moved, one way or another, to some holding area, as it were, most likely but not necessarily on the north bank of the Thames."

He swallowed. "Almost certainly on the north bank. If our mastermind is intent on making a political statement of some kind, then there's nowhere south of the river that would trump a long list of places north of the river."

"All right. So somewhere on the north bank, but, we believe, not yet at the final target site, as we have Saturday and Sunday to get through before all the offices and institutions fill again and an explosion at some government building will become a major event."

He nodded. "We know the four men Chilburn recruited came from the Phoenix Brewery, and although the bodies of two of the four haven't yet turned up, finding them won't get us any further."

"Not unless Jed Sawyer's body doesn't appear, suggesting he may still be alive. If so, and we find him, he might be able to point us in the direction in which the barrels have gone, but..." Looking across the table, she met his eyes. "We're running out of time, aren't we?"

He held her gaze and didn't immediately answer, then he looked down at the remnants of his pie. "We don't know, and we can't say, but..." He paused, then went on, "Without laying our hands on the gunpowder, I can't see how we'll stop its detonation, not now it's so close to wherever it's intended to go." After a moment, his voice lower, he added, "I feel as if time is tightening, that we haven't got much of that commodity left."

He glanced up and realized that she was...not exactly dithering—he couldn't imagine that—but uncertain. His instincts sharpened. So did his gaze. "What is it?"

There was command enough in his voice to bring her gaze to his. After a second of further debate, she grimaced. "I can't help but wonder, given the date." She drew breath and said, "Is there any possibility that this"— she waved—"is some sort of rerun of Guy Fawkes?"

He regarded her for several silent seconds, then pushed away his plate. "Damn!" Grim—grimmer—he held her gaze. "I thought of that yesterday and told myself it was too ridiculously fanciful a notion. But if it's occurred to you, too..."

She shrugged. "Gunpowder. Plot. Fifth of November coming up. We have all the right ingredients, and Parliament is sitting as well."

He stared unseeing across the booth, then he refocused on her face, on her eyes. "I want to discount it as absurd, but is it?"

For several moments, they stared at each other, then he stirred and started to get to his feet. "I need to speak with Greville."

"No," she countered, collecting her reticule, "*we* need to speak with Greville. Preferably the others, too, but at least the two of us."

He arched an arrogant brow, but before he could disagree, she rose and rolled on, "And I know just when to approach him." She paused before him, met his eyes and held them. "The Home Secretary will be at Sebastian and Antonia's engagement ball tonight. All the ministers will be. We can cut Greville out from the crowd and speak with him privately."

He suddenly saw what she was offering. "Without Waltham."

"Exactly." She turned and led the way from the dining room. "I can confirm that Sir Harold's name is not on the guest list."

Drake followed her out of the inn, dwelling on the prospect of speaking with Greville without Waltham present. They'd reached the carriage before he realized that if he wished to avail himself of that golden opportunity, there would be a price. He grasped Louisa's hand and helped her up, then joined her in the carriage. He leaned back against the squabs and fixed his gaze forward. "All right. But just you and me—the others will all be too much in the limelight."

"Done."

He glanced sidelong at her and saw a small, intensely feminine smile curve her lips. But she didn't turn to catch his eye. Instead, she declared, "Now it's on to Scotland Yard to see if Sir Martin has any new dead bodies on his slabs. *Ugh.*"

CHAPTER 32

Sadly, Sir Martin had not one, not two, but three more bodies of men killed by garrote lined up in the morgue. Knowing that the Chartist militia had lost four men, but the bodies of only two had turned up, Sir Martin had alerted Inspector Crawford, who had sent for Mr. Beam.

The lanky secretary, looking even more pasty than on his previous visit, arrived on Drake's and Louisa's heels.

However reluctantly, Beam once again did his duty, steeling himself and inspecting the bodies. He instantly identified the first. "That's Malcolm Triggs—the other driver missing from the brewery." He examined the other two bodies, then backed away from the slabs on which they lay. "I've never seen those two before." He turned to Drake. "I'd take an oath that neither are—were—members of the association."

Drake narrowed his eyes. "So Jed Sawyer isn't here?"

Beam shook his head vehemently. "Those others, they're definitely not Sawyer."

Drake frowned.

Beam swallowed, then glanced at Sir Martin. "If that's all…?"

"Thank you, Mr. Beam." Louisa smiled graciously when Beam swung her way. "You've been most helpful. If these gentlemen have no further questions for you"—she arched a brow at Sir Martin, then turned her interrogatory look on Drake—"then indeed, I believe you can return to your office."

Beam bowed. "Thank you, my lady." He glanced at Drake. "My lord?"

Drake nodded. "Thank you, Beam. Yes, that's all—you may go."

Beam went.

As the door swung shut behind him, Sir Martin humphed. "That's interesting."

"In what way?" Louisa inquired.

"Well, with all these deaths, the River Police are being extra-vigilant about keeping their eyes peeled for floaters—*ahem*. Bodies in the water, that is." Sir Martin tipped his head at the first of the occupied slabs. "The Chartist brewery driver was killed between twenty-four and forty-eight hours ago. My best guess would be on Thursday morning." He moved on and looked down at the sheet-draped bodies of the as-yet-unidentified men. "These two, on the other hand, were killed last night."

"You're suggesting they're not of the same group," Drake said.

"Indeed—and as the River Police are now picking up the bodies more quickly after they've been put into the river, they say they're fairly certain these latest two were put into the water from the north bank, somewhere not far from Blackfriars Bridge, rather than from the south bank, which was where that Chartist chappie was slipped in, near where we found the bodies of his two friends."

"So not Chartists and most likely not workers from the Phoenix Brewery."

Louisa frowned. "So who are they? Why did our garrotter kill them?"

"That, my dear, is indubitably one of our pressing questions." Sir Martin raised his gaze and fixed his best stare on Drake. "But the most important question at this point is who this madman—our garrotter—is." He spoke with more passion than Drake was accustomed to hearing from the jaded surgeon. "You have to stop this beggar, Winchelsea. I keep calling him a madman, but he's certainly not mad. He's cool, calculating, and entirely coldblooded. We now have ten bodies—ten!—we can attribute to him, and if the other killings you say are associated with this plot are added to that, we're up to thirteen. In a bare week!" Sir Martin's glare gained in ferocity. "Find him, for God's sake! And make sure you stop him."

Stony-faced, Drake nodded stiffly. "We're trying—and yes, we'll try harder."

With that, he gathered Louisa with a glance and followed her from the morgue.

CHAPTER 33

On leaving Sir Martin's domain, together with Drake, Louisa walked upstairs, and they called on Inspector Crawford. They shared what news they had, and Drake warned that the Chilburn family might attempt to apply pressure to curtail the investigation, a possibility that left Crawford unimpressed. After confirming he had no new information to impart, she and Drake quit the building.

While at the brewery the previous day, she'd noticed a sign listing the brewery's opening hours. She halted beside Drake on the pavement. "The brewery will be closed by now. They shut at noon on Saturdays."

Drake humphed, then waved her to the carriage. "I'd hoped we wouldn't need another meeting, but Michael, or even Sebastian and Antonia, might have learned something, and if you and I are to bend Greville to our cause this evening, we'll do better knowing as much as possible."

He paused beside the carriage and drew out a tablet and pencil.

She watched as he swiftly penned two notes. After folding them and inscribing names and an address on each—one to St. Ives House, the other to Clarges Street—he beckoned to two of the boys lounging in a loose group opposite the Yard's main doors. In a murmur, he told her,

"The boys hang around hoping to be hired to ferry messages, not just by the constabulary but also by the newsmen and the various members of the public who find themselves in the vicinity and needing to contact family or friends."

The boys came pelting up and halted, all but quivering in their eagerness.

Drake handed one note to each boy, reading out the names and address on each. "You're to take these to the addresses first, but if neither the gentleman nor the lady are in and the butlers tell you they're somewhere else, you're to take the message on and deliver it so that it reaches either the gentleman or the lady. Can you do that?"

The boys assured him they could. He paid them handsomely and added that they would be tipped well on delivering the notes.

The pair sped off, tacking through the crowds filling the pavements and covering distance far faster than any carriage.

Drake opened the carriage door and offered his hand.

She grasped it, climbed up, sat, and met his gaze. "So where to for us?"

Drake stared at her for a moment, then stated, "Home." He looked up and directed the coachman to drive to Grosvenor Square, then joined her in the carriage.

As the horses leaned into the traces, he settled beside her. "What do you know of the timing of the various segments of Sebastian and Antonia's event?"

Obligingly, she ran through the schedule. "That, of course, is assuming nothing changes at the last minute, but that rarely happens at Mama's events."

He grunted. "I imagine not."

She tipped her head, clearly thinking. "It's hard to say when Greville will show his face. He might come early, he might come late. It'll be best if I get Crewe to have one of our footmen keep an eye out for the Home Secretary and let me know the instant he appears."

Drake envisioned the scene. "We'll need a medium-sized room—not as small as that antechamber, but not as big as your library."

She nodded. "I know just the place."

They fell silent. Long enough for Drake to notice how relaxed, how comfortable he now felt in her presence. Over the past days, he'd spent hours jolting about London, seated beside her in that carriage. Apparently, repeated exposure had smoothed the jagged edges from what had previously been a much more tense and senses-jarring experience.

Or perhaps the change was an outcome of their most recent private interlude and the decision he'd subsequently made.

Regardless, change had occurred, and he wasn't averse to the result.

CHAPTER 34

*B*y midafternoon, Sebastian had escaped from Berkeley Square only to be informed by his mother that his presence was required in the St. Ives House back parlor for a final council of war.

The ladies foregathered didn't use those words, but in Sebastian's opinion, Wellington and his adjutants were amateurs compared to this group. Every last little detail was subjected to a final exhausting scrutiny and a definitive decision declared.

Why he had to be there was a mystery; he would have happily delegated any influence he might have to Antonia and left it at that.

He owned to relief when a footman appeared with a note on a salver; he fell on it as evidence that life still went on beyond the purlieu of his engagement ball.

The note was from Drake. Sebastian unfolded the single sheet and read.

Antonia materialized beside him. "From Drake?" When, frowning, Sebastian nodded, she prompted, "What does he say?"

"That we have a meeting to attend at four o'clock in the Wolverstone House library." Sebastian glanced at the ladies engaged in a spirited debate about something. "Will we be able to get away?"

"For that, yes, although I hope that by then, we'll have reached the end of our deliberations." When his gaze returned to the note, Antonia shifted to read over his shoulder. "What else has he written?"

"He raises the prospect that this plot might be an attempt at a rerun of Guy Fawkes. Presumably with the intention of getting it right, this time."

"Good gracious! Guy Fawkes?" Antonia paused, then more cautiously said, "I suppose I can imagine why, but...who would actually have the gall to attempt it?"

"Indeed." After a moment, Sebastian raised his gaze and looked at the ladies—many of them society's grandes dames—arrayed on the various sofas and armchairs. There were three duchesses, a countess, and numerous aristocrats of other degrees.

A few seconds' thought had him walking forward until he stood at the circle's edge, beside one of the armchairs. When a break in the discussions occurred, he spoke up. "Ladies, this has nothing to do with the ball tonight. More, it's a somewhat sensitive question, one I hope you will keep under your collective hat." He had the attention of every lady in the group. "The question is this. Have any of you heard the slightest whisper—even if you assumed it was in jest—about anyone planning to recreate the efforts of Guy Fawkes?"

Silence ensued. The ladies all stared at him; every one of them had husbands who sat in the lords or were related to noblemen who did or, in Caro Anstruther-Wetherby's case, had a husband who sat in the Commons.

Then his mother looked at Drake's mother. Silks susurrated as the ladies exchanged glances around and across the group, wordlessly communicating.

Finally, after another shared glance with Drake's mother, Sebastian's mother raised her gaze and met his eyes. "No. We have heard nothing, not even a whisper, in jest or otherwise." After the barest pause, she asked, "Is such a plot afoot?"

Sebastian glanced at the note in his hand. "That's what we'd all like to know."

CHAPTER 35

$\mathcal{T}$he St. Ives town carriage Louisa had commandeered drew up outside St. Ives House. Drake descended to the pavement and handed her down.

She shook out her skirts, then looked up at her coachman and her groom. With a smile, she said, "I don't expect to need the carriage again today."

"Very good, my lady," the men chorused. Both saluted her, then the coachman shook the reins, and the carriage rattled off for the mews.

She turned and regarded the front door of her home.

After a moment, Drake inquired, "Aren't you going in?"

She wrinkled her nose. "I don't really want to." She glanced at him. "If I show my face, I'll be drawn into the arrangements, and I don't like my chances of creeping in undetected." She arched a brow at him. "What's the time?"

He drew out his watch and consulted it. "Twenty minutes short of four o'clock."

"You called the meeting for four. Do you mind if I wait at Wolverstone House?"

"Not at all." He turned, and side by side, they walked the short distance to his home. He ushered her up the steps, then unlocked the door with his latchkey. As he opened the door, he caught her eye. "I warn you—my father and some of my brothers might be in."

She smiled and followed him inside. "I daresay I'll cope."

Hamilton appeared from the rear of the hall. He bent a disapproving look on Drake and bowed low to Louisa. "Lady Louisa." Straightening, he said to Drake, "You'll find the duke and Lord Tobias in the library, my lord. The duchess is presently visiting St. Ives House, and the rest of the family are out."

"Thank you, Hamilton." Drake arched a brow at Louisa. "The library? Or would you prefer to wait for the others in the drawing room?"

"If we're not interrupting your father or Tobias, then we might as well go straight to the library."

Together, they strolled down the corridor, then Drake opened the library door, and she swept in.

Royce, Duke of Wolverstone, was seated behind the desk that dominated one end of the long room. As she and Drake entered, the duke's gaze rose from the letter he'd been perusing and fixed, rather disconcertingly, on them.

Blithely ignoring the effect of that dark and distinctly penetrating gaze, with a confident smile, she walked forward and curtsied deeply. "Your Grace." She rose. "It's a pleasure to see you again."

Drake's father had risen as she had. His smile—reminiscent of one of Drake's more charming efforts—bloomed as he rounded the desk. "Louisa." He took her hand and half bowed. "The pleasure is entirely mine, my dear." He glanced at Drake, who had been collared by Tobias, who had been lounging in one of the library chairs, then looked back at Louisa. "Minerva is with your mother, I believe, dealing with urgent social matters."

She grinned. "Indeed. The engagement ball of the Cynster heir is, I'm sure, destined to be the pinnacle of the social year."

The duke smiled in response, but his eyes were sharp, his gaze shrewd. "I would have thought you would be in the thick of it."

"I daresay I would have been, if other matters"—she gestured to Drake—"hadn't taken precedence."

His Grace's brows rose. "Precedence over such an event?" He turned to Drake as, along with Tobias, his heir joined them. "I take it"—and Louisa noticed the change in the tenor of the duke's voice—"that this more important happening is some evolution of the mission that's sent you hither and yon over the past weeks."

Drake nodded. "We've yet to get to the bottom of it, and the plot remains ongoing." He glanced at Tobias, standing beside him; at thirty-one years old the son of the house closest in age to Drake, Tobias was an elegant gentleman of much the same ilk as his older brother, but a touch more easygoing. Drake returned his gaze to his father's face. "I"—his gaze dipped to her, and he smoothly amended—"we were wondering if, in your estimation, a rerun of the Guy Fawkes plot is at all likely."

"Guy Fawkes?" The duke blinked, but did not dismiss the idea out of hand. He was silent for several moments, then said, "I would have said not, but there's always a chance of some fanatical faction deciding such a move will be in their best interests, especially in the wake of '48." The duke paused, then went on, "I always felt that the most disturbing aspect of the original plot was that it was only exposed through betrayal. Admittedly, the powder was damp and wouldn't have made much of an explosion, but the fact remains that the authorities of the day were completely unaware of the existence of the plot until one of the plotters broke ranks."

"A betrayal," Drake stated, "is unlikely to happen in the present case. To date, we've detected only two active agents, and presumably there's someone directing the whole, but other than that, there seems no evidence of wider involvement." Drake grimaced. "Or at least not intentional involvement in the true plot."

When the duke looked understandably puzzled by that cryptic utterance, Drake outlined the unwitting involvement of the Young Irelanders and the Chartists. "Although we've blocked further recruitment from Chartist ranks, we've no idea what group might be drawn in next."

"Hmm." The duke put a question and followed it with more.

Louisa watched as Drake's father drew a brief but essentially complete summary of their investigation from his heir.

Viewing the pair more or less face-to-face illustrated a circumstance she'd long considered a curious mystery—that Drake's golden eagle's eyes, which he'd inherited through his mother, should possess the same ability to make one feel all but dissected, mentally at least, as his sire's very dark, bitter-chocolate-brown eyes. Plainly, the effect owed its existence to the power of the mind behind the eyes rather than their shade; certainly, when it came to the former, Drake was very much his father's son.

When Drake mentioned his previous meeting with Greville and their hopes of swaying the Home Secretary that evening, the duke's brows rose cynically. "I see that, since my time, very little has changed. And at least I had the pressure of ongoing wars to spur the bureaucrats into action."

"I'm discovering that peace," Drake responded equally cynically, "is much more difficult to preserve than to achieve."

The duke softly snorted in agreement.

Drake glanced at the clock on the mantelpiece, then met his father's gaze. "It's nearly four o'clock. I called a meeting here for that time. For obvious reasons, we can't gather at St. Ives House. I suppose we could use the drawing room..."

"No, no." The duke collected Tobias with a glance. "This is a much better room for dealing with plots." With a subtle smile curving his lips, the duke took his leave of her, then followed Tobias to the door. There, the duke paused. With his hand on the doorknob, he looked back at Drake. "While this plot sounds intriguing, I'm rather glad it's in your hands and not mine." The duke's gaze rested on Drake's face. "As for dealing with Greville, I suggest you focus on what you, as my heir, can and should do, rather than on what Greville might authorize."

With that, the duke went out, and the door quietly shut behind him.

She looked at Drake; his expression had turned thoughtful. "What did he—your father—mean by that last remark?"

A frown in his eyes, Drake said, "I think—" He broke off as the door opened, and Cleo, followed by Antonia and Sebastian, walked in.

They exchanged quick greetings, then Michael arrived. He shut the door, nodded to them all, and joined Cleo at one end of the long sofa. "So where are we?" He directed the question at Drake, who had walked to stand before the fireplace while Louisa had claimed her now-customary armchair.

Concisely, Drake summarized what he and Louisa had learned that day—that of the four men Chilburn had recruited from the Chartist militias, the third had been found dead while the fourth remained unaccounted for, and in addition, two more unidentified men, apparently unrelated to the Chartists, had fallen victim to the garrotter.

"Their bodies had been put into the river from the north bank somewhere near Blackfriars," Louisa added from Drake's left.

"Any chance the fourth man—the apprentice Sawyer—might have escaped and be in hiding?" Sebastian asked.

Drake inclined his head. "Given Sawyer's body has yet to turn up, that's possible, but with Mrs. Sawyer denying she knows anything of his whereabouts and no evidence to the contrary, there's no way to tell. For all we know, Sawyer escaped, and his family has successfully hidden him, but we don't have time to pursue that now."

"Oh," Louisa said.

He looked at her, but couldn't make sense of her distracted expression. "What?"

She shook aside whatever it was. "Nothing—although I do think we should pursue Sawyer if we continue to have trouble putting paid to this plot."

Drake still wanted to know what she'd thought of, but left the point for later. Swiftly, he sketched the notion that the current plot might be intended as a rerun of the Guy Fawkes plot and his consequent decision to beard Greville that evening. Then he looked at the others. "So what have you learned?"

Sebastian and Antonia had spent all day corralled with relatives and close family friends, all of whom they'd previously questioned regarding Lawton Chilburn's possible associates. "So we got no further on that score," Antonia said.

"However," Sebastian said, "we were still trapped with the most powerful when your note reached us, mentioning the possible connection with Guy Fawkes. So I put it to them, but no one had heard any relevant whispers."

"But," Antonia said, "with our engagement ball tonight and the better part of the ton expected, now that those ladies have been alerted, if there are any whispers circulating of such an attempt, I believe we can feel confident we'll know of them by tomorrow."

Drake humphed, then conceded, "That's probably the best we can do on that front."

Michael then explained the help he'd received from Cleo's parents and their close friends. "Their names got me the assistance of those within the guards' administrations in positions to know what we needed to learn. That said, although I asked at all three barracks and in some cases spoke with friends, no one knew of any current or past military man with whom Chilburn was known to associate. Indeed, the consensus was that Chilburn had served for little more than a year, and after he sold out, neither he nor those with whom he'd served maintained contact."

"Actually"—Louisa glanced fleetingly at Drake, then looked at the others—"that's something we forgot to mention. Last night, Drake and I overheard Lawton's two oldest brothers and one of his cousins discussing who they thought had killed Lawton. They put it down to either a frustrated creditor or perhaps someone seedier with whom Lawton had become involved. However, they were far more concerned that the investigation into Lawton's murder might expose some underlying scandal that would tarnish the entire family." She shook her head. "They really weren't worried that Lawton was dead."

Drake snorted softly. "They were almost ready to applaud the murderer as long as his action didn't backfire on them."

Michael huffed. "Lawton Chilburn seems to have been a remarkably unloved individual—there aren't many men who have no close friends and, apparently, haven't had for years. Incidentally"—he looked at Drake—"I also asked at all three barracks if their records showed any member of the Chilburn family or their connections who had been in the guards and served overseas. The answer was a resounding no."

Drake faintly frowned. "We've assumed that Chilburn's associate, our garrotter, is English. There's no reason he has to be. Or alternatively, he could be English, but served solely overseas. He might not be in our army's records at all."

"Sadly, that's true," Michael said. "So when I called at Wellington

Barracks, I took Carstairs's advice and got a list of all the officers in charge of the details of guardsmen who'll be on duty around the capital over the next week." He drew the list from his pocket and handed it to Drake.

As Drake unfolded the list and scanned the names, Michael went on, "I know quite a few, and Sebastian"—Michael glanced at his brother—"I'm sure knows others, and you'll be familiar with still others." His gaze fixing on the list, Michael shrugged. "Just in case."

Drake handed the list to Sebastian, then his gaze returned to Michael. After a moment, Drake met Louisa's eyes. "That's what my father meant." He glanced at the others. "My father was here when we came in. We told him what we knew thus far. While he had no insights to offer regarding the plot itself, with respect to dealing with Greville, Papa suggested I concentrate on what I, as his heir, can and should do, rather than on what Greville might wish." He glanced again at Louisa. "I believe His Grace meant that, given the situation, if November fifth approaches and we still haven't found the gunpowder, then loyalty to one's friends and family overrides any consideration of political niceties. In other words, I, and Sebastian and Michael, too, should warn the officers in charge of the various detachments guarding buildings around the capital and alert them to the potential threat."

Sebastian nodded. "It would be dishonorable of us not to warn all the officers on this list. That's something Greville cannot legitimately prohibit us from doing. He can't ask us to act in such a way that would besmirch the honor of our houses."

Surveying the men's faces, Louisa noted that all three looked, if not happier, then at least less grim.

"Between us," Sebastian said, scanning the list again, "I'm sure we can drop a preliminary warning into all these ears by tomorrow, and if not then, by Monday at the latest."

"And so you should," Antonia declared. "The fifth is Tuesday—you can't wait until then and hope to catch everyone."

There was universal agreement that as the plot might be a rerun of Guy Fawkes, their time to find the gunpowder and stop any explosion might soon run out, and therefore, they should warn the officers regardless of what Greville might say.

"Speaking of Greville"—Drake glanced at Louisa—"Louisa and I plan to waylay him at the ball tonight, with a view to convincing him that a quiet search of Parliament, Whitehall, and all government buildings in the city is now warranted. I intend suggesting we label it an exercise and use the nearness to the anniversary of Guy Fawkes's plot to paint it as a move to reassure the public that such a plot would never be allowed to threaten the realm again."

The others, even Louisa, looked impressed. "I like the twist of using the anniversary to our own ends," she admitted.

He'd thought she would.

"And," she continued, "without Waltham putting in his oar, I feel confident we can get the Home Secretary to see sense."

Given her tone and her grasp of duchessly command, no doubt learned at her mother's and grandmother's knees, Drake was actively looking forward to seeing what direction she hit Greville from and how the Home Secretary handled a challenge he almost certainly had little experience dealing with.

The corridors of Whitehall and the rarefied halls of Parliament did not contain duchesses.

Not even duchesses-to-be.

Shaking aside several distracting images, Drake concluded, "Assuming Greville accepts my recommendation, I'll mention our warnings to our friends and connections and assure him all will be handled with the secrecy the ton normally reserves for family scandals."

The others all nodded.

"Time," Sebastian said. "From the first, this plot has been odd, running very much to its own schedule. But now we know the gunpowder is almost certainly north of the Thames…"

Grim again, Drake nodded. He swept his gaze over the others' faces. "I think November fifth is the longest we'll have to conclude this matter successfully."

Louisa rose, and the others followed suit. "That means we have only two more days in which to find the gunpowder and identify and seize those behind the plot and stop this madness."

CHAPTER 36

*L*ater that evening, as the highlight of their engagement ball, Sebastian led Antonia onto the St. Ives House ballroom's dance floor, twirled her into his arms, and with utterly besotted smiles on their faces, they stepped into their engagement waltz.

They moved effortlessly—instinctively—together, tall and graceful, the epitome of marquess and marchioness-to-be, regal and yet worldly. So very much of their time.

Antonia felt sure she was glowing; she felt as light as thistledown as Sebastian whirled her down the floor. She smiled into his eyes. "We made it."

His eyes hadn't left hers from the moment they'd taken the floor. "There were moments over the last few days when I had to steel myself and not run."

She laughed, and the sound sank to Sebastian's bones. Then she met his eyes again and murmured, "I would have run with you."

"We'd never have made it to Gretna Green. Someone would have seen us and wanted to know what we were about."

Grinning, they fell silent as they negotiated the tighter turns at the end of the room. When they were once more revolving up the long length, Antonia said, "Well, we're on the right road now, socially speaking."

His expression radiating unalloyed happiness, he nodded. "The one leading to the altar, and from that, we won't stray."

Antonia tipped her head. Lost in Sebastian's eyes, she uttered the words that sprang from her heart. "It was always you for me. For me, it was always going to be this, here, with you."

"And for me." His voice had deepened. A low rumble, it fell with absolute conviction on her ears. "I admit that I didn't exactly know that, but my eyes are now open, and all I see is you."

No more words were said, but volumes were spoken, of what each meant to the other, of their hopes and dreams.

Carried via the bridge of their gazes, sent winging with the power of what they'd discovered was the reality of what lived between them.

Both were entirely unaware when other couples joined them on the floor. They were lost to each other, transfixed by the promise of a future shaped by, anchored by, and driven by their love.

They revolved and dreamed of family and the future while the rest of the ton looked on.

CHAPTER 37

*A*t the end of the engagement waltz, Michael and Cleo found
themselves at the far end of the huge ballroom. Since the beginning of the
ball, in between greeting others and chatting with friends, both Michael's
and Cleo's, and ducking subtle inquiries as to when their own
engagement announcement and ball were to be—events that all involved
had relegated to sometime after the plot had been successfully foiled—
they'd kept their eyes peeled for any members or connections of the
Chilburn family.

Unsurprisingly, the viscount and viscountess had sent their regrets.
Lawton's eldest brother and his wife, appropriately attired in mourning,
had arrived, but had stayed for only fifteen minutes. After greeting the St.
Iveses and the Chillingworths and tendering dutiful congratulations to
Sebastian and Antonia, the Chilburns had departed. Presumably, they'd
been delegated to represent the family at the event.

Now, as Michael and Cleo made slow progress through the quite
staggering crowd, he bent and murmured in her ear, "I seriously doubt
any of Lawton's other siblings will appear."

"No." Walking more or less in front of him, Cleo leaned back and
spoke over her shoulder. "But I can't believe there's no one connected
with the family here—there must be someone we can usefully question. It

seems such a waste of an opportunity."

Given he felt much the same way—he had far more interest in furthering the mission than in being a part of the social throng—as he could see over most heads, he glanced around, paused, then bent to whisper in Cleo's ear, "I hesitate to suggest it, but Grandmama and Lady Osbaldestone are sitting on a chaise against the wall to our left." When Cleo directed an eager, questioning look at him, he added, "The thing is, you'll have to do the talking. Both of them well-nigh terrify me."

She gave a gurgle of laughter, then, searching his eyes, realized he'd meant what he'd said. She patted his arm. "Never mind. I'll protect you. Now, where are they?"

He led her to where the pair of ancient grandes dames were holding court; despite the encroaching frailty of age, there were few in the ton who did not comprehend that, should they so decide, both ladies still could—and would—wield significant social clout. That they occasionally did kept everyone on their toes.

As a Cynster, Michael ranked as one of the pair's favorites, yet he'd spoken truly. Whether it was through eyes of palest green or jet-black, that both ladies possessed an uncanny ability to see through any obfuscation or façade had from his earliest years made him intensely wary.

He loved his grandmother, but he respected her perspicacity even more.

When they finally reached the old ladies, Michael bent and kissed his grandmother's cheek, then accepted the gnarled hand Lady Osbaldestone held out to him and bowed over it.

Cleo had already spent time with both ladies before the dinner party prior to the ball; she faced them with a bright, expectant smile.

"Well, my dear." Helena, Dowager Duchess of St. Ives, took hold of Cleo's hand and studied her face. "How can we help you?"

Apparently, Cleo did not find the question unnerving. She lowered her voice to a confidential murmur. "I believe you know that we"—she waved to include Michael—"have, with the others, been trying to learn about any associates Lawton Chilburn might have had. We wondered if there are any Chilburn connections, no matter how distant, present tonight—ones with whom we have yet to speak."

Helena's fine brows rose. "Certainly there should be." She glanced at Lady Osbaldestone. "I believe several of Hawesley's siblings are here. I cannot imagine you would have thought to ask them, yet as we know so much of our grandchildren's lives"—Helena directed a soft smile at Michael—"so, too, they may know something of their nephew's. It will be worthwhile to ask."

"Indeed." Lady Osbaldestone shifted on the chaise and peered through the crowd. Then she beckoned Cleo closer and pointed. "There—the lady in the green turban and the one sitting next to her. They're Hawesley's older sisters. They have families of their own, and I doubt they will mind speaking of Hawesley's black sheep."

"Thank you." With a smile and a curtsy, Cleo took her leave of the old ladies. With deferential nods, Michael followed her lead.

It took them some time to make their way to the other ladies, but as he and Cleo were the secondary focus of interest at the ball, once they'd paused beside the ladies' small chaise, both ladies quickly moved to engage them.

He was impressed by Cleo's verbal deftness in turning the conversation to Lawton by apparently suddenly recalling that she'd heard he'd died.

The ladies exchanged a glance, then the turbaned one turned to Cleo and conspiratorially remarked, "He was no great loss, my dear. Terrible to say such a thing of one's nephew, but truly, he gave poor Lavinia—his mother, you know—gray hairs at every turn. Hawesley had quite washed his hands of him."

"Oh yes." The second lady tightened her shawl about her shoulders and took up the tale. "And that was years ago. He utterly denounced the boy—well, young man as he then was. A no-account profligate—I remember Hawesley calling Lawton that."

"Why, I recall..." The first lady, apparently Lawton's oldest paternal aunt, continued with a story illustrating, if nothing else, that Lawton's family had, indeed, had their patience tried to the breaking point.

And the tirade, delivered as a duet, didn't end there.

In the end, even Cleo had had enough. She put a hand on the turbaned lady's forearm. "I'm sorry to derail such a fascinating tale, but we've just been summoned by Michael's mama. If you'll excuse us?"

Keeping her smile in place, she curtsied, and Michael half bowed, and in rapid order, they made good their escape.

"Phew!" Once they were safely screened by the dense crowd, Michael caught her eye. "We already knew that the Chilburn family isn't exactly sincerely mourning Lawton, but after hearing all that, if I didn't know better, I'd be inclined to suspect one of the family had done the deed."

She threw him a warning look; it had been he and she who, firing simultaneously, had shot Lawton dead.

She looked ahead, then pointed. "I think I can see Sebastian and Antonia over there."

Michael looked, confirmed the sighting, took her arm, and steered her to safety.

CHAPTER 38

*D*rake whirled Louisa down the ballroom. Tonight, she was gowned in an ethereal confection of gauzy silks in a variety of greens arranged to resemble a cascade of leaves. Her bare shoulders rose from a delicate screen of small "leaves" affixed to the sheath of her bodice, while the full skirt was formed by layer upon layer of the same translucent silks cut in the shape of larger leaves.

The result, in his eyes, rendered her distinctly fey—a nymph or perhaps a dryad—and also beyond alluring, especially as she'd chosen to wear her pearls again. Pearl bobs dangled from her ear lobes, and single pearls were scattered through her black curls, while a short rope of smaller pearls looped around the comb that anchored her upswept hair.

Given the effect her appearance had on him and suspecting it would affect others equally if not more so, in light of his recent decision vis-à-vis her, he'd decided there was no point putting himself through the aggravation of dealing with her usual court. Since he'd arrived, he'd managed to monopolize her time, apparently to her satisfaction as much as his; she'd neither complained nor attempted to draw her coterie of admirers to her.

That she was holding herself ready to deal with Greville the instant the Home Secretary appeared hadn't hurt.

They swirled through the turn at the end of the room with elegant precision. As they once again started up the length of the ballroom, he scanned those congregated about the doorway.

"Stop looking," she warned, "or people will notice and start watching us just when we don't wish them to." When he dutifully returned his gaze to her face, she bent a chiding look on him, then her features eased to their customary confident serenity. "I've asked Crewe to send a footman to find me the instant Greville darkens the front door. With luck, we'll be able to intercept him immediately after he makes his bow to Mama and offers his felicitations to Sebastian and Antonia."

As far as it went, that was an excellent plan and one he saw no reason to quibble over.

"I've been thinking," she went on, and he refocused on her face and saw a frown lurking in her eyes, "about Lawton's lodgings. We searched his rooms, but we were looking for papers and letters—anything that might have indicated who he was working with."

He wondered where her unpredictable mind was leading her.

"And, indeed, someone had searched before us, and they, too, had been looking through his papers, so presumably there was something written— or at least the other party, the one who searched, thought there might be something written—that might implicate them. Them or others involved in the plot, or perhaps even details such as where the gunpowder was to go."

She paused, frowning more definitely.

He looked up and steered her on. "I'm following so far." Albeit rather less easily than, transparently without thought on her part, her feet followed his through the revolutions of the dance.

"We tacitly assumed," she went on, "that whoever had searched before us would have found anything overtly incriminating and taken it away— but what if he didn't find everything?"

It was his turn to frown, although he managed to keep the expression from his face. "Between us—that other party and the pair of us—I would have said the place was searched fairly thoroughly."

"For papers left lying around, yes. But we didn't search for any special hiding places. We didn't even search Badger's pockets."

"True." He'd been surprised that they hadn't found any address book or the like. Most men carried one, but Chilburn hadn't had one on him when he'd died, and they hadn't found anything like that in his rooms; he'd assumed whoever had searched before them had taken it.

"And we didn't really search Badger's little room—not properly. We didn't look for any hidey-holes in his area, either—at that time, we didn't know he'd been killed." She was warming to her theme. "If Badger hadn't known something, then why was he murdered? Yet he was, so ipso facto, it's likely he knew something the garrotter didn't want him to reveal." She raised her gaze and met his eyes. "We should check if Badger had written anything down and hidden it somewhere in his room."

It was a long shot, but...experience had taught him never to discount such a cast.

Especially when proposed by a source such as she. He was learning to respect her instincts. Her logic might not always be entirely robust, but there was that uncanny perspicacity that ran in her family...he felt as if ignoring that would be to invite peril.

He was about to open his mouth and agree when movement at the edge of the dance floor caught his eye. A footman stood, hand half raised, trying valiantly to attract their attention without alerting the entire room.

Drake changed course abruptly, but Louisa adjusted without any misstep. He whirled her to a halt; his arm about her waist, he guided her out of the stream of circling couples at the spot where the footman waited.

The footman looked intensely relieved. "Message from Crewe, my lady—your gent is on his way up the stairs..." The footman's gaze shifted to where the duke and duchess were still receiving. "And there he is now."

"Thank you, Gregory. You can return downstairs."

Gregory bowed and departed. From beside Drake, Louisa surveyed Sir George Greville as he made his bow to her parents. "He'll have to congratulate Sebastian and Antonia before we can whisk him away. Can you see them?"

"They're standing to the left." Drake paused, then said, "All right. Let's head that way."

They didn't hurry. By the time they approached the small group that now contained Sebastian, Antonia, Prudence Cynster, one of Louisa and Sebastian's cousins who was also a longtime friend of Antonia, and the Home Secretary, Greville had made his bow to the affianced couple, acknowledged Prudence, exchanged comments and pleasantries all around, and was on the verge of moving into the crowd.

Abetted by Drake, Louisa positioned herself so that when Greville withdrew from the group and turned, he found himself facing her.

The consummate politician, Greville smiled delightedly. "Lady Louisa."

"Mr. Home Secretary." She smiled and gave him her hand.

Greville bowed low. As he straightened, she flicked her fingers at Drake. "I believe you're well acquainted with Lord Winchelsea."

"Indeed." Greville exchanged nods with Drake. His gaze remained on Drake's face—that Greville wished to ask about the plot but knew better than to raise such an issue in the middle of a crowd was obvious.

She smiled more brightly. Stepping to Greville's side, she linked her arm in his; he looked at her in surprise. "If I might suggest, Sir George"—she began to steer him through the crowd—"a few moments in a more private setting might be useful. For all of us."

Drake fell in on her other side.

Greville noticed, and his resistance evaporated. "Indeed, Lady Louisa—a few quiet moments would be most helpful. I take it you have some place in mind."

"Indeed, sir." She guided him out of the ballroom into the large foyer, then along one of the wide corridors that led deeper into the mansion.

They didn't go far. She halted before the second door along the corridor, waited while Drake reached past her and opened the door, then led the way inside.

Drake waited for Greville to follow, then brought up the rear and closed the door.

He glanced around. The room had been prepared for their use. The wall sconces and two lamps had been lit and shed a warm glow throughout a comfortable small parlor.

Still very much in command, Louisa waved Greville to an armchair facing the single sofa, while with a swish of her skirt, she claimed one end of the sofa, leaving the other end to Drake.

Greville sat, his gaze going from Louisa to Drake and back again.

Louisa smiled. "I should tell you that, along with Sebastian and Michael—and Lady Antonia Rawlings and Miss Cleome Hendon—I've been assisting Drake with this investigation."

Greville looked uneasy. He glanced at Drake as if seeking confirmation.

Drake met his gaze levelly and said nothing.

Greville cleared his throat. "Have you found anything?" He directed the question to Drake.

"Something, but not everything, and not the most important thing—the gunpowder."

"It's still out there?"

"It is."

"Are you sure?"

"Quite."

"I should mention," Louisa smoothly interjected, "that we—all six of us—have seen the evidence of the existence of this gunpowder, all ten hundredweight of it. We know it's somewhere in London—almost certainly somewhere north of the Thames." She paused, then almost pensively added, "Knowledge is one of those odd things   you can't reverse it." As Drake watched, she calmly met Greville's eyes and quietly stated, "You can't unknow it."

Drake inwardly shook his head in wonder—and not a little awe. They'd barely started, and she'd already issued a very specific threat, one Greville had understood with perfect clarity if the faintly panicked calculation passing behind the Home Secretary's eyes was any indication.

It was, Drake judged, time to step in. "There are, as it happens, several complications." Greville's gaze had swung his way as if hoping for rescue, but the word "complications" destroyed that hope.

"What complications?"

"First, a murderer who is ruthlessly killing his own henchmen after they carry out his orders. He's killed ten men over the past week—we believe on the grounds that dead men can tell no tales. Add those to the three we believe Lawton Chilburn killed, and the count associated with this plot currently stands at thirteen. And there may be more bodies we've yet to find."

Greville stared. "*Chilburn?* I heard of his death, of course—are you telling me he was involved in this?"

His lips thin, Drake nodded. "He was one of the...to use a chess analogy, knights who've been active in executing this plot. There is at least one other—the aforementioned murderer who is still out there and active."

Greville looked faintly stunned. "So we have a murderer—a multiple-murderer—involved. And Chilburn—good Lord! Hawesley will have an apoplexy. Does he know?"

"Not yet. But," Drake said, "let's leave the ton scandals until they eventuate. Neither the existence of the murderer nor Chilburn's involvement is the reason we've sought this meeting." He paused, then said, "I'm sure you know what the date is. Put that together with ten hundredweight of gunpowder disguised as barrels of a popular ale and concealed somewhere in London on the north bank of the Thames, and Parliament is sitting."

Greville's eyes had progressively widened. "You can't mean to suggest..."

Drake continued as if Greville hadn't spoken. "And one last point which, in light of those facts, seems distinctly pertinent." He captured Greville's gaze and ruthlessly held it. "Unlike Guy Fawkes and company, these plotters have taken immense care to ensure that the powder they've amassed and, we suspect, are about to move into position at their chosen target is in excellent condition."

Greville wasn't a lauded politician for nothing; when his back was to the wall, he could think and scheme faster than most.

He didn't look away but stared at Drake as he thought through all he'd heard, through the implications, and all he now had to fear.

Eventually, his lips tightened. He held Drake's gaze for an instant longer, but finding no hint of softness there, finally asked, "What do you recommend we do?"

We, Drake noticed. Greville had realized that much, at least. "The least we should do is to mount a thorough search of all the likely buildings this group might target."

Greville opened his mouth, but Drake stayed his protest with an upraised hand. "We will describe this search, occurring in the lead-up to the customary celebration of the anniversary of the Guy Fawkes plot, as an exercise designed to demonstrate to all concerned, but most especially to the public, that such a plot would never be allowed to threaten the realm again."

Drake rather liked that turn of phrase; judging by Greville's expression, the Home Secretary found it appealing as well. "It might even be wise," Drake continued, "to encourage talk of such a search becoming an annual event to be triggered at some random date. Purely as an exercise in developing the necessary preparedness to deal with a similar plot should such a thing ever arise..." He smiled cynically at Greville. "I'm sure you can dress the matter up to best suit the government's case."

Greville's gaze grew distant. After a moment, he nodded. "I take your point." He refocused on Drake's face. "Points." Greville glanced again, briefly, at Louisa, then returned his gaze to Drake's face. "Very well. You have the authority—my authority—to institute such a search. I take it you need nothing else to make it happen?"

"Your directive will be sufficient." Drake paused, then continued, "I propose to conduct the search tomorrow, drawing in the guards to look for any of our specific type of ale barrels. It should be possible to complete a search of all government buildings within the day. However, it's perfectly possible that we'll find nothing tomorrow because the barrels won't yet be in place. But we can't know until we look."

Greville frowned. "If you don't expect the barrels to be there—"

"Greville, this plot hasn't followed any of the customary rules thus far." Drake allowed his frustration with political caution to seep into his voice. "I am not of a mind to take risks at this point. We know the barrels are close to their target. November fifth is Tuesday. How close to Tuesday the plotters will leave it before moving the gunpowder to their chosen target site is anyone's guess. If it is already in place, then the sooner we remove it, the better." He paused, then felt compelled to add, "My task is, as it always has been, to protect the realm from threats of this ilk. Your role in this is simple—to let me do the job I agreed to take on."

To give Greville his due, he didn't look away. After a moment, he inclined his head. "Yes. All right. So you'll conduct a search tomorrow, but you consider it an outside chance that the gunpowder will be found. Is that correct?"

"In essence, the Sunday search will be a dry run. It will allow the guards to note all the places in which barrels might be concealed and, if possible, reduce access. Subsequently, if we don't locate the gunpowder by late on Monday, I intend calling the guards out again, and we'll conduct a second search starting at midnight on Monday. If, as we suspect, the plotters plan to strike on Tuesday, they will almost certainly have moved the gunpowder into position by then. If we still fail to find the gunpowder, I propose ordering a strict embargo on all barrels even approaching those buildings. Until we have the gunpowder in hand, no one—politicians, bureaucrats, or even the military command—will be safe."

Greville had blanched. He was unconsciously twisting the ring on one finger.

Beside Drake, Louisa stirred. "We should perhaps stress that after the search on Sunday, which we expect to be unfruitful, we will continue pursuing the investigations that have brought Lord Winchelsea to this point and following all avenues those investigations suggest. Our aim is to locate the gunpowder, preferably before it's moved to the target site, but at the very least, before it's detonated."

Whether it was hearing words such as "gunpowder," " target site," and "detonated" uttered in Louisa's distinctly feminine tones or simply the implications of the words, Greville visibly shivered.

"There's one more thing." Without waiting for any encouragement from Greville, Drake went on, "While arranging for the search tomorrow, we—Earith, Lord Michael, and I—will simultaneously alert the officers in charge of the various guard details to the real nature of the threat. In short, that there truly is gunpowder to be found. There's no point in a search if the guards aren't aware that there may well be something dangerous to find."

Greville frowned. "Can't you…? I don't know. Invent something so there's no chance of panic."

"Not really, no." Drake's voice had taken on a gentle, almost hypnotic quality. From the corner of his eye, he saw Louisa cast him a wary glance, but he didn't take his gaze from Greville's face. "As you're aware, there's the matter of honor between families, at least among families such as the Cynsters and Variseys. And, of course, the Grevilles. Among the ranks of guard officers are many who are either friends or connections to whom Sebastian, Michael, and I owe a degree of loyalty. Not informing those gentlemen of the very real nature of the threat would be…put simply, not the done thing."

"It's certainly not something you can ask my brothers or Lord Winchelsea to do." Louisa's tone even more than her words made that beyond plain.

Greville was cornered, and he knew it. Tight-lipped, he nodded. "Very well. But I will ask you—and Lady Louisa's brothers"—that was said with a stiff tip of his head her way—"to stress the importance of keeping a very tight rein on this situation. Nothing must find its way to the newspapers or be bandied about in any public forum."

Drake inclined his head. "I'm sure all those with whom we will speak can be trusted to keep their lips shut."

Greville's jaw clenched, then he shook his head and muttered barely audibly, "Be it on your head."

Louisa smiled brilliantly, effortlessly capturing Greville's attention as, in a frothing of silks, she rose—bringing him, slightly flustered, to his feet. Her smile didn't dim as she kept it fixed on his face, but the edges it grew could have sliced steel. "But you've already ensured that it is, haven't you?"

It took Greville a second to connect the two sentences, then he flushed. Uncertain, thrown off balance by a threat he hadn't until then correctly gauged, he jerkily nodded to Drake as he, too, came to his feet. "If you'll both excuse me, I must get on."

With that stilted farewell, Greville bowed—from a distance—to Louisa, then made for the door in uncharacteristic haste.

As the door shut behind the Home Secretary, Drake found his lips curving in an irrepressible smile. He glanced at Louisa. "I hope your mama doesn't decide we've overstepped the mark in sending him fleeing."

Louisa blinked. "Heavens, no—Mama would have said much worse. Especially about his last comment. Really! He's lived all his life in the ton—he knows perfectly well what the unwritten rules are."

And she, as her mother and grandmother before her, was one of the socially acclaimed protectors of those rules. As was his mother, if it came to that.

Drake drew in a breath, rapidly reviewed, then stated, "There's nothing more I can accomplish here." He glanced at her and formally inclined his head. "If you'll excuse me—"

"Don't be silly." She looped her arm through his. "I'm going with you."

He hesitated for a second too long before asking, "Where are we going?"

"To Cross Lane, of course. To search through Lawton's lodgings in case there's more to find."

He gave serious thought to trying to deny her, yet looking into her eyes and seeing not only her stubbornness but also her obdurate determination and her unwavering commitment to forging ahead—by his side to the very end—he simply couldn't. He sighed and agreed, "Of course."

Together, they quit the room, went down the stairs, collected her cloak and his greatcoat, then walked out into the night.

CHAPTER 39

*G*riswade put paid to two of the merchant Hunstable's four delivery men that night. It was almost too easy.

He'd kept watch on Hunstable's premises over the past days and had discovered that two of his marks frequented the Crown and Anchor, the public house he'd previously used for his last meeting with the bargemen from the brewery.

So he'd already been familiar with the amenities the area afforded.

The bodies of the bargemen had slipped beneath the dark waters of the Thames the night before. In the darkness that engulfed the lower, riverward section of the street, it had been easy to cosh them senseless. Then the wire had come out, and he'd finished them off before rolling their bodies into the water at the nearby largely unfrequented water stairs.

Disposing of tonight's pair had been even easier. They'd never seen him before, so when they passed him in the street, they'd had no idea he'd harbored any interest in them. Much less a murderous intent.

The cosh had fallen twice in rapid succession, and the rest had gone without the slightest hitch.

As he slid the second body into the water, he regretfully acknowledged that he wouldn't be able to use the spot again. Luckily, the other men from Hunstable's he had yet to dispatch drank at a different pub. He would deal with them tomorrow.

His grisly task complete, Griswade straightened and listened, instinctively checking for any sound, any suggestion that someone had seen him. All that reached him was the near-hypnotic lapping of the river against the stone. He'd always found the sound soothing—a lullaby for the dead.

With midnight approaching and all done for that day, he let his mind turn to the next. To the matters still outstanding to which he needed to attend.

It had proved extremely helpful that the days preceding the culmination of the old man's plan included Saturday and Sunday. It was essential to remove all four of Hunstable's men in such a way that the merchant wouldn't have time to find experienced replacements before the crucial delivery. And killing four men in one night was stretching things, even for Griswade. But with the timing as it was, he'd been able to remove two tonight, and once he accounted for the other two tomorrow, there would be no obstacle left standing in the way of the grand finale.

Griswade smiled to himself, then peered across the dark water to make sure the latest body was slipping away on the tide. Reassured on that score, he turned and walked away from the river. As he trudged up the street and around the bend to where the lamp outside the Crown and Anchor still shed its welcoming light, his mind refocused on his one remaining niggle of uncertainty.

He'd killed Badger, then searched Lawton's lodgings. In hindsight, he might have done better to reverse the order. It would have been easier had he thought to ask Badger for Lawton's address book before strangling the little toad.

The problem was, he wasn't even sure Lawton had kept such a book. He hadn't found it when he'd searched, and he was reasonably certain Lawton hadn't been carrying it when he'd been shot. If he had, surely by now, someone would have come calling, asking questions at least, even if they could have no real notion of what was in the wind, much less that he, ex-Captain Bevis Griswade of the Royal Hussars, was involved.

Regardless, if Lawton had kept any record of Griswade's or the old man's address—even just a jotting to aid his memory, never mind anything more incriminating—then the chances were that any such evidence was still somewhere in Lawton's rooms.

When Griswade had searched, he hadn't looked for secret hiding places; he hadn't tested the floorboards or the bricks around the fireplace.

As he tramped through the night-dark streets, passing into and out of the cones of light shed by the streetlamps, his jaw set. He didn't appreciate the niggling awareness of potential vulnerability that hung over his head like a sword of Damocles. He didn't have time for distractions, not now, not while he needed to focus to ensure that the old man's plans ran smoothly. Not while he'd yet to secure the inheritance the old man had promised.

There was one surefire way of guaranteeing that no clue left by Lawton could come back to haunt him. His lips curving slightly at his own wit, he continued to stride west. He passed several available hackneys, but decided he didn't want one—there was no need for any jarvey to remember a fare heading toward Cross Lane. Besides, it was too early yet, and he had preparations to make. By the time he had everything in hand and reached Cross Lane, the moon would have set, and the night would be dark enough, the street deserted enough, for his purpose.

SUNDAY, NOVEMBER 3, 1850

CHAPTER 40

*I*t was after midnight when Drake, with Louisa beside him, walked into Cross Lane. With the St. Ives House staff so very busy, rather than attempt to have Louisa's usual carriage brought around, he'd suggested they walk the short distance to the Wolverstone House mews and take his private carriage instead.

They'd left the carriage in the charge of his personal coachman-cum-groom, Henry, in Long Acre and had walked to the corner of Cross Lane.

Now, as they picked their way over the lane's uneven cobbles with Louisa leaning heavily on his arm, Drake was rethinking the wisdom of acquiescing to her accompanying him. Cross Lane ran north to Castle Street, and just a few blocks to the west, Castle Street led into the notorious slum of Seven Dials, a fact of which he was all too aware. The potential for dangerous misadventure had been high enough when they'd first come there in the small hours of Thursday morning. Although nothing had occurred on that occasion, to again escort her, dressed in her finery with a king's ransom in pearls dotted about her person, up the dark, narrow lane felt too much like tempting fate.

At least she was once again swathed in her voluminous velvet cloak; she'd put up the hood and was holding the dark folds tight about her, effectively concealing the shimmering silks of her dress. Even in the poor light, those layers of silk would have gleamed like a beacon of wealth and riches.

Tonight, there was no hint of fog, but the sky was heavy with cloud; there was little moonlight to pierce the gloom.

His senses at full stretch, he scanned the shadows. As luck would have it, while there were several groups of people at the far end, the stretch of the lane they had to cover appeared deserted. Despite his misgivings, they reached the door between the bakery and the stationer's shop without incident.

As before, the street door was unlocked. They climbed the stairs, him in the lead, with Louisa's hand locked in his, while with her other hand she managed her rustling skirts. On reaching the narrow landing at the top of the stairs, he wasn't entirely surprised to discover that the door to Chilburn's rooms had been locked.

Louisa had halted one step down from the landing. He glanced at her; in the dimness, he could barely make out her face. He released her hand. "Wait there."

Predictably, she humphed, but stayed where she was.

He reached into his greatcoat pocket and drew out the lock picks he rarely went anywhere without. Courtesy of the prevailing darkness, he took more than a minute to ease back the bolt. After returning the picks to his pocket, he opened the door, stepped inside, and halted with his body blocking Louisa's path, giving his senses time to stretch and search for any lurking danger.

There was none; he knew beyond question that the rooms lay empty. Smoothly, he walked forward, allowing her to follow him into the main room.

Louisa put back her hood and glanced around. The window overlooking the street had been left uncurtained, but tonight, very little light seeped in, and the room lay shrouded in shadow. Drake had gone to the sconce on the wall; she waited for him to light it.

The flame flared, then steadied; Drake reset the glass, then walked to the window and closed the thin curtains.

She shut the door to the landing, then studied the space.

What furniture there was hadn't been moved, yet the room looked quite different from when they'd last visited—a great deal more bare. A collection of boxes was stacked on and around the circular table.

She went to the boxes, lifted the flaps, and peered in. "Someone's packed Lawton's effects." She checked the contents of all the boxes. "His papers, cups, plates, clothes, blankets, sheets, and all." She glanced at Drake; he'd walked to the doorway of Lawton's bedroom. "I'm sure you're more expert in finding secret places. I'll search through what's been packed while you look for any hiding place where Lawton or

Badger might have concealed something helpful."

Drake turned from surveying Lawton's room. "This room's been cleared out. Badger's closet, however, doesn't appear to have been touched."

She crouched and opened one of the boxes on the floor. "I'll look in there once I've finished with these."

From the corner of her eye, she saw Drake scan the room, then he walked to the desk and started examining it, hunting for secret drawers.

She left him to it and concentrated on checking through the contents of the boxes. All those on the floor contained household goods and linens and nothing else. She rose and opened the first of the four boxes on the table. "Hmm—they've put all his papers in one box. Do you want to look at them again?"

"Can you see anything other than papers in there? Any little black book or notebook?"

She hunted through the box. "No. Nothing but loose papers. Nothing that looks like something we haven't already examined."

"No use, then. Leave them."

She was only too ready to do so. She moved on to the next box, which contained Lawton's shaving brush, shoes, and other odds and ends, all of which she deemed entirely uninteresting. The last two boxes contained Lawton's clothes.

Drake left the desk and moved toward the front of the room, examining the floorboards and skirting boards and the old wainscoting along the way, until he reached the window seat built against the wall below the window.

Louisa lifted out Lawton's greatcoat. She put her hands in the pockets, then felt the seams and even ran her hands over the lining, to no avail. Next, she lifted out his smallclothes and set them aside, then quickly checked through his shirts. She humphed and set them on the pile as well. "These are of very good quality. Hoskins and Sons."

"No one said Lawton didn't have good taste."

"Despite this place, he certainly seems to have preferred the finer things in life." She reached deeper into the box and lifted out two coats of superfine. She carefully checked the pockets, even the linings. Nothing. A tweed hacking jacket yielded the same result. Grimacing, she laid the coats aside and peered into the box. Two pairs of buckskin breeches and one of twill lay at the bottom. She hauled them out and dutifully searched the pockets. Nothing in the buckskins, but from a pocket in the twill breeches, her questing fingers drew out a piece of note-sized paper.

She dropped the breeches on the pile and eagerly smoothed out her find.

"What is it?" Crouched beside the window seat, Drake had looked her way.

She read, then frowned. "That's odd. This is an accounting from the Three Feathers posting inn in Reading. For a meal and ale."

"What's odd about that?"

"The date. October twenty-fourth. That was...the Thursday before last." She paused and raised her gaze, staring unseeing across the room as she rapidly reviewed the details in her memory. "Chilburn met with the three Chartist leaders on that Thursday evening, here, in town. And he was here on Wednesday afternoon to receive that message from the shifty-looking character, along with the keys to the warehouse. He was actively engaged with running the plot, and it was moving ahead—all here in London." She looked at the bill. "So what was so important in Reading that he left his doings here and traveled out there?"

When she glanced Drake's way, he met her eyes and nodded. "Good question. Keep it." He turned back to the window seat. "Let's see what else we can find."

She tucked the note into the tiny pearl-encrusted reticule that dangled from a gold chain looped over her wrist. There was nothing else to find in Lawton's clothes. She put them back in reasonable order, then shut the boxes.

Drake had moved on to the fireplace; on the wall opposite the door, it was located closer to the window than the rear of the room, facing the center of what had been Lawton's sitting area.

Louisa turned and went to the doorway to Lawton's bedroom. Bare walls, bare floor, bedstead with a lumpy old mattress. She walked to the chest of drawers, drew out the drawers and checked the undersides, and also looked to see if anything was affixed to the underside of the top, but there was nothing there. She raised the mattress; there was nothing hidden between it and the straps supporting it. After letting the mattress fall, she scanned the floor, including under the bed, but could see no sign of any loose board. If Lawton had had a hidey-hole, it seemed more likely to have been in the main room.

She walked back through the doorway. Drake was still testing the fireplace bricks. She turned to her right and went into the small, not to say tiny and cramped room Badger had made his domain.

As in Lawton's bedroom, there appeared to be no sign of a loose floorboard or skirting board or even a place in the wall that might conceal any secret place. She felt the pockets and lining of the suit hanging on the back of the door and patted the spare shirt and collar on the shelf and found nothing.

She considered the bed, a simple truckle-like affair. Unlike Lawton's bed, it hadn't been stripped. Seeing no reason not to, she gripped the sheet and thin blanket and drew them off the pallet. She bent and examined the pallet, but found no slits or inexplicable lumps, bumps, or bulges; she even turned the pallet over, but other than stains, there was nothing to be found. Just to be thorough, she stripped the flat pillow and examined that, too, but still found nothing.

She tossed the pillow back on the bed and was about to turn away when a sliver of black wedged between the head of the bedframe and the wall caught her eye. She leaned over the bed and angled her head. A small, thin, black-covered notebook was jammed between the wooden post at the head of the bed and the side wall.

Leaning on the bed, she reached for the notebook. The bed shifted, and the book slipped down, out of sight. "Damn!" She started to straighten, intending to pull the bed from the wall—

Smash. Crash. BANG!

An explosion flung her onto the bed.

Whoosh!

She gasped, and her breath stung. She coughed and rolled. She fetched up against the wall at the head of the bed and looked at the doorway.

At a sheet of roaring flames.

Then a figure—Drake with some garment flung over his head—rushed through the wall of fire.

His face a mask of resolution lit by the flames, he seized her arm and hauled her to her feet.

Drake realized he couldn't carry her out; the doorway was too narrow. He released her, grabbed the hood of her cloak, and drew it up over her head. "Hold your cloak closed." Thank God she'd kept it on; the heavy velvet folds would protect her delicate skin.

"But"—she turned toward the head of the bed—"there's something there, down in the corner. A notebook!"

"Forget it! We don't have time." The crude bomb had been hurled through the window. He'd looked up in time to see the bottle sail over the table and the boxes and crash against the rear wall of the main room. Instantly, flames had engulfed the wall and spread to block the doorway to Badger's tiny room. "Come on!" He managed to keep all panic from his voice, but they had only seconds to flee.

He caught her hand, but she tugged back. Wide-eyed, over the horrendous crackling, she yelled, "The book!"

"*It's not important!*" Not as important as her life—or his.

The roar of the flames was rising. Setting his jaw, he tightened his grip to unbreakable and yanked her behind him. "Hold on to your cloak!"

She almost stumbled, but he hauled her upright, and in an escalating rush, raced them out through the wall of flames.

They stumbled to a halt in the main room. Smoke was billowing and thickening; courtesy of their rush and their consequent need for breath, they both started coughing. Smoke stung their eyes. He swiped at his, then flung aside Chilburn's greatcoat that he'd seized and used to cover his head.

Smoke swirled around them.

Bent over, his hands on his knees, he swung to assess the fire. It had got a lot worse since he'd plunged through to reach Louisa. The flames were devouring the entire rear wall and were spreading onto the ceiling and licking over the floor. The building was all old wood and plaster; it would burn like a bonfire.

Louisa, too, turned and uttered a shocked gasp at the sight. Then she gave a choked squeal. "Oh God!"

He glanced at her, then followed her gaze down to where flames were licking at the hem of her silk gown.

Her velvet cloak had survived, but the fine silks had caught. Any second...

He was on her in a heartbeat. He flicked back her cloak, buried his fingers in the frothing layers of her fanciful skirt, gripped, and wrenched.

The skirts ripped and parted from the bodice.

Working feverishly, he gathered what he hoped was the entire mass and flung the resulting, already-merrily-burning bundle away. A tumbling clump of gauzy silks, still in midair a bare yard distant, with a soft, sibilant *whoosh*, the material went up literally in a ball of flame.

Horror-stricken, Louisa stared at the burning, blackening mass.

Shaken to his soul, he grabbed her and turned her, his eyes raking her petticoats to see if they'd caught, but they hadn't.

Around them, the heat and smoke were intensifying, inexorably eating the air.

"Come on!" He bundled her up in her cloak and, with his arm around her, propelled her to the door.

At the last minute, he remembered and left her for a second to turn off the gas.

Then he wrapped his arm around her, hauled open the door—and from behind him heard the sharper crackle as the fire fed on the fresh air. He thrust Louisa onto the landing, squeezed out beside her, and pulled the door shut.

"Let me go first." In case she fell—she was rubbing her eyes and coughing. He found her hand, gripped, and started down as fast as he dared in the enveloping dark.

The air grew less smoky the lower they went, but even in the stairwell, the heat was building.

He reached the tiny foyer before the outer door. He paused and half turned, and Louisa all but fell into his arms.

He clutched her tight, locked her against him; over the rush of the flames and the sharp cracking of burning wood, he heard the rapid flutter of her breaths, felt the harried patter of her heart against his chest.

He wasn't thinking clearly. He couldn't work out—couldn't even guess—if any further danger might be waiting for them outside.

But they had to get out.

He found the knob of the outer door, hauled it open, and clutching her protectively against him, his head bent over hers, plunged out into the street.

With long, swift strides, he carried her straight across the lane. An alley joined it a few yards closer to Long Acre; he swung into its mouth and paused. At full stretch, hyperalert, his senses informed him there was no one else close, that relatively speaking, they were safe. He forced himself to ease his hold and let her slide down until her slippers met the cobbles. He closed a hand about one of hers, and as one, they slumped against the alley wall, dragging in deep breaths of the clearer air. After several long moments, they both turned their heads and looked at the conflagration swallowing Lawton Chilburn's rooms.

A fire it might be, but it was a chilling sight.

Drake's blood was still thundering in his ears. He was breathing far too quickly, too harshly. There was smoke in his lungs, and his eyes stung like Hades. He'd faced several life-threatening situations over the course of the years; none—not one, and some had been even closer shaves—had affected him to this degree.

He'd never before known panic like this, arising from such a deep, fundamental, psyche-rocking fear.

All, it seemed, because it hadn't been only his life that had hung in the balance.

He looked at Louisa. She was gripping his hand as tightly as he was gripping hers. She stood beside him, close enough that he was aware of her very real presence—still vibrantly alive, still definitely there.

His breathing slowed. The sharp taste of panic faded.

She seemed unable to drag her gaze from the blaze.

Through the cloaking shadows, he studied her face, garishly lit by the dancing flames that had started to push through the broken window and poke fingers through the shingle roof. She was pale—paler than usual— her features stark in her white face. She was still breathing too rapidly, her breasts rising and falling beneath her cloak in a cadence he felt to his bones, yet despite the shock evident in her face, she was very far from panicking.

Something in him eased, calmed.

Her eyes remained fixed on the burning building.

He followed her gaze.

"A little black book was hidden between the bed and the wall," she

murmured, her voice low and smoke-roughened. "But now it's gone."
"That couldn't be helped." He hadn't been about to risk her in order to
secure it. "Laying hands on it wouldn't have done us any good if,
consequently, we'd died."

She gave a soft humph.

After a moment, he murmured, "I can hear the bells. Braidwood's boys
and their fire engines will be here soon." The frantic ringing drew nearer.
He bent his head and murmured more insistently, "We need to go."

She sighed. "Yes. We do."

Instead of going out and down Cross Lane, where any of the many
people pouring out of the surrounding buildings might see and note them,
he led her down the alley. It connected with another, and a few minutes
later, they stepped into Long Acre.

Henry and the carriage were drawn up closer to the corner of Cross
Lane. They turned, and with Louisa's arm in his and her holding her
cloak closed to conceal her white, lace-bedecked petticoats, they strolled
back to the carriage, just another couple innocently walking the street.

As they neared the carriage, a fire engine rattled up. It swung around
the carriage and turned up Cross Lane.

Henry watched it go, his face a mask of indecision.

Drake tapped on the side of the carriage.

Henry looked around, his face lighting with relief—abruptly subsumed
by consternation as he took in their state.

Drake could imagine; Louisa's face was soot-streaked, and he was
surely similarly bedaubed. He threw Henry a warning look and opened
the carriage door. "Home." He helped Louisa climb up, then remembered
what was going on in Grosvenor Square that night and clarified,
"Wolverstone House—straight to the mews."

"Aye, m'lord." Henry's crisp nod told Drake he'd made the right
decision. "Just sit back, and I'll have you there in no time."

Which, Drake assumed, as he joined Louisa in the carriage and
dropped to the comfort of the seat beside her, meant that Henry would
take the back roads and avoid the melee that doubtless was clogging the
square as carriages waited and others jostled to ferry guests away from
Sebastian and Antonia's ball; as such events ran, it would be hours yet
before the pandemonium ended.

The carriage pulled smoothly away from the curb. Drake didn't bother
tracking what route Henry chose. Instead, he allowed his mind to revisit
and reconstruct what must have occurred…

After several long moments, he glanced at Louisa and felt compelled to
state the obvious. "That was…very close."

She was apparently staring out at the passing façades. "Did they—
whoever threw that bomb or whatever it was into the room—know we

were there?"

One of the more critical questions. He noted that he wasn't even surprised that her mind had followed the same track as his. "I'd drawn the curtains, but the light was on. He—whoever he is—had to have known *someone* was there. Whether he knew it was us, specifically...he could only have known that if he'd been in the lane when we arrived, and I'm fairly certain there was no one lurking at that time."

After a moment, she asked, "Do you think they were still outside, watching, when we came out?"

Another important question. "I don't know." Before he'd been able to make any assessment, others had come tumbling out of the houses. "There were too many others about to even guess."

"Hmm." She said nothing more, but a moment later, he felt her search blindly for his hand.

He met her questing fingers with his, let her grip, then gently gripped in return.

Her hand remained in his, their fingers twined, as they rolled through the streets toward Mayfair.

CHAPTER 41

*G*riswade had, indeed, dallied in Cross Lane to verify the results of his handiwork.

Quite aside from ensuring that any remaining evidence linking Lawton to cither him or the old man had been converted to so much ash, he'd been interested in learning who had been searching Lawton's rooms, assuming, of course, that they made it outside.

After scanning the street and concluding it was empty, he'd lit the cloth wick he'd jammed into the neck of a bottle filled with a volatile mixture of lamp oil, spirit of turpentine, and pitch and thrown the bottle as hard as he could through the lighted window of Lawton's rooms. Then he'd ducked under the overhang protecting a shop door farther along the street and waited to see who came rushing out.

The flames had taken hold very nicely.

He'd held his position, lingering despite the danger of some neighbor of Lawton's spotting him and connecting him with the blaze.

His patience had been rewarded when a gentleman protectively carrying a lady wrapped in a velvet cloak, possibly thrown over a ball gown, had come racing out of the door to Lawton's rooms.

The man had rushed the lady across the street and out of Griswade's sight. He'd had only a fleeting instant in which to study the pair.

He had no idea who the lady was, only that she was a lady. Absolutely definitely—the gentleman's attitude to her had blazoned that fact on Griswade's brain. Protectiveness of that steely, ruthless, unbending variety only seen with such clarity in the upper ranks of the aristocracy had all but glowed through the shadows wreathing the lane.

Which made some degree of sense. Because even though the fire had been behind the fleeing couple and therefore the gentleman's face had been in shadow, Griswade had recognized him.

Ever a prudent man, even before the old man had recruited him, Griswade had deemed it wise to identify those few individuals men such as he—with birthrights that, judiciously used, would shield them from the more mundane authorities—had reason to fear.

The gentleman who had rushed out of Lawton's rooms with some aristocratic lady in his arms had featured as the one ranked above all others on the list of those whose notice Griswade would prefer to avoid.

Yet Winchelsea had been in Lawton's rooms, presumably searching.

Why he'd had the lady with him was anyone's guess. Although Winchelsea was renowned for his long string of paramours, Griswade couldn't imagine a man such as he mixing pleasure with business. With dangerous intrigue.

Unless he'd had no choice?

The fire engines arrived and set about their noisy business. Griswade clung to concealment while he toyed with the prospect of learning the lady's name and, perhaps, using her to somehow spike Winchelsea's guns, to distract or even pressure him into looking away...

Griswade's brain snapped back into focus, and he realized how farfetched that scenario was—how riddled with unforeseeable dangers.

Realized, too, that the sight of Winchelsea exiting Lawton's rooms had rattled him enough to derail his thoughts.

He couldn't afford that, especially not now.

Not now he was so close to securing the old man's estate.

Smoke was billowing thickly, and there were dozens of neighbors milling in the lane, providing cover enough for Griswade to slip out of his hiding place into the edges of the crowd and unobtrusively make his way up the lane.

Once he reached Castle Street, he set out for his own rooms, his own bed. And turned his mind to the now-burning question of whether, even at this late stage, he should cut and run. Or whether he should hold his nerve and usher the old man's plans to their undeniably attention-grabbing end.

Step by step, he went over the old man's plans yet again. He reached the end and could see no real justification for balking.

When the gunpowder went up, he wouldn't be there.

As for the old man, he wasn't even in London.

And by that time, there would be no one left to point the finger at either of them.

Winchelsea might be on his trail—might have started unraveling the threads of the plot—but that was really all his appearance in Lawton's rooms suggested.

What had the old man said?

On cue, his mind supplied the old man's raspy, almost-quavering voice intoning: *On no account, no matter what happens, deviate from the plan. There may be slips—matters you can't control. Don't panic. Simply proceed, step by small step, and follow my directions to the end... and all will be well.*

The old man had played in these leagues far longer than Griswade had. Without doubt, he could rely on the old man's advice. Indeed, he had no reason to do otherwise.

Reassured, he strode on. He could and would steer the plot to its stunning climax, and he would walk away untouched and, even more importantly, undetected and unsuspected.

And once the old man's estate was legally settled on him, he would make sure he inherited in short order. Then he'd take a trip— perhaps to the Americas. A land big enough to get lost in.

With every step, he felt more confident, more assured.

As he turned into the Strand, he reminded himself that Winchelsea had no idea who he was.

And given how far along their path they'd already gone, it was as close to impossible as made no odds that Winchelsea would ever find out, and certainly, not in time.

CHAPTER 42

*L*ouisa remained silent as Drake helped her down from the carriage in the mews behind Wolverstone House. Still compulsively clutching his hand, she walked by his side up the shadowed walk from the rear gate to the side door and didn't even ask why he'd brought her there.

He presumed she understood that with the ball still in full swing at St. Ives House, neither of them was in any state to attempt to smuggle her inside and to her room. Even trusting to the Cynster staff's discretion and using the servants' stairs was, in the circumstances, an unacceptable risk; it would need just one nosy guest to glimpse either of them in such disreputable state, and the news would be all over the ton come lunchtime.

At this hour, the side door was locked, but he had the key on his chain. The door opened into his mother's morning room; after unlocking it, he ushered Louisa in, followed her, then shut the door and relocked it.

She waited beside him without a word.

Retaking her hand, he guided her past the chaises and chairs to the door.

A secondary set of stairs was his favored route to his apartment. With all his family in residence, but thankfully presently several doors away at the Cynster ball, Hamilton would be awake and in the kitchen, awaiting their return. Finnegan, too, would be up and dressed, but he knew better than to present himself unless Drake rang for him.

Not even Drake had managed to fathom how Hamilton always seemed to know the instant any of the family set foot on the tiles of the front hall, no matter how quietly they crept in. Personally, Drake suspected Hamilton had rigged some sort of alarm to the front door, one he, his father, and his brothers had never been able to discover.

Luckily, Hamilton never showed up when Drake used his alternative route. His hand locked about Louisa's, he led her up to the first floor, inwardly debating whether Hamilton's absence was due to the lack of an alarm on the side door or...

His mind was rambling. After the shock, now that the demands of the moment—of dealing with getting them there, removing her to a place of assured safety—were past, the inevitable impact of the night's terror was making itself felt and doing a passable job of scrambling his usually reliable faculties.

He was accustomed to dealing with shock. He knew the best—the fastest—way to absorb and move past it was to simply let it roll through him as it would.

In that respect, Louisa lacked his experience. He assumed that was why she hadn't uttered a word for so very long; for her, ten minutes was close to infinity.

He had to admit that when she was silent, he noticed her—focused on her—more intently. In his experience, her being silent usually indicated she was plotting something, and therefore at those times, she was at her most dangerous.

Except, of course, if her speechlessness was due to shock.

His mind was still rambling.

They reached the suite of rooms that was his; at the end of one wing, his bedroom overlooked the gardens at the rear of the house. He opened the door and, finally drawing his fingers from hers, guided her through, then followed.

Putting back her hood, she walked in a little way, then presumably realizing that large though it was, the chamber was his bedroom, she turned to face him. The gaslights on the wall had been left turned low. In the soft light, he could see her face.

Could have easily read her expression had there been anything he understood in it.

She studied him for a moment, then sighed. "I'm...annoyed that we had to leave that little black notebook behind. Who knows what clues it contained?"

That was what she'd spent the past half hour and more dwelling on?

He froze for a second, then he pushed the door closed and walked, slowly, toward her. He knew she wouldn't shift, wouldn't take a step back. He stopped with less than a foot between them, ensuring she had to tip up her face to meet his eyes.

And that she could see them.

Her eyes had widened fractionally, but she met his gaze without any evidence of nervousness—even of awareness...

His brain felt overheated. "When I saw the bomb hit that wall and the flames spring up, cutting you off, trapping you in that room..." His tone was equable, even gentle, giving no hint of the turmoil raging inside him. "Do you know what I felt?"

She opened her eyes slightly wider, wordlessly inviting him to tell her. She knew perfectly well he intended to regardless.

"I would have predicted," he continued, his eyes locked with hers, "that I would feel battered by myriad emotions, but the truly curious thing was that there was only one. One compulsive feeling. A need to get you out of there safely—it threw every other thought, feeling, emotion, or need out of my head."

His voice hardening, he stated, "That single feeling trumped everything." Fractionally, he shook his head. "Nothing else mattered. The black book didn't matter. The mission didn't matter. The realm—even my honor—didn't matter when measured against that. When measured against you."

He paused, then more evenly reiterated, "In that moment, nothing was more important than getting you to safety."

Peridot eyes wide, she stared at him as if, for once, she saw him clearly, without any screens, any shields, without any sophisticated veil to mute his personality.

Several heartbeats passed, then she simply said, "Oh."

"Oh, indeed." His tone said it all—all he'd given up trying to hide. He'd already faced their reality. Now she could face it, too.

He stared into her eyes as they stood there, all but toe to toe in the soft gaslight, and as he'd expected, he saw not one iota of a suggestion that she was rethinking her—now their—direction.

Good.

He forced himself to turn and walk to the door to the adjoining bathroom. "We're soot-streaked, bedraggled, and we reek of smoke." He hadn't realized how dreadful they looked until he'd seen her in better light and had caught a glimpse of himself in the mirror over the mantelpiece; small wonder Henry had looked appalled. "We'll both need to bathe before I can take you home."

She followed him and, crossing her arms, leaned against the doorframe, watching as he turned up the lights, then set the gas burner on the big copper boiler roaring. He gave silent thanks for the plumbing his mother had insisted be installed; at least they could bathe without involving half the staff fetching and carrying water up the stairs.

He dropped the plug in the bathtub, then set the taps running. Water gushed, and steam rose.

He waved her to the tub. "Soap, towels. There's a bathrobe there, too. While you're bathing, I'll get Finnegan to fetch one of my sister's gowns."

She studied his face for several seconds, then straightened and pulled the ties of her cloak undone.

He moved to take the heavy, scorched, and smoke-drenched garment from her.

She half turned, allowing him to lift the cloak from her shoulders. "I doubt it's salvageable, but if someone could bundle it up, I'll take it home and let my maid decide what to do with it."

He nodded and carried it into the bedroom.

He laid the cloak on a chair against the wall. When he turned, she'd come back into the bedroom and was walking to the other side of the massive four-poster bed.

Across the rich, old-gold silk tapestry that covered the expanse, he watched as she unhooked the pearl drops from her ears and laid them on the small table beside the head of the bed.

"I'd better leave my pearls here. I don't want any swirling down the drain."

Instead of watching her unwind the long string from about her throat, he walked to the bellpull hanging beside the fireplace and tugged. Then he moved to the door.

Less than a minute later, Finnegan's rap fell on the panel.

Drake had already grasped the doorknob, preventing the Irishman from flinging open the door and theatrically waltzing in, as was his wont.

But when Drake opened the door, using his body to block Finnegan's view of the room, he saw Finnegan, his expression attentive and spuriously innocent, standing back a good yard from the door.

To have arrived so quickly, Finnegan had to have been on the first floor when Drake rang the bell; there was a maid's station at the top of the stairs in which the bells rang, as well as ringing on the main board in the servants' hall.

Finnegan had, of course, been tipped off by Henry, with whom Finnegan worked hand in glove, that Drake had returned with a lady— with Lady Louisa Cynster—in tow.

So Finnegan, being the very shrewd servitor he was, was on his best behavior.

Henry knew, and Finnegan knew, that Louisa was in Drake's bedroom. Drake decided he didn't need to do anything about that; he would—

and frequently had—trusted both men with his life.

He met Finnegan's innocent gaze with a very direct look. "Go to Meredith's room and fetch one of her walking dresses. One of the gray ones. Do not ask her maid or anyone else for permission."

Meredith was his oldest sister and most similar in height and build to Louisa. Unfortunately, there the similarity ended; their coloring and style were very different, and no evening gown of Meredith's would do for Louisa. But a walking gown in one of Merry's favorite grays would do for a short time.

Finnegan couldn't resist. He blinked owlishly. "You want one of Lady Meredith's gowns?"

"Yes."

"It won't fit you."

Drake narrowed his eyes and lowered his voice to the gentle tone that to those who knew him screamed a warning. "I know. Just fetch it."

Struggling to hide his grin, Finnegan saluted. "Yes, my lord."

Drake shut the door in Finnegan's face.

He turned to find Louisa, in her petticoats and what remained of her gown—just the bodice—ambling around the room, apparently idly studying this and that.

He—his nerves, his senses, and his emotions—had had enough.

He glanced into the bathroom and judged by the steam that the deep bath was half full. Enough for her to sit in while it continued filling.

She'd stopped by the wide window and was peering out, into the dark of the garden below. Jaw firming, he strode across the room. He'd intended to capture her hand and tow her to the bathroom, but she turned as he reached her.

Her expression serene and untroubled, she pointed to the back of her head. "There should be three more pearls, but I can't find them. Can you?"

She turned and gave him her back.

The three pearls were easy to see even in the low light; surrounded by the dark mass of her black hair, they glowed with an unearthly radiance—highly reminiscent of her skin.

He gritted his teeth and plucked the pins free, shaking each loose from the clinging tendrils of her hair. The curls brushed his fingertips, silky soft and curiously warm, and he couldn't stop his mind from leaping to the image of her hair brushing over his naked skin, his naked—

Ruthlessly, he dragged in a breath and shut off such thoughts. With her there, in this setting where she really shouldn't be, he didn't need the extra aggravation.

"Here." He offered her the pins on his palm.

She picked them up, then walked—glided with her customary almost-floating gait—to the bedside table and added the three to the small mound of her jewels.

Then she swept back to him. Her eyes on his, as she drew closer she murmured, "The bath must almost be ready." She halted before him, swung around, and presented him with her back. "You'll need to undo the buttons. I can't reach."

He stared at the row of tiny buttons that ran down her spine from below her shoulder blades to just below her waist. She could probably reach them if she tried, but not easily. He clenched his jaw and set his fingers to the task.

He couldn't count the number of times he'd performed the same office for some other lady, yet for some unfathomable reason, with her...

Gritting his teeth harder didn't lessen the impact.

Only when the last button slid free did he realize the inevitable result. The bodice had no sleeves.

No longer anchored about her, the bodice slithered free...with a practiced movement, she caught it in one hand.

"Thank you," she murmured, in that sultry tone that told him very clearly where her thoughts were roaming.

Then she glanced over her shoulder, met his eyes for a heartbeat, then her lips curved slightly and she looked forward and walked—slowly— away from him.

She swung the ruined bodice from her hand. As she neared the bathroom door, with a flick of her wrist, she sent the bodice flying to land on the chair with her cloak.

Drake barely noticed. His gaze had fixed on the delicate bones of her shoulders and upper back revealed above the low line of her corset's back. Fascinated by the play of light over those sleek curves, he couldn't drag his eyes away. By the time he did, she'd reached the bathroom door. There, she paused and looked back at him. All but purred, "I won't be long."

Then she went into the bathroom and shut the door.

Leaving him debating whether or not he was glad she wore corsets that laced up the front.

A knock on the main door dragged him from Louisa-induced distraction.

He crossed to the door, opened it, and found Finnegan with a gray gown draped across his arms.

"Best I could do." Finnegan handed the gown over. "It has some green in it."

Drake grunted. "Thank you."

Finnegan reverted to his innocent look. "Will you need me to assist you to bed, my lord?"

Drake just looked at him, then closed the door.

In the spacious bathroom, Louisa sank into the water with a sigh. For long moments, she focused on what she was there to do, lathering and rinsing her hair, then picking up a sponge and setting to work cleansing her body, uncaring that Drake's shampoo and soaps carried the distinctly masculine scent of sandalwood.

Yet as the soot sloughed from her skin, she grew aware of a burgeoning feeling that she was shedding other elements, too—not her past, for that was an intrinsic part of her, but certainly past beliefs. Past restrictions, inherent restraints that, even as Lady Wild, she'd accepted and obeyed.

No longer.

That moment when, lying on the bed in that tiny room, she'd looked back and seen a wall of flames cutting her off from both past and future was etched in her mind, never to be lost or erased. Then Drake had burst through the fiery screen, intent on rescuing her.

Whatever the cost.

She'd seen the raging flames, had felt their hunger and violent heat. She couldn't quite imagine the steely resolve one would have to have, viewing that wall from the other—the safe—side, to race through it into life-threatening danger.

Yet without hesitation, Drake had come for her.

And the declaration her bemoaning the loss of the black book had provoked had set the seal on his direction. For a man like him to so determinedly and deliberately set her above his honor? More, for him to tell her so? His words had communicated all she needed to know regarding his decision about her, about them.

Nothing could have been clearer.

She rose from the water, wrung out her long hair, bent and released the plug, then stepped out of the bath. The towels were fresh and soft. She rubbed her hair, then wrapped a towel turban-like around her head. Using another towel to dry her skin, she stared into the bath, watching the soot circle the drain, then vanish.

She reached for the cold-water tap, turned it on, and sluiced the last remnants of soot down the hole.

Gone. Just as her reserve regarding him, regarding them and their future, was gone.

Washed away by the events of the night.

A piece of advice her grandmother had once offered her echoed in her mind. *In order to make a dream into a reality, you have to reach for it— with your hands, with your heart, with all you have in you.*

Active, unquestioning, unconditional commitment. That was what a wealth of experience had stated was needed, and that was what she would give.

It was time to convert her most precious dream into a reality.

CHAPTER 43

*D*rake sat on the end of his large four-poster bed, with Merry's dress spread on the counterpane beside him, his gaze fixed on the bathroom door and his mind…circling, wanting to dwell on what was happening behind the door, if only he would let it.

He was determined not to—to keep his wits his own, under his control. He still had to get Louisa home.

Then he heard her approach the door, saw the knob turn, then the door opened, and he had to fight to keep all reaction from his face. He couldn't stop his eyes from devouring the mesmerizing, enticing, delectable sight of her. Even though she was engulfed in the folds of his bathrobe—more of her would have been visible had she been wearing a ball gown—the flush on her skin, the alluring promise of warm limbs and curves, the way the turban pulling her hair high revealed the sculpted lines of her jaw and cheekbones and drew attention to the upward tilt of her large eyes, all combined to make him itch with the desire to unwrap her.

Like a present.

One he was due.

But not tonight. They still had a mission to complete.

Later. He promised himself that. And when the time came, he was certain she wouldn't argue.

She moved diagonally across the space between them.

He rose from the bed and waved at the gray walking dress. "Merry's dress."

She glanced at the gray gown and regally inclined her turbaned head. "Thank you."

He finally registered her expression—untrammeled and serene. She halted in the middle of the room and swung to survey the fire. Then she turned her head and arched a brow at him. "I'll need to dry my hair."

Without a word, he crossed to the fireplace. The fire was already burning nicely; it was the work of a few minutes to stoke it into a roaring blaze.

He rose and was about to turn toward her when he sensed her drawing near. He—everything in him—stilled, then he felt her hand on his upper arm.

"Thank you." Gently, she pushed him toward the bathroom. "Now go and get clean."

He dropped an iron gate in the path of the impulses her being so close provoked, then turned and went.

Louisa watched him go; after the bathroom door had closed behind him, she allowed a slow smile to curve her lips. Even with the fire, her hair wouldn't dry enough to allow her to put it up; while damp, the mass was simply too heavy. And she certainly couldn't risk being seen slipping into her home with her hair down—she glanced at the clock—not at two o'clock in the morning, at any rate.

Not that it mattered; she wasn't going home any time soon.

After unwinding the towel from about her head, she knelt before the blazing fire and, with her hair over her head, drew her fingers through the heavy strands, holding them out to the warmth.

While the heat from the flames took the worst of the dampness from her hair, she weighed and considered how best to return the gauntlet Drake had flung at her feet in the wake of Lady Cottlesloe's ball.

CHAPTER 44

*D*rake rushed through his ablutions. The instant he was dry, he reached for his robe and remembered Louisa had taken it.

He glanced at the pile of his discarded clothes—unwearable even for a minute—and that was when he noticed hers.

Her petticoats, her corset, and a pair of fine lace-trimmed drawers were neatly draped over a low stool in one corner.

If her underthings were there, what was she wearing at that moment?

His mind supplied the most likely answer, but he refused to accept it—to leap to that conclusion—not until he'd seen the evidence.

The question of: She wouldn't, would she? had only one answer.

With no alternative offering, he wound a towel around his hips, gave his thick hair one last, vigorous rub, then he opened the door and stepped into his bedroom.

He halted just over the threshold.

She'd doused the lights. The room was lit only by the rosy glow of the fire and the moonlight slanting in through the uncurtained windows. Yet even in the dimness, he could make out Merry's dress laid over the back of one of the armchairs before the fireplace.

Visually, he quartered the large room, but couldn't see Louisa.

Face setting, he approached the side of the bed—the side he slept on, nearer the door.

Only when he drew close could he see—confirm—that the other side of the heavily shadowed bed was occupied.

She lay beneath the covers, her head on the pillow, her black hair spread above and around her face, a veil negligently fanned over the ivory pillowcase.

She'd warned him—had it been only five days ago?—that she would find her way there. Even then, he'd known she'd meant it, that her bold statement hadn't been empty words.

She lay on her side, facing his way. She appeared to have fallen asleep. Through the shadows wreathing the bed, he could hear her soft breaths and track the gentle rise and fall of her breasts screened by the silk of his sheets.

One arm lay over the covers, her bare shoulder a testament to what she was wearing.

To what he would find if he joined her between the sheets.

He stood beside the bed and stared at her.

At his destiny.

He could leave his bed to her and sleep in one of the guest chambers, but was he really such a coward that he would run from this challenge? He who thrived on challenge.

He'd long ago learned that attempting to outwit Fate never worked. If he tried to be clever, to manipulate matters and direct them rather than simply accepting Fate's decrees, invariably, ultimately, Fate would outwit him.

For him, to him, Louisa had ever been Fate's queen.

He'd decided that they should wait until the mission was ended, until all was done and squared away, and he—and she—could focus on what even he accepted was written in their stars.

Obviously, Fate—and Louisa—thought differently.

He stood there, all but swaying as he grappled with the twin urges of his kind—the unbending need to be in control, to dictate his own path at least, and the even more primitive need to seize what she, by her very actions, was transparently offering.

In the end, he accepted the inevitable. Who was he to argue with Fate—much less Louisa?

He loosened the towel and let it fall to the floor, raised the covers, and joined her in his bed.

She stirred, murmured, but didn't wake.

He settled beside her. Propped on one elbow, he studied her face—her expression more serene than ever in repose—then he raised his hand, cupped her jaw, bent his head, and proceeded to kiss her awake.

She responded, her lips softening, then moving beneath his.

Then she came alive on a soft murmur, and her body shifted beneath the sheets, seeking his.

Louisa's palms and fingers met hard muscle, warm and tempting skin. She raised her lids enough to assure herself of the reality—that he was truly there, in the bed alongside her. Sliding her arms up, over his shoulders, her lips curving under his, between one slow, drugging kiss and the next, she murmured, "About time."

Those two words encapsulated their past—a past they were clearly about to leave behind.

When next their lips parted, he murmured back, "I can think of far better uses of our mouths than to swap witticisms."

She laughed, husky and low. From beneath her lashes, she let her eyes meet his, glowing golden beneath heavy lids. "So can I."

She might be innocent experience-wise, but she'd heard enough, imagined enough…she thought she had some idea.

What followed opened her eyes.

He was ruthless in denying her the reins. Every time she thought to press him, every time she tried to take charge, he deflected her, distracted her, with some new and even more intense sensation.

She'd thought she'd known what his kisses were like, but the evocative, provocative fashion in which he explored her mouth, like a conqueror taking ownership of surrendered lands, was something else again. Something that drew her further, deeper into the exchange, that anchored her in the kiss and awoke some primitive instinct within her that sent shivers of anticipation coursing through her.

His chest, the breadth and extent of it, the heavy bones of his shoulders, and the thick muscles sheathing them were familiar, yet being able to savor his naked skin, to feel the heat burning beneath her sliding palms, to run her fingertips through the dark crinkly hair that adorned the wide muscle bands, to be able to trace each steely band—all that was a supreme distraction in and of itself.

And then there was the weight of him—the sheer physical impact of his powerful body as he lay alongside her. The inherent promise of it—of the heaviness, the hardness, and the potent strength every feminine wit she possessed told her lay within that body, his to command.

A fold of the silk sheet lay between them, yet as his tongue lazily, almost languidly tangled with hers—as if claiming her mouth was his right—even though he held his weight above her, she still felt the ineluctable effect of his nearness pressing against her senses, an enticing flame licking over her from head to toe.

Then he pushed the sheet aside and closed one hand about her breast, fingers firm and knowing, kneading and dragging her senses and wits to focus there—just as his fingers closed and tightened about her nipple. On a smothered gasp, she arched. Rising, her body connected with his. Inspired, she turned the movement into a long, sinuous caress—and was rewarded with his sudden hiss of awareness.

At last! One point to her.

Inevitably, he reacted. Retaliated.

Between one heartbeat and the next, the kiss turned incendiary, and then the sheet between them was completely gone, and he let his body down atop hers—and she lost contact with the world.

Lost all awareness of anything beyond his body, hers, and the sudden tumult of her senses. Called forth by the intimate contact, the undeniable, almost brutally clear statement of intent, desire and passion surged in a maelstrom of hunger and giddy, demanding need.

That need overwhelmed her. Every nerve she possessed sprang to attention. Her wits fractured, fragmented as her mind raced here, there, greedily seeking to absorb and savor every single point of contact—every touch, every pressure, every feel of his skin against hers.

Throughout, the kiss—now a ravaging, plundering, senses-scaring engagement—raged.

Drawn from him and her both, consuming passion swelled and surged, and compulsive need sank claws deep into her—and given his suddenly ragged breathing, into him, too—and drove them on.

Drake fought to slow down, to harness the sudden rush of desire and rein them both in, the better to savor, the better to experience…this. Her first time.

And, in some strange way, his.

His with her—which even in this early phase of the engagement, his senses saw as different. As special. As one engagement it was imperative he draw out and experience fully. In every little degree.

Yet the allure of her body, naked and so tempting, cushioned by the mattress beneath his, with her sumptuous breasts pressed to his chest and her long, slender legs tangling with his, called to the essential conqueror in him.

But this wasn't a time to simply seize.

He wanted more than a simple surrender.

From her, he wanted…so much more. A "more" he couldn't even define.

Yet the battle with his own impulses, the effort to corral them, had never been so fraught.

And she, with her greedy, grasping, hot little hands searching and sliding over all of him she could reach wasn't helping in the least.

In a move that reeked of desperation, he broke from the kiss and sent his lips cruising across her jaw, then down the long, arching line of her neck. He found the pulse hammering at the base of her throat, laved, then suckled.

Her hands gripped his upper arms, fingertips sinking in as she fought for breath, her body bowing, pressing up against his in instinctive invitation.

Before the inevitable effect, the compulsion to respond, could seize him, he moved on, skating across and down, leaving a trail of hot, open-mouthed kisses across her upper chest to where one plump, pert, tightly furled nipple begged for his attention. He obliged, licking, laving, then drawing the tight bud deep and suckling.

Her only partially smothered shriek was music to his ears. That sound and her suddenly harried breathing egged him on, and he settled to feast.

Louisa couldn't find her feet. Not in the real world, not even in her mind. Passion and need had swept her from her moorings, and the continuing bombardment of sensations commanded every iota of her awareness. All she knew was the escalating heat, a burning compulsion that made her yearn to fling herself headlong into the flames and be consumed. All her mind could focus on was the tug of his mouth, the sensation hot and searing, and the spike of sharp feeling every tug sent lancing through her, somehow evocatively tightening her core. Stoking the building tension.

His free hand lay heavy about her other breast, strong fingers kneading, provocatively possessing...

Possession. The word surfaced from the cauldron of feelings and impulses whirling in her brain, and in a flash of lucidity, she recognized that truth. But as an act, possession worked both ways.

The insight allowed her to catch her mental breath, to realize and respond—not against him, not to counter him, but to join him.

To align her passion, her desire, with his.

Her awareness expanded, taking in his heavy limbs, the weight of his torso pinning her to the sheet. She set her hands exploring again, absorbing and drinking in the reactive quiver of his muscles at her touch.

Emboldened, she stroked up the long length of his sides, then slid her palms down to his waist and the tops of his hips, then across his back, reaching as far as she could to hold, to own, to embrace.

Drake shuddered, trapped by that simple, almost-innocent caress. Caught by a need to metaphorically lean into her touch, to accept it.

But the fire between them wasn't about to fade; stoked by her blatant encouragement, it roared.

As her hands moved over his skin, need flared anew; set alight, more forceful, it drove him to slide lower in the bed. Gripped by a compulsion laced with wonder, he reared back enough to trace—first with his eyes, now accustomed to the dimness, then with his palms and fingers—the unutterably feminine lines of her breasts and lower ribs, the indentation of her waist, the slight curve of her belly and the triangle of black curls screening her mons, over the evocative shape of her hips, moving ultimately to caress the long, firm, yet femininely yielding expanse of her thighs.

He reached further still, circling her knee, then sliding his palm along the back of her calf to her ankle. He reversed the caress, returning to grasp her knee and move it up, out.

Then he shifted, anchoring her raised knee with his shoulder while he repeated the slow, almost-mesmerizing caress on her other leg, before lifting that knee up and outward, too.

One glance at her face showed her lashes low, her expression not blank but turned inward, her senses holding her mind captive as they followed his touch, absorbing the sensations.

Before she could regather her wits enough to think, he settled between her now-widespread legs, bent his head, and set his mouth to her softness. To sup and taste the ambrosia he knew he would find pooling there.

The shock that jolted through her, the way her hands frantically clutched at his hair, at his head, the convulsive viselike clamp of her thighs against his shoulders, both reassured and drove him on.

Louisa couldn't breathe. Her eyes had snapped open in shock, but she saw nothing. Couldn't focus enough to see...

Then she hauled in a breath on a panting gasp; shallow pants were all she could manage as her senses swam.

As he licked and savored...

Good Lord! She'd heard of this, but the knowledge hadn't prepared her for the reality. For the indescribable sensations as he fed upon her softness. Then the tip of his tongue found the tight nubbin of nerves hidden among her folds and swirled...

She shrieked. Her body bowed, her head tipping back in instinctive reaction as her fingers compulsively clutched.

He moved, shifting up the bed, then he cupped her with his palm, touched her with his fingers, and her senses overloaded.

Drake stroked through the delicate folds, swollen and slick with the honey-like moisture his ministrations had drawn forth. Resting his weight on one shoulder, he leaned over her and, as she drew breath after a sobbing moan, captured her lips again, claimed her mouth again, and ruthlessly waltzed her into passion's fire.

In this realm, he was a recognized expert, while she...might be a novice, but even in that moment, he accepted and savored the prospect of her being a very willing and apt pupil.

As if confirming that, her hands gripped his head and held him to the kiss as, with her lips and tongue, she did her damnedest to match and challenge him.

Her damnedest was impressive. Even with his fingers dallying at her entrance, she caught his attention and held it for several seconds.

But the thrum of desire pounding through his veins wasn't to be denied.

The scalding slickness bathing his fingertips drew him back to the overriding urgency, to the compulsive need swelling between them. He stroked, then slid his fingers farther, pressed one slowly in, and reached deep.

Through their ravenous kiss, she made an incoherent sound; instead of pulling back, she pressed into him and all but wrapped her limbs about him.

No order could have been clearer. With the part of his brain that still functioned informing him just how tight she was, he held to his reins, withdrew that first questing finger, and slowly but forcefully inserted two.

She was all heat and urgency as he stretched her, readied her, her hands gripping, tugging, wordlessly inciting.

When, still clinging to control with something close to desperation, he withdrew his hand from between her thighs and shifted to cover her, rising above her on braced arms, she sank her nails into his upper arms, then lifted under him, wriggling her hips, widening her thighs, and wrapping her long legs about his.

The movement dragged her scalding wetness over the painfully engorged head of his erection.

Passion surged, more violent and powerful than he'd ever known it; it raced through him in a boiling, devastating wave, washing his intentions, his will, and his wits away.

His reins snapped and whirled away in the tumult.

Unleashed, ungoverned, and driven by instinct to answer her primitively evocative call, he pressed in, then with one powerful thrust, he forged into her sheath and filled her.

Her half-swallowed shriek left her gasping.

He only just managed to stop himself from immediately plundering. Only just caught the flickering ends of control and managed to force himself to freeze, to hang his head and breathe through the impulses battering him and hold still within the scorching clutch of her sheath long enough to let her catch her breath.

To let her join him.

With her eyes closed and her lips parted, in that moment of fractured reality, Louisa had nothing but what she could feel, what she could hear, to anchor her. As she lay wrapped in the shrouding shadows of the bed, the only sounds that came to her ears were her short, rasping breaths and his deeper, harsher ones.

What she could feel...all but consumed her mind.
She now understood why they termed this intimacy. She couldn't imagine any act more so. The feel of his erection, hard, hot, and rigid, buried inside her, stretching and filling her and reaching so high within her, shook her to her core, yet...

There was something more there—something more to feel, to know. Something else.

A nebulous something hovering just out of reach, as if tempting them to try for it. To seize it and hold it and claim it as theirs.

On the thought, she felt her inner muscles—muscles that had convulsively contracted at his invasion—start to ease.

A second later, almost tentatively, he moved, withdrawing just a little before surging back, but more gently this time.

She discovered she could breathe again, albeit shallowly. She forced her lids to obey her and opened her eyes.

He was hanging over her, suspended on braced arms, the muscles of which, under her now lax hands, felt like granite; she had to tip her head back to see his face.

She met his eyes, slivers of beaten gold showing between his dark lashes. His jaw was clenched, every feature locked in what even she recognized as a passion-etched mask.

He held her gaze and said nothing, simply moved again, that same gentle rocking that in some strange way seemed to call to her.

The next time he did it, lost in his eyes, in his golden gaze, she mirrored the movement, rocking against him as he thrust in, then prompted by instinct, she tightened her inner muscles and held him, clung as he slowly—very slowly—withdrew. The sensation felt exquisite.

He shuddered and closed his eyes.

And held still for a heartbeat, the tip of his erection just within her entrance, then he thrust in again.

More forcefully this time, but as sensation rolled through her and pleasure bloomed, she only gasped and, with her hands, with her newly awoken body, wordlessly urged him on.

Once again, theoretical knowledge was eclipsed by reality. Pleasure welled, swelled, and wrapped her in its heat; passion and desire ran alongside, rising simultaneously, pricking and driving, investing them both with a building urgency, a swelling need that compelled them into a plunging, pounding rhythm of thrust and retreat.

Of meeting and matching and reaching and racing.

The force, the power, of their desperate joining should have shocked her, at the very least given her pause, but instead, she reveled in the potency, the intensity, the escalating, excruciatingly demanding compulsion as together they strove to seize that elusive prize that yet hovered beyond their reach.

Tension gripped her, tightening with every thrust, with every thudding beat of her heart.

They raced on. And that tension ratcheted tighter. Tighter.

They climbed, pushed on—higher, farther. She reached. Stretched...

Abruptly, the tension fractured into a million shards of brilliant, scintillating sensation that streaked down her every nerve and frazzled what remained of her senses. A wave of reaction caught her, swept her up, and once again, sensation soared.

He held her there. Together, for one finite instant, they quivered on the pinnacle of ecstasy, then they fell.

She shattered, broke apart, her mind overwhelmed by pleasure beyond her wildest imaginings even as she sensed his own release take him.

Head tipping back, he went rigid above her. Deep inside, in the heated cavern of her womb, she felt the fierce spurt of his seed. Her limbs were too weak to cling, but when he collapsed upon her, she wrapped her arms about him and cradled him.

As oblivion reared and rolled over them.

An irresistible tide, it swelled to engulf them. A sea of golden calm, the aftermath of pure, incandescent pleasure, it claimed them both.

Buoyed on the soothing waves, sated and reassured, they lay together and let slumber have them.

CHAPTER 45

$\mathcal{D}$rake woke before dawn. Regretfully rejecting the numerous alternatives his overactive libido suggested, he forced himself to carefully ease free of Louisa's clinging warmth. Leaving her sleeping, he rose, found the robe she'd discarded and shrugged into it, then he crossed the room, turned up the gaslight above the desk in one corner, sat, and wrote a letter to her father.

It was without question the trickiest letter he'd ever had to write. Explaining to a duke—one who happened to be a close friend of his own father—why said duke's only daughter wasn't, as that duke had every right to suppose, innocently asleep in her own bed but instead sprawled bonelessly in his, wasn't a communication that could be dashed off.

Claiming the right to keep her, now she was where she was, didn't require quite so much erudition.

Once the letter was completed, signed, and sealed, he penned notes to Sebastian and Michael. That done, Drake paused, thought, then quickly scrawled two separate notes to Antonia and Cleo. The four notes had required little thought, merely calling for a meeting over breakfast downstairs.

He rose from the desk and turned out the light.

With all five missives in hand, he checked on Louisa and found her still sound asleep. He stood looking down at her for several minutes, drinking in a sight he doubted he would ever get tired of—asleep and with the warmth of satiation still tinting her skin, she looked like a well-pleasured angel. Finally, he stirred, crossed to the bellpull and tugged it, then headed for the door.

The household had started stirring some time before; maids and footmen were crisscrossing the front hall.

Drake met Finnegan, dressed but still rubbing sleep from his eyes, in the gallery at the top of the stairs. After handing over the five letters and instructing Finnegan to arrange immediate delivery, Drake headed for his parents' apartment.

The clocks around the house were striking seven when he tapped gently on his parents' door.

He didn't have to wait long. Wrapped in a dressing gown much like the one he wore, his father joined him in the corridor, gently closing the door behind him.

His father rarely missed an implication. He met Drake's eyes and arched a brow. "I take it you have something of significant importance to tell me."

Drake tried not to grin. "I thought you and Mama would want to know that I've just dispatched a letter to St. Ives House, to the duke, requesting Louisa's hand in marriage."

"Ah. I see." After a moment, his father went on, "I feel I should have warned you to think long and hard about venturing in that direction, but there really is very little to be gained by attempting to resist the inevitable."

Drake wryly nodded. "Just so."

"Well, then." Smiling, his father clapped him on the shoulder. "Congratulations! And welcome to the club."

Drake refused to ask which club; given the mock-commiserating look in his father's eye, he suspected he could guess.

"I'll tell your mother." His father turned back to his room, then halted, looked back, and caught Drake's eye. "I take it you'd like me to warn her not to plan anything until after this current mission of yours has ended."

"Please." The thought... "Both Louisa and I will be unavailable, socially speaking, until the mission is concluded. Hopefully, that won't be longer than a few days—a week at most—so if Mama and Honoria could hold off until then..."

His father grinned a touch evilly. "I'll suggest that if they will pretend to ignorance for a few days to a week, then you—and Louisa, of course—will be suitably grateful."

Drake grimaced. "I wasn't intending this to happen now, but..." He shrugged.

"Fate runs to her own timetable, which is beyond the bounds of all mortal influence."

"Indeed." With a last filial nod, Drake parted from his father.

He returned to his bedroom to find Louisa still sprawled as he'd left her. But when he slid into the bed beside her, she turned to him, eyes bright under heavy lids.

She scanned his face, then smiled lazily. "What have you been about?"

He told her.

Unsurprisingly, she approved.

As it transpired, she was as little interested in further sleep as he. But celebrating their new relationship in decidedly uninhibited fashion was her—Lady Wild's—idea.

Given that in light of her novice status, her direction commenced with a sensual version of tit for tat, Drake decided it behooved him to lie back and let her have her way.

Later, of course, he had his way with her.

Consequently, it was long after eight o'clock when they finally stumbled from the ruins of his bed.

They made it to the breakfast parlor, with Louisa wearing Meredith's gown, a bare five minutes before the doorbell pealed.

Pausing in the act of sipping tea, Louisa caught his eye and smiled a distinctly smug smile.

He found himself smiling back. After they'd served themselves from the platters adorning the sideboard, he'd settled her in the chair alongside his.

Hamilton had been in and out, ferrying in coffeepot, teapot, and toast. Now, he returned to announce Sebastian and Antonia.

Sebastian appeared, leading Antonia by the hand; both were smothering yawns. But when, without a word, Drake waved them to the sideboard, they fell on the offerings with obvious appetite.

The doorbell pealed again, this time heralding Michael and Cleo. Apparently, Michael had gone first to Clarges Street to fetch Cleo, whom he ushered into the room.

To Drake's eyes, despite their appetites, the others all looked more tired than he felt.

He glanced sidelong at Louisa, taking in the bloom in her cheeks and the brightness of her eyes. Evidently, spending the night in his bed had agreed with her as much as it had agreed with him.

He waited until the others had taken their seats, and before Antonia, frowning as she noticed Louisa's not-quite-perfectly fitting gown, could make any comment, he stated without preamble, "I suspect you have yet to hear the news, but there will be another Cynster wedding." He inclined his head to the other four. "Following yours, of course."

It took Sebastian and Michael a second to work it out.

Their ladies, however, were far ahead of them. Antonia's and Cleo's eyes had flown wide, then with sounds startlingly like squeals, they were up and out of their chairs and rounding the table to hug Louisa, kiss her cheek, and exclaim and hug her again.

By then, Sebastian and Michael were grinning. Hugely.

Sebastian studied Drake and, still grinning, shook his head. "Of all the females in the ton…how the mighty have fallen. Still, I'm glad it's you."

"Indeed." Michael pushed back his chair and rose. "She and all her works will henceforth be on your head—and of all the gentlemen in the ton, you're arguably the most likely to survive."

Drake laughed. He rose as Michael and Sebastian came to thump his back and wring his hand.

Then Antonia and Cleo pushed Sebastian and Michael Louisa's way and took their turn to hug Drake and kiss his cheek.

The exclamations and questions continued for some minutes, then Drake called everyone to order and waved them back to the table.

He resumed his seat and looked around the faces. "As with Michael and Cleo"—he glanced at Louisa—"our news will be held strictly within the families until this mission is concluded."

They all nodded and turned their attention to their breakfasts. Hamilton came in, bearing more coffee. He poured, then glanced at Drake.

Drake nodded a dismissal. Once Hamilton had left and quietly closed the door behind him, Drake said, "Louisa and I spoke with Greville last night. We succeeded in getting his agreement to a search of all government and Parliament buildings, said search to be disguised as an exercise intended to reassure the public that a plot such as that shortly to be commemorated on Guy Fawkes Day will never be permitted to occur again."

"The Home Secretary has also accepted," Louisa added, "that should the climax of such a plot be imminent, it would not be appropriate to expect us to keep the information to ourselves and not warn—for instance—the officers in charge of the guards on duty at the various sites around town."

Sebastian's brows rose. "Greville agreed to that?"

"Not so much agreed," Louisa said, "as understood it to be inevitable."

Sebastian's lips twitched. He glanced at Drake, who shrugged.

After a second, Drake went on, "As we discussed yesterday, it would be best to organize and conduct the search today. Being Sunday, there'll be hardly anyone other than the guards about. Even if the gunpowder has yet to be moved into position—meaning we find nothing—we can't ask for a better time to do a dry run, as it were."

Sebastian and Michael exchanged glances, then Michael said,

"Consider us at your disposal."

Sebastian set down his cutlery and pushed away his empty plate. "I assume you expect to have to conduct another search in the small hours of Tuesday morning."

Drake nodded. "That would be my guess." He leaned back in his chair. "However, while we're organizing our search today, we're also going to whisper that warning of ours to all the officers in charge. At this point, for their ears only. We'll ask that, in the wake of today's exercise, they instruct their men to keep their eyes peeled for any strangers, anything unusual, any barrels of anything that seem out of place."

"You might suggest," Antonia said, "that they tell their men that it's possible a test might be conducted to see how alert the guards truly are."

Drake tipped his head to her. "An excellent idea." He paused, then went on, "While we hold no real hope of finding the barrels today, we should at least pinpoint all the possible places in which a cache of gunpowder of that size might be assembled. Then, if we haven't located the gunpowder by tomorrow night—the night of the fourth of November—regardless of any ructions it might cause, I propose rousing all the guards and conducting a thorough search, starting with the seventeen army messes the Phoenix Brewery supplies with ale, and continuing through every last store and cellar until we locate the gunpowder—even if that takes us all day."

Grimly, Sebastian nodded. "Acting might cause ructions, but not acting would be worse."

"Which"—Drake met Louisa's eyes—"brings us to the other relevant happening of the night. Namely, the fire that destroyed Chilburn's lodgings."

"What?" came from several throats.

Succinctly, Drake outlined why they'd returned to Cross Lane and described in bare-bone terms the subsequent firebombing of Chilburn's rooms.

"You were in there at the time?" Aghast, Cleo stared. "You might have been killed!"

Beneath the table, Drake felt Louisa's hand brush his thigh; he reached for her hand and felt her fingers grip, then twine with his.

But there was no hint of even mild perturbation in her face or her tone when she stated, "But we weren't."

A second passed, then Sebastian asked, "Did whoever threw the bomb know you were in there?"

"He must have known someone was because, of course, we'd turned up the lights," Louisa replied.

"Plainly," Drake dryly observed, "he didn't care."

"Such callousness fits our garrotter," Michael said.

"Indeed." Drake drummed a finger on the table. "And while we don't know if whoever flung the bomb was still there to see us leaving, given he knows someone was in Chilburn's rooms—his locked rooms—then I believe we can assume he now knows someone is investigating. That someone is after him." Drake glanced around the table. "I don't see that as a problem. If it increases the pressure on him enough to push him into a mistake, well and good."

"But," Louisa said, "we're under pressure, too. We have to find that blasted gunpowder before it's used."

No one had anything to add to that.

Drake, Sebastian, and Michael discussed the arrangements necessary to conduct their search-cum-exercise. It was agreed that while Drake drew up a list of all the relevant buildings and army messes, Sebastian would walk Antonia home to Green Street, and Michael would take Cleo to Clarges Street, then both Cynsters would return to Wolverstone House and, with Drake, would head to Whitehall.

The three couples rose from the table and walked into the front hall. Hamilton assisted with greatcoats and cloaks. While Drake found Louisa one of Meredith's cloaks for the short walk to St. Ives House, several unwelcome scenarios evoked by his recent words circled in his brain.

Arm in arm, he and Louisa followed the others out of the door, down the steps, and onto the pavement.

Michael's carriage was waiting; Michael helped Cleo up, then with a wave to the others, followed her.

As the carriage rattled off, Sebastian and Antonia led the way west along the north side of Grosvenor Square. They paused outside St. Ives House to farewell Louisa and Drake, then continued on, heading for the Chillingworths' town house in Green Street.

Drake followed Louisa up the steps of her home. When Crewe opened the door, Drake ushered Louisa into the front hall and allowed Crewe to shut the door behind him.

Crewe came to take Louisa's cloak. Lifting the garment from her shoulders, the butler looked faintly puzzled.

Drake caught Louisa's eye. "I'll get Hamilton to send over your cloak."

She inclined her head. "Thank you. I'll have Sukie deal with it."

Drake hesitated, searching for the best way to state what he felt he had to say. In the inimitable way of first-class butlers, Crewe read the undercurrents and vanished toward the rear of the hall.

When Louisa opened her eyes wide and arched a questioning brow, Drake sighed and simply said, "The man who flung that bomb was most likely one of the plotters. As Michael pointed out, he might well have been our garrotter. He might have seen us leave Chilburn's lodgings, might now know it was us—you and me—searching the rooms." He paused, his gaze on her eyes, watching for her reaction. "It's unlikely, but so much about this plot has been unexpected that I have to assume it's possible that he, whoever he is, might consider taking a hostage, especially at this late stage." He drew breath and evenly continued, "I would be very much obliged if you would remain indoors for the rest of the day."

Louisa blinked, but she didn't shift her gaze from his eyes. She saw—because he allowed her to see—lurking behind the beaten gold, the impulses that prompted his…request.

No order. Definitely a request.

Such as a nobleman might make of a noble lady who was his acknowledged Achilles' heel.

She understood that—understood that the position she had for so long coveted and now had claimed was precisely that.

This, then, was a part of their new relationship, indivisible from all the rest. Last night, or rather early that morning, she'd seized the rest with both hands—this could, thus, be seen as her moment of reckoning.

Or to put matters in a slightly different light, her first challenge.

Slowly, she nodded. "I believe I can manage to find distraction within doors, at least until we meet again at four o'clock." They'd arranged to meet at Wolverstone House so the ladies could learn of the outcome of the search.

Relief showed fleetingly behind Drake's eyes.

She widened hers. "But I do have one question."

Wariness overcame relief. "Which is?"

"If I agree to remain indoors until you come to fetch me, just how obliged are you going to be?"

His gaze sharpened. "Very—as in extremely—obliged."

She smiled delightedly and patted his arm. "In that case, we have a deal."

He laughed softly and shook his head at her. Smoothly, he caught her hand, raised it to his lips, and kissed her fingers, then his eyes darkened, and he drew her closer, bent his head, and brushed a tempting, over-far-too-soon kiss across her lips.

He straightened and met her eyes. "Behave, and I'll come to fetch you at four o'clock."

Her expression was all expectant delight as he released her and she stepped back. "Just as long as you deliver on being extremely obliged, and I don't have to behave later."

Drake was smiling as he left the house—a revealing expression he spent the short walk to Wolverstone House attempting to wipe from his face.

CHAPTER 46

*T*hey gathered in the library at Wolverstone House at the end of their day.

For once, the ladies had played no active part, but Drake, Sebastian, and Michael accepted the wisdom of keeping their coinvestigators fully apprised of developments, even when those developments amounted to very little.

"As predicted," Drake said from his usual armchair, "we found no sign of any barrels of ale that were not filled with liquid."

"Nor," Michael added, "were any other suspicious barrels or packages found."

The ladies looked at each other, then Cleo asked, "So what now?"

Louisa watched as Drake raked both hands through his hair. It wasn't a gesture she'd seen him make before; frustration was clearly riding him hard.

After several seconds, he lowered his hands. "Where is the gunpowder now?"

Understanding that to be a leading question, she promptly supplied, "As far as we know, it's in ale barrels, and given the effort expended to disguise it in that way, there's no reason to suppose our plotters would have transferred the gunpowder to some other receptacle. So the gunpowder is still masquerading as fifteen barrels of Phoenix Brewery's Bright Flame Ale, and it's somewhere in London, most likely north of the Thames in one of the places to which the brewery delivers."

"Although," Antonia said, "it's possible the barrels were removed from the brewery at night, in which case, we have no way of knowing where they might be."

"I don't think the gunpowder was taken out at night," Michael said. "I had Tully check with all the footmen and grooms who had been on watch—none of them saw any ale barrels moved at night. Apparently, delivery-wise, the area is virtually a graveyard at night, so they're confident that if any barrels had been moved then—at night, between Monday night and Thursday night, during which period the watch was maintained without a break—they would have seen them and noted the sight as odd."

Sebastian nodded. "So our fifteen barrels were moved out of the brewery as part of a delivery—therefore either by dray or by barge."

"If," Drake said, fingers now steepled before his face, "we accept that the barrels were sent out as part of an ordinary delivery by Friday morning at the latest, then presumably the delivery's destination was always a part of the plotters' plan."

"Except for one thing." Michael looked at Drake, then at Sebastian. "Over the past hours, we've checked hundreds if not thousands of barrels of ale. How?"

After a silent second, Drake's lips tightened. "Indeed. The instant the Phoenix delivery men picked up the barrels containing the gunpowder, they would have known the barrels didn't contain ale."

"Exactly." Grim-faced, Michael went on, "And Flock, the manager, insisted he was missing only four men—the ones we now know helped Chilburn on Monday night."

"The three of those four who've been found dead were killed by the garrotter on Wednesday and Thursday morning." Drake leant forward. "Two of those men drove drays. Might they have delivered those particular barrels on Tuesday, before they were killed?"

Silence reigned as they all considered that. Louisa eventually stated, "That's possible, certainly, but regardless, any such delivery would have gone to one of the customers on our lists." She paused, then continued, "However, there's also the possibility that the killer waited until all deliveries were completed on Friday and, sometime after that, murdered two of Phoenix's delivery men. If so, Mr. Flock might not be aware that he's missing more men."

"If our plotters wanted to make their trail as hard to follow as possible," Drake said, "then killing the delivery men on Saturday and Sunday, closer to the day we presume they intend to use the gunpowder,

makes perfect sense—it leaves us very little time to check." He glanced at
the others. "For argument's sake, let's say that a delivery team from the
brewery was bribed to take the gunpowder-containing barrels out of the
yard. Were the barrels delivered as part of some customer's normal
order? Or were the barrels left unmarked and taken somewhere else by
the delivery team?"

Louisa and Cleo exchanged a glance. "I don't think," Cleo said, "that
the barrels would have been left unmarked. From what I gathered while
there, any barrels left unmarked could be taken to make up extras for this
customer or that—a group of fifteen barrels would have been broken up
and distributed to numerous customers, and that distribution is decided by
the order clerks, not the delivery teams."

"I doubt the plotters would have chanced that," Louisa said. "They
would have had to bribe many more men, and the brewery isn't missing
any order clerks."

"Yet," Drake said, then inclined his head. "However, I agree that
scenario is unlikely. There's too many steps, too many people involved,
and too many stages at which things could go wrong. Conversely, if all
fifteen barrels were sent out as part of a customer's regular order, then
other than the delivery team—assuming they carry the barrels into a
customer's warehouse—the plotters wouldn't have to bribe anyone else."

Again, silence fell.

Louisa broke it. "Correct me if I'm wrong"—she fixed her gaze on
Cleo—"but *unless* our fifteen barrels were sent out for delivery as part of
a regular order to some customer, they wouldn't have left the brewery,
not all together, and as we know the barrels *had* left the brewery by
Friday morning, then they couldn't have been diverted elsewhere by the
delivery team. If they had, then some customer would have realized,
certainly by Friday afternoon, that they were fifteen barrels of Bright
Flame Ale short and have sent a complaint to the brewery. If not by
Friday, then at least by Saturday morning. The brewery was open until
noon. If Mr. Flock had received any such complaint, he would have sent
word—he knows we're looking for fifteen barrels supposedly of Bright
Flame Ale."

Drake's lips thinned, but again, he nodded. After a moment, he said,
"This is all speculation, but at the moment, that's all we have to work
with. Let's say our fifteen barrels were delivered successfully to some
customer's cellar somewhere north of the river. Why wouldn't any of
those barrels be tapped by the customer?" He looked at Cleo and arched a
brow. "Wouldn't that be a major risk?"

Louisa sat straighter. "As I understand it, that might not be a risk if
they've chosen the right customer—one who isn't the final customer for
those barrels." She paused, then said, her tone increasingly enthusiastic,

"Think of our lists." She looked at Cleo. "The delivery had to be one of ninety-three, so let's take it as settled that our barrels are with one of those ninety-three customers. But there were two hundred and eighty-seven possible *final* customers, and we don't know when the barrels will be moved to those final customers, so our barrels might well be sitting in some wine-and-ale merchant's warehouse, still waiting to be delivered."

The others all frowned.

Louisa looked at Drake. "When you were hypothesizing about how you would run this plot, you said you wouldn't move the barrels to the target site until less than twenty-four hours before blowing them up. So by that logic, the barrels should be one move away from their final destination."

Suddenly alert, she looked around. "Where are those lists?" She spotted her reticule, dived on it, and wrestled the tightly cinched neck open. She reached in and hauled out the folded lists. She unfolded them, scanned them, then tucked several sheets back and held out the rest to Cleo. "You have a pencil."

Cleo hunted in her significantly larger reticule, pulled out a stub of a pencil, and reached for the lists.

"Assuming the gunpowder is not at the target site," Drake said, "cross all the non-merchants off the list."

"Once we do that, how many are left?" Her gaze on Cleo, Louisa all but jigged. "Will it be possible for us to search them all?"

Cleo ignored everyone and concentrated on working her way down the sheet, crossing entries off as she went. Eventually, she returned to the top of the list and counted down. "Thirty-six," she announced.

"That's a lot better than ninety-three, let alone two hundred and eighty-seven," Louisa pointed out.

Drake looked at Sebastian and Michael. "Can the four of you search thirty-six merchants' premises tomorrow? Louisa and I have other avenues we need to pursue."

Michael looked at Sebastian and Antonia. "Now your engagement ball is over, we can get most of the footmen army released to us, at least for the day."

Sebastian nodded. "With the ball behind us, we'll be free—or at least can legitimately lie low socially."

"Sadly," Antonia said, "you speak for yourself." She looked rueful as she met Sebastian's eyes. "Now I'm officially your marchioness-to-be, there are countless events I absolutely must attend—starting from luncheon tomorrow."

Sebastian blinked. He looked faintly horrified. "I don't have to go, do I?"

Antonia's smile was wry. "No—you're not expected. This is purely the female half of the ton—and I hope you appreciate the sacrifice I'm making on our behalf."

Sebastian closed his hand about one of hers and squeezed. "Oh, I do. I definitely do."

Michael waited a beat, then clapped his hands together. "Right, then. Sebastian and I—"

"And me," Cleo stated.

Michael turned a smile on her. "*And* Cleo will just have to manage. If we divide the thirty-six warehouses and the footmen army between us, we should be able to get it done."

Antonia sniffed and waved a hand. "I'll hold the fort ton-wise. Just find that gunpowder."

Sebastian looked at Drake. "What will you and Louisa be doing?"

"One of the four missing brewery workers has yet to turn up dead." Drake paused, his gaze on Louisa, then said, "Neither Louisa nor I was convinced by the man's wife's behavior."

"It wasn't that she wasn't anxious," Louisa quickly said, "but it wasn't clear what she was anxious about—whether she feared he was already dead or, instead, feared a threat to his life."

"Meaning," Drake said, "that he's still alive. If he managed to escape the attentions of the garrotter, then if we can find him, it's very possible he might know something that will help us find the damned gunpowder." He raised his brows. "Or even the garrotter."

After a moment of imagining that, Drake glanced at Sebastian. "We also need to attend Chilburn's funeral. I doubt the garrotter will show his face, but Chilburn's family and connections and any acquaintances he still had will almost certainly be there. Someone among them must know something—who he was friendly with most recently, who he might have been working with, if he had any particular obsession he might have chosen to act on." He looked again at Louisa. "There has to be something more we can drag from his nearest and dearest."

None of the others needed it explained that of them all, Louisa was the most likely to succeed in drawing useful confidences from bereaved members of the ton.

Drake looked around the circle. "All right. So we know our plan of action for tomorrow."

With murmurs of agreement, as a group, they rose. They walked out of the library and down the corridor into the front hall.

Louisa glanced at the others' faces. She was keenly aware—and was sure they were, too—of a pressing sense of time running out. In essence, they had one more day in which to find the gunpowder. If they didn't, Drake would go out on a political and social limb and institute a search that would send public and governmental pigeons into a frenzy.

Despite the implication that they were losing this race, that the mastermind would triumph and something terrible would occur, far from being downcast, all of them were determined to push on—to battle to the very end.

That, ultimately, was who they were.

She halted two yards behind the others.

Michael and Sebastian helped Cleo and Antonia don their cloaks.

Drake brought Louisa's cloak and, from behind her, draped it about her, then he rested his hands briefly on her shoulders.

She raised a hand, placed it over his, and glanced up and back to meet his eyes. And whispered, "I'll see you later."

With a last, deliberately provocative smile, she faced forward and walked to join the others.

Drake lowered his hands and strolled behind her as she glided out of the door. Michael led Cleo to his waiting carriage, handed her up, then followed. Sebastian and Antonia, together with Louisa, paused on the pavement to wave the pair off, then with a last wave to Drake, the trio set off along the pavement toward St. Ives House.

Drake stood on the porch and watched them go. His gaze resting on Louisa's straight back, he wondered what she'd meant by "later."

CHAPTER 47

*H*er "later," he discovered, meant eleven that night.

The clocks throughout the house had just chimed the hour when, anticipating a full and frustrating day ahead, leading to a very long night of searching, Drake walked into his bedroom and learned the answer to his earlier question.

Louisa lay curled on her side in his bed and was already asleep.

He had no idea how she'd got there, but decided that question could wait until the morning.

For now…

He stood looking down at her for several minutes—simply enjoying the sight and plotting. Then he stirred and ambled about the room, going through his habitual routine before stripping, raising the covers, and joining her between his sheets.

Louisa woke to the sensations stirred by large, hard, hot hands roving over her body. Over the dips and curves, delving into the hollows. Warmth rolled over her, through her, and brought her fully awake on a crest of pleasure.

Smiling, she reached for him, drew his lips to hers, and kissed him.

Was kissed in return and slowly devoured. Slowly, with steely control, he led her along a path of burgeoning passion, of escalating desire, and building need.

Hunger prowled behind his façade of sophistication, a hunger she wanted to welcome, to release and embrace.

Challenge.

It would, she felt sure, always lie between them, in this sphere as in all others. Not a direct challenge, one against the other, but more a contest wherein each was challenged to be all and everything they could be.

Only with him did she feel that link; only to her did he respond in that way.

That was a part of the unique connection that had always existed between them.

Now, with lips and tongue, with her hands and her body, she pushed and pressed and urged him on—dared him to show her more.

He, meanwhile, insisted that instead of rushing ahead as she wished, they let the passion surging between them build and build, grow and swell—until need burned like wildfire down every vein and set every nerve ablaze.

Drake clung to patience. Pressed by her artful, willful play, he'd used his weight, his strength, to manage her, to hold her back from plunging recklessly on and, instead, give passion time to flare from smoldering embers to a firestorm.

But now they were burning, their breaths short and shallow as desire's flames licked their skins, and he finally gave way, rolled to his back, and with his hands about her waist, lifted her over him.

He set her down astride his hips.

The look on her face as she felt his straining erection nudge her entrance was priceless.

Then eagerness flooded her expression. Gripping his forearms, she took her weight on her knees and, with her eyes locked with his, slowly— excruciatingly slowly—slid down, impaling herself on his rigid length.

She took him all. Then she caught her lush lower lip between her teeth and wriggled—then she used her inner muscles to squeeze…

He felt his eyes crossing and lowered his lids.

Then he felt her hands flatten on his chest. He quickly opened his eyes to find her leaning forward on her braced arms. She shifted her hips experimentally, then arched a sultry brow at him and commanded, "Show me."

He was only too happy to comply.

As usual, she was a quick study.

Soon, they were both panting, their skins awash with passion's heat as she rode him with flagrant abandon.

She was an excellent rider, her thighs firm and strong. He watched and marveled at her open enthusiasm, at her reckless delight as she whipped them both on.

He swept his hands up from her waist to cup her breasts, kneading, then tweaking her tightly budded nipples. She was gasping, reaching, demanding yet more from them both. Sensing the tide rising within her, he half sat and set his mouth to her breasts.

He suckled, and she shattered.

He held her, held still within her until the ripples of her contractions faded, then he rolled, taking her with him, her thighs anchored on either side of his hips.

He set her beneath him, lifted her knees to his shoulders, and plunged deep.

She gasped, eyes opening to stare up at him in sensual shock—which with his next thrust converted to sensual appreciation.

She wrapped her arms as far about him as she could reach and held on as he rode her.

Hard, fast, straight into oblivion.

Into satiation so deep, it swallowed them whole.

MONDAY, NOVEMBER 4, 1850

CHAPTER 48

*T*heir final day in which to find the gunpowder dawned gray and cool, yet wrapped in each other's arms, Drake and Louisa slept on.

Beyond the windows and outside the door, the morning unfurled, and others started their day.

A peremptory knock fell on the door.

Before Drake could even blink, much less growl a prohibition, the door opened, and Finnegan strode in.

Drake's eyes flared, but before he could utter a word, Finnegan hurriedly said, "Don't shoot." He halted yards from the foot of the bed and studiously kept his gaze fixed forward. Staring at the window, he continued, "It's so dark in here, I can't really see anything, and even if I could, I would never breathe a word."

Drake sat up and pushed his hair off his face. "What the devil?"

"A message from Inspector Crawford, my lord. Urgent. They've fished out more bodies from the river, murdered in the same way as before, so they assume it's the same murderer. The inspector and Sir Martin send their regards, and can you come and take a look as soon as possible?"

From beneath heavy lids, Drake stared at Finnegan, then he humphed and slanted a glance at Louisa; she'd been sleeping on her side beside him, but had come up on her elbow to peer at Finnegan and was now wide awake and looking interested. "All right." Glancing at Finnegan, Drake added, "Coffee, tea, and toast in the breakfast room in five minutes. Now get out."

"Indeed, my lord." Finnegan bowed toward the window. "Consider me gone." He spun on his heel and made for the door.

Louisa fell back on the pillows. The instant she heard the door click shut, she said, "More dead bodies." A second later, she added, "I wonder whose."

Drake had remained sitting up. He reached over and slapped her derriere. "Up! Apparently, the day has started without us. We need to catch up."

CHAPTER 49

*G*riswade sat at the window of the tavern on the eastern corner of Lower Thames Street and nursed a pint of ale while he watched the world go by.

Truth be told, he had no interest in the activity on the river or about Tower Stairs, just visible across the cobbles. His attention was fixed on the steady stream of carts and drays making their biweekly or weekly trip through the arched entrance of Middle Tower, rumbling into the Outer Ward to make their deliveries of all things comestible.

Including ale.

Apparently idly—outwardly as patient as the day was long—Griswade waited and watched. He felt like biting his nails; anxiety over this one-but-last step, the need to ensure that nothing went wrong at this penultimate stage, pricked worse than burrs under his skin.

More than any other stage of this long-winded plot, this one held the greatest potential to go awry. The old man had insisted that this step be accomplished by subterfuge alone, without any direct involvement. That would definitely not have been Griswade's choice, but the old man's planning had been exemplary thus far; although it went against his grain, Griswade had stuck with the old man's plan.

Now he waited and sipped and watched.

Then he saw them. He almost doubted his eyes, but there they unarguably were—two drays marked with the distinctive logo of Hunstable's Wines and Ales rolling slowly along in the queue of carts waiting to pass into the outer precinct of the Tower, both drays driven oh-so-carefully by the lads Hunstable had been forced to hire to replace his missing delivery men.

The lads were mere boys, so inexperienced they wouldn't register that some of the barrels they'd loaded for delivery to the Tower that morning hadn't felt right.

From where Griswade sat, peering through the smeared glass of the small leaded panes of the tavern window, he could see that the goods stacked on the drays included the critical barrels.

Relief flowed like wine through his veins, a far more potent elixir than the weak ale he was drinking.

And that relief was further sweetened by a rising sense of impending triumph. He—and by extension, the old man—was nearly at the end of the plot. Success was in sight. Once the delivery was completed, there was only one more stage to go, and that was entirely in Griswade's hands. As he wasn't about to fail at the very last hurdle, ultimate success was as good as assured.

The old man's estate was virtually in his grasp.

Nevertheless, it was time to make sure of the delivery.

He drained his mug, set it down on the small table, then pushed to his feet and made his way to the tavern door.

He stepped into the street, paused for an instant to take stock, then walked with a confident, assured stride toward the archway that passed through Middle Tower. As he went, he drew out his gloves and tugged them on. He'd dusted off his old uniform; once he was attired in it and properly accoutered, there was nothing to say he wasn't a serving officer. He'd long been told that even in mufti, everything about him screamed "guardsman." It tickled him to bend what others saw as a weakness to his advantage; within the wards of the Tower, he would be entirely unremarkable—as good as invisible.

Without the slightest hitch in his stride, he walked straight to the entrance, nodded briskly to the guards stationed there, and passed on and through.

Once in the Outer Ward, he marched on.

He'd seen the lads driving Hunstable's drays ask directions. As expected, the guards had directed them to the Bloody Tower and the passageway that led to the Inner Ward. As Griswade approached, the drays rumbled through the arched passageway and continued on. With another round of crisp, officer-like nods to the guards stationed there, he followed.

The shadows of the Bloody Tower fell behind him. Walking purposefully but without hurry, Griswade continued straight ahead, on course for Waterloo Block. No one would think anything of an officer making for that block, presumably heading to one of the many offices located within it.

Although he gave no sign of looking around, Griswade surreptitiously checked his surroundings, but no one gave him a second glance. Not one of the numerous military men he passed took any special notice; only the officers bothered to actually look. Of course, none recognized him, so the extent of their interaction was the typical officer-to-officer dip of the head.

He remained on the gravel path leading to the main doors of Waterloo Block until a corner of the White Tower screened him from the Bloody Tower and the guards at the passageway. Not that he imagined they would be watching him, but there was no need to take chances. To do anything unexpected that might fix him in their memories. Once out of the guards' sight, he smoothly corrected his course and headed toward Martin Tower.

Anchoring the northeast corner of the Tower, Martin Tower housed several offices and barracks, but Griswade didn't need to go farther than the corner of Waterloo Block to confirm that the lads from Hunstable's had been given the correct directions; as he halted by the corner, the two youths were already unloading casks and barrels from the drays, which they'd drawn up in the shadow of Martin Tower.

Griswade watched as one of the youths opened the trapdoor set at ground level in the side of the building that clung to the inner curve of Martin Tower and scrambled down into the cellar. The second youth rolled the first of the Bright Flame Ale barrels stamped with the Tower's logo to the trapdoor, and between them, the lads manhandled the barrel down the ramp and into the depths. One lad remained inside, receiving and presumably stacking the barrels in the cellar, which had been claimed for storage by the officers' mess located in Waterloo Block.

Griswade seized the moment to study the building in the cellar of which the barrels were being stored. The two stories stood hard against the stone of Martin Tower, but were constructed primarily of timber rising above stone foundations. Considering the preponderance of stone all around, Griswade found it frankly astonishing that particular building had been built in timber.

So very easy to blow to kingdom come.

Amused by his unintentional play on words, he smiled, then he turned and walked away.

On passing the White Tower, he picked up his pace and determinedly retraced his steps out of the Tower and into the weak light of the gloomy gray day. He had a few final preparations to make, and then… What had the old man said? Smiling, Griswade murmured to himself, "All will be well."

CHAPTER 50

$\mathcal{D}$rake and Louisa arrived at the morgue to find Sir Martin scowling at the cloth-covered mounds occupying two of his marble benches.

Predictably, he turned his scowl on them. "Two more!" he rapped out. "And what's more, they were pulled from the area just east of Castle Street—same as the last two." Sir Martin waved farther down the room to where the bodies they'd seen two days before lay unclaimed. "That's the first time we've had him put bodies into the river from exactly the same place. The river rats tell me the spot he used is certain to be the steps at the bottom of Castle Street. Yet the first two were found on Saturday, and I'm as sure as I can be that they were killed on Friday night, while he did for these two"—Sir Martin nodded gravely at the most recent bodies—"on Saturday night."

Sir Martin grimaced. "The River Police are going to keep a close eye on that stretch, although what are the chances he'll slip more of his victims into the water just there, heh?" Sir Martin blinked, then humphed. "Then again, who can say with a madman?"

Drake eyed the shrouded bodies, but made no move to lift the sheets. "Same method of killing?"

"Exactly the same. Almost perfect copies." Sir Martin frowned. "Actually, that's a point you might want to consider. He's trained, so to speak. He's done this—killed like this—a lot, I would say."

From beyond the doors, they heard the clomp of boots approaching. "Ah—that will be the brewery manager," Sir Martin said. "Crawford remembered that one of your four missing brewery workers hasn't yet turned up, so he sent for the manager. Thought we'd give that poor Chartist chappie, Beam, a rest."

The tramping footsteps slowed, then halted. A burly sergeant swung open the door and ushered a thoroughly reluctant Mr. Flock inside. "In you go, sir. Won't take but a minute."

Wide eyed, Mr. Flock took one step inside and halted. He looked around rather wildly, saw Louisa and Drake and blinked in surprise, then jerkily bowed. "My lady. My lord."

"Good morning, Mr. Flock." Louisa took pity on the man and went forward to meet him. Flock was deathly pale and was compulsively turning his bowler hat around and around in his hands. Gripping his arm, she led him to where Sir Martin waited. "We truly appreciate your willingness to assist the authorities, Mr. Flock. If you'll just do as Sir Martin requests, this will be over in just a few minutes."

She released Flock to Sir Martin with a warning look at the surgeon.

Sir Martin elected to take pity on Flock as well and attempted to be gentle. "If you would, sir, we'd like you to take a look at these two men and tell us if either is your still-missing worker."

Flock's eyes grew wider. "Our apprentice cooper?"

"Was he an apprentice?" Sir Martin blinked. "I hadn't heard that. These men are older and both have calluses from reins, so I imagined..." Abruptly, Sir Martin shook off his distraction. "But now you're here..."

Sir Martin reached out and gripped Flock's arm in what the surgeon probably thought was a comforting grip, but appeared more like an implacable restraint. He drew—almost dragged—the reluctant manager forward, then with a certain reverence, Sir Martin lifted the sheet from the first corpse's face. He glanced questioningly at Flock.

Flock looked and paled even further. But then he gulped and resolutely shook his head. "He's not one of ours."

He was less reluctant to look at the second man; once he had, he shook his head decisively. "No." Some color returned to his face. As with a frustrated grunt, Sir Martin let the sheet fall over the second corpse's face, Flock looked hopefully at Drake and Louisa. "So...can I go now?"

Louisa had been thinking. "Are all your workers Chartists, Mr. Flock?"

"No, my lady. Only some of them."

"I see." She glanced at Drake, then looked at Sir Martin. "We only asked the secretary of the association to look at the two bodies retrieved from the river on Saturday." She turned her gaze on Flock. "For completeness's sake, sir, if you wouldn't mind, given, as Sir Martin mentioned, that you are here…" She waved Flock and Sir Martin toward the end of the room.

"Good idea!" Sir Martin seized Flock's arm again and towed the manager to the other two slabs.

Flock appeared to sigh and waited patiently as Sir Martin raised the sheet from the first body. Flock glanced at the corpse's face. His entire body went rigid.

Louisa swept down the room with Drake on her heels. "What is it, Mr. Flock? Do you recognize him?"

His gaze riveted on the dead man's face, Flock nodded woodenly. "Yes. It's… My God, that's Mellon." Flock raised his head and, eyes wide with shock, stared at Louisa. "He's one of our delivery men."

She nodded. "But he's not a Chartist."

Flock swallowed. "Not as far as I know, my lady."

"And the other?" She waved to the other corpse.

Flock visibly steeled himself, then gestured to Sir Martin, who raised the sheet so Flock could look.

One glance was all it took; Flock straightened, gulped, and nodded. His voice was weak when he said, "That's Cook. He's—he was Mellon's partner." A frown gradually appeared on Flock's face. "Just before I received the inspector's summons and left the brewery, my head clerk came in to say that they—Cook and Mellon—hadn't turned up." Puzzled, he looked at Louisa, then at Drake. "I've never known them to be late, but how could they be here…?" Flock swung to stare at the sheet-draped bodies.

Sir Martin harrumphed. "We believe these two were killed on Friday night."

Flock's frown deepened. "I suppose that's possible…" He turned to Drake and Louisa. "Cook and Mellon are bargemen, and the barges don't go out on Saturday, so if they'd been killed on Friday night, we wouldn't have known—we wouldn't have noticed until this morning when they didn't turn up."

"Indeed." Having exchanged an alert and meaningful look with Drake, Louisa asked, "Are you sure Cook and Mellon made their scheduled deliveries on Friday?"

Flock blinked, then lightly shrugged. "They must have, or we would have heard from our customers by Saturday morning." He shook his head. "We didn't have any complaints come in, so they must have completed their deliveries before they were killed."

"To whom do they deliver?" Louisa asked. "Merchants, individual inns, or both?"

"Well, they have the barge, so they usually only take the big orders."

"So they delivered to merchants." Drake kept his voice even as he asked, "Can you tell us to which merchants Cook and Mellon delivered over the four days from Tuesday to Friday last week?"

Flock shook his head. "But that will be in the ledgers. Mellon and Cook were experienced men, and they've been with us for an age, so they have a regular schedule." Flock nodded at Drake. "I can get your lordship a list as soon as I get back to the office."

"In that case"—Drake glanced at Louisa, then turned to Sir Martin— "if you could convey the gist of this to the inspector, Cranthorpe, her ladyship and I will accompany Mr. Flock to the brewery, avail ourselves of his ledgers, and compile the list of merchants whose premises we need to search."

Sir Martin nodded his shaggy head. "I'll tell Crawford." He waved them to the door.

Louisa led the way, with Flock behind her and Drake bringing up the rear.

As Drake reached the door, Sir Martin bellowed after him, "And don't forget I've still got two unidentified bodies here."

CHAPTER 51

$\mathcal{D}$espite the fact it was Monday morning and the streets were choked
with every sort of conveyance, at Drake's directive to get them to the
brewery with all possible speed, Henry whipped up the horses, employed
a style of city driving that only an employee of a ducal house would dare
attempt, and in record time, had them in Stoney Lane, drawing up at the
curb before the gates of the Phoenix Brewery.

Although rendered white-faced all over again, once his feet were on
solid cobbled ground, Mr. Flock led Drake and Louisa straight to the
office, and in just a few short minutes, the head clerk was compiling the
required list.

Drake asked and was assured that the loading of barges as well as
drays was overseen by clerks and that only barrels earmarked for
particular customers were sent out. Fifteen barrels that weren't on the
clerks' lists could not have found their way onto any barge and been
removed from the brewery as a pseudo-delivery.

Ten minutes later, Drake and Louisa walked out of the office and
halted in the yard. Together, they scanned the list Drake held.

Drake quietly swore. "Over those four days, Cook and Mellon
delivered to merchants all along the river from Westminster to east of the
Tower. Virtually every major government building as well as all the

Parliament buildings lie within easy reach—delivery reach—of that stretch of riverbank."

Louisa was busily counting the deliveries. "They did three deliveries each day. We need to send word to St. Ives House—someone there will know where Sebastian and Michael are. Their thirty-six merchants just reduced to twelve."

She glanced at Drake and sensed his impatience, not that any emotion showed in his sharply cut, angular features. "That's promising. Sebastian, Michael, Cleo, and the others can easily search twelve premises within the day."

When Drake made no response, she closed her hand about his wrist. When he looked at her, she met his eyes. "We need to leave searching the merchants to them and concentrate on the avenues they aren't in a position to pursue. You've said it several times—we can't afford just to find the gunpowder, we have to expose who's behind this plot as well. If we don't, we'll never know if the threat—the mastermind—is still there, thwarted in this instance, but able to come about and try again." Studying his eyes, she raised her brows. "As things stand, we don't even know who or what his target is."

Drake held her gaze for several seconds, then exhaled. "You're right." His lips set in a grim line. He reached into his pocket and drew out his fob watch, checked the time, then tucked the watch back. "It's just after ten o'clock. Let's send word to the others, then—"

"We should check again with the family of the missing apprentice, who, as we now know, still numbers among the missing."

Not only had the apprentice not turned up dead, but no one at the brewery had heard anything of him, either; Mr. Flock had inquired of his workforce while their list was being made.

"That," Louisa insisted, "was what we were scheduled to do."

Drake frowned as she linked her arm in his and started them walking toward the brewery gates. He noted the particularly belligerent tilt to her chin, the set of said chin, and the militant glint in her eye... He shrugged and faced forward. "I suppose we have time for a quick foray to the Sawyers', given their house is so close."

She tipped her head his way. "Thank you."

They halted beside the carriage. Drake penned a note to Sebastian and Michael while Louisa scribbled out a copy of the list of twelve merchants to whom Cook and Mellon had delivered.

Drake had had the forethought to bring along two young grooms for the purpose of ferrying messages; he sent one off to St. Ives House with his note and the copied list of merchants, while Louisa tucked the original list back into her reticule.

Drake wondered how it was that all the lists in this affair seemed to end up in one reticule or another, but forbore to comment. Instead, he handed Louisa into the carriage and told Henry to drive to Barnham Street.

CHAPTER 52

*T*hree minutes later, Henry drew the carriage to a halt in Barnham Street, just around the corner from Tooley Street.

Drake helped Louisa down to the cobbles. Side by side, they walked down the street toward the house Jed Sawyer had shared with his wife.

Louisa had been surveying the houses ahead. She put a hand on Drake's arm and slowed him.

He halted and looked at her questioningly and saw a frown in her eyes.

"I wonder..." Then her face cleared, resolution plainly taking hold. She tapped his arm and stepped away. "Can you please stay there? Far enough back so whoever answers the door can't see you. I want to try something else first."

He had no idea what she was about, but obediently remained where he was. At that time of day in a street such as this, not even she was likely to find danger.

Instead of continuing to the Sawyers' door, Louisa stopped before the steps of the narrow house next door. She paused as if rehearsing her words, then reached out and rapped smartly on the door.

Drake leaned against the wall beside which he'd halted and swiftly surveyed the street. A few children played at the far end, but at that moment, there were no women at any doors, and no curtains appeared to be twitching.

He heard the Sawyers' neighbors' door open and returned his gaze to Louisa; from where he stood, he couldn't see whoever had answered the door, and they couldn't see him. He was, however, near enough to hear the exchange that followed and appreciate Louisa's performance.

"Good morning." Louisa now held her reticule before her, both hands clasped about the top in a supplicatory manner she would never normally affect. She smiled brightly at whoever had answered the door. "I do hope you can help me. I represent the Athena Agency—we place respectable men and women with households in Mayfair. Your neighbors"—with a tip of her head, she indicated the Sawyers' house—"have filed an application with us, and we've had interest shown from the household of the Marquess of Winchelsea. That's what brings me here, you see—I need to check the character references the Sawyers have given us."

Louisa's features arranged themselves into an expression of embarrassed contrition that, if he hadn't known it to be entirely spurious, would have fooled Drake. Lowering her voice, she confided, "But now I'm here, I find I've brought the wrong application." She brandished what he suspected was the list of merchants they'd got from the brewery. "Of course, I meant to bring the Sawyers' application—they had listed as referee one of their relatives who I know lives close by." She glanced rather warily at the Sawyers' door. "I don't like to knock and ask the Sawyers directly." She gave a tittering laugh. "No one likes to admit to such a silly mistake. So"—she opened her eyes wide and trained them on whoever stood at the door—"I wondered if you knew where the Sawyers' nearest relative lives? If I have to go all the way back to the Agency—it's in Knightsbridge, you see—I won't be able to complete their application today, which won't please the Winchelsea housekeeper."

"Well, we can't have that. Sure as eggs are eggs, it's the Morgans you'll be wanting, miss." A large woman stepped out onto the stoop. She pointed down the street. "Just continue down to Crucifix Lane at the end there, and the Morgans' house is two…no, it's three doors from the corner on the right."

"Thank you so much." Louisa's face positively radiated gratitude. "You've been a great help."

"Aye, well." The woman heaved her massive shoulders. "It's what neighbors are for, ain't it?"

With further expressions of thanks, Louisa took her leave of the woman. Without glancing at Drake, she started walking in the direction of Crucifix Lane.

Drake waited until he heard the woman shut her door, then he strode swiftly after Louisa.

He caught up with her just around the corner in Crucifix Lane. She'd halted and was waiting for him. Curious, he asked, "What gave you the idea of asking for nearby family?"

"You did." She looped her arm in his, and they strolled on very slowly. "At our meeting in the library on Saturday. You said that Sawyer's family might have hidden him—and I realized that seeking refuge with family would have been the most obvious thing for him to have done." She tipped her head so her hair brushed Drake's shoulder. "I realize that by 'family' you meant his wife, but that wouldn't have worked. The garrotter could simply have kept watch on his house."

They drew level with the third door on the right, and she halted. "It would be difficult for Sawyer to hide at his home, but he wouldn't want to leave his wife and flee to the country, either. And if his wife went with him, not only would that signal to everyone that he was alive, but they would probably lose their house. I thought it most likely he would want to lie low and wait for this business to blow over—somewhere close and with people he trusted to hide him and keep it a secret." She met Drake's eyes. "So with family nearby."

He recalled her sudden abstraction at that point in Saturday's discussion. He nodded, then looked at the Morgans' door. "Now what?"

"Now you lead the way. I'm sure you can convince the Morgans that you know they're hiding Sawyer and that he needs to speak with you."

Drake humphed, but didn't disagree. He had a very well-developed line in intimidation. He lowered his arm, but caught her hand in his and, towing her behind him, approached the Morgans' door.

As it was Monday, Morgan was working. It didn't take Drake long to impress on Mrs. Morgan that she needed to convince her cousin—having established that Jed Sawyer was her first cousin—to come to the door and speak with him.

Left on the doorstep, his boot wedged in the door so it couldn't be closed, Drake listened to the heated argument inside. He'd already decided that Jed Sawyer had to have had his wits about him to escape the fate that had befallen his three coworkers. Consequently, the fact that someone had traced him to the Morgans and, courtesy of Mrs. Morgan's actions, now knew he was there would sink in soon enough.

Two minutes later, a tall, lanky man came out of a room at the rear of the house and, with obvious trepidation, approached the door. When he drew close enough to see Drake clearly, Sawyer frowned, but hung back in the shadows of the narrow hall. "What do you want?"

Drake straightened from the doorframe against which he'd been lounging. "You would be wise to continue to lie low." As he'd anticipated, that advice paradoxically reassured Sawyer. The apprentice wasn't that young, but at Drake's question, Sawyer confirmed he was apprenticed to Mike Jones, one of the master coopers at the Phoenix

Brewery.

"Of course, Mike's dead now—or so my wife heard." Sawyer looked glum. "I guess I'll be out of a job by the time this blows over."

"I doubt it." Drake watched Sawyer closely, but the man seemed exactly as he appeared. "We believe the matter will come to a head over the next few days. After that, once we're sure we have the killer who murdered your three friends behind bars, you'll be able to return to the brewery. I'll even put in a good word for you with Flock, although he seemed genuinely saddened to lose you as well as the other three."

Sawyer blinked. "Is that right?" He stood a fraction straighter.

"Of course," Drake continued, "you being able to return to your job and your home depends on us catching the killer. How did you get away from him? Did you see him?"

Sawyer had relaxed his vigilance. Readily, he shook his head. "No—it was in the fog. I used to meet up with Mal Triggs on my way in. He would wait for me in a little pocket in Vine Yard, then we'd cut through a ginnel that joins up with Stoney Lane and go in through the main gates." Sawyer paused, his face tightening. "That morning—it was Thursday last—I was early. I stopped at that little pocket where Mal usually waited, but he wasn't there, and I couldn't see anything in the fog—pea-souper, it was. I waited, but Mal didn't show. I started to walk on, but then..." He blanched. "I heard creeping footsteps coming up behind me and...well, I just knew. Mike and Cec hadn't been in the day before, and no one knew what had happened to them. They were supposed to be on second shift, but they disappeared on their way to work..." His gaze fixed unseeing on the stoop, Sawyer swallowed. "I just took to my heels, and I didn't stop running until I was safe indoors. Then later, I came over the fences and down the back alleys to Jenny's." He looked curiously at Drake. "I figured no one would think to look for me here, and my Suzie visits Jenny all the time."

Drake nodded reassuringly. "I doubt anyone else will think to look here." He glanced sidelong at Louisa, then looked back at Sawyer. "But as I said, I would strongly suggest you remain inside until I send word that it's safe to resume your life." Drake drew his card case from his pocket, extracted a card, and handed it to Sawyer, who received it and read the inscription with something like awe. "I'll send another card like that with any message, so you'll know it's from me and it truly is safe to emerge."

Sawyer nodded.

Drake waited until the man had tucked the card carefully away, then said, "Now, I need you to tell me what you and your three friends—Mike Jones, Cecil Blunt, and Mal Triggs—did on Monday night." When Sawyer's head came up, alarm flaring in his eyes, Drake continued, "We know you were hired to do something by a gentleman whose real name was the Honorable Lawton Chilburn—he had a scar from his lips to his jawbone." Drake drew a line on his own face.

Sawyer blinked slowly.

"We also know that you were told that the action was part of a plot the Chartist hierarchy had approved." Drake trapped Sawyer's eyes. "That wasn't true. The man with the scar and the man who's been killing your friends are, indeed, running a plot, but they wanted to get Chartists involved so that the movement would be blamed for it."

Sawyer looked stunned, then devastated. "Oh God. We thought…we all thought it was for the cause. We'd never have done it if it hadn't been approved. But the militia leaders told us…"

"Sadly, all three militia leaders, all of whom met Chilburn, have turned up dead. Killed, we believe, by him in order to ensure they could never identify him or speak to anyone of the plot if they became suspicious."

"They're dead, too?" In his shock, Sawyer stepped closer to the door.

Drake felt Louisa shift from where she'd been standing, largely hidden from Sawyer by Drake's greatcoated bulk and, he'd presumed, keeping an eye on the reassuringly quiet street. "Unfortunately, yes," she said. "But Mr. Beam from the association has been helping us."

Sawyer blinked rapidly, assimilating Louisa's presence as well as her information.

"If you want to help us and avenge your friends—the three from the brewery as well as the militia leaders—then you really do need to answer Lord Winchelsea's questions." Louisa slanted a look at Drake. "We need to learn the truth as quickly as we can."

Sawyer stared at her for a moment, then the lanky man nodded and drew himself up. "I'll do whatever I can to help." He looked at Drake. "We—me and Mike—were waiting in the brewery for Cec and Mal when they brought the barrels of gunpowder over from Shepherd's in Morgan's Lane. Earlier, that fellow—Major Sharp, he told us he was called—had explained what he wanted us to do, and he'd given Mike the money for the oilskin. Mike and I got busy lining the ale barrels while Cec and Mal fetched the gunpowder. When they rolled in, we broke open the gunpowder barrels and tipped the stuff into the oilskin-lined ale barrels. Then Mike and I sealed the ale barrels with the oilskin bags inside up tight."

Sawyer frowned. "We thought Major Sharp was supposed to come and check over the work, but he hadn't exactly said he would, and when he didn't turn up…" Sawyer shrugged. "The others got busy stamping the barrels—the ale barrels that now contained the gunpowder. They said as I could go, so I left—I knew Suzie would be waiting up for me."

"The stamp that was put on the barrels," Louisa said. "What stamp was it?"

"It was the one for Hunstable's warehouse—Mike said that was the stamp Major Sharp said had to go on all those barrels."

"So the barrels were delivered to Hunstable's," Drake said.

Sawyer shrugged. "I assume so, but I don't rightly know for certain."

"Was there another mark put on the barrels?" Louisa asked. "One for an eventual customer?"

His gaze growing distant, Sawyer frowned. After several moments, he nodded. "Now you mention it, Mike did have another stamp waiting on his bench to go into the brazier." Sawyer looked at Louisa. "For heating it up, you see, to burn the mark into the wood."

"Which customer's stamp was it?" Both Drake and Louisa said the words in unison. They glanced at each other, then looked back at Sawyer.

But the lanky man grimaced. "I'm sorry. I can't say. I didn't see the stamp itself—it was lying on the bench facing the other way, and I left before Mike got to using it."

Disappointment warred with relief over having got at least one definite step forward. Drake nodded to Sawyer. "Thank you—that's all we need to know."

Sawyer grasped the edge of the door, but kept his eyes on Drake's face. "That was gunpowder we were handling—illegally and all. Will I be up before the beak for that?"

Drake shook his head. "The authorities now know that you and your friends—and others, too—have been taken in by this group. You were led to believe things that weren't true, and as you're helping us to unravel the plot, and it's those behind it we're actually after, I can't imagine the police or anyone else thinking to come after you."

Louisa nodded in affirmation. "But you definitely should remain indoors until Lord Winchelsea sends word it's safe to go about again."

"I will." Sawyer started to close the door. "And thank you, my lord. My lady." With awkward bobs, he closed the door.

Drake and Louisa exchanged a glance, then as one, turned and started walking quickly back to the carriage.

On the way, Louisa wrestled open her reticule and hauled out the list of merchants again. She ran her eyes down it. "As you might expect, Hunstable's is on the list of deliveries Cook and Mellon made." She glanced sidelong at Drake. "They delivered to Hunstable's on Friday morning."

Drake swore. He gripped her arm, and they hurried along even faster. "So we missed the barrels by just a few hours."

Louisa kept reading. "Hunstable's Warehouse is on Chatham Square. That's at the north end of Blackfriars Bridge." She glanced at Drake. "We can call in there on our way back to Grosvenor Square to change for the funeral."

He nodded curtly. "Precisely my thoughts."

The carriage lay ahead. Less than a minute later, they were in it, and Henry was heading for Blackfriars Bridge.

CHAPTER 53

*A*s they rattled over the bridge, Louisa looked down and across and spotted the large warehouse with "Hunstable's Wines and Ales" blazoned above a pair of double doors that stood open to a wharf at which flat-bottomed river barges lined up to off-load barrels, kegs, and crates of bottles. One barge was currently unloading. A reed-thin individual in clerk's garb was standing to one side of the doors, marking off barrels on a list as the bargemen carried them past.

Louisa tugged Drake's sleeve and pointed. "The bargemen carry the barrels inside. If Chilburn or whoever it was bribed Cook and Mellon to deliver the gunpowder barrels to Hunstable's, they wouldn't have had to bribe anyone else to get the barrels into the warehouse."

Drake had glimpsed what she'd seen. He faced forward. "I'm now more concerned with learning for which customer those barrels were destined—and if the damned gunpowder is still in the warehouse." After a moment, he added, "Pray God it is."

"One step at a time," she counseled.

They'd reached the end of the bridge, and the carriage swerved sharply to the right, turning into a graveled yard before the street-facing façade of the same large warehouse.

Before the carriage had properly halted, Drake opened the door and swung down. Louisa didn't wait for him to help her out, but in a froth of skirts and petticoats, scrambled out after him.

She shook down her skirts and looked up at the warehouse as, grim-faced, Drake strode for the warehouse doors. There, too, a handsome sign proclaiming the premises as housing Hunstable's Wines and Ales was mounted above the open double doors.

Their arrival had not gone unnoticed. As she hurried to catch up with Drake, a dapperly dressed, middle-aged man with a beaming smile wreathing his face walked out to meet them. With Drake approaching at pace, the man halted and bowed. "Sir. Madam." Straightening, he fixed a look of inquiry on Drake. "How might we at Hunstable's be of service, sir?"

Drake returned Hunstable's look levelly and told him, omitting only to mention that the "contraband material" hidden in the doctored barrels of Bright Flame Ale was gunpowder.

Nevertheless, by the time Drake reached the end of the information he'd elected to share, the man's florid complexion had turned chalk white. "Dear Heaven!" he exclaimed. "Doctored barrels." His voice grew weak. "My reputation... I'll be ruined!"

"Not"—Drake's tone sliced through what appeared to be Mr. Hunstable's imminent hysterics—"if we can secure the barrels before they're delivered."

Hunstable leapt on the suggestion. "Yes—of course! Excellent idea." He turned and rushed back into the warehouse.

Louisa and Drake strode after him.

Hunstable halted in the middle of a dimly lit space surrounded by stacks of barrels of various sizes. "Higgins! I say, Higgins! Damn it, man, where are you?"

The reedy-looking clerk Louisa had seen on the wharf came hurrying up a ramp that led down to the lower level of the warehouse. "Yes, Mr. Hunstable?"

Hunstable waved the man over. When Higgins presented himself, Hunstable, after furtively glancing to either side, waved at Drake and Louisa. "These, er..."

"Representatives of the authorities," Drake supplied in a tone that left no room for doubt.

"Quite, quite." Hunstable half bowed to them, then continued to Higgins, "These representatives of the authorities have brought word of a mix-up at Phoenix. It seems some blighters have swapped the ale in fifteen barrels of Bright Flame for some contraband stuff. Not ale."

Higgins frowned.

Hunstable rolled on, "Apparently, the fifteen barrels of er...contraband material were delivered here on Friday morning." Hunstable fixed his gaze almost beseechingly on Higgins's worn face. "Please tell me we still have those fifteen barrels and can return them."

Higgins looked increasingly wary. He glanced at Drake and Louisa, then looked back at Hunstable. "It's Monday, sir. I'm afraid almost all the Bright Flame barrels that arrived on Friday will have been sent out."

Hunstable groaned. "I'll be ruined—ruined!" Then his expression abruptly cleared, and he turned to Drake. "But perhaps this wasn't a regular delivery? Who was it destined for?"

"As to who, we don't know, but we understand the barrels were stamped by Phoenix for delivery to one of your regular customers." While Hunstable groaned anew, Drake fixed his gaze on Higgins. "How many different regular customers could have been the one supplied with the fifteen barrels of Bright Flame Ale delivered on Friday?"

Higgins's gaze turned inward; he was clearly counting.

As the silence stretched, Drake grew more tense.

Finally, Higgins refocused and announced, "Eighteen. Since Friday."

Drake felt like groaning, too.

Louisa asked Higgins, "Can you tell us how the deliveries work? Did you deliver the barrels you received on Friday morning on Friday afternoon or Saturday?"

"Well, miss, that depends. We receive upward of ten barge-loads of barrels from Phoenix between Thursday morning and Friday afternoon, and most all of that is for regular customers. But Phoenix knows all our standing orders, and they fill them as and when they fit—as works out best for their runs, you see, because most of the customers want all of their order to come from the one run."

Louisa nodded. "Yes, I understand that part—the clerks at the brewery explained it to me. But how does that influence your deliveries to your customers?"

Higgins seemed to warm to her. "Well, let's take a fer-instance. The Ship's Anchor down by London Dock takes twenty barrels of Bright Flame delivered last thing Saturday. But the barrels to fill that order might come in any time from Thursday morning to Friday afternoon."

His hands gripping his hips, Drake had been listening. "Can you tell us which orders were filled with the Bright Flame barrels delivered this last Friday morning?"

Higgins sucked his teeth. He glanced at Hunstable, who made a get-on-with-it gesture, then Higgins looked back at Drake. "No, sir. We have a sheet that gets ticked off as the barrels come into the warehouse, but that's to make sure everything that's due comes in. We've never needed to know on what day a particular customer's order of Bright Flame comes in, only that the order is here, ready to be delivered in time to meet our customer schedule. As long as all the barrels for our orders are here by

Saturday midday when the brewery shuts for the week, then all's well. That's all we check for."

Drake exhaled through his teeth and looked down at the floor. After a moment, he raised his head. "All right. We know the barrels were delivered here on Friday morning. Tell us about the deliveries made after that—the ones involving fifteen or more barrels of Bright Flame. All the deliveries that might have included the doctored fifteen barrels."

"Well," Higgins said, "like I mentioned, there are eighteen customers that fit your bill, and most of those deliveries, all except three, get done between Friday early afternoon and Saturday late afternoon. Most places want their stock in for Saturday night, you see. Then the last three deliveries roll out first thing Monday morning."

The open doors of the warehouse were behind them. Louisa heard a heavy cart draw up rather jerkily, almost skidding on the gravel of the yard. She turned and looked outside.

Two lads in tabards bearing the Hunstable name and logo climbed down rather gingerly from the box seat of a dray. They were eyeing the two huge workhorses in the traces as if the beasts might kick or bite at any moment.

She frowned, then glanced disapprovingly at Hunstable. "Are all your delivery drivers so young?"

"Heh?" Hunstable followed her gaze and saw the two lads slinking into the warehouse.

Higgins turned and directed the pair to a stack of barrels set to one side of the doors. The boys—they were really not much older—bobbed their heads, went and picked up a barrel each, and staggered with them out to the dray.

Hunstable sighed gustily. "No—that's another crisis. I have four regular drivers. They've been with me for years. Experience tells in this game, you see—those four know all the shortcuts that can fit a dray, where all the cellar doors are, and so on. But the four of them—all four!—didn't turn up for work this morning, and I literally had to hire lads off the streets." He tipped his head toward the pair trooping back and forth with barrels. "At least those two can manage the reins."

More missing men. Louisa exchanged a look with Drake. More deaths, and they'd missed the barrels again.

She took the bit between her teeth and laid a hand on Hunstable's arm. "Mr. Hunstable, I would most strongly urge you to go—or send someone who knows your missing drivers well enough to recognize them—to Scotland Yard."

Drake had already pulled out his card case and was scribbling on the back of a card. "Take this." He handed the card to Hunstable, who had blanched. "Show it to the man on the desk and ask for that name—

Inspector Crawford. Tell him who you are, that I've sent you, and that you're missing four deliverymen. He'll know where to take you." Drake paused, glanced at Higgins, then said, "This is part of a much larger plot, and it sounds as if your regular drivers have got caught up in it."

Hunstable stared at the card—at Drake's title. When he looked up at Drake, his color was pasty, his expression grave. "Something's happened to those men—my drivers—hasn't it?"

Fleetingly, Louisa met Drake's eyes, then once again laid a comforting hand on Hunstable's sleeve. "We strongly suspect they've been killed. Murdered."

"That said," Drake added, "it's possible two or more escaped and have gone into hiding, too frightened to show their faces here, where someone might be watching and waiting."

Hunstable frowned, then glanced around. "Higgins and the others—the boys." Hunstable peered outside where the two lads were lashing barrels to the dray. "Are they in any danger?"

"No." Drake's tone carried conviction. "It's the Bright Flame barrels containing the contraband material that are behind all this, and those barrels are no longer here."

Hunstable nodded. "Yes—I see." He stared again at the card, then raised his head and squared his shoulders. "I'll go straightaway. It's the least I can do." He managed a creditable bow to Louisa, then to Drake. "If there's anything more we can do to assist you, my lord, just ask Higgins here."

"Thank you." Drake inclined his head to Hunstable, who then turned and walked heavily out into the yard.

Drake looked at Higgins. "I'm the Marquess of Winchelsea, and in this matter, I'm acting with the authority of the Home Secretary. We need— urgently—a list of those eighteen deliveries that might have contained the fifteen doctored barrels of Bright Flame Ale."

Higgins saluted. "At once, my lord."

"Two copies, please," Louisa added. "And addresses would greatly help."

"Right away, miss—my lady." With a bobbed bow, Higgins rushed off to a small office to the left of the open doors.

Drake walked to the nearest stack of barrels and leaned against them. Louisa went to where a nearby barrel of brandy offered her a place to sit. They waited without words; neither needed words to know what the other was thinking—what thoughts and conjecture were flying through their brains.

In less than ten minutes, Higgins came rushing back, waving two sheets of paper as he came. "Two copies, as requested." He presented one sheet to each of them with a little bow, then stepped back and watched them scan the entries.

When Drake looked up, Higgins offered, "I double-checked our ledgers—there were no other deliveries that included fifteen barrels of Bright Flame, not since Friday morning. And the only barrels of Bright Flame we have left came in on spec—meaning not stamped for any customer—last Tuesday."

"They won't be the barrels we're seeking." Drake's gaze fell again to the list.

Louisa looked up from perusing her copy. "Thank you. You've been a great help."

Drake finally grunted, folded his copy, and stuffed it into his pocket. He nodded at Higgins, then took Louisa's elbow, and they walked out into the yard.

They stopped beside the carriage. Drake released Louisa, drew in a deep breath, then raked one hand through his hair. "Damn it! Are we ever going to catch up with these barrels? Before they're set off?"

Louisa read his frustration—for once, on display—in his face, and calmly replied, "Yes. Of course we are."

Her tone—one which brooked no denial, much less disbelief—brought Drake's gaze to her face. He stared at her for a moment, then humphed and reached for the carriage door.

"I suppose we are." He gave her his hand, helped her up, then followed. As he dropped onto the seat beside her, he added, "When it comes down to it, no other outcome is possible."

"Indeed."

Henry gave the horses the office, and the carriage rolled out and into the traffic, heading west toward Mayfair.

Several minutes later, his gaze on the passing façades, Drake asked, "Can you handle the funeral alone?"

"No. I've already thought, and I can't. I can't cover both the gentlemen as well as the ladies, and we can't tell from whom a vital clue might fall." She glanced at him. "It has to be me and you both. Nothing else will do." She tried to read his mood from his profile, then went on, "No matter how much you want to be in the thick of things, you have to trust the others to manage the search—you know they will."

When his jaw tightened and he made no reply, she glanced out of the window; they were on the Strand. "When we get back to St. Ives House, while I change, you can talk to Tom or Tully—whoever is currently acting as footmen-army liaison. Divide up the eighteen..." She glanced again at the list of deliveries she still held in her hand. "Well, it's fifteen customers if we discount the deliveries made this morning." She frowned and glanced at Drake. "Or do we?"

A minute ticked by, then Drake stated, "If the plotters—and the garrotter—adhered to their pattern of killing those drawn in as helpers immediately or as soon as possible after they've accomplished their allotted task, then it's the deliveries on Saturday we should focus on."

Still frowning, she said, "Isn't that contrary to the best way of going about things? You thought—and it seemed to me for excellent reasons— that they wouldn't move the gunpowder to the target site until twenty-four hours or less from the time they intended to blow it up."

He grimaced. For several moments, he stared at the list in her hand, then said, "This plot has frequently deviated from established precepts, but whether that strengthens the case for the deliveries on Friday and Saturday or the deliveries made this morning being the critical ones…" He shook his head. "It's impossible to predict. However, as we've significantly reduced the number of cellars your brothers and their helpers have to search, I'll suggest they start with the fifteen Friday and Saturday deliveries, and if they find nothing there"—he shifted and reached for his watch—"we should still have time to search the other three places later today." He glanced at his watch. "It's half past eleven."

"And who knows?" She looked down at the list. "At the funeral, we might get some clue as to which of these customers or addresses is the target."

Drake shifted closer so he could read the list. After scanning the addresses, he humphed. "Most of the locations are not ones we've searched. But these two"—he pointed—"are close to Whitehall, possibly close enough to do serious damage." He pointed to a third entry. "And that inn is next door to the Hungarian Embassy. In contrast, all three deliveries made this morning went to government and army sites we searched yesterday. Those cellars and stores were clear of gunpowder then." He sat back and added, "Of course, there's nothing to say they still are."

"Hmm." She refolded the list. "And as we still have no idea of motive…"

"Indeed. We can't discount any of the sites."

She loosened the ties of her reticule, tucked the list inside, and cinched the neck shut. "If you send word to Sebastian, Michael, and Cleo to concentrate on the places Hunstable's delivered to on Friday afternoon and Saturday, between them, they should be able to search all fifteen today. Meanwhile, if you and I learn nothing useful at the funeral, we can start at the bottom of the list and visit the three messes that received barrels from Hunstable's this morning."

Drake grunted an assent and looked out of the window. Impatience rode him, exacerbating a sense of an unseen clock inexorably ticking, of sand sliding through an hourglass where, all too soon, no more grains would be left to fall.

The thought of joining the search after the funeral—it would be a wonder if they learned anything about the location of the gunpowder there—went some small way to appeasing that side of him that hungered for action. That wanted to get out and do.

But Louisa was right. Of the six of them now actively immersed in the mission, he and she were the most appropriate—most usefully skilled—to do the rounds of the family and friends who would gather for Chilburn's funeral service.

And no matter the compulsion he felt to hunt and locate the barrels of gunpowder, he could not afford to forget that it was equally important—and ultimately possibly even more crucial—to identify the mastermind behind the plot.

They couldn't afford to ignore any opportunity to learn more about the elusive man—or, indeed, woman—who had recruited Lawton Chilburn to a plot that had brought about his end.

CHAPTER 54

$\mathcal{D}$rake held the heavy door of St. George's open for Louisa to slip
through, then silently followed her.

They'd timed their arrival perfectly; the doors had already been shut,
but a glance toward the front of the nave showed the minister had yet to
appear.

Almost on the thought, the minister entered from a side door and made
his stately way to the pulpit, which rose above the right front corner of
the nave. He climbed the stairs to the raised platform, looked down on the
congregation, then after a brief statement of their purpose in being there,
he opened the service with a call to prayer.

With Drake beside her, Louisa had halted to the rear of the massed
mourners filling the width of the nave. Standing in loose clusters, the
crowd reached more than halfway up the church. Her head slightly
bowed, she scanned the faces she could see, then rose on her toes to peek
over the wooden partitions that ran along each side, confirming that the
older family members had retreated into the box pews.

The prayer ended, and everyone shifted, resettling their weight as they
prepared to endure the rest of the hour-long service. Studying faces and
stances, Louisa detected few who appeared to have any real interest in
being there. Most had attended out of a sense of duty, not because they

truly mourned Lawton.

The minister embarked on a sonorous recitation of what was clearly a heavily edited account of the highlights of Lawton Chilburn's life.

Drake bent his head and whispered in her ear, "I doubt the Chilburn elders of either gender would have any idea of what Lawton was up to."

Turning her head Drake's way, she murmured back, "I doubt any of the younger ones—those much younger than he—would, either."

"Which leaves those of his generation." He met her eyes as she glanced up at him. "You take the females, I'll take the males—let's see what we can tease from them."

She nodded. It was a challenge of sorts; she was still convinced that someone of Lawton's family had to know something useful. The issue, she suspected, was that they—his brothers, sisters, or closest cousins—didn't realize that what they knew was relevant to his murder.

Moving all but silently, she and Drake parted. She glided to where two clusters of ladies stood, giving every appearance of dutifully listening. Drake, meanwhile, ambled forward and stopped just short of a group of well-dressed gentlemen—close enough to overhear any shared comments, no matter how muttered; the acoustics of the nave were wonderful for eavesdropping.

Louisa trained her ears to the low-voiced conversations of the ladies on either side. Although the members of both groups noticed her, they merely inclined their heads politely and returned to their comments, making no effort to curb their tongues.

Lawton was, after all, dead, and he was the subject of their observations.

Louisa listened avidly. All she heard reinforced their already-formed view of Lawton Chilburn as a scapegrace who had blotted his copybook several times too often for his family's taste. She wasn't surprised to learn that the family and all connections had agreed to make a point of attending the service—held at the church most favored by the haut ton—and all the gentlemen were to attend the burial at St. James in Highgate in the hope that such a turnout would mute any talk of the schism between Lawton and the rest of the Chilburns, thus downplaying Lawton's shortcomings and allowing the family to bury any lingering whispers along with him.

While she understood their reasoning, to her mind, such overenthusiastic attendance only underscored how deeply Lawton had fallen out of favor with his family—to the extent they all, root and branch, felt a need to exert themselves to whitewash his name.

Under cover of the minister's drone, she looked around more carefully, noting faces and putting names to most. All the family members she had heard of had answered the call. Shifting silently to the side, she peered briefly into the pews, noting the older generations, including Lawton's aunts and several aunts-in-law, along with his mother and her bosombows, the ageing Mereton spinsters; the few who saw her recognized her and stiffly inclined their heads.

She nodded back, then looked searchingly around again. The most notable lack among the mourners was the dearth of any who might be classed as friends or acquaintances. Lawton's cousins and the sons of several connections, all of whom Louisa could place, were the only males of that age group present.

Drake had already moved through their ranks, exchanging nods and, occasionally, a few whispered words. He'd eventually fetched up by the side of an ancient earl, with whom he was quietly talking. No one who knew of Drake and Louisa's involvement in breaking the news of Lawton's death to his family would be surprised to see them at the funeral, if nothing else as representatives of their respective houses. There were several others present in that capacity—like the earl to whom Drake was chatting—their appearance purely a courtesy to Hawesley and his viscountess. In general, however, such representatives were of the older generations, lords and ladies who could easily make time to pay their and their families' respects. Louisa nodded to several such older ladies and gentlemen, all of whom recognized her and were, patently, wondering why she was there. She acknowledged them, but steered clear.

Returning to the groups of ladies clustered in the nave, she halted close to Lawton's sisters and two of their cousins, all largely dry-eyed, and listened to their murmurings. All she heard merely confirmed that those ladies knew no more than they'd already shared.

Finally, the dull and uneventful service drew to a close. After the benediction, the minister invited the ladies present to return to the Hawesleys' Hill Street residence for the wake, while those gentlemen so inclined would follow the coffin to its final resting place in Highgate cemetery before returning to Hill Street.

Across the nave, Louisa met Drake's eyes. Lips thin, he shook his head. He wasn't going to Highgate.

Louisa hid a grimace. Presumably, he'd been as unsuccessful as she in learning anything of value. That left pursuing the barrels as their only way forward; she had no excuse to waste more time searching for those among Lawton's family and friends who—she was still convinced—must know something about his recent activities.

In her experience, it was well-nigh impossible to hide private schemes, especially illicit ones, from family and close friends; those who attempted it often believed they'd succeeded, but invariably—*invariably*—someone picked up some clue.

However, accepting that they'd run out of time to pursue her favored angle—dejected over what she saw as her failure to discern *something* that would point to whoever Lawton had fallen in with or even the cousin he'd thought had sent Cleo to follow him—she joined the other ladies as they moved up the nave toward the doors and the gray day outside.

She found herself beside one of Lawton's more cheery cousins, a Miss Tippet, a comfortable spinster of middle years. As they waited to file through the double doors onto the church's covered porch, purely by way of making conversation, Louisa murmured, "The family certainly answered the call and put on a good show."

"Yes, indeed." Miss Tippet smiled benevolently. "We've all come to support Hawesley and Lavinia through this. Such a thing to happen." She raised her head and glanced around at the crowd before and behind them. "Almost everyone made the effort, which speaks well for the family, don't you think?"

Louisa blinked. *Almost* everyone? "Indubitably." After the barest pause, she asked, "So who isn't here?"

"Oh, Uncle Hubert isn't, of course, but no one expected to see him." Miss Tippet lowered her head and her voice to add, "He's positively ancient and rather infirm and lives in Berkshire. I don't believe he even leaves the house." She raised her head and looked around again. "The only other who isn't here is Bevis—Bevis Griswade." Miss Tippet's tone and expression turned disapproving. "Heaven only knows why he didn't turn up. I know Monica, his sister, called on him on Saturday to make sure he knew about the funeral and tell him he was expected to attend." Miss Tippet humphed. "I really don't know what's going on with him, but he hasn't been attending family gatherings for a while."

Prodded by an impulse too powerful to resist, Louisa asked, "By any chance was Mr. Griswade—Bevis—in the army?"

"Why, yes." Miss Tippet looked at Louisa. "How did you know? Perhaps you've met him—he was in the guards. I forget which regiment."

"Did he serve in India?"

"Hmm." Miss Tippet appeared to be consulting her memory. "I don't believe so, but the last time I saw him—and thinking back, that must be close to ten years ago. How time does fly! But that was before he sold out, and he'd become quite obsessed with Oriental ways." She paused, frowning, then added, "Actually, he did go to India, but that was more recently, after he sold out of the guards. I believe he was with the East India Company troops."

"Ah." Louisa nodded as if pleased she and Miss Tippet had solved a minor social puzzle; she even managed to keep her tone within bounds as she said, "That must be it."

That was it!

Those before them shuffled forward, and Louisa and Miss Tippet emerged into the pearly light of the overcast day. They moved to join the other ladies and the gentlemen not attending the burial, who were congregating to either side of the doors to allow the coffin to be ceremonially carried past and placed in the waiting hearse.

As soon as she and Miss Tippet had settled, Louisa quietly said, "One of my cousins is interested in joining the East India Company. I know he would appreciate speaking with someone who has served over there. Do you happen to know Mr. Griswade's address?"

"I don't," Miss Tippet said, "but Monica"—she pointed to a fashionable matron standing farther along the porch—"Mrs. Monica Trevallayan, is his sister. She knows."

"Thank you." Louisa didn't dare allow the full measure of her gratefulness to infuse her tone. She rested her hand briefly on Miss Tippet's arm. "If you'll excuse me?"

Tamping down her rising excitement, keeping it from her face and her eyes and out of her voice, was imperative. Quitting Miss Tippet's side, she sidled unobtrusively step by polite step through the crowd, eventually halting beside Monica Trevallayan.

Mrs. Trevallayan glanced at her, recognized her, and smiled and nodded politely, transparently pleased to have Lady Louisa Cynster by her side.

Graciously, Louisa nodded back. After a quick glance to confirm that the coffin had yet to be carried out, she turned to the other woman. "Mrs. Trevallayan, I believe you might be able to assist me."

After being assured that Mrs. Trevallayan would, of course, do anything possible, Louisa repeated her tale of a cousin interested in learning about the East India Company and thus wishing to speak with, for example, Mrs. Trevallayan's brother, Mr. Griswade.

"Well, I'm rather miffed with Bevis at the moment. After I took the trouble to go to his lodgings and tell him of this event, he claimed he had a prior engagement." Mrs. Trevallayan sniffed. "A prior engagement— pshaw! What could be more important than a family cri—er, gathering such as this?"

"I agree unreservedly. So lacking in feeling." A second later, Louisa prompted, "And his lodgings…?"

"Oh yes—in George Street, Lady Louisa, just down from the Strand."

"Thank you." Louisa looked around, searching for Drake. She spotted him off to one side at the bottom of the porch steps, on the very outskirts of the crowd and transparently—at least to her—impatiently waiting for her.

Even though he was champing at the bit, wanting to get on and search for the gunpowder, by the time she'd slid through the crowd and reached him, he'd read the building excitement in her face.

The instant she joined him, he gripped her arm and turned her toward where Henry and the carriage were waiting around the corner in the square. "What did you learn?"

Walking briskly by his side, she tipped her head at the carriage, only paces away. "I'll tell you on the way home."

He helped her climb up, directed Henry to make for Grosvenor Square, then followed her.

She waited only until Drake had shut the door and dropped onto the seat before declaring, "The garrotter is Mr. Bevis Griswade. He's Lawton's first cousin—the last child and fourth son of Alice, Lady Griswade, who is the viscountess's sister. Bevis Griswade is the cousin Lawton thought had sent Cleo to follow him—perhaps checking on him, on how well he was managing the plot."

Drake's eyes had narrowed and fixed on her face. "Of all Lawton's many cousins, why decide it's Griswade?" His tone stated that he didn't disbelieve her but wanted proof.

"You must have noticed all the family attended the funeral."

He nodded. "I assumed they made a point of it, intending to douse any rumors that Lawton had been shunned by the family, which, of course, he had been."

"Precisely. But there were two family members who didn't attend. One, an old Uncle Hubert, who I think must be Lord Hubert Nagle—the viscountess's much older brother. He's a bachelor and also the Marquess of Faringdale's uncle—and Faringdale himself did attend. However, no one expected to see Lord Hubert because he's ancient and keeps to his house in Berkshire. But the other non-attendee was Bevis Griswade. His sister Mrs. Trevallayan took him the summons personally, but he said he had a prior engagement."

She held up a hand to stay any question and increasingly excitedly continued, "The most critical point, however, is that Bevis Griswade was in the guards. Then he sold out and served with the East India Company in India!"

Drake sat back and stared across the carriage. "How the devil did we miss him?"

"I think we just didn't ask quite the right questions. Griswade sold out about a decade ago—it could have been more. The guards' files—the ones they have at their fingertips in their offices—probably don't go back that far, so Griswade simply didn't show up. He'd be older than Chilburn by several years, and they didn't serve concurrently. And although Griswade served in India, it wasn't with the army. Michael checked for any connection of Chilburn's who had served in India *with the guards*, so of course, Griswade's name didn't come up."

She paused, then went on, "I don't know in which regiment Griswade served, but apparently when he sold out, he was already obsessed with all things Oriental, so he went off and joined the East India Company."

Slowly but definitely, Drake nodded. "He's our man. Thank God we now have a name." He glanced, more sharply, at her. "I saw you speak with Monica Trevallayan—did you get Griswade's address?"

"Yes—it's George Street, south of the Strand. He has lodgings there."

Calculation flared in Drake's eyes, and she hurriedly said, "*Before* you race off to hunt Griswade down—and as it's just lodgings and he supposedly had some prior engagement at this time, he's unlikely to be there at the moment—" She broke off and frowned. "A prior engagement—could that be something to do with the plot? Even though it's the fourth and not the fifth…" She arched her brows and met Drake's eyes. "Could Griswade be overseeing the gunpowder being moved to the target site?"

Drake's expression turned grim. "That's entirely possible."

She thought for a moment, then pressed her point. "Regardless, we can't just race willy-nilly around London hoping to stumble on the right place or on him." She met Drake's gaze; he was clearly unconvinced. "Do you know what Griswade looks like? Would you recognize him?"

Drake's lips thinned, then he admitted, "No. You?"

"I might via a family resemblance, but in general, no—I don't think I've ever met him."

Drake glanced outside. The carriage had been rolling slowly along Brook Street; they'd nearly reached Grosvenor Square. "If Griswade is our man and he's involved in some action very possibly to do with the gunpowder being placed at the target site, then our best bet is to do as we'd planned—leave the others to check the twelve earlier deliveries, and with all possible speed, search the three messes to which Hunstable's men delivered this morning."

Something about the morning's deliveries tugged at Louisa's mind, but she nodded. "Yes—but I have to change, and you, meanwhile, need to send word to Sebastian, and Michael and Cleo—and Antonia, and Inspector Crawford, too—that Griswade is the garrotter."

"That won't take long."

"Changing my gown will take only a few minutes." She glanced at her pale-gray silk skirts; the material was far too fine to serve if they were racing about chasing killers and searching for barrels, and she wanted something sturdier on her feet—half-boots instead of her pumps.

And there was something else niggling in her brain, like a hairpin poking insistently into her scalp. "I also want to ask Grandmama and Lady Osbaldestone about Lord Nagle. It sounds as if he's far too old for me to have met him, yet I'm sure I've heard his name mentioned in passing, although in relation to what I can't recall, other than that it was some time ago. I've heard nothing about him recently." She looked at Drake. "Do you know anything about him?"

He thought, then shook his head. "I've never met him, but I recall much the same as you—I've heard his name, but it was long ago, and I know next to nothing about him." He paused, then said, "I could ask the pater."

"If he's at Wolverstone House, please do."

The carriage rocked to a halt outside St. Ives House. Louisa gripped Drake's hand and climbed down to the pavement. She straightened her full skirts while Drake called up to Henry that they wouldn't be long.

Then Drake took her arm, and they quickly climbed the steps. Crewe was on duty; he swung open the door, and they walked into the front hall.

When Drake released her arm, Louisa swung to face him. "I'll change and check with Grandmama and Lady Osbaldestone while you send your messages and talk to Tom"—Michael's man was hovering toward the rear of the hall, on duty as the central command for Sebastian, Michael, Cleo, and the footmen army—"and check with your father. And *then*"— she held Drake's gaze—"we'll go after Griswade and the gunpowder."

Drake hesitated, then, grim-faced, nodded.

Louisa nodded decisively back, turned, and rushed for the stairs.

CHAPTER 55

She didn't waste a moment. She raced up the stairs, into the west wing, and flew into her room.

Sukie, her maid, was already there; Louisa had warned her she would return to change her gown after the funeral.

"Quickly!" Louisa turned and gave Sukie her back. While the maid's fingers made quick work of the buttons running down the back of the gown, Louisa kicked off her pumps. "If I don't get changed and down soon, Winchelsea will go without me."

"He wouldn't dare." Sukie's tone was entirely confident.

Louisa stripped the long sleeves from her arms. "Unfortunately, yes, he would." Letting the gown fall to the floor, she stepped out of it and all but jigged with impatience while Sukie picked up the walking dress in dark-blue twill that had been laid out on the bed. The maid gathered the skirts, then lifted them over Louisa's head.

She wriggled the skirts down and thrust her arms into the sleeves. "And I need to speak with Grandmama and Lady Osbaldestone—are they up, do you know?"

"Must be—I saw Colleen taking them a nuncheon, so I'd say they'll be ready to talk."

"Good—my black kid half-boots and the matching gloves." While

Sukie raced to the armoire, Louisa checked her reflection in the mirror above her dressing table. Her hair was still neat and in place, and the subdued pearl collar she'd donned for the funeral would do well enough with the dark-blue dress; she needed to appear properly turned out if she was to present herself before her grandmother and the even more eagle-eyed Lady Osbaldestone.

Sukie returned with the boots and knelt to hold them so Louisa could slip her feet inside. While Louisa held up her wide skirts, Sukie deftly did up the lacings. "There." Sukie sat back on her ankles and looked Louisa over with a critical eye. Then she nodded. "Yes. You'll do."

"Excellent." Louisa grabbed up the reticule she'd carried earlier and left on the dressing table stool; the list of Hunstable's deliveries was inside. She headed for the door. "Now for Grandmama and Lady Osbaldestone."

Those two grandest of grandes dames were seated at a round table set in the window embrasure of her grandmother's sitting room. They'd finished their light meal and were sipping tea, and were very ready to welcome Louisa.

Indeed, their eyes lit up when, rising from a graceful curtsy, she declared, "I need to pick your brains, and I don't have much time."

Her grandmother held up a cheek for a kiss and arched her fine brows. "And why is that—your lack of time?"

"Because if I take too long, Drake will lose what little patience he has and go off without me." She didn't know if he would, but he might, and she wasn't about to risk it. She dutifully kissed her grandmother's cheek, then drew up a straight-backed chair to the table and sat. "I need to know everything you can tell me about Lord Hubert Nagle. His name has cropped up in relation to Drake's current mission."

"The one you are all helping him with?" Helena asked.

Louisa nodded. "Yes. That one."

"Nagle, heh?" Therese Osbaldestone exchanged a look with Helena. "Now there's a name we haven't heard in an age."

"But you know about him, don't you?" Louisa couldn't imagine that they wouldn't.

Lady Osbaldestone snorted. "Of course, we do—patience, child. Now, let's see. Lord Hubert Nagle is the younger brother of the late Marquess of Faringdale. His nephew currently holds the title."

"Yes—I knew that. And Viscountess Hawesley is his sister, and his other sister is Alice, Lady Griswade. But that's all I know about Lord Nagle. Was he notable in any way?"

"Whitehall," Helena said. "He was one of the principal private secretaries for many, many years. I can't recall what ministry." She looked questioningly at Lady Osbaldestone.

"Home Office," Therese Osbaldestone supplied. "Dear Gerald was Foreign Office, of course—"

Louisa knew "dear Gerald" was Lady Osbaldestone's way of referring to her late husband, who had died many years ago.

"—so we didn't cross Nagle's path all that often, but he was very much the Whitehall mandarin. He wielded significant power, always had the ear of his minister—indeed, in his later years, he was known to positively *guide* the Home Secretary."

"Hmm. Nagle was considered quite brilliant, as I recall," Helena put in.

"Oh, indeed—and in that arena, 'brilliant' means quite ruthlessly clever and cunning." Lady Osbaldestone frowned. "As far as I know, there was never any scandal attached to his name—not while he was in office, at least. And he's been gone from London for, what? More than fifteen years?" She looked interrogatively at Helena.

"At least fifteen years," Louisa's grandmother stated. "Remember, it was when the Queen, then Princess Alexandrina, was on one of those horrendous tours her mother used to drag her around the country on that he was introduced to her, and that was what triggered all the subsequent brouhaha." Helena's hands gracefully swept upward, indicating an eruption. "That must have been in '34 or '35, and he'd been retired for a few years by then."

Louisa sat forward. "What brouhaha?"

Helena waved dismissively. "It was all ridiculously silly. A typical piece of male conceit."

Lady Osbaldestone snorted. "Indeed. Nothing more than injured male pride."

"But what happened?" Louisa asked.

"That harpy, the princess's mother, had driven the poor gel too hard, and she—the princess—fell ill."

"And she was never one to take to all the fuss, anyway," Helena said. "Indeed, she still isn't."

Louisa, who had spent a year as one of the Queen's ladies-in-waiting, knew that to be true.

"Quite so." Lady Osbaldestone nodded. "But the long and the short of it was that when Alexandrina was introduced to Nagle, ill and barely able to function, she more or less cut him. Not intentionally, but from all accounts she had reached *point non-plus* and couldn't carry on any longer. He, however, unaware of her difficulties, was infuriated that she didn't acknowledge the long and valuable service he'd rendered to Crown and country. Well, with that mother of hers as mentor, I doubt the poor gel even knew of it. But Nagle...well, let's just say that it was as well that he was already retired. He roundly denounced the princess as unfit to rule, to ascend the throne."

"Good Lord!" Louisa could only stare; she'd never heard of this tale, and fifteen and more years on, after more than thirteen years of Victoria as monarch, she found it difficult to credit.

"Oh yes." Helena's pale-green eyes, so very like Louisa's, seemed to see her granddaughter's difficulty. "He spoke out against her, and he was exceedingly loud about it."

"Naturally," Lady Osbaldestone said, "several ladies of the court tried to explain what had happened—that the princess had not been properly briefed as to his past contributions, and that she had been ill and, indeed, had later been forced to take to her bed—but Nagle would have none of it. He continued to trumpet her inappropriate behavior—meaning her lack of recognition of him—as clear evidence she was unfit to rule."

Helena snorted and managed to make the sound both French and elegant. "That Alexandrina was female had more to do with it than anything else. I firmly believe Nagle would have found fault regardless— Alexandrina's illness and poor preparation simply played into his hands. Lord Hubert was definitely of the old school—he would have recommended patting ladies on their heads and advising them— nay, instructing them—to stick to their embroidery."

Lady Osbaldestone humphed. "You will have noticed he remains a bachelor to this day." After a moment, she went on, "As I recall, Nagle created sufficient noise by way of letters to the news sheets that William—the King—dispatched several gentlemen to explain to Nagle that speaking so of his future sovereign came perilously close to treason." Lady Osbaldestone squinted at Louisa. "Indeed, I suspect Wolverstone was one of those sent. I can certainly imagine he would have been most persuasive. And after that, Nagle shut up, and as far as I know, he sank back into complete obscurity somewhere in the Home Counties."

"Berkshire," Louisa supplied. Something clicked in her brain. Reading was in Berkshire. According to the bill she'd found in his pocket, Lawton Chilburn had visited Reading in the very middle of managing the plot. Suddenly, facts and thoughts were whirling in her brain. "Thank you." To her ears, her voice seemed to come from far away. She rose. "I think that's all I need to know."

Both her grandmother and Lady Osbaldestone eyed her intently, then Lady Osbaldestone said, "Just be sure to come back and tell us the whole story once you and that dragon of yours get to the bottom of it."

"Incidentally," Helena said with a gentle smile, "do bring him with you next time. You may tell him we wish to interview him."

Not even the prospect of telling Drake that and seeing how he reacted was enough to pull Louisa free of the whirlpool of conjecture swamping her mind. She nodded woodenly. "Again, thank you both."

She curtsied, then walked quickly to the door.

Her mind continued to spin. She tried to pulls facts free, tried to order them, tried to list those she had to tell Drake—those he didn't as yet know.

She made it to the head of the stairs before, like a kaleidoscope swirling, then clicking into position, the various facts she'd gathered swung and revolved one last time and snapped into place.

She saw the whole—the horrendous whole—and she gasped. She reached out blindly and gripped the bannister while, in her mind, she searched the picture that known facts, thoughts, and conjecture had shaped, desperately seeking a weakness—a break in the fabric that would indicate the picture wasn't true. Instead, the harder she looked, the more closely she studied it, her mental image only gained in clarity; within it, every single fact fitted and locked into place.

She'd solved the riddle of the mission.

What she saw chilled her to her marrow.

She jerked back to reality, to the here and now. Frantic, she pulled open her reticule, hunted, and hauled out the list of Hunstable's deliveries and scanned down the list… Her heart literally stopped.

Then it started thumping furiously.

"Oh dear God!" She picked up her skirts and all but flew down the stairs.

Startled, Crewe looked at her. "My lady?"

She skidded to a halt on the tiles. "Drake—Lord Winchelsea?" Close to panic, she searched the hall. "Where is he?"

"The marquess went to Wolverstone House to speak with—"

She reached the front door, hauled it open, grabbed up her skirts, and raced onto the porch—

Straight into Drake. He'd been climbing the steps when she'd rushed out, but had braced himself so when she barreled into him, they didn't go tumbling to the pavement.

"Oof!" She rebounded and staggered.

He caught her and steadied her. "What's happened?"

She flung back a curl that had tumbled forward, seized his sleeve, and looked into his eyes. "We have to stop her. Now!"

"Stop whom?"

"The *Queen!*"

Drake glanced around. A few startled passersby had heard. "Inside." He didn't give Louisa a chance to argue; his hands on her shoulders, he propelled her backward into the front hall.

Crewe had been holding the door; Louisa jigged with impatience while he shut it. She barely waited until the latch clicked before stating, her voice tighter, her tone more rigid and absolute than Drake had ever heard it, "Lord Hubert Nagle, a now-ancient, once-exceedingly-powerful ex-

Whitehall bureaucrat, is your mastermind. He's plotted to blow up the Queen, but not tomorrow. Today! *Now*—this afternoon. In fact"—she glanced at the clock on the wall—"within the hour." Her gaze swung back to lock with Drake's. "If we don't stop her."

He blinked, trying to envisage such a scenario. "Calm down. There's no way they'll get the gunpowder into the palace."

"*Not* the palace!" Her tone was beyond adamant, and he realized that whatever she was saying, she didn't just believe it was true—she knew it was. As if to prove that, she brandished the list of Hunstable's deliveries in his face. "He's going to blow her up at the Tower."

"What?"

She pointed to one entry on the list. "See? A delivery to the Waterloo Block officers' mess of fifteen barrels of Bright Flame Ale."

He felt his features blank. "There was nothing there yesterday afternoon. Sebastian checked."

"The delivery"—she poked at the list—"was this morning."

"But the Queen—"

"Is on her way to the Tower as we argue!"

He frowned. "Why, for heaven's sake?"

Louisa felt giddy, but this was no time to swoon. She forced herself to draw in a deep breath, and with her eyes fixed on Drake's, succinctly said, "Parliament has commenced sitting, so there's a state banquet to mark the occasion tonight. That's a permanent feature in the court calendar. It's sheer luck that this year, it's fallen so close to Guy Fawkes Night."

He nodded. "And the banquet is at the palace."

"Yes, but this afternoon, as she always does before a state banquet, the Queen, accompanied by Prince Albert, will go to the Jewel House in the Tower to choose which of the crown jewels she'll wear tonight."

Drake paled. "The officers' mess...it's in the cellar beneath the Jewel House."

"I know! We have to stop the Queen before she reaches the Tower."

Drake seized her hand and strode for the door. "You can tell me the rest on the way." Crewe was at the door; he opened it, and they rushed down the steps and across the pavement to where Henry had the carriage waiting.

Drake all but flung Louisa up into the carriage and called to Henry, "The Tower! As fast as you can."

When he tried to get into the carriage, Louisa pushed him back and twisted to call up to Henry, "Go via the Strand."

Drake didn't contradict her. To Henry and the footman beside him on the box, he said, "We need to intercept the royal coach."

"It'll be the small black one," Louisa added, "but it'll have outriders—

guardsmen. Look for the helmets."

She pulled back into the carriage, and Drake dived in. He fell onto the seat as Henry, an ex-jarvey and nothing loath, obeyed Drake's orders and literally whipped up his horses in Grosvenor Square.

Drake straightened and clutched at the strap swinging by his head.

Beside him, Louisa was clinging to the strap on her side for dear life. "Obviously," she gasped, as Henry took the first corner at speed, "if we don't catch them before the Tower, it won't be for lack of trying."

Drake quashed the impulse to demand Louisa tell him the whole from the beginning; if her conjecture was correct, they didn't have time. And if she was correct, they'd have plenty of time later—after they saved the Queen.

Of course, that meant he was accepting that she'd got everything right, but if he'd learned anything of her, it was that when she was this clear, when she felt this strongly and spoke so adamantly, she wouldn't be— wasn't going to be—wrong.

Accepting that, the first thing he needed to do was work out what lay ahead. "You know the Queen's movements from your time as one of her ladies." Like all the daughters of the higher nobility, she had served a year in the royal household as lady-in-waiting to the Queen.

She nodded. "And one thing you can say about Victoria, she stringently adheres to established protocols." She glanced at him and briefly met his eyes. "It's after two o'clock, so she's already left the palace and is either on or almost on the Strand."

The carriage rocked violently, and he caught her against him. Only when the carriage had righted and shot forward again did he ease his hold.

"We have to catch her carriage before it reaches the Tower." Louisa peered out, noting the streets they were passing. "It'll be much harder to send her back to the palace if she gets past the entrance—you can trust me on that."

He was trusting her over a great deal more than that, but halting the Queen's carriage before it reached the Tower fitted well with his evolving plan of how best to spike Griswade's gunpowder and end the threat from Lord Hubert Nagle.

They hadn't yet reached the Strand. "Papa was out, so I didn't learn anything about Nagle, but clearly you did. Tell me."

Her nerves unbelievably tight, Louisa took a moment to order her thoughts—to strip her mental picture to its bare bones. "For years, Nagle was principal private secretary to the Home Secretary. He became one of Whitehall's most powerful mandarins. For various reasons, he believes that Victoria—Princess Alexandrina as she then was—snubbed him years ago. He publicly declared her unfit to rule. He was already retired and was told to shut up. Was more or less told that not doing so would be treason—and it's possible your father was involved in that telling."

"Ah." Drake felt his jaw set. "This always felt like it had a...personal aspect to it."

"In Nagle's mind, it probably does. He would want to outwit you— you're your father's heir in more ways than one."

"So Nagle set out to blow up Victoria?"

"It might not be just Victoria but Albert as well. A lot of Nagle's generation didn't approve of Victoria marrying a German prince."

"True. Presumably, he's planning to remove both Victoria and Albert and establish a regency with Edward on the throne."

"That might be why he's waited this long to act—to be sure Edward was going to survive childhood and to have sufficient other heirs that there's no chance of the line failing." She paused, then went on, "Who knows what his reasoning was? The important point is that if you put Nagle into position as the mastermind, everything else falls into place. Every skill and talent, all the experience you've hypothesized the mastermind must have, Nagle surely possesses. We knew we were looking for someone with a deep understanding of the Young Irelander and Chartist causes, who knew how each organization is run, how to hoodwink their members into doing what he wished and so implicating both organizations, and for all that, Nagle qualifies—arguably better than anyone else."

She drew breath. "On top of that, Nagle is a bachelor and has no immediate heirs—his estate is his to leave as he pleases, and I imagine it's not inconsiderable. Lawton told his sister that he was expecting to inherit from someone—that's what Nagle offered him for his help, a part of his estate. Griswade is also one of Nagle's nephews and, as another fourth son, might also be in need of funds. Nagle plotted and planned, and then once he was sure his plot was perfect to the last degree, he needed two henchmen to carry it out. Who better than two younger relatives, both with military backgrounds, both hungry for funds, and both—as Nagle almost certainly knew—with very few scruples and no qualms about killing in pursuit of their goals."

She looked at Drake and met his eyes. "That's how it was done—Lord Hubert Nagle planned his revenge, and Lawton Chilburn and Bevis Griswade executed it."

He held her gaze, then nodded. "Yes, that fits."

She flung her arms wide. "*Everything* fits. Down to the smallest detail. You've said many times that this plot didn't follow the usual patterns— that's because Nagle expected to have you as his...well, opponent. He knew you would become involved and planned for that, too. For instance"—she turned toward him, her features animated—"his latest piece of misdirection was killing Hunstable's deliverymen. Not *after* they'd done what he wanted, as had been his habit until then, but before—that made us concentrate on the Saturday deliveries. We sent Sebastian and Michael to check those, rather than the deliveries on Monday. If we hadn't realized it was Nagle behind this, possibly none of us would have got to the Tower in time to seize the gunpowder before it's used." She sobered. "We still might not be in time."

"You said Victoria always adheres to her schedule. What time does she usually reach the Jewel House?"

Louisa thought, then replied, "For once, I find myself grateful for Her Majesty's majesty, so to speak. She's a monarch and behaves as one— she never rushes. She invariably stops to talk with the guards at both entrances—the Middle Tower and the Bloody Tower. The Keeper of the Jewels will meet her just inside the Bloody Tower, and she'll chat to him before the carriage rolls on at a walking pace and stops outside the Jewel House. Then she usually spends a few more minutes chatting to Mrs. Proudfoot, the Keeper's wife. Victoria is quite fond of Mrs. Proudfoot."

"Time-wise, when would she go inside the Jewel House?"

"I would say she normally goes through the door at about ten minutes before the hour."

Drake hauled out his watch. "It's twenty minutes past two." He glanced out of the window. They were now in the Strand. "I'll place my faith in Henry. And the royal coach never goes quickly, not with the traffic and the guards hemming it in."

After a moment, he frowned at her. "You were saying that Nagle had Hunstable's men killed before…ah." His expression blanked. "I see."

"Indeed—you said all along that the best way to move the gunpowder to the target site was to disguise it as something that would normally be found there—in this case, ale—*and* to have it moved into position by people completely innocent of what they were doing. I doubt you could find more complete innocents than the lads Hunstable was forced to hire to replace his missing drivers."

Drake softly swore. "He really did think of damned near everything."

"I suspect he's been planning this for years. He had to force Hunstable to hire lads on the spot. That way, even if they noticed the difference in weight and lack of movement within the ale barrels, having just got the job, they would be unlikely to start asking questions or making any fuss, at least not right away."

They heard Henry call that he had the royal carriage in sight.

Drake shifted focus. "Correct me if I'm wrong. The Jewel House stands against the inner face of Martin Tower. The side wall of Waterloo Block faces the Jewel House door." He looked at Louisa. "I've never been inside. Tell me everything you can remember about it."

"Facing the door from outside, there are five steps to a small porch. There's a cellar door at ground level to the left, but no window to the cellar."

"All right. If I go through the front door, what will I see?"

"There's a rectangular hall, and the stairs to the upper floor where the jewels are kept lie directly in front of the door, starting about two thirds of the way down the hall. There's a passage to the left, which leads into the rooms the Keeper and his family use."

"Family—any children?"

She shook her head. "I've never seen any. If there are, they must be away at school."

"We can hope. So the stairs go up, and the jewels are on the first floor. Are there any guards there?"

"Usually there are four—at least there are whenever the Queen visits."

"How many on the lower level—the level of the Keeper's rooms?"

"None—I've never seen a guard on the lower level. All four are always on the upper level."

"All right. Where's the cellar door?"

She glanced at him. "I've never had to go to the cellar."

"Guess."

She thought, then said, "It must be somewhere on the Keeper's level, but at the same time, must be readily accessible to the workers in the officers' mess to take barrels out of and so on. So I would guess that it's along the corridor to the left of the stairs—the one that leads to the Keeper's rooms."

He nodded. "That makes sense."

Drake's footman called down, "The royal carriage is some way ahead on Fleet Street, my lord."

On the words, the carriage jerked sharply to the right, then back the other way.

Drake swore and pushed to his feet. Clinging to the upper frame of the door, he pushed up the trap in the ceiling and called, "Henry, do whatever you have to and close the distance as fast as you can."

"Aye, m'lord!"

Immediately, the carriage jerked to the side. Drake all but fell back onto the seat. He caught Louisa as she was flung against him.

Louisa clung to Drake as Henry displayed a degree of ruthless force that fully matched that of his master.

Five minutes and several sharp tacking moves later, the groom called down, "The royals are three carriages ahead, my lord, and the guardsmen have noticed." A second later, the groom reported, "Two are riding back."

Drake pulled himself up and called to Henry, "Slow, but don't pull to the curb."

Even before the carriage slowed, Drake opened the door and stepped out onto the step.

Louisa watched him look ahead, then he yelled, "Winchelsea!"

Two seconds later, a puzzled "My lord?" floated back.

Drake responded, "I have urgent business with Her Majesty. On the authority of the Prime Minister, stop her coach."

Louisa scooted to the other window, hung out, and peered ahead. She saw one of the guards who had ridden their way wheel his horse and spur back to the royal carriage.

Still half out of the door, Drake ordered, "Push forward as far as you can, then stop."

To Louisa's amazement, Henry managed to squeeze them one place closer, then he hauled his horses to an abrupt halt.

"Come on." Louisa turned to see Drake beckoning. He'd already dropped to the road. She wasted no time in grabbing his offered hand and joining him, then together, they raced around the carriage and horses now wedged between the royal carriage, which had halted in the middle of the road, and Drake's now-stationary carriage.

Given the milling guardsmen, not one driver or passenger was complaining.

Drake reached the royal carriage, glanced at Louisa and fleetingly met her eyes, then he faced the carriage, opened the door, and bowed deeply. "Your Majesty. Your Highness."

Beside him, Louisa sank into a full court curtsy.

"My lord Winchelsea." The Queen's tones were those of the matron she was and also somewhat peevish. "What is the meaning of this?"

Drake raised Louisa, then faced the Queen. "With our deepest respects, Your Majesty, this matter is urgent. You must turn back and return to the palace." The prince had leant forward to look past the Queen; Drake met his eyes briefly before saying to the Queen, "Lady Louisa will explain. I must hurry to the Tower, where an ambush has been laid, unbeknown to any of the guards."

The Queen's expression was tightening. She could, on occasion, be exceedingly stubborn. "But I need—"

"*Liebchen.*" Albert placed his hand on her arm and spoke quietly. "I believe we should do as your faithful Lord Winchelsea suggests." Albert knew Drake and could be counted on to react as necessary whenever any threat to the Queen surfaced. "We should take no risks—none whatsoever. We can decide and send a courier to retrieve the pieces you wish to wear tonight. If something is afoot at the Tower, we should not drive needlessly into it."

The Queen uttered a sound that in a lesser mortal would have been called a grunt. After a second, she fixed her protuberant eyes on Louisa, waiting beside Drake for permission to enter the carriage. "Very well." The Queen waved Louisa up and huffily said, "Lady Louisa may come up and explain everything to us as we travel back to the palace."

As Albert gave orders to the guards' officer who'd drawn up by the carriage on Albert's side to turn their small cavalcade around and return to the palace, Louisa gripped Drake's hand, and he helped her up into the carriage.

Then he stepped back and bowed low. "With your permission, Your Majesty?"

"Yes, yes." Lips thin, Victoria waved him away.

Drake shut the door and raced back to his carriage. Louisa felt a tug in her chest as his dark head vanished from her sight, hidden behind the jostling bodies of the guardsmen's horses.

Still standing, she waited as Lady Anthea Gorton, Victoria's lady-in-waiting for this trip and an acquaintance of Louisa's, lifted Victoria's heavy, ermine-trimmed cloak and shuffled along the rear-facing seat to make room, then Louisa sat and faced the Queen and Prince.

"Your Majesty. Your Highness." She drew breath and plunged in. "It appears that an old gentleman has plotted to blow you—both of you—up."

The heavy black carriage rocked into motion, then turned left up a street to come around; through the window, from the corner of her eye, Louisa glimpsed Drake's carriage dash past and on toward the Tower.

To the cellar of the Jewel House where, if their deductions were correct, Bevis Griswade had assembled ten hundredweight of gunpowder that he intended to detonate at close to three o'clock, a time when, had Victoria followed her customary routine, the Queen and Prince Albert would be in the upstairs chamber of the Jewel House, making her selections for the state banquet that evening.

Louisa knew the Queen well enough to know better than to attempt to gloss over the bald facts. Her Majesty had survived at least two attempts on her life and was definitely no longer the sort of woman to fall into hysterics, if she ever had been. As quickly and as concisely as she could, restricting herself to the essential elements of the plot, she related the gist of what they had uncovered, what they now understood, and what they now believed.

Prince Albert was a godsend. While Victoria wanted to know this or that, and was inclined to demand answers to a host of minor questions, the prince grasped the critical nature of the situation with admirable swiftness. "I take it," he said, "that Lord Winchelsea has gone on to the Tower to attempt to halt the explosion."

"Indeed, sir." Louisa seized her chance and went on, "With Your

Majesty's permission, I would like to follow and lend what assistance I can." The farther the carriage traveled and the distance from the Tower increased, the more the compulsion to leap out and race after Drake grew. "Lord Winchelsea will focus on what needs to be done, and he will not have sufficient time to explain to the guards and others there what I've just told you—he will use his authority to clear his path. But there are many officers, guards, and other workers in the Tower who will not know what's going on—I can assist in minimizing the inevitable confusion, and that might be vital in securing the outcome we would prefer."

Albert met her gaze directly, and before Victoria could huff and puff—she did not like her ladies-in-waiting to go gallivanting about, as she termed it—the prince stated, "You and Lord Winchelsea have rendered us a great service this day, Lady Louisa." Albert patted Victoria's hand and continued, "I believe we must accede to your request."

It wasn't quite a question, but the Queen understood the message. She fixed Louisa with a searching look, then nodded. "Very well. By all means go, but at the first opportunity, we will expect you both at the palace to report on the outcome."

"Yes, Your Majesty." Gracefully, Louisa bowed low—the best she could manage while seated in the carriage.

Albert called for the carriage to halt. Louisa edged along the seat and gripped the door handle.

"If there is anything we can do, Lady Louisa—any assistance we may offer—you have only to ask."

The Queen's unexpectedly supportive words, uttered, Louisa knew, in all sincerity, gave her pause. Then she glanced at Lady Anthea before looking at Victoria. "Actually, Your Majesty…"

Three minutes later, she was being helped to the saddle of one of the guardsmen's horses. Having to ride astride meant her skirts were rucked, but Victoria's heavy velvet cloak fell past the shortened stirrups and concealed the scandalous sight.

Not that Louisa cared about being scandalous at such a time; she'd requested the cloak for another reason entirely.

"Are you sure you can hold him?" The worried guardsman she'd unhorsed reluctantly handed her the reins. "You could ride pillion."

The smile Louisa bent on him would have cut glass. "I've been riding since infancy, John Marlowe, including in Scotland, where most ladies ride astride. I can handle any beast you can—now get out of my way."

She barely waited for him to comply before she set her heels to the horse's flanks and sent him flying, tacking through traffic at breakneck speed.

Behind her, she heard the thunder of hooves as the three guardsmen the prince had ordered to go with her attempted to keep up.

They couldn't. She was much lighter. She was also more driven. Gradually, the guardsmen fell behind.

By then as one with the horse, Louisa all but flew toward the Tower.

Almost certainly, Griswade would be in the cellar of the Jewel House when Drake reached it.

The Queen and Prince Albert might now be safe, but that wasn't the end of the threat. There was no question in her mind that Drake would do whatever was needed to prevent the explosion.

But he might need help to come out of the encounter alive.

That was the possibility that thudded inside her with every beat of her heart.

Instinct, primitive and powerful, insisted she fly to his side, whispered that he might well need help, that he might need a distraction.

And no one delivered distraction more effectively than Lady Wild.

CHAPTER 56

*A*s he had that morning, ex-Captain Bevis Griswade walked confidently through the arched entrance of Middle Tower and into the Outer Ward. The guards stationed in the archway tipped their heads; he acknowledged them with the customary abbreviated nod.

In the excitement to come, they wouldn't remember him, one among so many officers passing them that day.

Griswade strode on around the Outer Ward and turned under the arched passageway of the Bloody Tower. The guards there—different guards from those on the morning roster—also acknowledged him. They were on their best behavior, knowing their queen would arrive shortly.

Griswade noted the thin, prim-faced, black-coated man waiting with a species of anxious expectation at the inner entrance to the Bloody Tower. Mr. Proudfoot, Keeper of the Crown Jewels. An extra guard stood beside him, and they were passing the time in idle chatter while they waited for their sovereign to appear.

Good. Griswade allowed himself a small smile at the confirmation of the old man's omniscience. As always, his intelligence had been accurate down to the smallest detail, and his suggested timing was nothing less than perfect. The Queen and her entourage would be arriving at the entrance to the Inner Ward in about ten minutes. Five minutes or so after that, she and her German prince would be in the upper chamber of the Jewel House.

Everything was proceeding according to plan.

Once again, as soon as the White Tower concealed him from those gathered at the Bloody Tower, Griswade smoothly altered course and walked steadily, unhurriedly, toward the Jewel House.

From the inside pocket of his coat, he drew out an official-looking checklist printed with the names of the various breweries and merchants who supplied the Waterloo Block officers' mess. Naturally, the list included the Phoenix Brewery. Griswade also drew out a pencil.

With no pause in his stride, he walked directly to the Jewel House and mounted the five steps to the narrow porch shading the front door. He rapped peremptorily, yet lightly, on the wooden frame—he didn't want to alert the four guards who, according the old man's information, would be on the upper floor.

He waited, praying that his knock would have been loud enough to be heard by Mrs. Proudfoot, who should have been somewhere on the ground floor, in the Keeper's rooms.

Eventually, he heard the sound of light footsteps approaching, then the door opened, and Mrs. Proudfoot, a tallish, thin, and rather gawky woman in her mid-thirties with pale-brown hair and pale-brown eyes, looked at him inquiringly, a tinge of surprise in her face.

Griswade brandished his list and kept his voice low. "I've been sent by Captain Conroy to take an inventory of the barrels in the cellar." Captain Conroy was the officer in charge of the officers' mess.

Mrs. Proudfoot made a disapproving sound. "Her Majesty is due at any moment. Can't it wait?"

Griswade summoned a genial smile. "I won't trip up Her Majesty—I won't even be seen. I'll be in the cellar."

Mrs. Proudfoot stared, but Griswade kept his smile in place and didn't give an inch.

Eventually, Mrs. Proudfoot heaved a put-upon sigh. She peered past Griswade at the White Tower—in the direction of the Bloody Tower— but as yet, there was neither sight nor sound of any arrival. "Oh, very well." Mrs. Proudfoot stood back and waved Griswade inside. "Come in, but you'd best get down there straightaway."

His next move was one on which the old man's intelligence had offered no insight; he knew of the Jewel House but had never been inside it. Griswade walked into the hall—all wooden walls, floor, and ceiling— and waited until Mrs. Proudfoot shut the door and turned his way before, with an apologetic look, he all but whispered, "I haven't been sent to do this before. Where's the door?"

Mrs. Proudfoot humphed. "I'll show you." She moved past him and led the way down a corridor to the left of the stairs. "I suppose you'll be wanting a lantern as well?"

"If you wouldn't mind."

She humphed again and halted, then she released a catch concealed in the paneling of the wall beneath the stairs, and a door swung open. "This way."

Griswade followed her into what appeared to be a storeroom under the stairs. Mrs. Proudfoot went to a narrow shelf that jutted from the underside of the stairs. Two lanterns stood waiting; she fumbled with a match and lit one. After adjusting the wick, she picked up the lantern, turned, and played the light over a heavy wooden door set into the opposite wall.

She crossed to the door, opened it, and pulled it wide. "There you are." She moved into the doorway, held up the lantern, and waved, encompassing the cellar's contents. "That's what you're after."

Silently, Griswade shifted closer and looked over her head. A small landing lay beyond the door, and from that, a set of stone steps led down into the flagstone-paved cellar. There was a stone wall to the right, supporting the landing and the steps and restricting his view of the space, but the area he could see was filled with low stacks of crates, and beyond, lining the walls, stood barrels of every description.

This was a critical moment. Griswade was acutely aware that only a single wooden floor separated him and the Keeper's wife from the guards above.

When Mrs. Proudfoot started to turn toward him to hand him the lantern and leave, his gaze on the barrels below, he stepped forward.

Instinctively, Mrs. Proudfoot stepped back onto the landing, then edged to the side, against the wall. She glanced down at the crates.

A quick tap on the head with his pistol butt sent her crumpling. He caught the lantern before it fell, then reached back and quietly shut the cellar door.

He looked down at the figure lying at his feet. So far, so perfect.

He stepped over Mrs. Proudfoot and went down the steps. Raising the lantern, he started searching. A minute later, he found the fifteen barrels of Bright Flame Ale stacked along the side wall to the right of the steps. Hunstable's new lads had copied the ways of their predecessors and stacked the barrels on their sides in a neat pyramid with five barrels in the bottom row. The cellar didn't run the full width of the building; Griswade estimated the stack of barrels stood two floors below and just a fraction to the right of the central section of the Jewel House.

He allowed himself a smile—at the appropriateness of the name emblazoned on the ale barrels and at the fact that Fate had once again smiled and he wouldn't need to reposition even one barrel. When detonated, the gunpowder would do what the old man intended.

Griswade returned to the landing, hefted Mrs. Proudfoot over his shoulder, and carried her down into the cellar. He laid her on the floor not far from the Bright Flame barrels. She remained unconscious, but he hadn't hit her that hard.

He pulled the scarf she'd used as a fichu of sorts about her throat and quickly and efficiently gagged her. Then he tore strips from the hem of her petticoats and used them to bind her wrists in front of her. She was only a woman; he didn't need to do more.

Conscious, now, of time ticking past, he pulled the long match cord fuse he'd prepared from his pocket. He'd spent over an hour testing and timing the rate of burn and had cut the length accordingly.

The old man had instructed him to light the fuse once the Queen and her party had gone upstairs. On this one point, Griswade had elected to improve on the old man's plan; he hadn't wanted to leave anything to chance. He'd cut a length long enough to be able to light it before the Queen arrived and still have time to ease his way unobtrusively from the house and walk briskly back across the Inner Ward until he was on the other side of the White Tower and effectively screened from the blast.

Better by far to add more fuse so he could ensure it lit properly and got going as it should and also to have a few extra minutes up his sleeve in case he was questioned on leaving and needed to produce his inventory as excuse.

Nothing but nothing was going to get in the way of him inheriting the old man's estate.

As he worked to ease out the bung in the central barrel on the bottom row, he went over the next steps in his amended plan. He would set the fuse in place, light it, wait until the royal party had climbed the stairs and were distracted by the business of choosing the Queen's jewels, then he would walk calmly but silently out of the cellar and out of the house.

Once outside, the guardsmen who would have escorted the Queen's carriage would see him, but they had no reason to suspect someone in a guard's uniform walking openly away from the Jewel House toward Waterloo Block. He doubted anyone would challenge him, but he had the inventory as his excuse if any did.

The bung popped free. He checked the fuse, selected the end he'd marked with a pencil to show how much should extend inside the barrel, then carefully fed the cord of treated hemp into the powder behind the bung.

Then he used the bung to wedge the cord in place.

He laid out the fuse, making sure there was nothing to interfere with its smooth burning. He arranged it on the flagstones in a set of looping curves running from the central barrel in the opposite direction from where Mrs. Proudfoot lay.

That done, he straightened and consulted his watch. He still had a few minutes, and even straining his ears, he could hear no activity to suggest the Queen was approaching.

He seized the moment to examine his preparations. To his great satisfaction, everything was perfectly in place. Considering the blast, envisioning how the effects would play out, he was once again struck by the elegance of the old man's strike. Despite the immense repercussions the incident would cause, relatively few people would die in the blast. The old man had found the perfect time and place in which to eliminate both the Queen and her husband. Aside from the royal couple and the two members of their household who would accompany them upstairs, only the Keeper, his already unconscious wife, and the four guards stationed upstairs would die. There might be further casualties depending on how close to the Jewel House the royal carriage and the outriders waited, and also on the impact of the blast on the structure of Martin Tower.

Should Martin Tower be breached sufficiently that it crumpled, it would fall outward into the Outer Ward. A few might be killed there, but the numbers would be limited. That wasn't a public area. Meanwhile, in the Inner Ward, the side wall of the relatively new Waterloo Block would take the brunt of the explosion and should contain the fallout from the blast. The much older White Tower was too far away to sustain much damage.

While Griswade himself didn't care much about such things—the trappings of state, as he thought of them—he suspected the old man did. He certainly wasn't against the monarchy—quite the opposite. If anything, he was the sort who had reveled in the trappings of it all his long life.

Monarchy, in fact, was the old man's obsession.

Mrs. Proudfoot stirred, uttered a small moan smothered by the gag, then lapsed back into unconsciousness.

Griswade still couldn't hear anything above stairs, but his watch informed him the time was nigh.

Victoria held to an inflexible schedule; she wouldn't be late for her death.

A smile on his lips, Griswade crouched, and at precisely five minutes before the Queen was due to walk into the room two floors above, he struck a lucifer, steadied the flame, then lit the fuse.

It fizzed, then settled to a smoldering burn.

CHAPTER 57

$\mathcal{D}$rake approached the Jewel House on silent feet.

He'd been forced to waste precious minutes establishing his credentials, giving orders for various evacuations, and dealing with the babbling Keeper and, despite the man's state, extracting vital information before having to give orders to the guards to restrain Proudfoot from following him to the Jewel House. Drake understood the man's wife was inside, along with four guards, although the guards would be in the jewel chamber on the upper floor.

The guards at both the main entrance and the passageway to the Inner Ward had confirmed that a guardsman they hadn't recognized but who fitted the description Inspector Crawford had compiled of the man suspected to be Connell Boyne's killer had walked past them between ten and fifteen minutes before. The guards at the Bloody Tower had thought the unknown captain was heading for Waterloo Block, but they hadn't actually seen him go inside.

As Drake climbed the steps to the porch of the Jewel House, he was perfectly certain that Griswade was inside, in the cellar with the gunpowder.

While they'd spiked Nagle's plot to blow up the royal couple, the threat was far from over. Quite aside from those who got caught in the blast, blowing up the Jewel House would strike at the very heart of the British Empire.

A blast of such size hard up against the walls of Martin Tower would almost certainly collapse that tower, along with buildings in the Outer Ward—buildings with people in them. Drake had ordered a silent evacuation of those buildings, but had no way of telling how quickly the area would be cleared. Equally importantly, the planned blast would blow the Crown Jewels—more or less all of them—to kingdom come. Over the centuries, crowns and state jewels had been lost from time to time, but never all at once.

The political and social fallout from such a blast—in the capital at a site synonymous with the endurance of the monarchy and also one of the most highly defended and defensive installations in the realm—would be immense. Incalculable.

Britain would be rocked to her foundations.

And as was men's wont, they would search for scapegoats; few would believe such an act stemmed purely from an old man's obsession sparked by a thirst for petty revenge.

Drake acknowledged such a tale bordered on the ludicrous. Unfortunately, in this case, it was the truth.

As silent as smoke, he opened the Jewel House door, entered the hall, and quietly shut the door behind him.

He glanced up the stairs. He couldn't risk warning the guards on the upper floor; their inevitable movements would alert Griswade, and he might act precipitously.

Drake's entire focus now was on preventing Nagle's explosion from taking place.

The door to the cellar that the nearly hysterical Keeper had managed to describe stood open, swinging across the corridor. Drake approached it cautiously. At this point, he had no real plan, and there was the Keeper's wife to be considered. He had no idea where she was—whether Griswade had already killed her and left her body somewhere in the Keeper's rooms or...

He didn't have time to debate the point, much less look for the woman. By his calculation, he had perhaps five minutes before Griswade—who Drake felt certain would know the Queen's schedule—realized the Queen's party was overdue.

Once Griswade woke up to the fact that the Queen wasn't putting in an appearance...Drake had no idea and even less faith in what such a man might do.

He rounded the swinging panel without touching it, then, ghostlike, slipped into the room beyond—the storeroom the Keeper had described. No lamps were burning in that space, making the light seeping from around the edges of the cellar door readily discernible.

Drake's eyes quickly adjusted to the gloom. He examined the cellar door. The latch was a simple lifting one, with no bolt or lock. According to the keeper, there was a small landing beyond the door, then nine stone steps down to a paved floor.

There were several places where the line of light showing around the door was wider. Drake discovered a gouge above the lower hinge; he crouched and put his eye to it.

He glimpsed a wall to the right of the landing—and past the wall's end, to the right beyond the last step, stood Griswade.

Drake smelt an acrid scent and silently swore. Griswade had already lit his fuse. Although Drake couldn't see the fuse through his peephole, Griswade, his hands on his hips, was looking down at the floor that was screened from Drake's sight by the wall.

The wall was a problem. Drake couldn't simply rush in, leap down, and stamp out the fuse, then grapple with Griswade.

Drake scanned the segment of the cellar he could see—from roughly one o'clock, where Griswade stood, counterclockwise to nearly nine o'clock. There was no sign of the Keeper's wife, but that didn't mean she wasn't there.

Obviously, Drake was going to have to do this the hard way.

He rose, shook his shoulders and arms, and flexed his hands. Then he grasped the latch, opened it, hauled the door wide, and leapt through.

He saw Griswade's eyes widen in shock. Saw the Keeper's wife lying by Griswade's boots; she was groggy but very much alive.

Drake landed in a crouch on the flagstones beyond the end of the steps.

Griswade moved with a speed Drake had rarely seen. Before Drake could spring, Griswade had hauled the woman—gagged and with her hands tied—up in front of him, cinched a wire garrote around her throat and, holding it tight with one hand, with the other pulled a pistol from his coat pocket and aimed it unwaveringly at Drake's heart.

Slowly, Drake straightened. His gaze on the pistol, his brain worked at lightning speed. Griswade wouldn't shoot, not if he could help it, because the sound would bring the guards rushing down.

Drake's gaze darted to the fuse, and he knew he had time. Griswade wouldn't want the guards down yet because the fuse had much too far to run. Griswade had used match cord, slow burning but harder to put out. There was, Drake estimated, more than five minutes yet to burn.

The Keeper's wife was ineffectually scrabbling at the wire about her neck. She uttered a choked sound. Without taking his eyes from Drake, Griswade tightened the garrote, and the woman came up on her toes, eyes starting from her head. She fell silent and stopped struggling.

Drake met her terrified eyes, with his gaze tried to will calmness into her, but suspected it was a lost cause. At least she'd given up her useless struggling.

Griswade was listening hard, assessing if the guards overhead had heard anything.

Drake could have told him they hadn't. He looked again at the pistol. It was standard military issue from several years back—a single shot, not a multi-shot revolver like the gun nestling in Drake's pocket. But there was no sense in drawing that, which was why he hadn't. With Griswade standing squarely in front of the barrels containing one hundredweight of gunpowder, risking a shot in a room with stone walls and stone floor... Drake had no idea if a single shot would be enough to detonate the powder and had no wish to find out.

No explosion at all was his aim.

And he had his knives. He'd intended to take Griswade down with one, but that was before Griswade had hauled the Keeper's wife up as a shield, with his garrote about her throat, no less. Nevertheless, now Drake had had a chance to assess the angles, if he threw true—and given the distance, there was no excuse for waywardness—then the Keeper's wife would survive, and either he or she would pull out the fuse...

As if reading his thoughts, Griswade abruptly swung the pistol and aimed at the front panel of the barrel where he'd teased out the bung to reveal the gunpowder inside. "One wrong move, and we all go up." Apparently immediately realizing that Drake might actually make that sacrifice in order to save the Queen, Griswade swung the pistol up, again aiming at Drake. "If you make the slightest move, I'll shoot you, kill her, then walk out and let the place explode. Do you want the lives of the guards, and her, and all the others who will die on your head?"

Drake feigned puzzlement—not that much of a stretch. "Aren't they going to be on my head, anyway?"

How long before Griswade realized the Queen wasn't coming? Drake had absolutely no interest in dying that day, and there was the Keeper's wife and everyone else to save. Let alone preserving the vested importance of the Crown Jewels and the inviolability of the Tower. He glanced at the fuse. He had at least a few minutes to work on bringing about his preferred outcome.

He looked at Griswade. "Is Nagle's estate really worth this?"

Griswade blinked.

Drake smiled cynically. "Oh yes. More than enough people know of that connection, and that Nagle recruited you and your cousin Lawton Chilburn to act as his henchmen."

Griswade shifted, growing more tense; he hadn't liked hearing any of that.

"Consequently, all of this"—Drake waved at the barrels of

gunpowder—"isn't going to get you anything. Even if you succeed in blowing this place up, you won't gain anything from it."

Griswade wasn't sure he believed him; Drake could see that in his face. After several moments, Griswade growled, "I'll take my chances." From the way his eyes repeatedly half flicked to his left, he wanted—badly wanted—to look at the fuse, but was too well trained to take his eyes from Drake.

From Griswade's point of view, not taking his eyes from Drake was undoubtedly wise.

Drake had rarely—possibly never—faced an opponent so experienced and disciplined. But if he could get close—closer—to Griswade, Drake knew he could take the man and swiftly incapacitate him, but unless Griswade gave him an opening, there was the pistol, the gunpowder, the Keeper's wife, and the fuse ...

Stalemate.

Griswade was waiting for the fuse to burn down to the point he could shoot Drake, kill the Keeper's wife, and race out of the house before the guards clattered down from above and the gunpowder exploded.

He would have only one chance, and he had to judge it correctly even though he couldn't afford to look at the fuse.

Drake, meanwhile, couldn't act unless Griswade gave him an opening—or Griswade reached that critical point, and his finger tightened on the trigger.

Until one or the other happened, Drake's only option was to wait, and that was no good option at all.

He needed a distraction, but God alone knew—

The front door of the Jewel House opened on a wave of voices; the words were indistinct, but one voice held a distinctly familiar, regal tone.

Drake's blood ran cold. Had Louisa somehow failed to divert the Queen? Horror swamped him.

Then from above their heads came "I was thinking of the diamond cross and perhaps the Scottish crown. What do you think, my dear?"

The voice was unmistakably Victoria's.

But she hated the Scottish crown, said it made her look dumpy...

Drake stopped breathing. It was an effort to keep his feelings from his face.

With his eyes locked on Drake's face, Griswade hissed, "Not a sound, or she's dead." He put his face close to Mrs. Proudfoot's. "That goes for you, too."

Footsteps, those of four people—three men and a woman in heels—tramped over their heads as the party climbed the stairs.

"Wait! Where's Mrs. Proudfoot?" The woman's heels halted, then reversed direction, coming down the stairs. "Go ahead, Albert dear. I'm just going to have a word with Mrs. Proudfoot."

Mrs. Proudfoot looked anything but thrilled. She tensed as if to struggle anew, presumably in an effort to save the Queen. That was the last thing Drake and his distraction needed. He shifted his gaze to Mrs. Proudfoot's face, trapped her eyes, tried desperately to will her to calm—to silence and stillness; he risked infinitesimally shaking his head and finally, puzzled, Mrs. Proudfoot eased back from the brink.

The woman's lighter footsteps drew nearer. Drake recognized them—too light to be Victoria.

What the devil was Louisa up to?

"Mrs. Proudfoot? Are you there?" The Queen's voice rang out from the storeroom at the top of the stone steps.

Obviously, Louisa was a superb mimic. Then Drake remembered she was considered a past master at charades.

The door at the top of the stairs had swung partially closed. Now it was pulled fully open, and Louisa appeared on the landing, wearing a dark velvet cloak with its ermine-trimmed hood up and drawn forward to shade her face.

She was several inches too tall to be Victoria, but seen in isolation, unless the viewer was very familiar with the Queen, the difference wasn't easy to discern. The heavy cloak swathed her figure from head to ankles, disguising the lack of matronly weight, and the hood was so deep it effectively hid her features.

The cloak was one Victoria was frequently seen in, the ermine trimming distinctive.

Drake took in the spectacle with one swift glance, then refixed his gaze on Griswade's face. Drake realized he was holding his breath, yet even now with, as far as Griswade knew, his queen looking down on him, the damned man kept most of his gaze and most of his attention trained on Drake.

A muscle twitched in Griswade's jaw.

"Good *gracious*! What on earth is going on here?" Victoria's outraged accents fell on their ears.

Mrs. Proudfoot had frozen, her gaze fixed on the cloaked figure. She'd realized the woman wasn't Victoria. Drake thanked the Lord that, holding her as he was, Griswade couldn't see Mrs. Proudfoot's face.

"What is this all about?" Imperious demand rang in Victoria's voice. Then the cloaked figure swept regally, commandingly, down the steps. "Unhand that woman at once, sir!"

Griswade almost flinched. He didn't know what to do, but he plainly saw Louisa-Victoria as the lesser threat and stubbornly kept his gaze mostly trained on Drake. He hadn't eased his hold on the garrote, and the pistol he held never wavered.

Louisa had enough sense not to get between Drake and Griswade. She fetched up on Drake's right, blocking his view of the fuse still smoldering its way across the floor toward the barrels of gunpowder.

The cloaked figure regarded Griswade with the air of one stunned by his failure to immediately comply with her order. Then Louisa drew herself up with an aplomb that was pure Victoria and asked with terrifyingly regal disdain, "Do you know who I am?"

For a fraction of a second, Griswade's gaze flicked to her, but instantly, he swung his eyes back to Drake. "I…" Griswade clamped his lips shut. He only had to wait a few more minutes… Drake could almost read Griswade's mind. Shoot Drake, hit the Queen over the head, strangle Mrs. Proudfoot, and run like the wind.

"Great heavens! What's this?" Apparently, the cloaked figure had just noticed the burning fuse.

Before Griswade could react, she took three steps toward it.

"Stop!" Griswade's voice was a hoarse rasp.

The figure halted, reacting as if shocked that anyone would dare order her about. She was still more than a yard from the red end of the fuse.

His gaze still on Drake, Griswade licked his lips and pulled the wire tighter around Mrs. Proudfoot's neck, bringing the poor woman once more to her toes—then quick as a flash, he pointed his pistol at "the Queen." "Take one more step, Your Majesty, and your Mrs. Proudfoot dies. And so will you."

With the pistol aimed unwaveringly at Louisa-Victoria, Drake was still held at bay.

The cloaked figure regarded Griswade.

Assuming he had "the Queen" under his control, Griswade's gaze returned to Drake.

Then Louisa's voice said, "All right. Not one more step."

From the corner of his eye, Drake saw her bring her right arm out from under the heavy cloak. Almost unable to believe what he was seeing, he turned his head in time to see her send a pitcherful of water splashing and washing over the fuse.

The fuse sputtered and died.

Griswade froze, staring at the extinguished fuse in utter disbelief.

Drake was already moving.

Already plowing his shoulder into Griswade, driving the man against the barrels behind him, simultaneously locking both hands about the hand in which Griswade was holding the pistol and, by sheer, ruthless strength, forcing the pistol down.

There was only one safe place for a bullet to go.

With Drake's help, Griswade shot himself in the foot.

Louisa had rushed in. Instinctively, Griswade had released his hold on the garrote to grapple with Drake; Louisa grabbed Mrs. Proudfoot and pulled her away.

On a bellow of pain, Griswade dropped the spent pistol and lunged for Louisa.

For Drake, it was a moment when the world stood still.

Louisa saw Griswade attack, but with Mrs. Proudfoot sagging in her arms, weighing her down, was unable to move—

Griswade didn't so much as touch the ermine-trimmed cloak.

He might have been a coldblooded killer, but he'd finally crossed paths with someone even more ruthless. Even more skilled.

Drake clapped his hands on either side of Griswade's head and sharply wrenched.

Louisa could barely believe how quickly and silently a man could be killed.

Or as the case was, executed.

After that one swift jerk, Drake removed his hands, and Griswade's body crumpled to the floor.

For a moment, Drake looked down at Griswade's still-twitching form, then he raised his golden eyes—solid beaten gold—to meet hers. "I'm sorry you had to see that."

His voice was deep, his tone harsh.

She held his gaze for a heartbeat, then haughtily arched her brows. "I'm not. If he'd lived, I would have insisted on a front-row seat at his execution."

Somewhat to her relief, Drake's distant, impenetrable, and impervious expression softened fractionally, then his lips twitched—which seemed to surprise him. He turned away, then bent and ripped the fuse from the barrel into which it had been set and flung it aside.

Louisa returned her attention to Mrs. Proudfoot. The poor woman was struggling to breathe while holding in her sobs. Louisa hushed her, then set about carefully peeling the wire of the garrote from her neck.

Drake came down on one knee on Mrs. Proudfoot's other side and, with infinite care, took over the difficult task of easing the wire from the flesh into which it had cut.

Leaving him to finish the task, Louisa took one of Mrs. Proudfoot's hands between hers and lightly chafed it. "You were exceedingly brave." Drake eased the garrote completely free and tossed it aside, then together, he and she helped Mrs. Proudfoot to her feet.

Above them, heavy boots thundered down the stairs just as a rush of equally heavy footsteps came bursting through the front door. The two groups met in the front hall and milled, uncertain.

Mrs. Proudfoot had jumped. Louisa calmly patted her hand. "The cut on your neck needs to be bathed and salved, but no one will see any scars—not unless you wish to show them off, of course." When Mrs. Proudfoot shot her a startled look, Louisa smiled. "Not many ladies can claim to have been wounded while assisting in saving the Queen from assassination."

Mrs. Proudfoot blinked, then looked much struck—and much less cowed.

Thumping footsteps raced closer, then a gaggle of guards led by Mr. Proudfoot burst into the cellar. The Keeper rushed down the stairs, his eyes only for his wife, who he dragged into his arms and frantically clutched to his bosom. Quite overcome, he rocked from side to side. "Glynis! Glynis! I thought I'd lost you."

"No, dear." Mrs. Proudfoot patted his shoulder. She was rapidly regaining her composure. "Apparently it will take more than the likes of him"—she glanced at Griswade's body and sniffed—"to make away with me. This gentleman came, and then Lady Louisa as well, and it all turned out all right."

To Louisa's mind, Mrs. Proudfoot's precis was an accurate condensation of the essential facts. Drake had come, then Louisa had arrived, and now all was, once again, safe and sound and right in their world.

It took her and Drake, working together, fifteen more minutes to reassure the numerous senior officers of the Tower that the threat was, indeed, at an end. The realization that, purely on the basis of a uniform, Griswade had been able to freely enter the Tower and, without being challenged, gain access to the Jewel House mere minutes before the Queen had been due to arrive resulted in several red faces. The revelation that the officers' mess housed ten hundredweight of gunpowder caused an even bigger furor and a great deal of discomfort. Better care would be taken in checking items admitted to the Tower henceforth.

Finally, Drake and Louisa, now hand in hand, freed themselves from the melee on the grounds of needing to report to the palace.

They emerged from the Jewel House to find guardsmen everywhere, but Henry, perched on his box in the shadow of the White Tower, saw them and set his horses pacing, guiding the carriage through the crowd to pull up as close as he could manage to the steps.

They descended and walked to the carriage. Drake opened the door, handed Louisa in, then called to Henry, "Buckingham Palace. I gather we're expected."

He followed Louisa into the shadows and the leather comfort of the carriage. He sank down beside her and leaned back against the squabs. His heart had slowed from its earlier thundering, but was still beating too fast.

The carriage rattled out of the Inner Ward, through the archway of

Middle Tower, and out onto the street.

The side-to-side rocking as the wheels negotiated a gutter pitched Louisa against his shoulder. Instead of straightening and shifting away, she settled closer. Seconds later, he reached for her hand just as she reached for his. Their palms slid together, and they gripped, then twined their fingers and rested their linked hands on his thigh.

Uncounted minutes later, once the reality of her soft warmth beside him had finally penetrated to every level of his brain and the iron vise about his lungs at last released, he drew in a deep breath and, with his gaze fixed ahead, in an almost conversational tone murmured, "I have no idea how I feel about you doing what you did. Walking into a situation like that with only a pitcher of water for protection. It's"—raising his free hand, he rubbed his temple—"a little hard to…accept."

She didn't immediately reply, then he felt her lightly shrug. "I didn't have much time to plan. I'd crept to the door and smelt the fuse burning, so I went and got the pitcher of water and then organized some of the guards to help me pretend that the Queen had arrived."

Drake couldn't imagine the scene that must have ensued when she'd arrived at the Tower gates; he wondered how long it would take for the guardsmen she must have lorded—ladied?—it over to recover from the experience.

Matter-of-factly, she went on, "I couldn't think what else to do, and in the end, it worked. The explosion didn't happen, and the garrotter is dead. We won. The mastermind lost." She glanced at him. "What more needs to be said?"

Her last sentence translated to: What else had he expected?

He decided she was right, or at least that there was no point arguing. Not yet. Perhaps later, when they were alone and not likely to be interrupted, and he'd worked out what he should do about her. About a wife as focused, as determined, as single-minded and as relentless as he.

One who would stand with him shoulder to shoulder and hold the line and never surrender.

A quiet voice in his mind softly scoffed. What could he say?

What could he do?

Effectively nothing, other than accept that being her husband looked set to be the ultimate, even predominant, challenge of his life.

CHAPTER 58

*B*oth the Queen and Prince Albert needed to prepare for the state banquet that evening, which restricted the time available for Drake and Louisa to report on their foiling of the plot. Regardless, the royal couple insisted on hearing sufficient details to understand what had transpired. They received Drake and Louisa in Albert's private drawing room, with only the prince's private secretary and the Queen's equerry in attendance.

After they'd performed the usual low bow and curtsy, Victoria waved them to sit in armchairs facing the royal couple, who were seated on the sofa side by side. "Very well," Victoria said. "Lord Winchelsea, Lady Louisa, please start at the beginning. Lady Louisa's earlier account was decidedly scant on detail."

Advised by the equerry, who had met them downstairs and escorted them to the drawing room, of the need to be concise, Drake and Louisa were only too happy to oblige. They stripped the plot to its bare bones, commencing with the events at Pressingstoke Hall and the consequent involvement of Scotland Yard, then proceeding to the arrival and subsequent disguising and transporting of the gunpowder, noting the many murders ruthlessly committed to conceal the trail, eventually leading to the explosive being stored as ale in the cellar beneath the Jewel House.

Throughout their recitation, Drake made a point of ensuring that the suborning of several Young Irelander sympathizers and the hoodwinking of Chartist militiamen was seen for what it was—a deliberate manipulation to cast blame on the two organizations, blame that was not deserved. "Neither organization was involved in the slightest."

"Good gracious." Victoria shook her head as if overwhelmed by the scope of the intrigue. "I am greatly relieved to hear that."

Albert looked grave. "The gunpowder is now in the hands of the Tower guards?"

Drake confirmed that was so and that all was now safe.

Albert looked directly at Drake. "And the men who executed this plan are both dead?"

Again, Drake confirmed that. "But they were merely the henchmen of the man who devised the entire scheme."

"And who was that?" Victoria demanded. "Lady Louisa merely called him 'an old gentleman.'"

Revealing the identity of the man they now knew to be the mastermind behind the entire plot required a certain degree of tact, given that it was Victoria's own long-ago behavior, excusable though that had been, that was the root cause of the entire episode.

Drake left Louisa to skate over those facts, a feat she accomplished with her usual skill.

If Victoria recalled her run-in with Lord Hubert Nagle, she gave no sign; her only comment was that the Faringdales and Hawesleys would be devastated to learn that one of their own had acted so traitorously.

After inquiring as to the health of Mrs. Proudfoot and being assured the lady had taken no serious injury, Victoria regally thanked Drake and Louisa and extended those thanks to Sebastian, Antonia, Michael, and Cleo. "We are greatly indebted to you all. In times such as these, it is a relief to know we have such staunch supporters."

Correctly interpreting those words as a dismissal, Drake and Louisa rose. Drake bowed low. Louisa sank into a deep curtsy.

"I have one last question," Victoria said as they straightened. "We have been informed, of course, of the impending nuptials of the Marquess of Earith and Lady Antonia." The Queen opened her protuberant eyes wide. "Should we expect to hear any further announcements of that nature?"

Drake glanced at Louisa, then held out his hand.

She grasped his fingers and smiled at Victoria. "Lord Michael and Miss Hendon expect to announce their engagement shortly. And..." She glanced at Drake.

"And"—his gaze trapped hers, his tone resolute as his fingers tightened on hers—"Lady Louisa and I expect to announce our engagement soon after. We anticipate marrying early next year."

Her eyes danced, their teasing brilliance somehow conveying the words "Will we now?" yet she made no move to correct his statement, just beamed her happiness at the royal couple.

Victoria looked pleased and distinctly approving. "That is excellent news. Please accept our congratulations and do convey our felicitations to your brothers and their ladies, my dear."

"Indeed." Albert, too, was smiling. "We are always happy to hear of such events among those we hold in our highest regard."

Drake bowed again. Louisa dropped into another curtsy.

The Queen nodded a gracious, smiling dismissal, and together, Drake and Louisa stepped back two paces, bowed and curtsied again, then turned and walked toward the door.

The prince's secretary and the Queen's equerry immediately descended on Victoria and Albert, but the prince left the group and walked after Drake and Louisa.

He caught up to them as they reached the door.

Drake faced him. "Your Highness?"

Albert glanced up the room, saw the Queen engaged with his secretary and her equerry, then looked at Drake and Louisa and murmured, "I am concerned that even after the response to the previous attempts on Her Majesty's life, Lord Nagle felt able to instigate this plot—one that very nearly succeeded." Albert glanced at Louisa, then met Drake's gaze levelly. "Even you, my lord, would not have been in time to prevent a great catastrophe had you not had help from a most unexpected source. By that, I mean no disrespect or censure—none indeed, you have my wholehearted thanks as I believe you know—but rather to point out that official vigilance alone has not, in this instance, deterred a nobleman from attempting to kill the Queen. It is therefore unlikely that even heightened official vigilance will succeed in that respect in the future." Albert paused and looked down, then went on, "Of all the attempts on Her Majesty's life, this one is unarguably the most serious. In the past, Her Majesty had always argued for leniency." Albert raised his gaze to Drake's face. "That cannot happen in this case. Lord Nagle must pay the full account for his crime. More, that judgment must be seen and understood by all."

His gaze still on Drake's face, Albert cocked his head. "What are your thoughts on this, my lord?"

Drake didn't have to think to understand Albert's reasoning. He nodded. "I concur, Your Highness. No one would wish to have such an incident occur again." He bowed a courtier's bow. "As ever, I am the Crown's to command."

Albert's expression eased. "Thank you." He inclined his head. "I will leave dealing with Nagle in your ever-capable hands."

"I am"—Drake glanced at Louisa and amended—"we are honored by your trust."

Albert smiled at that. He reached past them and opened the door.

With a final inclination of her head, Louisa gracefully led the way out. She waited until Drake joined her. Once the door had shut behind him, and they'd started strolling along the corridor, heading for the side door where they'd left the carriage, she asked, "Nagle?"

After several moments of ambling by her side, his gaze on the carpet ahead of them, Drake replied, "As it appears he's ensconced in deepest Berkshire, and I believe he would have had no other agents in town, then he won't receive any report of what has or has not occurred. He'll be waiting, expecting to hear of the calamity he engineered, almost certainly expecting Griswade to arrive with the news. When Griswade doesn't turn up...I think Nagle won't know how to react. He won't know whether the explosion occurred, won't know if Griswade was caught, or if he succeeded but has subsequently been delayed." His voice firming, he stated, "Nagle will remain where he is for the moment, waiting to hear what's happened."

Drake turned his head and met Louisa's gaze. "I rather fancy taking him the news myself first thing tomorrow."

Louisa smiled her sharp-edged smile. "An excellent idea. We can leave early—I believe we have no major engagement tonight."

Drake wondered if he should try to dissuade her from accompanying him and decided that would be wasting breath.

He was learning.

CHAPTER 59

*C*ontrary to Louisa's expectations and unbeknown to them, they did, indeed, have an unavoidable engagement awaiting them at Wolverstone House, where their families—all the members now in residence who hadn't been directly involved—had gathered to hear their news.

But they called first at St. Ives House; it was after six o'clock when they climbed the front steps. Milling in the front hall, they found Sebastian and Antonia, Michael and Cleo, and the entire footmen army. They'd all recently returned to check with Tom, only to be informed by Crewe of Louisa's discoveries and Drake and Louisa's subsequent race to intercept the Queen on her way to the Tower; the company was waiting on tenterhooks to learn the outcome.

The instant Drake and Louisa came through the door, the entire gathering swung to face them, and her brothers started bombarding them with questions.

Drake held up his hand and waited until silence descended. Then, with a slight, irrepressible smile curving his lips, he stated, "This is what happened."

Having so recently gone over the same ground with Victoria and Albert, Drake and Louisa made short work of describing the day's events—what had proved to be the final stages of a long-running and extremely well-orchestrated plot to assassinate the royal couple.

Despite not being, as Sebastian put it, "in on the kill," everyone looked thoroughly pleased, the tension that had spiked when they'd heard of the true nature of the threat and the ticking clock that had so nearly run its course releasing in an equally intense relief.

Drake ended by conveying their sovereign's approbation and thanks, then added his own. "We would never have succeeded in checkmating this plot if we hadn't had the support of every last one of you."

The footmen and grooms looked thoroughly chuffed.

Drake glanced at Louisa, and his expression turned wry. "And while I hesitate to invite the inevitable preening, we couldn't have prevailed without the Dowager Duchess's and Lady Osbaldestone's excellent memories. We'll have to give them due recognition."

"Speaking of which," Sebastian said, "a footman from Wolverstone House brought a summons for the six of us. My mama and your mama learned the latest from Crewe, and we're expected there to report on the final act, and describe, explain, and elucidate the entire plot, first to last with no detail omitted, for the edification of our assembled families."

Louisa looked her disbelief. "The footman did not say that."

Sebastian inclined his head. "The poor footman didn't have to." He drew a note from his pocket and held it out to her. "Mama wrote it."

"Oh." Louisa took the note and scanned it.

"And"—Michael leaned over to point—"Drake's mama—your future mama-in-law—countersigned it."

"Ah." Drake stared at the note in Louisa's hands. When she looked up, he met her eyes, then sighed. "In that case, we'd better get around there."

The footmen army had already started disbanding, with Crewe and Tom shaking hands with their peers and sending those from the other Cynster houses on their way.

Flanked by Sebastian and Antonia and Michael and Cleo, Drake and Louisa, again hand in hand, went out of the front door.

They walked slowly along the pavement.

Halfway to Wolverstone House, Louisa sighed gustily. "After days of rushing hither and yon, always one step behind the gunpowder and the plotters, it's…difficult to take in that it's finally over."

Close behind her, Sebastian humphed. "For my money, it won't be over until Nagle is taken up." He glanced at Drake. "When's that going to happen?"

Drake exchanged a glance with Louisa, then told the others of their plans.

Naturally, all four invited themselves along.

Drake looked ahead and didn't argue.

Yes, he was learning.

They entered Wolverstone House to find an unexpectedly large gathering filling the drawing room and waiting impatiently for them to appear.

"At last!" Minerva, Drake's mother, exclaimed. "We were about to send a second summons to St. Ives House."

"Obviously," Royce, Drake's father, said, having scrutinized their faces, "all has ended well."

"Almost." Drake halted not far inside the door and felt the others flank him, all six of them facing the assembled company. Somewhat to his surprise, all his five siblings were present, grinning at them, along with Cleo's parents as well as her three brothers, who must have recently returned from the Americas. The Earl of Chillingworth and his countess—Antonia's parents—were there, along with her three siblings. And, of course, in pride of place on the sofa opposite the one occupied by the two duchesses sat Helena, Dowager Duchess of St. Ives, and Therese, Lady Osbaldestone.

Drake drew in a breath.

"First to last," Honoria, Duchess of St. Ives, instructed, "with not one single detail omitted." Her stern expression softened, and she added, "If you please."

Honoria might be a duchess, but no matter how insistently she demanded, she was not going to get every single detail; there were several to which Drake had no intention of admitting, and he suspected that went for the five surrounding him as well.

"It all began," he said, "with an invitation from Lord Ennis to a house party."

After describing in a few words the situation that had led to him enlisting Sebastian's aid, he passed the baton to Sebastian, who took up the tale of explanation and elucidation, ably assisted by Antonia. Drake looked around, then touched Michael's sleeve, and they fetched straight-backed chairs for their ladies. When Sebastian and Antonia reached the point of them returning to London after Connell Boyne's murder, Drake took over briefly to explain the connection, or lack thereof, to the Young Irelanders, after which Michael and Cleo took center stage.

Sebastian fetched a chair for Antonia and placed it in line with those occupied by Louisa and Cleo. Once Antonia sat, Sebastian took up a stance similar to that of Michael and Drake, standing beside and leaning on the backs of their respective lady's chair.

The truth of the death of Lawton Chilburn made those who had yet to learn of it blink, but by then the twists and turns of the plot had captured everyone's attention. The gathering was hanging on their words when Michael and Cleo handed the telling of the tale back to Drake.

After their visit to the palace, he and Louisa made short work of their report, although Michael and Cleo and Sebastian and Antonia had their own contributions to make.

But when their story reached the point where Louisa had realized who the mastermind was and therefore who he was targeting, and her experience in the Queen's household had allowed her to make the deductive leap that had sent her and Drake chasing the royal carriage and turning the Queen away from the Tower, the entire company was on the edge of their seats.

As Drake described the situation as he'd found it in the cellar below the Jewel House, Mrs. Proudfoot's presence, and his resulting exchange with Griswade, one could have heard the proverbial pin drop.

When he explained how Louisa, pretending to be Victoria, had appeared in the cellar, both her father and his paled.

In contrast, Drake noted that their mothers—indeed, all the ladies present—continued to look intrigued and absorbed.

He glossed over how he'd killed Griswade, simply saying that he'd forced the man they had labeled the garrotter to shoot himself and he'd subsequently died. Louisa stepped in to assure the company that Mrs. Proudfoot had recovered quickly from her ordeal.

Drake looked at his father. "Once the Tower commanders arrived and we could leave dealing with the situation to them, we went to Buckingham Palace as ordered and reported to the Queen and Prince Albert."

His father nodded. "And?"

"And Albert made it clear he wanted Nagle to be made an example of." Drake paused, then said, "I have to agree. If this is not dealt with appropriately, there will be more attempts like it, and one of them will succeed."

His father grimaced. "Despite the inevitable repercussions, I, too, agree. It must be done."

"So!" Lady Osbaldestone, who had remained uncharacteristically silent along with everyone else, thumped her cane on the floor. "When do you propose to visit Nagle?"

Drake reluctantly admitted, "Tomorrow." He said nothing about the other five accompanying him, and for their part, they kept their lips shut.

"Excellent." Lady Osbaldestone nodded decisively, with the full weight of authority of one who had ruled the ton for more years than any other there could count. She looked at the other ladies. "We must see what we can do about shielding the Faringdales and Hawesleys. Despite what the gossipmongers will surely say, one can hardly blame them for Nagle's actions—he always considered himself a cut above everyone else in his family."

That effectively distracted the ladies. Drake noted their siblings were exclaiming and commenting to each other, the various families intermingling, while their fathers had risen and gathered in a group to discuss... He strained his ears and confirmed they were discussing the possible political ramifications of Nagle's attempts to damage the Young Irelander and Chartist causes.

While men like their fathers did not openly sympathize with such organizations, they were not, in general, antagonistic toward the changes both groups wished to see implemented.

Drake turned to his five co-investigators. Whether it was because for him and Louisa, their recent performance had been the third time they'd described the penultimate and ultimate events, the reality that the mission was truly over finally hit him—that they had, despite all the hurdles so cunningly erected in their path, prevailed.

Relief—deep and powerful—rolled through him, sweeping away tensions, dispelling the shadows of lingering fears, leaving behind not peace but the prospect of that blessed state.

He looked at Louisa as she looked at him. She studied his eyes, then smiled the slow smile she seemed to reserve just for him.

Then his mother clapped her hands. When the noise faded, she declared, "I said seven for dinner, and it's past that now. So I suggest we adjourn to the dining room." She made a shooing motion toward the door.

Drake, with Louisa on his arm, led the way.

Sebastian and Antonia and Michael and Cleo were close behind.

They laughed and joked as they strolled into the dining room to find the long table extended and places set to accommodate the entire company.

Once they'd all found seats, and Hamilton and the footmen had done the rounds, filling the waiting glasses with fine champagne, with a celebratory mood already taking hold, Drake's father stood at the head of the table and raised his glass. "To our latest generation and all their works." His eyes met Drake's, and he inclined his head. "You've done us proud."

"Hear, hear!" and "To you all" came from all around.

His glass in hand, Drake waited only until the echoes died to push to his feet. From his position halfway down the table, he held up his glass to his father, then to all of their parents around the board. "I believe," he said, "that this is where I say: We've all been very well trained."

Laughter rolled around the room, then all their siblings shouted, "Hear! Hear!"

Beaming, Hamilton opened the dining room door to admit a line of footmen bearing trays.

Drake sat, and Louisa, sitting beside him, leaned close and, under cover of the tablecloth, patted his thigh. "Very well done." She sipped from her glass, then sidelong, met his eyes. "Do you think they've realized the full implications of that?"

He wasn't sure he had, but Hamilton intervened to present a platter of roast boar.

Drake realized he was famished. He served Louisa, then himself, as the company settled to a sumptuous feast.

Inevitably, with the dark menace of the mission eradicated and no other obstacle looming in the way, the older ladies steered the conversation to Sebastian and Antonia's upcoming wedding and the two engagements that had yet to be announced.

With that topic uppermost in their minds, said ladies led the company back to the drawing room. Drake, Sebastian, and Michael had all hoped for a quiet interval while passing the port and brandy, but their fathers showed no inclination to linger in the dining room. Instead, the company's gentlemen brought up the rear and filed back into the drawing room in the ladies' wake.

Consequently, there was no escaping the older ladies' planning.

Venues were weighed and dates discussed and eventually decided.

Drake let it all pass over his head. To him, the when and where didn't matter; making Louisa his marchioness was the only thing that did. As long as that happened relatively soon, he didn't care, and as she'd taken her place in the ladies' circle and he was fairly certain her views on that subject matched his, he felt confident he could leave the matter in her manipulative hands.

Yes, indeed, he truly was learning to share the responsibilities associated with his life.

He, Sebastian, and Michael stood by the windows with Jack Hendon, Drake's father, Sebastian and Michael's father, and the Earl of Chillingworth, and explored the various subjects thrown up by the recent mission, from the Young Irelanders and the Chartists, to the mode of transport of ale throughout the capital, the existence of the Worshipful Company of Carmen, the possibilities for more certain transport of gunpowder using oilskin bags, and the exotic beverages Sebastian and Michael and their helpers had unearthed in the cellars of various army messes.

Finally, the ladies decided to call an end to the evening. Buoyed on a wave of confident satisfaction, the company split into their constituent families, and the Cynsters, Rawlingses, and Hendons prepared to depart. Carriages were called. The Hendons left first, followed by the Rawlingses.

Drake had halted in the middle of the hall. He nodded to Sebastian and Michael as they turned to the door. Then to his surprise, Louisa materialized by his side; he'd thought she'd already left with her mother.

She smiled into his eyes, and for a moment, he wondered if she—Lady Wild—was about to shock everyone, even his unshockable parents, and insist on going up the main stairs with him…

Instead, she gripped his arm, leaned close, and murmured, "There's an extremely old ivy vine that grows up the wall all the way to my bedroom window."

She drew back as if she'd simply said goodbye, then with a distinctly provocative smile curving her lips, she patted his arm and, with a final general wave, rushed to follow her brothers out of the door.

Drake stood staring after her, then he blinked and turned to his father as the latter approached.

CHAPTER 60

It was significantly more than an hour later when Drake lifted the covers on Louisa's bed and slid between the sheets.

"Hmm." She rolled toward him, hot little hands reaching and claiming.

"Sorry I took so long." Drake lifted her over him and brushed her hair back from her face. "M'father wanted to talk."

"Did he?" She swooped in and captured his lips, then he captured hers, and passion, brought closer to the surface than either had realized by the pressures and fears of the day, ignited.

Erupted.

Finally, on a gasp, she broke the seal of their lips. Rising over him on her hands and knees, from beneath desire-weighted lids, she studied his face and smiled with sultry delight. "But you did brave the ivy"—she leaned low and swayed sinuously from side to side, brushing her already swollen breasts across his chest—"and you're here now." She caught her lush lower lip between her teeth and let her lids lower, then she released her lip and breathily declared, "So I believe I'll forgive you." She slid lower in the bed.

Those were the last words she or he managed for many long minutes.

Long-drawn minutes during which desire surged and passion raged, and the hunger and even more the blinding need scored and exacerbated by the day's events—by their inherent and instinctive fears, by the horror of so nearly losing the other, of losing their own lives and the promise of the future they'd so recently glimpsed—surged, overwhelmed them, and eclipsed all control.

They rolled among the sheets, panting, gasping, moaning, he muffling her shrieks when they became too loud, and burying his face in the tumbled mane of her hair as he reached his own completion.

Finally, pleasured and sated, they lay bathed in the soft moonlight that washed through her uncurtained window.

For him, no release had ever reached so deep, and no lover had ever fed his needs with such gloriously uninhibited generosity. For her, their connection, the depth and breadth of that ineluctable link, was all and more than she'd dreamed it might be.

Moments passed while they lay with her slumped on his chest, his arms loosely holding her as their hearts, still thudding, slowed, and their senses gradually returned to the physical world.

Drake glanced down at her dark head, then lifted a hand and idly picked up one thick, curling, black lock and let it slide through his fingers. He repeated the exercise, mesmerized anew by the silky texture.

Soothed in some way he didn't understand by the warm weight of her lying boneless atop him.

His wits weren't in charge, and for once, he felt no need to bring them to bear. The words that formed on his tongue didn't spring from his intellect, but from somewhere much deeper. "You know I never wanted to allow you into this mission—that for years, I've done everything I could to keep us far apart." He paused to consider if he wanted to go on, but apparently he did. "I didn't want you near because I knew if you came close enough for long enough, we'd end like this. Together. Married." Even though she'd moved not one muscle in response, he knew she wasn't sleeping, that although her breathing had slowed, she was listening. "And I didn't think—couldn't bring myself to believe—that I would ever be able to trust you. Not as I have. As I do. As I've learned I can without losing…any part of me. Any of the strength that makes me me. If that makes sense?"

When he let silence stretch and waited, slowly, she lifted her head, folded her hands on his chest, and rested her chin upon them. From a distance of inches, from beneath heavy lids, she looked into his eyes. After several long moments, she softly replied, "You thought I'd be a chink in your armor. A liability."

He forced himself to meet her steady gaze, pale and mysterious in the moonlight. "Not a liability—a vulnerability. No matter how desirable you were in other ways, I always equated having you by my side— having you as my wife—as a weakness I couldn't afford."

Her gaze unwavering, she tipped her head. "And now?"

"Now... When you walked into that cellar today, when I saw you standing there in Victoria's cloak, pretending to be her..." Now the tensions had faded from his system, he could appreciate what his feelings—his true feelings—had been. "Instead of being paralyzed by fear for you, instead of being distracted from what I needed to do, frantic to protect you, I felt more confident, not less. It was...virtually the opposite of what I'd expected to feel. I knew you, and I trusted you to help me overcome Griswade. On some basis I don't even now understand but which I accepted without question, I saw you being there as giving me an irrefutable advantage. You...have somehow become an additional source of strength to me, rather than any weakness."

She smiled, satisfied by more than passion. "So no longer a vulnerability?"

He arched one brow. "Apparently, you were never that—never destined to be that for me."

"It's called working as a team. We're alike in many ways, but the parts of us that are different complement each other. That's why I make you feel stronger, and you make me feel more assured."

He arched a brow at that.

She tipped her head, studying his eyes and his face for a full minute, then she purred, "So you've reversed your earlier view of me and accepted that we should wed. That I should be your marchioness."

"Given where we are, you can take that as read."

"Hmm. But tell me, before you changed your mind, what was it that drew you to me? What force was it you were resisting in ensuring you were never in my orbit?"

Louisa held his gaze and waited. Her heart seemed to slow, thudding more heavily in her veins. Would he answer? Would he admit—

Without warning, he rolled and set her beneath him in the billows of her bed.

She laughed and locked her arms between them, each hand gripping her opposite elbow, and held him away enough so he couldn't kiss her—couldn't distract her—and she could still see his face. She found his eyes, trapped them. "Tell me."

His face was in shadow, but she could feel the heat in his eyes. He looked down at her for long enough for her to wonder if he would meet her challenge.

But then he softly sighed, fleetingly closed his eyes, and stated, "I swear I am only going to say this once." He opened his eyes, and they blazed into hers. "I love you. I have always loved you, reaching back as far as I can recall—even when you were a brat still in pigtails. I adored you even then. You always captured my attention, always held it effortlessly. I always knew you were mine. I just didn't know what of mine you would prove to be—my Achilles' heel or my salvation."

She smiled radiantly, letting her love for him light her eyes and face. "There." She released her arms, reached up, and draped them about his powerful shoulders. "That wasn't so hard."

"Says you." He looked down at her, his gaze drinking in all she allowed to show in her face. Yet his features remained hard, chiseled, unyielding. "Teamwork aside, I can't see our life together being easy. With our characters, our tempers—as you noted, so alike —it's certain our marriage will be no gentle ride in the park."

It was her turn to arch her brows. "Neither you nor I go for gentle rides, in the park or anywhere else. That's not our style"—she grinned— "as we've just proved yet again." She hesitated, then went on, "Yet would something we could do easily entice us? Satisfy and intrigue us?"

He was silent for several heartbeats, then his lips softened fractionally. "Is that what our marriage is to be? One long intrigue?"

She shook her head. "I misspoke." She looked into his golden eyes and smiled the smile she reserved just for him—warm, encouraging, and just a touch taunting. "Not an intrigue. Our marriage will be the one thing we both need it to be."

A hint of wariness flitted over his features. "What?"

"A challenge."

Drake tried to keep his lips straight, but failed. Even in this, they thought alike.

Then she widened her eyes, provocative and tempting, and as uninhibited as ever, undulated beneath him, using her sleek body to caress the hardness of his, and he bowed his head to hers, found her lips with his, and willingly embraced everything she and the power that now thrummed between them, a well-nigh tangible reality, offered.

Before him stretched a life with his one true love—his Lady Wild. She would undoubtedly challenge him, and he would return the favor.

Yet for a man like him, coping with love itself, its joys and its fears, its difficulties and delights, would forever remain the one, the only, greatest challenge of them all.

TUESDAY, NOVEMBER 5, 1850

CHAPTER 61

*T*he six of them arrived at the rear of Midgham Manor on foot.

They'd driven through Reading, then west along the Bath Road into the sleepy countryside. Drake had called a halt in the village of Midgham, and while they'd waited for Inspector Crawford and his constables to catch up with them, the three couples, along with Finnegan, Tom, and Sebastian's groom, Ned, had ambled and inquired of the locals as to the household of the nearby manor house. From three old farmers seated outside the inn, Finnegan had learned that Nagle employed at least one manservant to wait on him—a ferrety-faced man, according to the grocer. Tom had chatted with the grocer's wife and heard that the manservant, Reed, was the only member of the household who came into the village, but that two of the village women went in to cook and clean every second day. Louisa, Cleo, and Antonia had spoken with the two women, who had happily described the layout of the rambling old house; Drake, Sebastian, and Michael had stood near enough to hear.

Thus informed, when the large, ponderous coach carrying the men from Scotland Yard had finally rolled up, the three couples had returned to their curricles, and in procession, they'd set out for the manor.

The charwoman had told them that the master of the house, an irascible old man confined to a Bath chair, spent his days in the long parlor on the first floor, a room that overlooked the front garden and the drive. Accordingly, Drake took the lane that the inn's ostler had told Ned led to the stable via the rear of the estate.

They'd rolled to a halt a little way short of the stable. The six had left the curricles with their teams hitched to fence posts and Inspector Crawford busy deploying his men and, accompanied by Finnegan, Tom, and Ned, had made their way through a field and into a stand of old trees.

It was close to noon when Drake halted in the shadows cast by several oaks bordering the manor's rear garden; sufficient leaves still clung to the branches to give them some cover. Louisa, her hand in his, stood to his left, while Sebastian came up on Drake's right, with Antonia beside him. Michael and Cleo quietly slipped into place beside Louisa. All of them studied the rear face of the manor, searching for signs of life.

From what little they could discern through the small, leaded windows, the manor might have been deserted.

The house was a single rectangular block, mostly Tudor in construction. It had been well kept not long ago, but was developing signs of neglect.

A short stretch of untended lawn, scythed but not weeded, lay between them and the house. The kitchen garden, such as it was—overgrown with brambles and out-of-control berry canes—lay to their right. A narrow graveled path ran along the back of the house, a yard or so from the wall.

Crawford, accompanied by two of the five burly constables he'd brought with him, came tramping up behind them.

Drake winced. Speaking over his shoulder, he murmured, "When we approach the house, try to avoid the gravel."

With that, he started forward. They crossed the lawn in a loose line. The others waited at the edge of the path while Drake leapt over the gravel to the back stoop, tried the door, and found it unlocked. With the others at his back, he led the way along a narrow passageway and into a snug kitchen.

Across the room, an archway gave onto a corridor leading toward the front of the house. Drake rounded the deal table that stood in the middle of the room and signaled for Ned to remain on guard there, just in case.

Silently, Drake walked along the corridor's faded runner until the main stairs leading to the first floor loomed on his right and the front hall stretched before him. He halted at the foot of the stairs; he looked back at the others, clustering in the gloom of the corridor, and signaled for silence, then with his gaze searching the shadows at the head of the stairs, treading close by the bannister, he started up.

Somewhat to his surprise, he realized Louisa had allowed Sebastian to take the position immediately behind him...or perhaps Sebastian hadn't allowed her a chance to claim it. Regardless, Drake was grateful when, after he'd reached the top of the stairs and turned along the corridor leading to the room at the front of the house, a door ahead on his left opened, and a thin, lanky manservant stepped out directly into his path.

The man looked up and literally jumped, but had no chance to raise any alarm. Drake tapped him smartly on the jaw, caught him before he hit the floor, and manhandled his limp form to Sebastian.

"Reed?" Sebastian whispered.

Drake glanced at the man. "So I would think." Reed by name, reed by nature, it seemed.

As Sebastian beckoned Finnegan and Tom to take charge of the unconscious man, Louisa squeezed past Sebastian and looked into the room from which the man had come. She closed the door and whispered, "Bedroom. In use, but empty."

Drake nodded and led the way on. The door to the room that ran across the front of the house lay directly ahead.

With his hand on the latch, he paused to allow the others to regroup, then opened the door and walked in.

"H'rumph! Reed? Is that you?" Despite the querulous tone, Nagle's voice remained strong.

He was seated in a Bath chair facing the wide windows, but sufficiently far back that his view was of the trees and not the desolate grounds. Nevertheless, the chair was sited too far into the room to allow its occupant to turn his head and see who had entered; the position declared that Nagle harbored no fear of anyone and had absolute confidence in his own invincibility.

Drake strolled toward the chair. "I regret to inform you that Reed is currently indisposed."

Nagle's head whipped around as Drake came into view. "Who the devil...?" Then the light from the window fell on Drake's face. Nagle's eyes narrowed. After a second, he muttered, "Winchelsea."

"Indeed." Drake walked to the window and half sat on the wide sill. The others filed quietly into the room. While Sebastian and Michael came forward to stand one on either side and two yards or so from Nagle's chair, where he could easily see them, the three ladies, somewhat to Drake's surprise, hung back; it occurred to him they might have some notion of using their appearance to discompose Nagle at some point in the upcoming proceedings.

As Drake had instructed, Crawford and the two constables clung to the rear wall, present as witnesses but remaining out of Nagle's sight.

Nagle didn't spare even Sebastian or Michael a glance; his head tipped down, his chin tucked into a paisley silk neckerchief, he scowled at Drake.

In return, Drake studied Nagle—his mastermind. The opponent who had very nearly triumphed and who had repeatedly delayed and deflected Drake by tying him up in a distracting web of political intrigue.

Nagle was, as Louisa had warned, ancient. His skin was like that of withered fruit, wrinkled and shrunk. Hanks of gray hair, thin and greasy, straggled out from under his round cap to hang limply on either side of his face. He must once have been a commanding figure, tall and heavily built, but now his legs were scrawny beneath the blanket arranged over them, and under his old-fashioned velvet smoking jacket, his now-bony shoulders were hunched, his chest caved in. His hands were withered almost to claws, his gnarled fingers restless and rarely still.

His head now seemed too large for his body, the skull solid beneath the thinning skin. His face was deeply lined in a way that suggested expressions of anger and contempt were his norm. Shaggy grey eyebrows lowered over deep-set but faded browny-gray eyes; his lips were thin, his mouth pinched as if it had been a long time since he'd tasted anything sweet, much less smiled.

He might have passed for just another very old, cantankerous gentleman, except for the menacing intelligence in his eyes.

When Drake said nothing, when he reacted not at all to Nagle's glower, the old man grated, "Wolverstone's whelp. To what do I owe this questionable pleasure?"

"To your attempt to assassinate your queen and her husband by blowing up the Jewel House while they were inside." Drake kept his tone equable and engaging, as if he was discussing an intriguing play. "I have to admit there is one small point in that scenario that seems out of character. In blowing up the royals in that setting, you would also have destroyed all the regalia pertaining to the Crown."

Nagle waved dismissively. "No help for it—unavoidable collateral damage. A sacrifice necessary for the greater good."

Drake inclined his head. "That's another point on which I can only hypothesize—what was your ultimate aim? To place Edward on the throne with a regent?"

Nagle's face tightened. "An *English* regent." One gnarled hand clenched and thumped the chair's arm. "No more of these German upstarts! And no more weak, ineffectual females, either." His shoulders hunched tighter, and he stared at the floor. "Damned country's going down the drain all because we've a female on the throne, under the sway of a German prince."

"Strange." It was Louisa who spoke. She glided forward, passing behind Sebastian to halt between him and Drake. She leveled her gaze on Nagle. "Considering the continuing expansion of the empire under Victoria and the great strides made on the industrial stage, enthusiastically championed by Albert, few in the world would agree with your assessment."

It wasn't her words but her voice that shook Nagle. The tones were her own, regal, assured, with undertones of the power of the old nobility ringing clearly beneath.

Nagle looked at her—stared at her as if her appearance and her voice had finally jolted him into realizing why they were there. Then he switched his gaze to Drake.

Drake read the question in Nagle's faded eyes. After a moment, he deigned to answer. "Your plot failed. The explosion didn't occur. Lawton Chilburn and Bevis Griswade are dead."

Nagle frowned. "How?" His gaze on Drake, he slowly shook his head. "You couldn't possibly have unraveled the threads in time."

Drake dipped his head in acknowledgment. "Not alone."

Cleo took that as her cue; she walked forward to stand between Michael and Drake. "Your plot failed because many people—high and low, Young Irelanders, Chartists, carters and workers, lords and ladies—joined together to thwart you. To deny your ambitions."

"You failed"—Antonia came to stand beside Sebastian—"because it isn't up to you to define the future of our country. To manipulate and dictate to the nobility, to the commons—to anyone at all."

Nagle narrowed his eyes on Antonia, then his face set in dismissive, disdainful lines, and he raked his gaze over the six of them. "Bah! You're the so-called flower of the nobility, and none of you understands the first thing about power. Power isn't power unless you use it! And so we should! All of us! The country's going to wrack and ruin while that vapid woman on the throne looks on and wrings her hands. It's up to the likes of us to take charge and—"

"Nagle!" Although he'd barely raised it, Drake's voice sliced through Nagle's rant. Nagle glowered at him. Imperturbably, Drake went on, "What you've just said amounts to sedition. You can't seriously imagine we'll permit you to speak of our sovereign in such a manner, let alone agree with you. You may advance your arguments and your ideas for running the country to the judges at your trial, although I can't see their lordships being any more impressed than we are."

Nagle's face drained of expression. "Trial?"

"Why, yes." Drake rose and straightened. He looked down at the old man who, driven by his obsession, had so very nearly succeeded in plunging the country into utter chaos. "You can't possibly have thought that attempting to assassinate your sovereign wouldn't result in a public trial."

Some emotion flitted across Nagle's face. "But what about the Young Irelanders? The Chartists?"

Drake shook his head. "All innocent victims of yours, drawn into acting as pawns in your great game."

"You, Chilburn, and Griswade," Sebastian stated. "Chilburn and Griswade are dead. That leaves you to answer for the crimes committed—all of them."

Drake had nodded to Crawford. The inspector, flanked by the two constables, came forward. Crawford halted by the Bath chair and stared at the old man who was, ultimately, responsible for a total of twenty-four deaths. "Lord Hubert Nagle, I'm arresting you for the attempted assassination—"

"No!" His expression suddenly panicked, Nagle gripped the chair's arms and looked wildly around, then his gaze fixed on Drake. "This isn't how it works. You know that. Give me a damned pistol, and I'll do the gentlemanly thing."

Drake held Nagle's gaze for a long moment, then quietly said, "No."

Nagle blinked. "What?" Confusion filled his face. "But...you can't put me on trial."

"I assure you, we can." Drake held Nagle's gaze. "You'll be tried for treason, sedition, and numerous counts of murder. And whatever other charges the authorities think to press."

Nagle's expression set in mutinous lines. "No—you can't do that. That isn't the way things are done. Good God, man!" Seeing no hint of any softening in Drake's expression, Nagle came close to sneering. "Your father knew how to deal with matters such as this—he understood the ways of the upper echelons. *He* would have given me a pistol and privacy, and then the thing would have been done."

Drake regarded Nagle calmly, then evenly said, "That's another reason your plot failed. Times have changed. I am not my father. I"—he glanced at the others—"we represent the current generation." He brought his gaze, cold and darkened to amber, back to Nagle's face. "And in our world, this current world, traitors pay the full price for their perfidy."

Drake raised his gaze to Crawford and nodded, then reached out a hand to Louisa. She slipped her fingers into his, and they turned, and with Sebastian, Antonia, Michael, and Cleo, made for the door.

"Wait!" Nagle scrabbled in his chair, trying to turn and keep them in sight. "What about my family? What about the family name?"

Without slowing his march to the door, Michael growled, "You should have thought of that before you plotted with two of your relatives to kill the Queen."

"But I'm the son of a marquess! That has to mean something."

"Oh, it does." Louisa paused and looked back. Nagle had struggled around. She met his eyes. "It means your family will gain a great deal of sympathy when they denounce and disown you, along with Lawton Chilburn and Bevis Griswade." Nagle blinked at her. She smiled, the gesture carrying more chill than an Arctic gale. "You're correct in stating that the nobility has its ways. In our age, that means ensuring that the innocent aren't stained by the brush used to blot out the evil. The ladies of the haut ton are already closing ranks around the Faringdales and Hawesleys. At this very moment, several grandes dames are advising the family how best to distance themselves from you and all your works. I can assure you that your family will not be dragged to any metaphorical gallows along with you." Her voice lowered a notch as she added, "And therefore, in sentencing you, your judges will not be swayed by any consideration of…as you termed it, collateral damage."

With that, she turned and followed her brothers and their ladies out of the room.

Standing in the doorway, Drake watched as Inspector Crawford finished his statement of the current charges, then one of the constables stepped forward, set shackles about Nagle's wrists, and snapped them shut.

Nagle was shaking his head from side to side as if he still could not believe—could not accept—what was happening, but he didn't resist as the constables hauled him to his feet.

Drake turned and left.

He caught up with the others on the lawn beyond the back door. As they were all doing, he breathed deeply, needing fresh air to dispel the stale, close atmosphere of the house and the sense of malignancy that, miasmalike, had hung about Nagle.

Sebastian blew out a long breath, then said, "He'll cut a pathetic figure at his trial."

"I don't know about that." Drake glanced at the house, then he faced forward and waved toward the trees, and they started walking back to the curricles. "I suspect that when he's given the chance to speak, he won't be able to resist the temptation to flaunt his intelligence and his superior understanding. Indeed, I hope he'll seize the opportunity."

Antonia glanced at him. "Why?"

"Because Albert was correct. A public trial is the only way to demonstrate to the nation the true nature of malignantly arrogant intelligences such as Nagle—people capable of manipulating others on a grand scale and who believe they have the right to do so. To most people—even most in the corridors of government—that anyone could have got so far and come so close to wrecking the very foundations of the state is simply inconceivable. By and large, if you told Nagle's story, most would think it fabricated and not at all likely to be true. Establishing the reality and danger of men like Nagle—especially among those in Whitehall—is one thing a public trial will accomplish. But even more importantly, a public trial is the only way of reassuring the wider population that the old ways of screening the aristocracy from justice are well and truly past."

"When it comes to it," Louisa said, retaking Drake's hand, "justice is arguably the most important cornerstone of our nation. People need to see that it works regardless of status—financial, personal, or political. That it applies to everyone without fear or favor."

The others murmured agreement, and they walked on.

Louisa lightly squeezed Drake's hand and looked up at the trees, at the sky above the dying leaves. He looked, too.

"Finis," he murmured.

"Thank God," she replied.

Hand in hand, they walked through the shadows beneath the line of oaks, leaving the manor house behind with a sense of relief—with a sense of welling lightness as they looked ahead.

To where the carriages waited in the lane.

To their journey back to London.

To the rest of the day and the rest of their lives.

EPILOGUE

CHAPTER 62

Saturday, November 23, 1850
Lambourn Castle, Berkshire

*I*n the aftermath of what became known as the Second Gunpowder Plot,
the six who had been drawn into the investigation and experienced the
thrill of ultimately, at the very last gasp, foiling Nagle's revenge might
have endured a degree of deflation had it not been for the all-but-
immediate whirlwind of preparations and associated revelry attendant on
the wedding of the heir to one of the premier dukedoms in the land.

And then Sebastian and Antonia's wedding itself was upon them.

The service was held in the chapel within Lambourn Castle. That
morning, the castle had hovered in fairytale splendor above the mists
wreathing the Lambourn river valley, but the sun had shone through, and
by the time of the ceremony, shafts of sunlight were piercing the stained-
glass windows of the chapel, bathing the groom and his radiant bride in a
dappling of jewel tones as they stood before the altar.

Decked out in customary morning attire, Sebastian was his usual
resplendently handsome self. However, gowned in a creation fashioned
from her mother's lace and pearl-encrusted wedding gown, Antonia was
beyond stunning and riveted all eyes.

Clad in amethyst satin, Louisa filled the position of Antonia's principal
attendant, with Antonia's sister, Helen, by her side, flanked in turn by
Cleo, who had become an acknowledged sister-of-the-heart to both

Antonia and Louisa over the weeks-long mission. Michael was Sebastian's best man, and Drake had been persuaded to stand as Sebastian's groomsman, along with Julius, Antonia's brother. While Sebastian and Antonia had eyes only for each other, Louisa glanced along the line of the wedding party and could not rein in her smile.

Everything had ended perfectly. All was as it should be.

With a sense of satisfaction far greater and all-embracing than that engendered by their mission's success, she listened to Sebastian and Antonia exchange their vows. This, then, was the start of their future— Sebastian and Antonia's, Michael and Cleo's, and her and Drake's, but not just for them. For their families. And did the ton but know it, for the upper echelon of society as well.

This wedding was but the first of three—the first step of three that would establish alliances that would have far-reaching consequences for generations to come.

While the wider ton might not yet appreciate what was afoot, much less what that augured, the three hundred guests at the wedding assuredly did. As the ceremony ended and the newly-weds made their slow way up the aisle, receiving felicitations and good wishes at every step before leading the way into the grand ballroom where a magnificent wedding breakfast awaited, Louisa, on Drake's arm, heard numerous shrewd comments exchanged.

Numerous predictions made. Some, she thought, would definitely come true.

With all their Cynster cousins assembled, and virtually all the Rawlings family and connections present as well, the wedding breakfast was a joyous event that fell only just short of riotous. The speeches were pointed and witty, and some—such as Antonia's father's and Michael's— were subtly hilarious. But to Louisa's mind, the speech given by her own father, Devil, was the most poignant, referring as it did to a changing of the guard and the passing of the baton from his generation to theirs.

That, more than anything else, was the tenor of this time.

Attending large social gatherings had never been a favorite pastime of Drake's, but he survived the wedding breakfast in better case than he'd expected. Of course, a large part of his equanimity derived from having Louisa by his side; with her deep knowledge of the ton and her confident, effervescent personality, in this milieu, as long as she was on his arm, he could relax and let her steer them.

Let her take charge.

He might have been less comfortable in so completely surrendering the reins if he hadn't noticed Sebastian doing much the same. Matrimony, even pending matrimony, had, it seemed, benefits he hadn't foreseen.

Waltzing with Louisa was another such benefit. He'd forgotten how much he enjoyed the exercise, but only with the right partner. One who could effortlessly match him, as she did.

On every level—a fact that continued to be a source of joy and also of trepidation, albeit minor.

As he steered them through the revolutions of the dance, he looked at her face and found her regarding him with an alert, assured, confiding— private, just for him—expression. "One down, two to go." She grinned. "As a group, we're certainly causing ripples aplenty in the social pond."

He smiled. "I heard that Victoria was annoyed she couldn't attend."

"She wanted to attend all three weddings, but—thank goodness— Albert pointed out that if she appeared at even one, she would be expected to attend all such events forevermore."

"Just as well." Drake couldn't help grinning as he steered her through the turn. "Our gracious sovereign would not appreciate being cast into the shade and not being the cynosure of all eyes. She would frown, and that wouldn't go down well."

Louisa laughed. "Very true."

"So"—Drake set them precessing up the long room—"Michael and Cleo's announcement and engagement ball will be next week."

"Yes—everyone's looking forward to that, too. Sebastian and Antonia will stay in town for the event before heading off to Scotland."

"Scotland at this time of year. What were they thinking?"

"Sebastian is thinking of buying a hunting lodge, while as for Antonia, I believe he's beguiled her with talk of snug, wood-panelled rooms with huge stone fireplaces and roaring fires and no society for miles around."

"Hmm. I hadn't thought of that—I can see the attraction."

Predictably, Louisa sniffed. "I can survive isolation for three days. After that..."

Drake felt his smile deepen, but elected to remain silent on that point. "Mama mentioned that the details of our engagement announcement have been finalized."

"Yes—as we discussed, our engagement will be announced quietly on December thirtieth and celebrated with a very select New Year's Eve ball at St. Ives House." Studying his face, Louisa arched a cynical brow. "You should be pleased with that—the time of year means the guest list will be largely family, connections, and close friends."

He arched his brows back. "Our combined family, connections, and close friends number in the multiple hundreds."

"True, but if we'd made the announcement during the Season, we would have had every member of the ton and every last government minister and secretary angling for invitations. At least, this way, we've avoided that for our engagement."

He conceded that with an inclination of his head, along with the unstated implication that there was no way in hell they would avoid a cast of thousands for their wedding, which was scheduled for March fifteenth.

Still, as he glanced around at the other dancers and at the other guests gathered around the room, smiling, chatting, and adding to an ambiance of joy and happiness that buoyed them all, he had to admit to wondering what it would be like to stand at the center of such a gathering—that perhaps experiencing it just once in his life might even be enjoyable. Given it would be just once and given Louisa would be by his side.

He glanced down to find her regarding him quizzically.

"What are you thinking about?"

He looked down into her far-too-perspicacious pale-green eyes, then smiled. "If I told you, you wouldn't believe me."

CHAPTER 63

Saturday, January 18, 1851
Hendon Castle, Norfolk

*M*ichael and Cleo's wedding was a smaller, more private, but no less

joyous affair. Although chilly, the day was bright and breezy with not a
cloud in the wide, pale-blue sky.

Drake felt that, in many ways, this was England at her finest, when
Cleo and Michael stood before the ancient altar in the small, plain village
church at Brancaster and, surrounded by their families, in voices clear
and eager, exchanged their vows. As well as their relatives and
connections, the church was packed with an assortment of the
aristocracy—those who had worked with Cleo's father, and Drake's, in
years past. The same gentlemen—and their ladies—had joined with the
Cynsters, many of whom were present, more than once in apprehending
the miscreants behind various plots.

Drake had heard all the tales. More, the sons of some of those present
occasionally assisted him.

He and Louisa danced at the wedding breakfast, then as the company
settled to talk, he tugged on her hand, and they slipped away. They found
her cloak and his greatcoat and donned them, then climbed the tower
stairs to the battlements.

Despite the raking breeze that whipped and tousled her curls, Louisa
didn't complain. Her hand snug in Drake's, with every evidence of

content, she lifted her face to the breeze, shook back her curls, and paced regally by his side.

He studied her face, then smiled, gripped her hand more firmly, and looked ahead.

In the days prior to Christmas, she and her family had joined him and his family at Wolverstone Castle. Leaving their elders reminiscing, he and she had spent a pleasant few days riding and walking about the estate. They'd also ridden out rather more adventurously over the snowy hills, and he'd taken her across the border to meet his half uncle Hamish and his family.

Then everyone had headed south for Christmas, which the Varisey family routinely spent at Elveden in Norfolk—just an hour's drive from Somersham Place in Cambridgeshire, where the Cynster family always gathered en masse to celebrate the day. Drake had driven across in the afternoon and spent a few days at Somersham, meeting more of the Cynster connections.

Both families had returned to London just in time for their engagement ball, which, of course, had passed without a hitch. No such thing as a hitch was permitted, not at an event organized by that premier hostess, the Duchess of St. Ives, ably seconded by the equally august Duchess of Wolverstone.

Somewhat to his surprise, Drake had found the evening amusing and far less trying than he'd anticipated. Having not just Louisa but Sebastian, Antonia, Michael, and Cleo with whom to share the moment had had the added benefit of largely shielding him from the more difficult encounters—such as those with his aunts or certain other grandes dames.

It wasn't so much that he couldn't deal with such ladies as having to work to do so in a manner his mother, Louisa, and her mother would deem acceptable. Keeping a social guard on his tongue had never been his forte.

He could manage being in the midst of crowds for an hour or so at a time—he had been bred to the ton, after all—but as the minutes stretched beyond that point, inevitably, he started longing to escape, to get into the open, out of the crush, and simply breathe, and Louisa, thank heavens, seemed to understand that. Despite transparently suffering from no such sensitivity, she accepted his foible without so much as a comment.

Now, they strolled the battlements hand in hand, looking out over the Wash, watching the westering sun streak the shimmering expanse in a palette of pastel hues.

They halted at the northwest corner. He drew her around, settling her back against his chest, angling his body so his bulk protected her from the worst of the wind and wrapping his greatcoat about them both.

She relaxed against him, and they looked out over the wild and desolate, yet hauntingly beautiful view.

After a moment, she murmured, "You and Albert were so very right to push for a trial."

Nagle had faced the court just after the turn of the year. As he didn't hold a seat in the Lords, he wasn't entitled to a trial there but instead had faced proceedings like any other criminal.

Drake lowered his chin to rest on her bountiful black curls. "It was worth every tithe of the effort."

He, ably assisted by the other five, had spent long hours working alongside Inspector Crawford detailing the case—the full litany of crimes that could be laid at Nagle's door—and assembling and clarifying the evidence supporting the charges.

As Drake had hoped, Nagle hadn't been able to resist arrogantly elucidating for the judges his reasons for acting as he had, and as Drake had predicted, their lordships had taken a dim view of Nagle's justifications. They'd sentenced Nagle to a traitor's death, and everyone—led by his family, who, as Louisa had warned, had disowned and denounced him—had applauded the decision.

Nagle was no more.

Reflecting on the ultimate outcome of Nagle's scheme, Drake continued, "The reassurance to the public that the law will prevail, even in the case of perpetrators such as Nagle, was essential. And the boost to Scotland Yard's reputation—with the public, with higher society, and within the various arms of government—will stand everyone in good stead. On top of that, the revelation of Nagle's inspired attempts to manipulate existing prejudices—in his case, against the Young Irelanders and the Chartists—to maneuver the state into reacting in a manner which would, in fact, have been against the Crown's and the people's best interests was a warning long overdue."

Drake paused, then went on, "From whispers our fathers and others here have heard, it seems that point has finally struck home to those in Parliament and, even more importantly, those inhabiting the corridors of Whitehall. Unthinking prejudice is a weakness. Acting on it is outright folly."

"Speaking of those inhabiting the corridors of power"—Louisa twisted her head to look back at him—"I assume you'll continue to act for the Home Secretary on occasion."

He studied her eyes, but for once couldn't read her direction. "Would you rather I didn't?"

Her eyes widened. "Oh no. I can't imagine anyone more qualified for the task, and as we've just proved with this latest mission, yours is a vital role that someone suitable must fill." She wriggled around to face him, her hands rising to grasp his lapels. "Neither Greville nor Waltham—nor, indeed, any of their minions, much less Scotland Yard—would have had any chance of foiling Nagle's plot. If it hadn't been for you, me, and the other four, the country would now be in dire straits."

Understanding bloomed. "Ah. I see." Drake realized he should have foreseen her tack. "You want to be involved."

She blinked her huge, peridot eyes at him. "Well, as I'm sure you'll admit, my help was essential in outwitting Nagle."

He could hardly argue that. More, the events of the last months had opened his eyes on several fronts, not least to the contributions she, Antonia, and Cleo were capable of making whenever investigations veered into those domains in which they were expert—more expert than he or any other gentleman. Slowly, he nodded. "There will, no doubt, be further missions in the months and years to come." He met her eyes. "And I agree. The sons of the nobility are stronger and more able when the daughters of the nobility join them."

For a second, she stared at him, then she beamed. "I never thought I would hear you admit that."

He grunted. "I might be domineering, arrogant, and autocratic, but I'm not foolish enough to deny that I'm stronger and more able with you than without you."

Her smile took on a richly satisfied edge. "We're going to be a very powerful team."

She was right. She might be female, might be soft where he was hard, weak where he was strong, yet when it came to mindset, to wielding inherent and inherited power and possessing ruthless, unrelenting inner resolve, she was as warrior-born as he. Varisey and Cynster. And soon, through them, their houses would be linked.

"You do realize that once they've had a chance to absorb and assimilate our news, the ton is going to grow just a tad nervous over the degree of combined power, inherited and otherwise, we'll have at our disposal."

"I daresay." Her brows rose haughtily; her eyes were fixed on his. "But they'll just have to get used to it. We're here, we're together, and no power on earth will ever succeed in pushing us apart."

He looked into her eyes, then slowly smiled. "My thoughts exactly."

He bent his head, and she rose on her toes, and they sealed that declaration—one of intent and commitment—with a soul-deep kiss.

CHAPTER 64

Saturday, March 15, 1851
Somersham Place, Cambridgeshire

$\mathcal{T}$hey were married at Somersham Place, in the chapel in the grounds of her family home—a chapel that had seen countless other marriages throughout the centuries. Marriages that, if the tales told were true, had all been founded on love.

Surrounded by a vast gathering of family and friends, of connections and acquaintances, along with representatives of the other great houses, the royal family, and ministers of state, Drake and Louisa recited their vows in voices that, even in that setting, rang with their respective strengths, with the power they commanded, and the resolution each possessed.

And thus, two of England's most powerful dukedoms were joined.

Her hand in Drake's, her fingers gripping his, in a gown of shimmering ivory silk overlaid with gilt-edged ivory lace, as the minister, a benevolent smile on his face, pronounced them man and wife, Louisa felt, deep in her chest, a resonance as if a bass gong had been struck.

An acknowledgment, perhaps, that this was fated—that Fate had triumphed and claimed them as her own.

And that in this setting, in that moment, love was made manifest. That through this ceremony, their love was recognized and accorded its due.

Because she, most certainly, was marrying for love, and she knew it.

And no matter what he did or did not say, so was he.

And as, with a sidelong glance, he met her eyes, read them, and his fingers squeezed hers more tightly, she saw in the golden depths of his eyes that he knew that, too.

For several seconds, she could not have spoken as emotion, unbidden, rose and swamped her.

But then the minister gave Drake permission to kiss her, and he drew her into his arms, and all she could see was him.

Her anchor, her protector—her never-failing challenge.

In that second, he read her eyes and, apparently, saw all she was feeling. His lips curved as he bent his head and, quite deliberately, stole her thunder. "Finally!"

Refusing to be outdone, she flung her arms about his neck. "At last!"

Those near enough to hear—her brothers and sisters-in-law and the poor minister—had to smother their laughs while he and she engaged in a suitably restrained kiss.

Then Drake released her and took her hand, and smiling more delightedly than either ever had, they turned and walked up the aisle. Congratulations and felicitations rained upon them, then someone started to applaud—was it her grandmother or Lady Osbaldestone?—and the entire congregation and all those surrounding the chapel started clapping.

The insistent uplifting beat followed them as, laughing, they swung out of the door and, hand in hand, led the wedding party and all the guests over lawns strewn with rose petals back to the sprawling mansion, to the ballroom and the wedding breakfast the staff were waiting to serve.

Later, after the meal and the toasts and the speeches were done, and Drake and Louisa had led the company in the first waltz, and they'd subsequently enjoyed several more, he stood beside her before one of the huge arched windows and looked over the sea of heads.

She'd wound her arm in his; he could sense her eagerness—her enthusiasm for plunging into their future—like a tremor of happiness coursing through her.

He glanced down at her—and as was now usual, she felt his gaze and looked up and met his eyes. Briefly, he studied hers, then murmured, "How are you feeling?"

Her smile bloomed, radiant and joyous. "I told you—I feel utterly wonderful! Not every lady wilts at such a time."

The notion of her wilting, even given the cause...he had to admit he couldn't imagine it.

"And"—she leaned closer to whisper—"I'm fairly certain Antonia is expecting, too, and what's more, Cleo as well." She held his gaze, amusement shining in hers. "We're all so busy playing our cards close to our respective chests, I'm half inclined to organize an event—just for the six of us—at which the truth will out." She looked at the company, all chattering and exclaiming and talking nineteen to the dozen. "Can you imagine what the interest will be when the news gets out?"

"I really don't think I want to imagine it," he dryly replied.

She grinned at him. "Yes, but…" She tipped her head, her expression teasing. "I would think you three males will be exceedingly interested in one particular aspect."

Feigning aloofness, he arched his brows. "Boy or girl?"

She laughed. "No. Which baby arrives first!"

"Ah." After a second, he inclined his head. "I take your point."

Still laughing, she tugged on his arm, then caught his hand. Walking backward, with her eyes fixed on his in quite scandalously open and evocatively sultry challenge, she drew him through the guests—who parted like the Red Sea—and onto the dance floor.

Smiling—and he fervently hoped his expression wasn't besotted—Drake went.

By the ballroom wall, Devil and Honoria stood with Royce and Minerva. All four had watched the interplay between their recently wed children who were now whirling down the room in a waltz, oblivious to everyone and everything around them.

"Well," Minerva stated in her most duchessly voice, "that's those two taken care of."

Honoria sighed, the sound redolent of the utmost content. "And so very straightforwardly—or at least so it seemed once they'd finally undertaken to grapple with reality. Helena and Therese always maintained that this— the pair of them wed—was how it was supposed to be, and that once they were a couple, above all others, these two will shape their world."

Minerva nodded. "And they decreed that nearly a decade ago. Do you remember?"

"Indeed," Honoria replied. "It was the day following Louisa's come-out ball, after they'd watched Louisa and Drake waltz."

Over their wives' heads, Devil and Royce exchanged a glance. Then Royce shifted and said, "You were right in labeling this time—marked by these three weddings—as a changing of the guard."

Devil nodded. "You put it well today—that our generation's era of dominance is waning, and it's time for our children to step forward and take over the mantle of guiding the country."

"Their turn to take on the responsibility." Minerva linked her arm with Royce's.

"And ours"—Honoria looked up at Devil as she took his arm and smiled rather more understandingly than Devil would have wished—"to accept their rise and step back."

Both Royce and Devil frowned near-identical frowns.

Minerva and Honoria exchanged a knowing glance and, laughing, led their spouses to the dance floor.

When the waltz eventually concluded, at the far end of the floor, Louisa wound her arm in Drake's and, with a bright and eager smile on her face, determinedly steered him to one of the chaises at the very end of the ballroom.

Drake looked ahead and inwardly sighed. He'd hoped to avoid the occupants of that chaise, but resigned, he hid his reluctance and pretended to go willingly. While standing in the receiving line alongside Louisa, he had, of course, greeted and briefly spoken with her grandmother and her grandmother's even more ancient friend, Lady Osbaldestone. That exchange had necessarily been brief. He had hoped he wouldn't be called on to sustain any further exposure to the elderly ladies; in his admittedly limited experience, such exposure was always an unnerving experience.

"Grandmama!" Louisa halted before the elderly Dowager Duchess of St. Ives.

Apparently blithely unaware of his antipathy, Louisa shifted her bright gaze to Lady Osbaldestone, then back to the Dowager, and said, "I wondered if either of you had any advice for us."

Drake nearly closed his eyes and groaned...then he realized Louisa almost certainly meant socially. Social advice, which, arch-grandes dames that they indubitably were, the pair were supremely well qualified to give.

He started to breathe easier, then noticed that both beldames had fixed their eyes—one pair a similar shade of pale green as Louisa's, the other obsidian—on him.

They didn't give him a chance to retreat.

"My advice," Louisa's far-seeing grandmother stated, "is to never forget what brought you together."

He knew perfectly well she wasn't referring to the mission.

Lady Osbaldestone nodded sagely. "That's sound and wise counsel, to which I will add"—her black eyes narrowed on Drake's face—"when aggravation strikes, try harder."

Drake stared at the ancient old lady, and she stared unwaveringly—challengingly—back at him.

He didn't need telling; he already knew—had already accepted—that love and, even more, loving Louisa was and always would be the most exciting, most distracting, most exacting, most scarifying, most satisfying, and inevitably, the greatest challenge he'd ever faced.

The greatest challenge of them all.

That realization, his acceptance of it, allowed him to smoothly incline his head to both ladies. "I will endeavor to remember." He glanced at Louisa and reached for her hand. "And if I don't, I'm sure I can rely on my wife to remind me."

That comment put a glorious smile on all three ladies' faces.

With an elegant bow to the two older grandes dames, Drake looped Louisa's arm in his and led his own grande dame away—into their future, into whatever adventures and intrigues Fate might send them, into a life ruled by mutual passions and desires, by shared goals and shared challenges, by family, by loyalty, by honor and purpose, presided over by the one immutable power that held sway over all.

Love.

The old ladies were correct. Life began with, was sustained by, and ultimately was ruled by love.

CHAPTER 65

*M*uch later that night, in the sumptuous apartments of the Duchess of St. Ives, slumped beside her husband of nearly thirty-two years in the shadows of the huge four-poster bed, despite Devil's best efforts, Honoria was still wide awake.

Raising one hand, she poked Devil in the ribs. "I still can't believe it! We've married off all three—extremely well, if I do say it myself—and all in a matter of months!" She turned her head on the pillow to study his face. "Do you have any idea just how remarkable that is?"

His face half buried in the pillow, Devil raised one heavy lid. After several seconds of staring back at her, he ventured, "I thought they made up their minds on their own."

"Well, of course, they did! But it's getting them to that point that's so tricky." Honoria flung out her arms. "And we've managed it without having to push, or steer, or take any action at all."

Devil snorted and turned over. "Frankly, in the matter of you or anyone else pushing, steering, or manipulating any of our three in even the most minor way in that arena, I would have given a small fortune to watch."

"Huh." After a moment, Honoria said, "Well, it never came to that, and now they've all flown, as it were..." She turned and met Devil's eyes. "You said it yourself, when we were talking with Royce and Minerva and in your speech at Sebastian's wedding. It's their turn to run things now.

You might still be the duke, but you've trained Sebastian from the cradle—there's no reason he can't take on more of the daily chores."

Devil allowed his eyes to feast on the face he had never grown tired of seeing beside him. "If he did—and I'm sure he would if we asked—what would you like to do?"

She sighed and looked up at the canopy. "I've always wanted to travel. Remember? That's what I intended to do before I met and married you."

Before he'd seen her and seized her as his bride. The years rolled back in his memory. "Egypt." He glanced at her. "We could go and explore that country if you like. See the pyramids and all the rest. Float up the Nile. Visit Cairo and Alexandria."

She found his hand with hers and gripped; when she turned her head and met his gaze, her brown eyes were bright. "Yes! I'd love to see those sights—and finally doing so after seeing all our brood wed will be like coming full circle."

Abruptly, calculation overtook her eagerness. She frowned slightly. "But if we're to go, we'll need to go soon—we have to be back by the beginning of summer at the latest."

He frowned. "Why?"

The look she bent on him was the equivalent of telling him not to be stupid. "Because we need to be here, back at home, when the next generation—our grandchildren—are born."

"Good God! *Already?*"

"You're one to talk. By my calculation, any time after June, and they might well be starting to arrive."

Staring up at the canopy, a strange smile playing over his lips, Devil slowly shook his head. "I hadn't thought that far." His tone carried a hint of wonder. "Yet another generation...."

Another generation of Cynsters, Variseys, and Rawlingses and Hendons, too—and these would be only the first, the beginning.

Until that moment, he hadn't truly grasped the reality of his words, his prophecy.

Then another thought occurred, and he grinned, then he laughed. "Heaven might be smiling upon our houses, but all I can say is: God help the ton."

THE END

Dear Reader,

Louisa and Drake's romance has been in the wind for many years—it was a delight and a thrill to be able to finally write it. And what a ride it was! I never know until I write a particular romance how it will all unfold, so I was following these two through all the twists and turns of the plot, much as you have. I hope you've enjoyed this third and final act in the Devil's Brood Trilogy—if you feel inclined to leave a review, I would greatly appreciate it.

As with the previous two volumes in this trilogy, given the storyline incorporated real places, events, and institutions of those times, I've included an Author Note (see Table of Contents) in which I detail the historical facts that feature in this volume and have influenced what is otherwise a work of fiction. If you want to know: *How much of this is real?* that note is for you.

But now our tale is told, and three weddings have taken place, and Honoria and Devil are planning a trip to Egypt for a well-earned holiday. There will be more Cynster Next Generation stories to come, with Prudence and Christopher and several others lining up to take the plunge—or trying to avoid it, as the case may be. As might be expected, those who have already found their other halves will be there to cheer their second cousins on. Two new Cynster Next Generation novels are slated for release in 2019.

Until then, however, for your delectation, we have a new and very special Christmas short novel, set in 1810, in which Lady Osbaldestone finally retires to her dower property and discovers that life in a small country village can be far more entertaining than she'd imagined. See below for details of the first volume in *Lady Osbaldestone's Christmas Chronicles: Lady Osbaldestone's Christmas Goose.*

Next year, 2018, will see the release of at least two more Casebook of Barnaby Adair novels, along with a series of historical novels written, separately but in sequence, with a handful of your other favorite historical romance authors – look for The Legend of Nimway Hall books, coming in the first half of the year. In addition, the first of the Cavanaugh siblings, Lord Randolph Cavanaugh, will meet his match in May.

So lots more to come—stay tuned!

Stephanie.

For alerts as new books are released, plus information on upcoming books, exclusive sweepstakes and sneak peeks into upcoming novels, sign up for Stephanie's Private Email Newsletter
http://www.stephanielaurens.com/newsletter-signup/

The ultimate source for detailed information on all Stephanie's published books, including covers, descriptions, and excerpts, is Stephanie's Website www.stephanielaurens.com

You can also follow Stephanie via her Amazon Author Page at
http://tinyurl.com/zc3e9mp

Goodreads members can follow Stephanie via her author page
https://www.goodreads.com/author/show/9241.Stephanie_Laurens

You can email Stephanie at stephanie@stephanielaurens.com

Or find her on Facebook
https://www.facebook.com/AuthorStephanieLaurens/

COMING NEXT

The first volume in
LADY OSBALDESTONE'S CHRISTMAS CHRONICLES:
LADY OSBALDESTONE'S CHRISTMAS GOOSE
To be released on October 19, 2017

A lighthearted tale of Christmas long ago with a grandmother and three of her grandchildren, one lost soul, a lady driven to distraction, a recalcitrant donkey, and a flock of determined geese.

Three years after being widowed, Therese, Lady Osbaldestone finally settles into her dower property of Hartington Manor in the village of Little Moseley in Hampshire. She is in two minds as to whether life in the small village will generate sufficient interest to keep her amused over the months when she is not in London or visiting friends around the country. But she will see.

It's December, 1810, and Therese is looking forward to her usual Christmas with her family at Winslow Abbey, her youngest daughter, Celia's home. But then a carriage rolls up and disgorges Celia's three oldest children. Their father has contracted mumps, and their mother has sent the three—Jamie, George, and Lottie—to spend this Christmas with their grandmama in Little Moseley.

Therese has never had to manage small children, not even her own. She assumes the children will keep themselves amused, but quickly learns that what amuses three inquisitive, curious, and confident youngsters isn't compatible with village peace. Just when it seems she will have to set her mind to inventing something, she and the children learn that with only twelve days to go before Christmas, the village flock of geese has vanished.

Every household in the village is now missing the centerpiece of their Christmas feast. But how could an entire flock go missing without the slightest trace? The children are as mystified and as curious as Therese—and she seizes on the mystery as the perfect distraction for the three children as well as herself.

But while searching for the geese, she and her three helpers stumble on two locals who, it is clear, are in dire need of assistance in sorting out their lives. Never one to shy from a little matchmaking, Therese undertakes to guide Miss Eugenia Fitzgibbon into the arms of the determinedly reclusive Lord Longfellow. To her considerable surprise, she discovers that her grandchildren have inherited skills and talents from both her late husband as well as herself. And with all the customary village events held in the lead up to Christmas, she and her three helpers have opportunities galore in which to subtly nudge and steer.

Yet while their matchmaking appears to be succeeding, neither they nor anyone else have found so much as a feather from the village's geese. Larceny is ruled out; a flock of that size could not have been taken from the area without someone noticing. So where could the birds be? And with the days passing and Christmas inexorably approaching, will they find the blasted birds in time?

First in series. A novel of 60,000 words. A Christmas tale of romance and geese.

RECENTLY RELEASED

The first volume of the Devil's Brood Trilogy
THE LADY BY HIS SIDE

A marquess in need of the right bride. An earl's daughter in search of a purpose. A betrayal that ends in murder and balloons into a threat to the realm.

Sebastian Cynster knows time is running out. If he doesn't choose a wife soon, his female relatives will line up to assist him. Yet the current debutantes do not appeal. Where is he to find the right lady to be his marchioness? Then Drake Varisey, eldest son of the Duke of Wolverstone, asks for Sebastian's aid.

Having assumed his father's mantle in protecting queen and country, Drake must go to Ireland in pursuit of a dangerous plot. But he's received an urgent missive from Lord Ennis, an Irish peer—Ennis has heard something Drake needs to know. Ennis insists Drake attends an upcoming house party at Ennis's Kent estate so Ennis can reveal his information face-to-face.

Sebastian has assisted Drake before and, long ago, had a liaison with

Lady Ennis. Drake insists Sebastian is just the man to be Drake's surrogate at the house party—the guests will imagine all manner of possibilities and be blind to Sebastian's true purpose.

Unsurprisingly, Sebastian is reluctant, but Drake's need is real. With only more debutantes on his horizon, Sebastian allows himself to be persuaded.

His first task is to inveigle Antonia Rawlings, a lady he has known all her life, to include him as her escort to the house party. Although he's seen little of Antonia in recent years, Sebastian is confident of gaining her support.

Eldest daughter of the Earl of Chillingworth, Antonia has abandoned the search for a husband and plans to use the week of the house party to decide what to do with her life. There has to be some purpose, some role, she can claim for her own.

Consequently, on hearing Sebastian's request and an explanation of what lies behind it, she seizes on the call to action. Suppressing her senses' idiotic reaction to Sebastian's nearness, she agrees to be his partner-in-intrigue.

But while joining the house party proves easy, the gathering is thrown into chaos when Lord Ennis is murdered—just before he was to speak with Sebastian. Worse, Ennis's last words, gasped to Sebastian, are: *Gunpowder. Here.*

Gunpowder? And here, where?

With a killer continuing to stalk the halls, side by side, Sebastian and Antonia search for answers and, all the while, the childhood connection that had always existed between them strengthens and blooms…into something so much more.

The first volume in the trilogy. A historical romance with gothic overtones layered over a continuing intrigue. A full length novel of 99,000 words.

The second volume of the Devil's Brood Trilogy
AN IRRESISTIBLE ALLIANCE

A duke's second son with no responsibilities and a lady starved of the excitement her soul craves join forces to unravel a deadly, potentially catastrophic threat to the realm - that only continues to grow.

With his older brother's betrothal announced, Lord Michael Cynster is freed from the pressure of familial expectations. However, the allure of his previous hedonistic pursuits has paled. Then he learns of the mission his brother, Sebastian, and Lady Antonia Rawlings have been assisting with and volunteers to assist by hunting down the hoard of gunpowder now secreted somewhere in London.

Michael sets out to trace the carters who transported the gunpowder from Kent to London. His quest leads him to the Hendon Shipping Company, where he discovers his sole source of information is the only daughter of Jack and Kit Hendon, Miss Cleome Hendon, who although a fetchingly attractive lady, firmly holds the reins of the office in her small hands.

Cleo has fought to achieve her position in the company. Initially, managing the office was a challenge, but she now conquers all in just a few hours a week. With her three brothers all adventuring in America, she's been driven to the realization that she craves adventure, too.

When Michael Cynster walks in and asks about carters, Cleo's instincts leap. She wrings from him the full tale of his mission—and offers him a bargain. She will lead him to the carters he seeks if he agrees to include her as an equal partner in the mission.

Horrified, Michael attempts to resist, but ultimately finds himself agreeing—a sequence of events he quickly learns is common around Cleo. Then she delivers on her part of the bargain, and he finds there are benefits to allowing her to continue to investigate beside him—not least being that if she's there, then he knows she's safe.

But the further they go in tracing the gunpowder, the more deaths they uncover. And when they finally locate the barrels, they find themselves tangled in a fight to the death—one that forces them to face what has grown between them, to seize and defend what they both see as their path to the greatest adventure of all. A shared life. A shared future. A shared love.

Second volume in a trilogy. A historical romance with gothic overtones layered over a continuing intrigue. A full length novel of 101,000 words.

If you haven't yet caught up with the first books in the Cynster Next Generation Novels, then BY WINTER'S LIGHT is a Christmas story that highlights the Cynster children as they stand poised on the cusp of adulthood – essentially an introductory novel to the upcoming generation. That novel is followed by the first pair of Cynster Next Generation romances, those of Lucilla and Marcus Cynster, twins and the eldest children of Lord Richard aka Scandal Cynster and Catriona, Lady of the Vale. Both the twins' stories are set in Scotland. See below for further details.

BY WINTER'S LIGHT
A Cynster Special Novel

#1 New York Times bestselling author Stephanie Laurens returns to romantic Scotland to usher in a new generation of Cynsters in an enchanting tale of mistletoe, magic, and love.

It's December 1837 and the young adults of the Cynster clan have succeeded in having the family Christmas celebration held at snow-bound Casphairn Manor, Richard and Catriona Cynster's home. Led by Sebastian, Marquess of Earith, and by Lucilla, future Lady of the Vale, and her twin brother, Marcus, the upcoming generation has their own plans for the holiday season.

Yet where Cynsters gather, love is never far behind—the festive occasion brings together Daniel Crosbie, tutor to Lucifer Cynster's sons, and Claire Meadows, widow and governess to Gabriel Cynster's daughter. Daniel and Claire have met before and the embers of an unexpected passion smolder between them, but once bitten, twice shy, Claire believes a second marriage is not in her stars. Daniel, however, is determined to press his suit. He's seen the love the Cynsters share, and Claire is the lady with whom he dreams of sharing *his* life. Assisted by a bevy of Cynsters—innate matchmakers every one—Daniel strives to persuade Claire that trusting him with her hand and her heart is her right path to happiness.

Meanwhile, out riding on Christmas Eve, the young adults of the Cynster clan respond to a plea for help. Summoned to a humble dwelling in ruggedly forested mountains, Lucilla is called on to help with the difficult birth of a child, while the others rise to the challenge of helping her. With a violent storm closing in and severely limited options, the next generation of Cynsters face their first collective test—can they save this mother and child? And themselves, too?

Back at the manor, Claire is increasingly drawn to Daniel and despite her misgivings, against the backdrop of the ongoing festivities their relationship deepens. Yet she remains torn—until catastrophe strikes, and by winter's light, she learns that love—true love—is worth any risk, any price.

A tale brimming with all the magical delights of a Scottish festive season. A Cynster novel – a classic historical romance of 71,000 words.

THE TEMPTING OF THOMAS CARRICK
A Cynster Next Generation Novel

Do you believe in fate? Do you believe in passion? What happens when fate and passion collide? Do you believe in love? What happens when fate, passion, and love combine? This. This...

Thomas Carrick is a gentleman driven to control all aspects of his life. As the wealthy owner of Carrick Enterprises, located in bustling Glasgow, he is one of that city's most eligible bachelors and fully intends to select an appropriate wife from the many young ladies paraded before him. He wants to take that necessary next step along his self-determined path, yet no young lady captures his eye, much less his attention...not in the way Lucilla Cynster had, and still did, even though she lives miles away.

For over two years, Thomas has avoided his clan's estate because it borders Lucilla's home, but disturbing reports from his clansmen force him to return to the countryside—only to discover that his uncle, the laird, is ailing, a clan family is desperately ill, and the clan-healer is unconscious and dying. Duty to the clan leaves Thomas no choice but to seek help from the last woman he wants to face.

Strong-willed and passionate, Lucilla has been waiting—increasingly impatiently—for Thomas to return and claim his rightful place by her side. She knows he is hers—her fated lover, husband, protector, and mate. He is the only man for her, just as she is his one true love. And, at last, he's back. Even though his returning wasn't on her account, Lucilla is willing to seize whatever chance Fate hands her.

Thomas can never forget Lucilla, much less the connection that seethes between them, but to marry her would mean embracing a life he's adamant he does not want.

Lucilla sees that Thomas has yet to accept the inevitability of their union and, despite all, he can refuse her and walk away. But how *can* he ignore a bond such as theirs—one so much stronger than reason? Despite several unnerving attacks mounted against them, despite the uncertainty racking his clan, Lucilla remains as determined as only a Cynster can be to fight for the future she knows can be theirs—and while she cannot command him, she has powerful enticements she's willing to wield in the cause of tempting Thomas Carrick.

A neo-Gothic tale of passionate romance laced with mystery, set in the uplands of southwestern Scotland. A Cynster Second Generation Novel – a classic historical romance of 122,000 words.

A MATCH FOR MARCUS CYNSTER
A Cynster Next Generation Novel

Duty compels her to turn her back on marriage. Fate drives him to protect her come what may. Then love takes a hand in this battle of yearning hearts, stubborn wills, and a match too powerful to deny.

Restless and impatient, Marcus Cynster waits for Fate to come calling. He knows his destiny lies in the lands surrounding his family home, but what will his future be? Equally importantly, with whom will he share it?

Of one fact he feels certain: his fated bride will not be Niniver Carrick. His elusive neighbor attracts him mightily, yet he feels compelled to protect her—even from himself. Fickle Fate, he's sure, would never be so kind as to decree that Niniver should be his. The best he can do for them both is to avoid her.

Niniver has vowed to return her clan to prosperity. The epitome of fragile femininity, her delicate and ethereal exterior cloaks a stubborn will and an unflinching devotion to the people in her care. She accepts that in order to achieve her goal, she cannot risk marrying and losing her grip on the clan's reins to an inevitably controlling husband. Unfortunately, many local men see her as their opportunity.

Soon, she's forced to seek help to get rid of her unwelcome suitors. Powerful and dangerous, Marcus Cynster is perfect for the task. Suppressing her wariness over tangling with a gentleman who so excites her passions, she appeals to him for assistance with her peculiar problem. Although at first he resists, Marcus discovers that, contrary to his expectations, his fated role *is* to stand by Niniver's side and, ultimately, to claim her hand. Yet in order to convince her to be his bride, they must plunge headlong into a journey full of challenges, unforeseen dangers, passion, and yearning, until Niniver grasps the essential truth—that she is indeed a match for Marcus Cynster.

A neo-Gothic tale of passionate romance set in the uplands of southwestern Scotland. A Cynster Second Generation Novel – a classic historical romance of 114,000 words.

And if you want to catch up with where it all began,
return to the iconic
DEVIL's BRIDE

the book that introduced millions of historical romance readers around the globe to the powerful men of the unforgettable Cynster family – aristocrats to the bone, conquerors at heart – and the willful feisty women strong enough to be their brides.

AUTHOR'S NOTE

Certain of the historical facts that feature in this volume are described more fully below. In addition, as usual, the streets I have my characters strolling, running, or skulking down are real to the time. The map I use as reference is by Cross, dated 1850.

So to the nuggets of history buried in this book. Due to space constraints and also the easy availability of information on topics such as the Tower of London, what follows is not an exhaustive history but more a recounting of the facts pertinent to the story in this book.

1) The London Working Men's Association (LMWA)
Was founded in 1836 by cabinet-maker William Lovett and publisher Henry Hetherington, with assistance from tailor Francis Place, and printers John Cleave and James Watson, to provide a meeting place for Chartists in the southeast of England and further the ideas espoused by the Chartist movement, with a particular bent toward achieving political reform. As well as disseminating information to London's working poor, the association had as its aim "to seek by every legal means to place all classes of society in equal possession of their political and social rights."

Further to this, the pivotal People's Charter, presented in 1838 (see Author's Note in the previous book for more details), was written by the LMWA's secretary, William Lovett, with the help of Francis Place.

From its inception, the LWMA concentrated on securing political reform via appealing to public opinion to sway Parliament. The association was small in size, with only a total of 279 members, but was instrumental in organizing much larger gatherings of the working class in support of the policies the association espoused.

Note that I was unable to unearth any facts regarding the association's headquarters. It is entirely possible that no such building existed, as it was common for London trade and political societies to meet in the back rooms of taverns, coffee houses, or clubs. However, there always was a secretary, and there had been a very large demonstration organized by the association on Kennington Common in south London in 1848, so I placed the association's "office" in that area.

2) The Guards and their barracks
The British Army includes regiments of Horse Guards and Foot Guards.

The duties of the various guards regiments includes ceremonial appearances, but their members are fully operational soldiers.

Since the reign of Charles II, the Queen's Guard (unmounted) and the Queen's Life Guard (also known as the Household Cavalry) have been responsible for guarding the Sovereign's residences. In the London of 1850, those residences numbered three—Buckingham Palace (which became the London residence of the British monarch on Victoria's ascension in 1837), St. James Palace, and the Tower of London.

At any given time, the Queen's Guard was formed from one of the five regiments of foot guards—those being the Grenadier, Coldstream, Scots, Irish, and Welsh Guards. Whichever regiment was on duty provided detachments of guards for sentry and security duty at Buckingham Palace and St. James Palace, as well as a detachment to guard and secure the Tower of London.

Meanwhile, the Queen's Life Guard provided mounted escorts to the royal family whenever the royal family ventured about the capital.

The Household Cavalry Regiment (the Life Guards) operated out of the Hyde Park Barracks in Knightsbridge. The foot guard regiments were in the main stationed at Wellington Barracks, between Birdcage Walk and Petty France, close to Buckingham Palace. In 1850, army headquarters and general command of all regiments was located in Horse Guards, a Palladian building located between Whitehall and Horse Guards Parade (parade ground). Horse Guards served as the office of the commander-in-chief of the Armed Forces until 1904.

3) The London fire brigade of 1850

In 1833, the London Fire Engine Establishment was founded by James Braidwood. It was a private enterprise funded by insurance companies with the stated purpose of saving material goods from fire. Braidwood was the first to introduce protective uniforms for firefighters. The London Fire Engine Establishment boasted 13 fire engine stations and 80 firefighters.

Braidwood himself was famous for turning out to help fight fires with his men, leading to the moniker used by Drake to refer to the firefighters: "Braidwood's boys."

4) The Cemeteries of London in 1850

In the early 1800s, the principal burial sites previously used—common burial grounds located around the city and the church yards, vaults, and crypts within the city—became overcrowded, and after several outbreaks of cholera, in 1832, Parliament authorized several private companies to establish cemeteries on London's outskirts.

There were seven large cemeteries, most styled after the famous Pere Lachaise cemetery in Paris, that became known at the Magnificent Seven, including one at Kensal Green, but in 1850, the most fashionable was the "very impressive" St. James in Highgate, which had opened in 1839.

5) The Tower of London
Little about the layout of the Tower of London has changed since the late 1200s. However, over the centuries, buildings within the walls have been demolished, some rebuilt, and others erected from scratch. The buildings of the Tower of London described in this book are those that existed in 1850. Of particular note, Martin Tower is one of the thirteen towers of the curtain wall enclosing the Inner Ward, and stands at the northeastern corner of the Inner Ward. The White Tower is the original medieval keep and stands in the middle of the Inner Ward. The Waterloo Barracks were constructed in 1845 along the north side of the Inner Ward, facing south toward the White Tower and with the Bloody Tower directly opposite on the other side of the Inner Ward. Essentially, with one notable exception, the layout and buildings of the Tower of London described in this book as existing in 1850 remain the same to this day.
The single exception is the Jewel House.

6) The Jewel House of 1850 and the Keeper of the Crown Jewels
The tradition of storing at least a part of the Crown Jewels in the Tower of London dates from Henry III's reign. The position of "Keeper of the Crown Jewels" was created in 1207. On 1378, the original Jewel House in the Tower of London was built specifically to house the royal regalia and was located near the White Tower. There was also another Jewel House located in Westminster Abbey that housed part of the collection; over the centuries, this secondary Jewel House was moved from place to place within the abbey, until in the 1530s, the entirety of the Crown Jewels were brought together at the Tower of London, almost certainly for security's sake, and housed in the rebuilt Jewel House on the south side of the White Tower.

In 1669, after the Restoration, the then-130-year-old rebuilt Jewel House was demolished, and the largely newly-recreated Crown Jewels were moved into Martin Tower.

Over the centuries, the title of Keeper of the Crown Jewels underwent various changes of duties and of title. In 1814, the appointment became known as the Keeper of the Jewel House, with responsibility for the day-to-day custody of the jewels. The Keeper was permitted to allow members of the public to view the Crown Jewels for a fee. This practice became hugely popular, to the point that the government became alarmed. Consequently, the Treasury planned and built a new Jewel House attached to the south face of Martin Tower; this new Jewel House opened in 1842. The Crown Jewels were displayed in glass cases in the middle of the main chamber so that people could walk around and view them. Critically, this new Jewel House was constructed primarily of wood.

This was the Jewel House that existed in 1850 and which features in this book.

Note that I have found no information on the layout of this short-lived Jewel House, but the Keeper and his family did live on the premises, so the upstairs/downstairs plus cellar structure I have described may well be what existed at that time.

Of all the various Jewel Houses in the Tower of London, this one lasted for the shortest time. In the late 1850s it was declared a fire hazard. A new chamber was constructed on the upper floor of Wakefield Tower, another tower in the Inner Ward, and the Crown Jewels were moved there in 1868.

The Wakefield Tower Jewel House remained in use until 1967. Today, the Jewel House is located in the Waterloo Barracks.

I hope you've enjoyed learning of the snippets of historical fact that have contributed to the backbone of the stories in this trilogy.

Stephanie.

ABOUT THE AUTHOR

#1 *New York Times* bestselling author Stephanie Laurens began writing romances as an escape from the dry world of professional science. Her hobby quickly became a career when her first novel was accepted for publication, and with entirely becoming alacrity, she gave up writing about facts in favor of writing fiction.

All Laurens's works to date are historical romances ranging from medieval times to the mid-1800s, and her settings range from Scotland to India. The majority of her works are set in the period of the British Regency. Laurens has published more than 60 works of historical romance, including 38 *New York Times* bestsellers and has sold more than 20 million print, audio, and e-books globally. All her works are continuously available in print and e-book formats in English worldwide, and have been translated into many other languages. An international bestseller, among other accolades, Laurens has received the Romance Writers of America® prestigious RITA® Award for Best Romance Novella 2008 for *The Fall of Rogue Gerrard*.

Laurens's continuing novels featuring the Cynster family are widely regarded as classics of the historical romance genre. Other series include the *Bastion Club Novels*, the *Black Cobra Quartet*, and the *Casebook of Barnaby Adair Novels*.

For information on all published novels and on upcoming releases and updates on novels yet to come, visit Stephanie's website: www.stephanielaurens.com

To sign up for Stephanie's Email Newsletter (a private list) for heads-up alerts as new books are released, exclusive sneak peeks into upcoming books, and exclusive sweepstakes contests, follow the prompts at Stephanie's Email Newsletter Sign-up Page.

Stephanie lives with her husband and two cats in the hills outside Melbourne, Australia. When she isn't writing, she's reading, and if she isn't reading, she'll be tending her garden.

CPSIA information can be obtained
at www.ICGtesting.com
Printed in the USA
LVOW13s1803180717
541773LV00015B/1439/P